Daniel Defoe

THE FORTUNES
AND MISFORTUNES OF THE
FAMOUS MOLL FLANDERS

Edited by
PAT ROGERS

DeBartolo Professor in the Liberal Arts,
University of South Florida, Tampa

EVERYMAN
J.M. DENT · LONDON
CHARLES E. TUTTLE
VERMONT

This title first published in Everyman 1930
Previous paperback edition first published 1982
This edition first published 1993

J. M. Dent
Orion Publishing Group, Orion House
5 Upper St Martin's Lane, London
WC2H 9EA
and
Charles E. Tuttle Co.
28, South Main Street, Rutland,
Vermont 05701, USA

Typeset at The Spartan Press Ltd,
Lymington, Hants
Printed in Great Britain by
The Guernsey Press Co. Ltd,
Guernsey, C.I.

British Library Cataloguing in Publication Data for this
title is available upon request

ISBN 0 460 87287 7

CONTENTS

A NOTE ON THE AUTHOR
AND EDITOR

Daniel Defoe was born in London probably in 1660, the son of a tallow-chandler. He grew up in the City of London, and witnessed both the Great Plague of 1665 and the Great Fire of 1666. He studied at a dissenting academy in Stoke Newington and was intended for the ministry, but abandoned this plan. Instead he embarked on a varied career in trade, starting out as a wholesaler in the hosiery trade. His career was interrupted when he went to fight for the Duke of Monmouth and was captured at Sedgemoor in 1685, subsequently gaining a royal pardon. In 1692 he went bankrupt for the first time; a few years later he suffered bankruptcy again after the failure of a brick-making business. He also spent some time in a debtors' gaol. His first book was not published until 1697. A pamphlet called *The Shortest Way with the Dissenters* (1702) caused official outrage and Defoe was put in the pillory. Afterwards he became a political agent and spy, and observed the Union with the Scottish parliament whilst in Edinburgh (1707). After publishing a huge array of varied works on politics, economics, travel and theology, he eventually produced the first part of *Robinson Crusoe* in 1719. This was followed by his other novels including *Moll Flanders* (1722) and *Roxana* (1724). His works in the last decade of his life include a *Tour* of Britain (1724–26) and a manual on *The Complete English Tradesman* (1726). Defoe died, in hiding from creditors, on 24 April 1731, aged about seventy.

Pat Rogers, DeBartolo Professor in the Liberal Arts at the University of South Florida, has written books on Pope, Swift, Defoe, Fielding and Johnson, as well as general studies including *Grub Street*, *The Augustan Vision* and *Literature and Popular Culture in Eighteenth-Century England*.

A CHRONOLOGY OF DEFOE'S LIFE

Year	Age	Life
1660		Defoe's probable year of birth, in London
1665	5	Taken to the country to avoid the Plague
1666	6	
1667		
c.1670	10	Goes to study at Rev. James Fisher's school at Dorking, Surrey
c.1674–79	14–19	Studies at dissenting academy in Stoke Newington, outside London, under Charles Morton
c.1682	22	Decides not to enter the Ministry
c.1683	23	Begins career in trade as a wholesaler in the hosiery business, located in Cornhill in the City of London
1684	24	Marriage to Mary Tuffley, daughter of prosperous tradesman
1685	25	Joins the rebellion of the Duke of Monmouth and captured after the battle of Sedgemoor; eventually receives a royal pardon
1688	28	Greets the incoming army of William III at Henley
1689	29	
1690	30	Travels to Chester with King William, and visits Liverpool on business
1692	32	Business failures lead to first bankruptcy
1694		

A CHRONOLOGY OF DEFOE'S TIMES

Year	Literary Context	Historical Events
1660		Restoration of monarchy in England under Charles II; Royal Society founded
1665		Devastating Plague in London
1666		The Great Fire of London
1667	Milton, *Paradise Lost*	
1670		
1674		
1682	Dryden, *Mac Flecknoe*	Shaftesbury's trial as culmination of Exclusion Crisis
1683		
1684		
1685		James II succeeds to throne; Monmouth rebellion in the West Country, put down savagely
1688	Alexander Pope born	Glorious Revolution; James flees on the invasion of William; William III and Mary II accede
1689	Richardson born; Lady Mary Wertley born; Aphra Behn dies	Bill of Rights confirms Protestant succession
1690		
1692		Salem witchcraft trials, Massachusetts
1694	Voltaire born	Foundation of Bank of England

Year	Age	Life
1695	35	Gains small government post
1696	36	Manager of official government lottery
1697	37	*An Essay upon Projects*[1]
c.1698	38	First visit to Scotland
1700	40	
1701	41	*The True-Born Englishman* (verse satire)
1702	42	Political satire, *The Shortest Way with the Dissenters,* causes furore; forced to flee from authorities
1703	43	Arrested, convicted of sedition; escapes and then recaptured. Stands in the pillory. A collection of his early works published.
1704	44	Inception of the *Review,* a journal of news and (chiefly) opinion, which Defoe conducts singlehanded until 1713.
1706–10	46–50	Resident in Scotland for long periods, as agent and spy for the leading ministers Harley and Godolphin
1707	47	
1708	48	
1709	49	Proposes scheme for settling refugees from the German Palatinate
1710	50	
1711	51	
1712	52	Visits Derbyshire to take the waters at Buxton
1713	53	Arrested and imprisoned in the Queen's Bench gaol for indiscreet pamphlets
1714	54	
1715	55	Tried for libel but the case dropped

Year	Literary Context	Historical Events
1695		Queen Mary dies
1696		
1697		
c.1698		
1700	Congreve, *Way of the World*; death of Dryden	
1701		Act of Settlement (concerning Hanoverian line)
1702		Death of William III; accession of Queen Anne
1703		Great Storm
1704	Swift, *Tale of a Tub*	Battle of Blenheim
1706		
1707	Fielding born	Union of English and Scottish parliaments
1708		Further success for Allies under Marlborough in War of the Spanish Succession
1709	Pope, *Pastorals;* Johnson born	
1710		Sachverell trial; fall of Godolphin ministry, Harley succeeds
1711	Addison and Steele, *Spectator* (runs until 1712)	
1712	Jean-Jacques Rousseau born	Handel settles in England
1713	Diderot born	Treaty of Utrecht
1714	Pope, *Rape of the Lock* in five cantos	Death of Queen Anne; George I succeeds; fall of Harley
1715	Le Sage, *Gil Blas*, vols. 1–2	Jacobite rising put down; death of Louis XIV

Year	Age	Life
1717	57	Starts to write for highflying Tory newspaper, Mist's *Weekly Journal*
1719	59	*Robinson Crusoe*, Part 1
1720	60	*Captain Singleton; Memoirs of a Cavalier*
1721	61	
1722	62	*Moll Flanders; Journal of the Plague Year; Colonel Jack*
1724	64	*Roxana;* first volume of *Tour of Great Britain*
1725	65	Second volume of *Tour; Complete English Tradesman;* pamphlets on criminals including Jonanthan Wild
1726	66	Third volume of *Tour*
1727	67	
1728	68	Lawsuit over old debt, obliged to go into hiding
1729	69	
1730	70	
1731	70/71	Death in London, still as a fugitive. Buried in Bunhill Fields on north of the city.

[1] Defoe wrote over 500 separate books and pamphlets. This Chronology lists those for which he is chiefly remembered today. See pp. 310–12 for bibliographical surveys of Defoe's writing.

Year	Literary Context	Historical Events
1717	Pope, *Works* collected	Triple Alliance
1719		Peerage Bill
1720		South Sea Bubble, following collapse of Mississippi scheme in Paris
1721		Robert Walpole comes to power
1722		Atterbury's Jacobite plot uncovered; death of Marlborough
1724	Swift, *Drapier's Letters*	
1725		Death of Peter the Great, Russian Emperor
1726	Swift, *Gulliver's Travels*	
1727		Death of George I, succeeded by George II: death of Newton
1728	Pope, *Dunciad*; Gay, *Beggar's Opera*	
1729	Swift, *Modest Proposal*	
1730	Fielding, *Tom Thumb*	
1731	Prévost, *Manon Lescaut*	

INTRODUCTION

I

A cult-book must first of all be a popular book, but it has to be something more than that. There needs to be an intangible quality of myth, which makes the work eloquent beyond its immediate literary purposes, and resonant in ways its author can never have planned. An interesting case in point is *Lord of the Rings*, the fantasy world of a dry philologist which has come alive in the imagination of youth across two continents. Tolkien's success did not come overnight, yet the process was instantaneous when set alongside the curious history of *Moll Flanders*. For two hundred years Moll struggled on, always the outsider, refused admission to the highest literary company in case her muddy boots soiled some precious figures in the carpet. The warmest praise she received in that time was the touching but seemingly uncomprehending testimony reported by George Borrow in Chapter 31 of *Lavengro*. The narrator has met an old fruit-seller on London Bridge; she tells him that her son has been transported to Botany Bay, and persuades herself that his thefts were not really crimes, since a certain 'blessed woman' has published an account of her own adventures and final delivery. It turns out that the author of this pious tract is none other than 'blessed Mary Flanders'. Borrow attempts to buy the book from the old woman, but she refuses his offer of two silver crowns for the greasy old copy. He reflects, 'This is a singular book . . . but it does not appear to have been written to prove that thieving is no harm, but rather to show the terrible consequences of crime: it contains a deep moral.' The old fruit-seller is unconvinced. She replies, 'I am glad you like it, which shows I was right about you, after all; you are one of our party.' The autobiographer retires, apparently nonplussed.

A singular book it is indeed. But until the present century, no one had thought that *Moll Flanders* was more than a vivid rogue's tale. It was the generation of Virginia Woolf, James Joyce,

E. M. Forster and André Gide which discovered new depths in the prosy, gossiping narrative. In the heyday of 'realism', bourgeois optimism and the no-nonsense story-telling, Defoe had seemed just a primitive forbear. With the coming of a more inward and consciously poetic style in fiction, he suddenly made a quantum leap in significance. Virginia Woolf could claim that he anticipates Meredith and Ibsen, and further that 'he deals with the important and lasting side of things and not with the passing and trivial'. His supposedly sordid areas of concern no longer got in the way of readers' enjoyment – it is worth recalling that as late as 1916 the leading academic authority of the day observed of Moll, 'It is not a book to be recommended to young readers – perhaps it is not a book to be recommended to anyone, which is one of the reasons why no selections are given in the present volume.' Prudery did not vanish in an instant and only now is Moll Flanders beginning to be included amongst the set books for English school examinations.

Yet elsewhere Moll has come into her own, and her story has been variously dramatised for film and television audiences. From the start, indeed, she found herself transmogrified in surprising ways. Only a year after the novel first appeared, a private bookseller issued an abridgment which contained an extra section at the end describing Moll's will, death and burial, familiar components of the penitential biography. She was identified as really one Elizabeth Atkins, deriving from Galway (obviously this picks up the hint of the heroine's original name 'Betty'). Another adaptation, in 1730, filled out the picture even further. Garnished with an astounding title, Fortune's Fickle Distribution, this version tacked on to Moll's life and death two further parts: one dealing with the governess, here dubbed Jane Hackabout, and the other giving the full career of the Lancashire husband, now christened James MacFaul. Defoe's creation was almost squeezed out of the action; it is as if an abridgment of Hamlet should cut down on the prince's role in order to pursue the girlhood of Shakespeare's heroine.

Later still Moll became the target of chapbook compilers. These were small, badly printed texts sold to poor people by itinerant pedlars at fairs and markets; the narrative is usually pared down to a bare summary, and crude illustrations are supplied. In fact one chapbook version of about 1750 contains rather better woodcuts than most examples of this genre.

Considerable care has been devoted to getting out an enticing title-page, since this was a major promotional factor in the days before dust-jackets and sales literature. In addition to the experiences chronicled on the original title-page, the chapbook informs us that the heroine was eleven times in Bridewell, a total of thirty-four times in other gaols, and twenty-five times in Newgate itself. Her collected misfortunes include being on fifteen occasions whipped at the cart's arse, and four times burnt in the hand. The compiler drives home his moralistic message in various doggerel lines ('Man's fate is ordered by God's just decree') and concludes by quoting the epitaph written for Moll after her death in Virginia:

> Newgate thy dwelling was, thy beauty made thee
> A goddess seem, and that alone betray'd thee.
> Twelve years a whore, a wife unto thy brother,
> And such a thief there scarce could be another.
> Unweary'd traveller, whither dost thou roam?
> Lo! in this place remote to find a tomb
> Transported hence, to heaven, 'tis hoped thou'rt sent,
> Who wicked liv'd, but dy'd a penitent.

That Moll could so easily be fitted into the stock pattern of popular homiletic fiction is a clue to the enduring power of her story. Again, as late as 1776, the Irish connection was strengthened with a further adaptation entitled *The History of Laetitia Atkins, vulgarly called Moll Flanders*. This claims to make use of new manuscripts which set Defoe's account to rights, and fills out Moll's last days in an implausible fashion.

The only living, breathing Moll – the one totally unfabricated creation – is the character Defoe invented, 'vulgarly called Moll Flanders'. In bare outline her career can be made to fit the procrustean framework of didactic fiction, aimed at people too uneducated to have recourse to 'serious' books. But the insights of *Moll Flanders* afford complexity and richness, human depth and not moralistic diagrams. There may be lessons to be learnt, but they will not be the easy formulae of improving literature. Perhaps in the end, Borrow's fruit-woman was right: we feel something approaching love for Moll at times, not in spite of her failings but more nearly *because* of them. The strange metamorphoses which her story has undergone indicate a primal current of life which surges through her being; but only the original novel releases this power into a truly expressive artistic statement. A woman like

Moll can furnish the basis of myth, and the cult will draw on this underlying quality in her nature. But the novel exists independently of the cult; though she seems to fit our times, she is not properly of our times. A true response to the book must mean liberating Moll from some of the mythic accretions, and getting back to the eighteenth-century woman displaced by the twentieth-century archetype.

II

It is to the eighteenth century, assuredly, that Moll belongs. The literal position is that the story is supposed to have been 'written in the year 1683', as we are told at the end. At this point the heroine is 'almost seventy years of age', which would of course fix her birth at about 1614. Moll's mother is supposed to have been transported to the plantations when the girl was six months old, which is radically unhistorical – there was at this date no real colony in Virginia, and transportation did not begin until the 1650s. In addition, the kind of mass transportation which Moll observes at first hand, late in the novel, was a very recent phenomenon when Defoe wrote. It was only after an Act of Parliament passed in 1719 that such widespread shipping of convicts became the rule: this measure regularized the procedures for dispatching felons to the American colonies. This is not the only slip Defoe makes, and we would be justified in reading the book as a contemporary narrative in all essential features. For his own tactical purposes Defoe wants us to think of Moll as a character safely removed in time, but the world he makes her inhabit is recognizably the landscape of very recent memory.

Indeed, it is quite possible that *Moll Flanders* has a direct basis in topical events. The first hint we get of its intellectual genesis comes in a letter signed 'Moll' which appeared in Applebee's *Weekly Journal* in July 1720. John Applebee employed Defoe for a number of years, both as a contributor to his newspaper and as the writer of dying speeches for condemned criminals, his main speciality line. The letter is said to be written from Rag Fair, a notorious locality in the East End of London associated with sharpsters, stolen goods (especially clothes) and what a historian of London called in 1720 'small, nasty and beggarly streets'. This Moll describes herself as 'an eminent pickpocket', who had prospered until caught in the act by 'a plaguy hawk-eyed journeyman mercer'. She was tried and convicted, but 'pleaded her belly', that is petitioned for mercy on the grounds of her pregnant condition. She was transported to America, but at the time of writing the letter she has returned to England before her term has expired – another capital offence. She is now being blackmailed by an old accomplice, and asks the public for advice. It is overwhelmingly probable that Defoe was responsible for this item, as for so many others in Applebee's columns. If so, it is the first clue that he was in the throes of conceiving his novel.

But as well as the invented 'Moll' from Rag Fair, there may easily have been a real-life analogue to Defoe's heroine. A strong candidate put forward in recent years is a certain Moll King, who went by a variety of aliases and has proved hard to pin down in the criminal files of the age. But, thanks to the skilful research of Gerald Howson, we do know a little about her. In June 1721, six months prior to the publication of *Moll Flanders*, Moll King was prominently featured in the *Daily Journal*, another newspaper for which Defoe wrote extensively. She was labelled 'one of the most notorious pickpockets of the town, and eminently famous for assisting in stealing watches at ladies' sides at church'. The report informs us that she has been sent back to her old home, Newgate prison. Fifteen months later, that is some time after the novel appeared, she was back in the same newspaper; she had returned from transportation and had on this account yet again found herself in Newgate. She appears in other news-stories and in pamphlets for a year or two more. Mr Howson was able to trace a little of her earlier history, and deduced that in 1718 Moll King had been sentenced for stealing a watch in St Anne's, Soho: for some reason she was not transported until early in 1720. After returning illegally from the colonies she was apparently employed for a time by the great Jonathan Wild, godfather of the entire London criminal system. She was caught and ought to have suffered hanging this time: but somehow she escaped (probably by informing against another criminal) and instead received another sentence of transportation. Even that was not the end of the story, but her subsequent adventures cannot have influenced the shape of the novel.

Not all the details square exactly with the career of Defoe's fictional Moll, but there are enough parallels to make it likely that he had Moll King's story in mind for the latter part of the book.

Defoe habitually embroiders upon actuality: his imaginative works tend to start from some true-life episode, though they never stick to the original with absolute fidelity. It is interesting to consider the history of Moll King, which Defoe must have known about and which he may well have written up for journalistic purposes. Nevertheless, the novel which actually emerged is far more than mere padded-out criminal biography. It is true that in years to come Defoe was to turn into something of a specialist in Tyburn narratives: he wrote the life of thieves and pirates like Jack Sheppard, Jonathan Wild, Edward Burnworth and many others. But the great majority of these books postdate *Moll Flanders*. I do not mean to suggest that in 1721, when the novel was probably in the process of composition, Defoe knew nothing of criminal matters. He must already have been well acquainted with footpads and highwaymen, pickpockets and fences, and must have observed the growth of organised crime (mainly the result of Wild's adroit managerial techniques) with the dual interest of a moralist and a journalist. But most rogue biographies were perfunctory things, unsubtle in construction and often hazy in detail. Even if Defoe had been, as he was not, a regular practitioner of such forms before he wrote *Moll Flanders*, the experience would never have equipped him to produce such a book. Much of the ephemera of Dublin newspapers goes into *Ulysses*, but we do not on that account suppose that Joyce's art is 'explained' by their presence.

In this connection one other point is worth a brief mention. At the end of 1721 advertisements began to appear in the press for a new book called *The History of Flanders, with Moll's Map*. It is the sort of work Defoe would have been tempted to buy; he had a lifelong interest in geography and world affairs, with a library well-stocked in these branches of study. Herman Moll, the greatest map-maker of the age, provided cartographic materials to some of Defoe's own books, and in one case may have supplied him with a plot – Defoe's *New Voyage Round the World* (1724) hinges on a trek across the Andes, in reality more or less impossible, which one of Moll's maps suggested as feasible. At all events, the collocation of the nouns in this often-repeated advertisement is a likely trigger for Defoe's invention. (If so, the novel cannot have been finalized until the eve of publication.) 'Flanders' also meant contraband Flemish lace, a nicely ironic *nom de guerre* for a woman like Moll to adopt. 'Moll' may allude to the true-life criminal, but it seems to have been a generic name, like Betty for a servant. In 1730, in his last book, Defoe was using 'Moll Harvey' as the type of a female Fagin, training young women up to practise street robbery.

It is no casual feature of the design that Moll should be born in Newgate, any more that her mother should have been transported, or that she should find herself in Newgate later in the novel. The prison is both setting and motif for much of the literature and art in Defoe's lifetime. In an important book, *Imagining the Penitentiary* (1987), John Bender has argued that the way people envisaged places of confinement – along with the kind of buildings they erected for the purpose, and the sites where these were located in the city – points to deeply engrained habits of thought in the eighteenth century, paralleled in some of the procedures of the novel form itself. At all events, it is certain that the prison recurs in Swift's *Tale of a Tub*, in Gay's *Beggar's Opera*, in Fielding's *Jonathan Wild*, in Hogarth's 'progress' pieces, and elsewhere. Newgate above all is the symbolic centre of the nation's crime and punishment. It should also be stressed that gaols were not primarily places for long-term punishment by incarceration. They held chiefly two catagories of prisoner: first, debtors, and secondly those awaiting trial on serious felonies. The sentence for these latter offences (if a conviction was obtained – quite often judges, lawyers or juries conspired to soften the rigour of the law by dismissing the charge) was either the death penalty or remission to a period of transportation, such as Moll endures. Prison, in short, was not used for custodial sentences as it is today. For most people accused of serious crime, then, the gaol was a limbo to be encountered between arrest and a savage, often final, retribution on behalf of society. (It is a paradox that Moll should undergo moral conversion in a place not designed for reformation.) Moll's obsessive fear of Newgate reflects this particular set of historical circumstances. It is largely an adventitious fact that Defoe himself had known the inside of Newgate prison in 1703, after fleeing from justice in the wake of an injudicious 'libel' named *The Shortest Way with the Dissenters*; he was indicted at the Old Bailey as 'a seditious man and of a disordered mind, and a person of bad name, reputation and conversation'. But when we add to this his spell in the pillory, his trial at the Guildhall in 1714 for 'scandalis[ing] and vilify[ing] the memory of the queen [Anne]', his commital to the Fleet Prison as a debtor in the 1690s, and, we may add, though it still lay ahead, his death in an obscure hiding-place whilst again on the run from creditors – if we put all these together, we may see why he was capable of rendering Moll's terror with peculiar intensity.

III

The first edition of *Moll Flanders* was published on 27 January 1722, an ordinary enough Saturday in most respects. Defoe was already into his early sixties. He had experienced a varied, not to say chequered, life. The son of a London tallow-chandler, he had originally been set for a career in the dissenting ministry, but around the age of twenty-two he decided against such a calling. Instead he went into trade, building up a number of business enterprises, in the export/import field mainly. He also made an advantageous marriage. But a vein of imprudence mingled in his nature with the crafty, opportunist side which his enemies liked to stress. He went off to fight for the Duke of Monmouth during the rebellion of 1685: this was an action in accord with his political convictions, but it was slightly quixotic for a rising young businessman. He was captured by the king's forces and escaped being strung up on the West Country gallows only by dint of a royal pardon. Things took a turn for the better again with the Glorious Revolution of 1688, since the young man inhabited a world less inimical to dissent and more hospitable to his enterprising spirit. But he got himself into trouble again, rashly dabbling in marine insurance during a period of fierce naval warfare. He found himself bankrupt and then in the debtors' gaol. Slowly he recovered, and by the turn of the century he had acquired some favour from William III. He held minor official positions; he had turned his unimpressive particle of a surname, Foe, into the aristocratic Defoe. He had also begun to write on political and social questions.

Within two or three years he had spoilt everything again. A scandalous pamphlet incurred the government's displeasure and landed him in Newgate as well as at the pillory. A brick-making concern in Essex failed and once more he was carted off to the debtors' prison. His patron King William died, and Defoe could look for no favours from the new monarch, Anne. His deliverance this time came from the politician Robert Harley, who employed him as agent, spy, pamphleteer and surreptitious public relations officer. For a decade these tasks sent Defoe the length and breadth of the nation, with a lengthy sojourn in Edinburgh to help cement the fragile Union of the English and Scottish parliaments. All this time he was writing extensively, with satire and economics among his preferred areas of operation. When Queen Anne died in 1714, and at the same time his patron Harley fell from power, Defoe was middle-aged; his health was uncertain, his literary modes beginning to look old-fashioned, and he had all the appearance of yesterday's man.

Remarkably, he had new and greater achievements still to come. First he wormed his way into favour with junior ministers in what would today be called the Home Office; he was permitted to write for a high Tory opposition journal, with the supposed aim of toning down its more extreme criticisms. Only Defoe could have persuaded the government to allow him such a peculiar role. For a time the ups and downs continued as before, but suddenly in 1719 – when almost sixty – Defoe produced his masterpiece, the first part of *Robinson Crusoe*. It was a great commercial success, and gave a huge lift to the writer's entire literary career. He had twelve more years to live, and in this period he produced a flow of exciting and original books. A new surge of confidence entered his spirit; he was again living urgently in the present, and his works were more boldly innovative than ever before. Many of these late books are non-fiction of the highest quality – for example, his splendid *Tour through the Whole Island of Great Britian* (1724–6), a great cache of information and ideas for anyone interested in the birth of modern Britain. His *Complete English Tradesman* (1725–7) is a hymn to the business ethic, a dramatisation of mercantile values (thrift, energy, self-help, and so on) which anticipates Benjamin Franklin as it outdoes him for point and vitality.

All the same, it is the novels Defoe composed during this phase which are best remembered, and which ensure him readers today. After the original *Robinson Crusoe* came a rather disappointing sequel, lacking the taut immediacy of its forerunner. Then followed some stronger efforts: 1720 saw the appearance of *Memoirs of a Cavalier*, a vigorously conceived picture of seventeenth-century warfare, and *Captain Singleton*, a dramatic and unsentimental study of piracy. The year 1722 began with *Moll*, and then yielded two other major works, *A Journal of the*

Plague Year and *Colonel Jack*. The latter contains an outstand-ingly vivid evocation of the hero's youth as a pauper in the streets of London. But the *Journal* is better integrated and more inwardly alive; it re-creates history, but also it animates a personality, the tenacious city saddler H. F., who tells the story. Finally in 1724 Defoe brought out *Roxana* and *A New Voyage Round the World*; both are marred by technical flaws, but the awkwardness is redeemed by other features of the writing – intense collisions of personal feeling in *Roxana*, and an exciting quest theme in the *Voyage*.

Moll Flanders seems to have enjoyed reasonable success when it appeared, but nothing really spectacular – *Robinson Crusoe* had fared a good deal better. The novel came out anonymously; this was the normal procedure anyway, but the pretence of an 'editorial' hand made it essential in this case. How many readers at the time were deceived into thinking the book an authentic recital by a real woman, we cannot now be sure. The likely printing run would be of the order of 1,000 copies, possibly 1,500; but again firm evidence is lacking. We cannot say what sum he received for his work; it must be assumed that the success of *Crusoe*, well known in the trade, had increased the market value of a manuscript by Defoe, but a realistic guess would not put the figure above fifty to seventy-five pounds.

Nor is it possible to speak of a critical reception in the full sense. The practice of reviewing new books was in its infancy, and novels did not qualify for the few learned journals which undertook it. Though contemporary writers occasionally linked the book with the memoirs of whores and pickpockets – such as the notorious Sally Salisbury, who attained extraordinary promi-nence as a courtesan much involved with great figures of state like Lord Bolingbroke – there is very little by way of serious comment. The audience for *Moll* is unlikely to have been exclusively lower-class, though a catchy verse couplet suggests that her memoirs should be kept below stairs:

> Down in the Kitchen, honest Dick and Doll
> Are studying Colonel Jack and Flanders Moll.

Such evidence as there is suggests that the emerging novel did reach a broad spectrum of the reading public. In other words it was read by a high proportion of the existing literary audience as well as satisfying the tastes of readers hitherto excluded from serious culture.

As we have seen, *Moll Flanders* was pirated in 1723, and again in 1730. It maintained a shadowy existence throughout the eighteenth century, often in garbled forms, but it was generally omitted in any accounts of Defoe's life and works. In 1770 a bookseller was able to buy up a job-lot of copyrights, including both *Moll Flanders* and *Roxana*, for a matter of eight guineas. Later still, in 1789, a correspondent to the *Gentleman's Magazine* mentioned *Moll* as one of Defoe's unknown books which yet had some currency, stating that Defoe's novels 'are much in vogue among country readers'. He thought that 'on account of their moral and religious tendency' these works might counteract 'the pernicious effects produced by the too-general circulation of modern novels'. This surprising judgment was not to herald a Victorian revival: *Crusoe* stood alone as the embodiment of practical and patriotic virtues. The rebirth of *Moll's* fame was delayed until a time when she would be neither recommended for her improving tendencies nor banned on the score of her immorality. Around 1920 the shift in taste became unmistakable, and *Moll Flanders* acquired a relevance and interest it has never since lost.

IV

It is necessary, then, to see *Moll* in her time; the background furnished by such things as the vogue for criminal biography supplies a context and an ideological frame of reference. But we read the novel today for its closeness to our own moral experience, for its capacity to touch on raw nerves of twentieth-century sensibility, for its revelations of psychic ordeals we understand only too well. In an age of feminism we are intrigued by the career of a woman attempting to advance herself in a heavily male-dominated society. Moreover, the absurd stops and starts of Moll's life, the pointless wandering from one place to another, the fraught encounters of her muddled urban existence – all these strike immediate reverberations in the modern sensibility. We respond to Moll, not as a stranger from a distant era, but as one trapped in the same labyrinths of diurnal living as we ourselves are.

This authenticity proceeds from a variety of factors, which might be summarised under the heading of expressive literalism. Defoe ensures that Moll will always maintain total fidelity to her impressions, and he restrains her from elaborating upon the basic data of her experiences. A good example occurs in the passage describing Moll's frenzied reaction to the news that she cannot have the elder brother at Colchester, that is either as a husband or a protector. She tells us that 'the agonies of [her] mind threw [her] into a high fever', which raged so intensely that her life was despaired of. The narrative charts her spell of delirium with scrupulous care, filling out the spaces in the calendar with an almost pedantic accuracy:

> It was near five weeks that I kept my bed; and though the violence of my fever abated in three weeks, yet it several times returned; and the physicians said two or three times, they could do no more for me, but that they must leave nature and the distemper to fight it out. After the end of five weeks I grew better, but was so weak, so altered, and recovered so slowly, that the physicians apprehended I should go into a consumption.

Samuel Richardson, and many novelists after him, would have delighted in spinning out this episode, with abundant recollections of hallucinatory visions and half-waking impressions. The fever would be instilled into the narrative, with a convulsive prose echoing the bouts of delirium. Moll gives us nothing of the kind. She will not editorialise, or reconstruct the scene. Instead she renders directly the succession of events as they now appear to her. What she is interested in is not the texture of feeling from moment to moment, but the ongoing course of her life. Unlike many subsequent writers, she refuses to supply a graph of every tiny judder in emotional temperature. Rather she sticks to the 'facts', even where these concern her inward state – in this instance, the progress of a nervous breakdown. The doctors' prognostications are quoted in exactly the same tone of voice as her own observations of her condition.

It is not, as some critics have suggested, that Moll concentrates on event and leaves out feeling. Her emotions are abundantly present in the book, perhaps most strongly of all in this early episode with the two brothers in Essex, a masterpiece of comic realism. What happens is that the feeling is usually reported with a later judgment built in. Thus, when Moll describes her seduction by the elder brother, she defines her situation in these terms:

> I had wholly abandoned all such thoughts, and was taken up only with the pride of my beauty, and of being beloved by such a gentleman. As for the gold [given to her by the lover], I spent whole hours in looking upon it; I told the guineas over a thousand times a day. Never poor vain creature was so wrapt up with every part of the story as I was, not considering what was before me, and how near my ruin was at the door; and indeed I think I rather wished for that ruin than studied to avoid it.

The final verdict is something the later Moll, telling the story, is fully capable of reaching. It is a formulation the younger Moll might have resisted, yet it renders the inner urges she was driven by at that time. We have in effect a narrative of emotional second thoughts.

All this might sound a recipe for blunting the human import of Moll's experiences; but somehow this does not occur. It has often been noticed that there is a clash within the book's emotional logic, that is between the active participant Moll (or Betty) and the reflective narrating Moll. The surprising thing is that this dual viewpoint adds richness and vigour to the novel. One commentator has observed that 'the crafty, young, (and sometimes sentimental) Moll capers through the tale the aged penitent tells'. It is of no importance whether or not we *trust* the ancient teller or the youthful tale; nothing hinges on this, as far as the imaginative life of *Moll Flanders* is concerned. Some readers find the repentant note at the end unconvincing, and they see the narrator as a sort of lady Polonius, uttering trite maxims of high-sounding inutility whilst the real world goes about its grubby buiness. What matters is not the respect we have for sinning Moll, or the credence we attach to penitent Moll. The drama plays around both sides of her character. And it should be added that youth is not really a crucial element in the equation. By the time Moll gets to Newgate, she is already well on into middle age, and yet the same disparities of judgment are apparent:

> I had no trouble, no apprehensions, no sorrow about me; the first surprise was gone; I was, I may well say, I know not how; my senses, my reason, nay, my conscience, were all asleep; my course of life for forty years had been a horrid complication of wickedness, whoredom, adultery, incest, lying, theft; and, in a word, everything but murder

and treason had been my practice, from the age of eighteen, or thereabouts, to threescore; and now I was engulfed in the misery of punishment, and had an infamous death at the door; and yet I had no sense of my condition, no thought of heaven or hell, at least that went any farther than a bare flying touch, like the stitch or pain that gives a hint and goes off. I neither had a heart to ask God's mercy, or indeed to think of it.

There is a strong iambic rhythm running through much of this passage ('the first surprise was gone'; 'I was, I may well say, I know not how'; 'my course of life for forty years'; 'no thought of heaven or hell'; 'the stitch or pain that gives a hint'; and so on). This pulse reflects the anxiety of the moment even as the expressions used place a critical gloss on Moll's responses.

The 'horrid complication' of guilt pervades her criminal career, and distinguishes the account from the majority of rogue's tales. Just as the novel is remote from traditional picaresque – where the central figure is young, swaggering, male, footloose, playful, unreflective – so the book departs from the normal Tyburn biography, where the hero is full of bravado up to the last moment. Even Jonathan Wild, who attempted suicide with a draught of laudanum the day before his execution, is presented by Defoe as resisting all calls for repentance, refusing to go to the prison chapel and avoiding thought of his own spiritual plights. The *Life and Actions* of Wild, published by John Applebee in 1725, informs us that he was never 'in any suitable manner sensible of his condition, or concerned about it, very little sign appeared of his having the least hope concerning his future state; but as he lived hardened, he seemed to die stupid'. There are, of course, stock penitential motifs in other books, but they seldom give any strong impression of a tortured soul. Often the tone of crime literature is a jaunty one as in a letter to Applebee's *Weekly Journal* for 21 November 1724. (Again Defoe is the probable author). A certain 'Betty Blewskin' writes in to describe her love for the escapologist and housebreaker Jack Sheppard, then bound for the gallows. She remarks that she was born in Newgate, niece of 'the famous Moll Flanders' – perhaps a puff for the novel, which employed that phrase on its title-page. Her activities as a pickpocket are recounted with a genial insouciance, as though she were describing a fishing trip:

I never went to Salters-Lecture [a dissenting chapel], or St Lawrence's church, and came away without a gold watch, or a tweezer, or some other valuable prize in my life. I rarely came empty handed from the theatre, especially if the play was anything popular: I assure you, *Cato* [Addison's play] was worth above 100 guineas to me, and yet I reckon the things taken, as we generally sell such things; namely, at half value.

There could not be a greater contrast with Moll's idiom of temptation, necessity, snares, misery, want, distress and so on. Betty Blewskin revels in her trade; Moll sees her 'advēntures' as threatening, and constantly dreads capture – for this would mean exposure as well as punishment. The governess acts as a kind of anti-conscience, but also as a secret sharer of the guilty truth. Fellow-thieves are likely to be imprudent and unreliable: hence her resolve 'to be very cautious how I adventured with them'. There is little sense of a community of kindred spirits, for Moll never feels that she is part of the criminal subculture: she keeps a little of herself back. Just as Oliver Twist clings on to his genteel patterns of speech through all his days in Fagin's den, so Moll Flanders can never fully join her accomplices. Her desire is to be a paid member of orthodox society, and so she is fated to remain marginal to a group of marginal men and women.

Throughout the book, in her sexual exploits and in her escapades in crime, Moll strives for respectability, not just because it connotes status but also because it means quietus, the stilling of that insistent drum-beat which urges her on to desperate action. She is perpetually insecure; she wants to arrive, less out of the desire to reach any particular destination than out of incapacity to travel hopefully. Her successive marriages are like Gulliver's repeated voyages into the unknown, undertaken to ward off the horrors of stasis, yet having a Houyhnhnm-like passivity and innocence as their ultimate goal. There is a remarkable percipience in the strange Yeatsian doggerel of the chapbook compiler:

> Unweary'd traveller, whither dost thou roam?

V

Crucial to the effect of all Defoe's fiction is his highly individual manner of writing. His style is sometimes dismissed as dull, baldly referential, lacking in colour and texture. It is true that he uses a

rather dry idiom, that is a narrow and repetitive range of
expressions and a loose-jointed syntax where such things as
subsequence and consequence can be blurred. He has an extraordinary fondness for certain verbal devices, such as the so-called
'economical statements' used to cut a long story short (*in a word*,
etc.) or the parenthetic *as I may call it*. Nevertheless, Defoe was
able to squeeze out a remarkable wealth of implication from this
penurious stock of language. He is particularly good at
dramatising moral debate within a character; *Moll Flanders* is full
of little exercises of weighing good and bad in a given situation,
provoked by what G. A. Starr aptly terms 'local crises'. An
example is the passage where Moll considers what she ought to do
with her five-year-old son, fathered by the gentleman she met at
Bath.

> And now I was greatly perplexed about my little boy. It was death to
> me to part with the child, and yet when I considered the danger of
> being one time or other left with him to keep without being able to
> support him, I then resolved to leave him; but then concluded to be
> near him myself too, that I might have the satisfaction of seeing him,
> without the care of providing for him. So I sent my gentleman a short
> letter that I had obeyed his orders in all things but that of going back to
> Bath; that however parting from him was a wound to me that I could
> never recover, yet that I was fully satisfied his reflections were just, and
> would be very far from desiring to obstruct his reformation.

A large amount of the stylistic work here is done by tiny particles,
inobtrusive conjunctions for the most part ('And now'; 'and yet';
'then'; 'but then'; 'so;' 'that'; 'yet'). Often Defoe injects an
element of drama into apparently directionless prose by stressing
adversative notions with 'but', 'yet', 'however', etc., where the
sense might seem to require ordinary linkage by a word like 'and'.
The language is constantly changing the point of attack: by small
shifts in emphasis Moll creates the impression of moral confusion,
without any recourse to heavy ethical terminology.

One of the most striking features of the style is its closeness to
ordinary material reality. It is a concrete and object-filled prose,
eloquent in its precise registration of such things as size, price,
time and location:

> To prevent being known, I pulled off my blue apron, and wrapt the
> bundle in it, which was made up in a piece of painted calico; I also
> wrapt up my straw hat in it, and so put the bundle upon my head; and

it was very well that I did thus, for coming through the Bluecoat Hospital, who should I meet but the wench that had given me the bundle to hold. It seems she was going with her mistress, whom she had been to fetch, to the Barnet coaches.

Note how the opening phrase here, in omitting the expected possessive pronoun, appears to mimic Moll's urge to conceal herself. The specificity of reference depends on several facts mentioned earlier in the narrative – that Moll was dressed in deliberately 'mean' clothes, including a blue apron and a straw hat; that she had by chance taken her station near the alehouse from which the Barnet coach left; that the maid has gone off to fetch her mistress, leaving Moll in charge of the parcel. Almost all the essential facts in the quoted passage have a collateral in the previous snatch of narrative. We are never allowed to get far away from the raw phenomenology of the scene: the prose insists on the key facts (like the bundle and the straw hat) and makes the reader's attention hold on fast to them.

When Moll gets this bundle back safely to her accomplice, the governess, she itemises the contents: 'There was no money, plate, or jewels in it, but a very good suit of Indian damask, a gown and petticoat, a laced head and ruffles of very good Flanders lace, and some other things, such as I knew very well the value of.' (Moll's familiarity with textiles and dress-materials is one of her few concessions to traditional femininity.) Characteristic here is the final dismissive phrase. A studied vagueness is common to all Defoe's fictional narrators, but Moll is particularly cagey in the way that she doles out her information. It is true that occasionally we get exceedingly detailed accounts, as with the three bills presented to Moll by the governess by way of estimate for a quarter's boarding. 'However, it is much more common to get deliberate blurring of the precise figures. The narrative is studded with approximations: 'about fifteen miles, as I remember', or 'near three weeks', or 'worth only about £6'. The effect is partly to reinforce our sense of an effort to recall facts: by committing herself to a slightly inexact quantity, Moll persuades us that she is keeping scrupulously to the truth in all other particulars. In addition, the trick works to suggest that she is concerned about the broad pattern of events, and will not vouch for every single item mentioned. In theory these impressions might seem to pull in different directions; but subliminally they coexist peaceably enough, and most readers are not disturbed by the contradiction.

Moll's style is in large measure Defoe's own habitual style, and he makes only small adjustments to suit the sex and circumstances of his narrator. But then, although he had never been a transported felon, a kept mistress or a widow, he had seen enough of his heroine's milieu to make an intelligent guess at her feelings and likely expressive needs. If he did not go round robbing women while their houses burnt to the ground, he did at least (in his early days) try to cheat his mother-in-law by selling her civet-cats which were already under a writ of seizure. Of course, I do not suggest that naked biographic experience accounts for Defoe's understanding of Moll; his sense of her being proceeds from much deeper psychic sources, and like all great novelists he invented much more than he copied direct from life. But it is true that he needed to do no special research in order to embark on this story. His background in the hosiery trade and insurance; his work as a spy; his writings on social questions; his journalistic forays into crime, bankruptcy and economics; his own conflicts with the law – all these gave him a broad understanding of Moll's world. The travels she makes about England often follow in precise detail the journeys recounted in the *Tour*. The characters she encounters sometimes resemble the kind of people he knew best, and in one instance (the 'amphibious creature, this land-water thing, called a gentleman-tradesman') there is an uncomfortable similarity to Defoe himself.

In the last analysis, however, *Moll Flanders* stands as a remarkable imaginative feat. Diurnal eighteenth-century England and Virginia are there, but transposed and illuminated by Defoe's intense and personal vision of the human condition. Moll leads a panicky, muddled, disturbing life, and it is possible to feel that Defoe got himself in a muddle at times when he sought to render this quality of being. But there is also a luminous attribute in her character, a courage and indomitable will which makes her struggle for survival very far from grim reading. Gusto and energy pervade the recital of this chequered life-history. So the old apple-woman on London Bridge got nearest the truth, after all. There ought to be a 'deep moral' at the heart of it, but what we take away from our reading is a sense of heightened life, a penetration of one woman's inner being, an abiding affection for this outcast who overcame all the pressures of a hostile society.

A NOTE ON THE TEXT

As remarked in the Introduction (p.xxii), *Moll Flanders* appeared in late January 1722. The likely print run would have been around 1000 copies, possible as many as 1500, but firm evidence is missing. The title-page carries the date '1721', which most likely reflects a delay in publication. Six months later the second edition appeared; there are in fact two variant editions, with different title-pages (listing a different group of booksellers, i.e. publishers) but otherwise identical. This text is shorter than the original version, containing mostly small deletions, with the aim of saving space predominating over any literary considerations. It is not out of the question that Defoe had a hand in this operation, which reduced the length of the novel by something like a twentieth part: but it is more likely that he knew nothing of the whole exercise, having sold his copyright for an outright fee. A so-called 'third' edition in December 1722 was in reality a straightforward reissue of the second edition with a cancelled title-page. In other words, there are basically only two versions, the unabridged text published in January, and the shortened text appearing in July and December. Though the later version makes a few improvements in matters such as grammar, the first edition has stronger claims to authenticity. The disparities are not so marked that any signficant literary consequence is entailed. The book was also serialised in the *London Post* over the course of several months in 1722–23.

For a comparison of the first and third editions, noting the kind of changes made, see J. Paul Hunter's edition of the novel (New York, 1970), pp. 353–67. The present text, like most modern reprints, is based on the third edition, modernised in spelling, in accidentals (e.g. use of italics and initial capitals), and conservatively in punctuation (lightening the heavy use of commas in the original). This text was prepared for the first Everyman edition in 1930, but since it has been reset for its new publication in 1993, I have examined its readings throughout to confirm accuracy.

AUTHOR'S PREFACE

The world is so taken up of late with novels and romances, that it will be hard for a private history to be taken for genuine, where the names and other circumstances of the person are concealed; and on this account we must be content to leave the reader to pass his own opinion upon the ensuing sheets, and take it just as he pleases.

The author is here supposed to be writing her own history, and in the very beginning of her account she gives the reasons why she thinks fit to conceal her true name, after which there is no occasion to say any more about that.

It is true that the original of this story is put into new words, and the style of the famous lady we here speak of is a little altered; particularly she is made to tell her own tale in modester words than she told it at first, the copy which came first to hand having been written in language more like one still in Newgate* than one grown penitent and humble, as she afterwards pretends* to be.

The pen employed in finishing her story, and making it what you now see it to be, has had no little difficulty to put it into a dress fit to be seen, and to make it speak language fit to be read. When a woman debauched from her youth, nay, even being the offspring of debauchery and vice, comes to give an account of all her vicious practices, and even to descend to the particular occasions and circumstances by which she first became wicked, and of all the progressions of crime which she ran through in threescore years, an author must be hard put to it to wrap it up so clean as not to give room, especially for vicious readers, to turn it to his disadvantage.

All possible care, however, has been taken to give no lewd ideas, no immodest turns in the new dressing up this story; no, not to the worst part of her expressions. To this purpose some of the vicious parts of her life, which could not be modestly told, is quite left out, and several other parts are very much shortened. What is left 'tis hoped will not offend the chastest reader or the modestest hearer and as the best use is to be made even of the worst story, the moral, 'tis hoped, will keep the reader serious, even where the story might incline him to be otherwise. To give the history of a wicked life repented of, necessarily requires that the wicked part should be made as wicked as the real history of it will bear, to illustrate and give a beauty to the penitent part, which is certainly the best and brightest, if related with equal spirit and life.

It is suggested there cannot be the same life, the same brightness and beauty, in relating the penitent part as in the criminal part. If there is any truth in that suggestion, I must be allowed to say, 'tis because there is not the same taste and relish in the reading; and indeed it is too true that the difference lies not in the real worth of the subject so much as in the gust* and palate of the reader.

But as this work is chiefly recommended to those who know how to read it, and how to make the good uses of it which the story all along recommends to them, so it is to be hoped that such readers will be much more pleased with the moral than the fable, with the application than with the relation, and with the end of the writer than with the life of the person written of.

There is in this story abundance of delightful incidents, and all of them usefully applied. There is an agreeable turn artfully given them in the relating, that naturally instructs the reader, either one way or another. The first part of her lewd life with the young gentleman at Colchester has so many happy turns given it to expose the crime, and warn all whose circumstances are adapted to it, of the ruinous end of such things, and the foolish, thought-less, and abhorred conduct of both the parties, that it abundantly atones for all the lively description she gives of her folly and wickedness.

The repentance of her lover at Bath, and how brought by the just alarm of his fit of sickness to abandon her; the just caution given there against even the lawful intimacies of the dearest friends and how unable they are to preserve the most solemn resolutions of virtue without divine assistance; these are parts which, to a just discernment, will appear to have more real beauty in them than all the amorous chain of story which introduces it.

In a word, as the whole relation is carefully garbled* of all the levity and looseness that was in it, so it is applied, and with the utmost care, to virtuous and religious uses. None can, without being guilty of manifest injustice, cast any reproach upon it, or upon our design in publishing it.

The advocates for the stage have, in all ages, made this the great argument to persuade people that their plays are useful, and that they ought to be allowed in the most civilised and in the most religious government; namely, that they are applied to virtuous purposes, and that, by the most lively representations, they fail not to recommend virtue and generous principles, and to discourage and expose all sorts of vice and corruption of manners; and were it true that they did so, and that they constantly adhered to that rule, as the test of their acting on the theatre, much might be said in their favour.

Throughout the infinite variety of this book, this fundamental is most strictly adhered to; there is not a wicked action in any part of it, but is first or last rendered unhappy and unfortunate; there is not a superlative villain brought upon the stage, but either he is brought to an unhappy end, or brought to be a penitent; there is not an ill thing mentioned but it is condemned, even in the relation, nor a virtuous, just thing but it carries its praise along with it. What can more exactly answer the rule laid down, to recommend even those representations of things which have so many other just objections lying against them? namely, of example of bad company, obscene language, and the like.

Upon this foundation this book is recommended to the reader, as a work from every part of which something may be learned, and some just and religious inference is drawn, by which the reader will have something of instruction if he pleases to make use of it.

All the exploits of this lady of fame, in her depredations upon mankind, stand as so many warnings to honest people to beware of them, intimating to them by what methods innocent people are drawn in, plundered, and robbed, and by consequence how to avoid them. Her robbing a little child, dressed fine by the vanity of the mother, to go to the dancing-school, is a good memento to such people hereafter, as is likewise her picking the gold watch from the young lady's side in the park.*

Her getting a parcel from a hare-brained wench at the coaches in St John's Street;* her booty at the fire, and also at Harwich, all give us excellent warning in such cases to be more present to ourselves in sudden surprises of every sort.

Her application to a sober life and industrious management at last, in Virginia, with her transported spouse, is a story fruitful of instruction to all the unfortunate creatures who are obliged to

seek their re-establishment abroad, whether by the misery of
transportation or other disaster; letting them know that diligence
and application have their due encouragement, even in the
remotest part of the world, and that no case can be so low, so
despicable, or so empty of prospect, but that an unwearied
industry will go a great way to deliver us from it, will in time raise
the meanest creature to appear again in the world, and give him a
new cast* for his life.

These are a few of the serious inferences which we are led by the
hand to in this book, and these are fully sufficient to justify any
man in recommending it to the world, and much more to justify
the publication of it.

There are two of the most beautiful parts still behind,* which
this story gives some idea of, and lets us into the parts of them, but
they are either of them too long to be brought into the same
volume, and indeed are, as I may call them, whole volumes of
themselves, viz.:1. The life of her governess, as she calls her, who
had run through, it seems, in a few years, all the eminent degrees
of a gentlewoman, a whore, and a bawd; a midwife and a
midwife-keeper,* as they are called; a pawnbroker, a child-
taker,* a receiver of thieves, and of stolen goods; and, in a word,
herself a thief, a breeder up of thieves, and the like, and yet at
last a penitent.

The second is the life of her transported husband, a highwayman, who, it seems, lived a twelve years' life of successful villainy
upon the road, and even at last came off so well as to be a
volunteer transport, not a convict; and in whose life there is an
incredible variety.

But, as I said, these are things too long to bring in here, so
neither can I make a promise of their coming out by themselves.

We cannot say, indeed, that this history is carried on quite to
the end of the life of the famous Moll Flanders, for nobody can
write their own life to the full end of it, unless they can write it
after they are dead. But her husband's life, being written by a third
hand, gives a full account of them both, how long they lived
together in that country, and how they came both to England
again, after about eight years, in which time they were grown very
rich, and where she lived, it seems, to be very old, but was not so
extraordinary a penitent as she was at first; it seems only that
indeed she always spoke with abhorrence of her former life, and
every part of it.*

In her last scene, at Maryland and Virginia, many pleasant things happened, which makes that part of her life very agreeable, but they are not told with the same elegance as those accounted for by herself, so it is still to the more advantage that we break off here.

THE FORTUNES AND
MISFORTUNES
of the Famous
MOLL FLANDERS

My true name is so well known in the records or registers at Newgate, and in the Old Bailey,* and there are some things of such consequence still depending there, relating to my particular conduct, that it is not to be expected I should set my name or the account of my family to this work; perhaps after my death it may be better known; at present it would not be proper, no, not though a general pardon should be issued, even without exceptions of persons or crimes.

It is enough to tell you, that as some of my worst comrades who are out of the way of doing me harm (having gone out of the world by the steps* and the string,* as I often expected to go), knew me by the name of Moll Flanders,* so you may give me leave to go under that name till I dare own who I have been, as well as who I am.

I have been told, that in one of our neighbour nations, whether it be in France or where else I know not, they have an order from the king, that when any criminal is condemned, either to die, or to the galleys, or to be transported, if they leave any children, as such are generally unprovided for, by the forfeiture of their parents, so they are immediately taken into the care of the government, and put into an hospital called the House of Orphans,* where they are bred up, clothed, fed, taught, and when fit to go out, are placed to trades, or to services, so as to be well able to provide for themselves by an honest, industrious behaviour.

Had this been the custom in our country, I had not been left a poor desolate girl without friends, without clothes, without help or helper, as was my fate; and by which, I was not only exposed to very great distresses, even before I was capable either of understanding my case or how to amend it, but brought into a course of life, scandalous in itself, and which in its ordinary course tended to the swift destruction both of soul and body.

But the case was otherwise here. My mother was convicted of felony for a petty theft, scarce worth naming, viz. borrowing three pieces of fine holland* of a certain draper in Cheapside.* The circumstances are too long to repeat, and I have heard them related so many ways, that I can scarce tell which is the right account.

However it was, they all agree in this, that my mother pleaded her belly;* and being found quick with child, she was respited for about seven months; after which she was called down, as they term it, to her former judgment, but obtained the favour afterward of being transported to the plantations, and left me about half a year old, and in bad hands you may be sure.

This is too near the first hours of my life for me to relate anything of myself but by hearsay; 'tis enough to mention, that as I was born in such an unhappy place, I had no parish to have recourse to for my nourishment in my infancy; nor can I give the least account how I was kept alive, other than that, as I have been told, some relation of my mother took me away, but at whose expense, or by whose direction, I know nothing at all of it.

The first account that I can recollect, or could ever learn, of myself, was that I had wandered among a crew of those people they call gipsies, or Egyptians; but I believe it was but a little while that I had been among them, for I had not had my skin discoloured, as they do to all children they carry about with them; nor can I tell how I came among them, or how I got from them.

It was at Colchester,* in Essex, that those people left me, and I have a notion in my head that I left them there (that is, that I hid myself and would not go any farther with them), but I am not able to be particular in that account; only this I remember, that being taken up by some of the parish officers of Colchester, I gave an account that I came into the town with the gipsies, but that I would not go any farther with them, and that so they had left me, but whither they were gone that I knew not; for though they sent round the country to inquire after them, it seems they could not be found.

I was now in a way to be provided for; for though I was not a parish charge upon this or that part of the town by law, yet as my case came to be known, and that I was too young to do any work, being not above three years old, compassion moved the magistrates of the town, to take care of me, and I became one of their own as much as if I had been born in the place.

In the provision they made for me, it was my good hap to be put to nurse, as they call it, to a woman who was indeed poor, but had been in better circumstances, and who got a little livelihood by taking such as I was supposed to be, and keeping them with all necessaries, till they were at a certain age, in which it might be supposed they might go to service, or get their own bread.

This woman had also a little school, which she kept to teach children to read and to work; and having, I say, lived before that in good fashion, she bred up the children with a great deal of art, as well as with a great deal of care.

But, which was worth all the rest, she bred them up very religiously also, being herself a very sober, pious woman; secondly, very housewifely and clean; and, thirdly, very mannerly, and with good behaviour. So that, excepting a plain diet, coarse lodging, and mean clothes, we were brought up as mannerly as if we had been at the dancing-school.

I was continued here till I was eight years old, when I was terrified with news that the magistrates (as I think they called them) had ordered that I should go in service. I was able to do but very little, wherever I was to go, except it was to run of errands, and be a drudge to some cookmaid, and this they told me often, which put me into a great fright; for I had a thorough aversion to going to service, as they called it, though I was so young; and I told my nurse, that I believed I could get my living without going to service, if she pleased to let me; for she had taught me to work with my needle, and spin worsted, which is the chief trade of that city, and I told her that if she would keep me, I would work for her, and I would work very hard.

I talked to her almost every day of working hard; and, in short, I did nothing but work and cry all day, which grieved the good, kind woman so much, that at last she began to be concerned for me, for she loved me very well.

One day after this, as she came into the room, where all the poor children were at work, she sat down just over against me, not in her usual place as mistress, but as if she had set herself on purpose to observe me and see me work. I was doing something she had set me to, as I remember it was marking some shirts, which she had taken to make, and after a while she began to talk to me. 'Thou foolish child,' says she, 'thou art always crying' (for I was crying then). 'Prithee, what dost cry for?' 'Because they will take me away,' says I, 'and put me to service, and I can't work house-work.' 'Well, child,' says she, 'but though you can't work house-work, you will learn it in time, and they won't put you to hard things at first.' 'Yes, they will,' says I; 'and if I can't do it they will beat me, and the maids will beat me to make me do great work, and I am but a little girl, and I can't do it'; and then I cried again, till I could not speak any more.

This moved my good motherly nurse, so that she resolved I should not go to service yet; so she bid me not cry, and she would speak to Mr Mayor, and I should not go to service till I was bigger.

Well, this did not satisfy me, for to think of going to service at all was such a frightful thing to me, that if she had assured me I should not have gone till I was twenty years old, it would have been the same to me; I should have cried all the time, with the very apprehension of its being to be so at last.

When she saw that I was not pacified yet, she began to be angry with me. 'And what would you have?' says she. 'Don't I tell you that you shall not go to service till you are bigger?' 'Ay,' says I, 'but then I must go at last.' 'Why, what,' said she, 'is the girl mad? What! would you be a gentlewoman?' 'Yes,' says I, and cried heartily till I roared out again.

This set the old gentlewoman a-laughing at me, as you may be sure it would. 'Well, madam, forsooth,' says she, gibing at me, 'you would be a gentlewoman; and how will you come to be a gentlewoman? What! will you do it by your fingers' ends?'

'Yes,' says I again, very innocently.

'Why, what can you earn,' says she; 'what can you get a day at your work?'

'Threepence,' said I, 'when I spin, and fourpence when I work plain work.'*

'Alas! poor gentlewoman,' said she again, laughing, 'what will that do for thee?'

'It will keep me,' says I, 'if you will let me live with you'; and this I said in such a poor petitioning tone, that it made the poor woman's heart yearn to me, as she told me afterwards.

'But,' says she, 'that will not keep you and buy you clothes too; and who must buy the little gentlewoman clothes?' says she, and smiled all the while at me.

'I will work harder then,' says I, 'and you shall have it all.'

'Poor child! it won't keep you,' said she; 'it will hardly find you in victuals.'

'Then I would have no victuals,' says I again, very innocently; 'let me but live with you.'

'Why, can you live without victuals?' says she. 'Yes,' again says I, very much like a child, you may be sure, and still I cried heartily.

I had no policy in all this; you may easily see it was all nature; but it was joined with so much innocence and so much passion that, in short, it set the good motherly creature a-weeping too, and at last she cried as fast as I did, and then took me and led me out of the teaching-room. 'Come,' says she, 'you shan't go to service; you shall live with me'; and this pacified me for the present.

After this, she going to wait on the Mayor, my story came up, and my good nurse told Mr Mayor the whole tale; he was so pleased with it, that he would call his lady and his two daughters to hear it, and it made mirth enough among them, you may be sure.

However, not a week had passed over, but on a sudden comes Mrs Mayoress and her two daughters to the house to see my old nurse, and to see her school and the children. When they had looked about them a little, 'Well, Mrs—,' says the Mayoress to my nurse, 'and pray which is the little lass that is to be a gentle-woman?' I heard her, and I was terribly frighted, though I did not know why neither; but Mrs Mayoress comes up to me, 'Well, miss,' says she, 'and what are you at work upon?' The word miss was a language that had hardly been heard of in our school, and I wondered what sad name it was she called me; however, I stood up, made a curtsey, and she took my work out of my hand, looked on it, and said it was very well; then she looked upon one of my hands. 'Nay, she may come to be a gentlewoman,' says she, 'for aught I know; she has a lady's hand, I assure you.' This pleased me mightily; but Mrs Mayoress did not stop there, but put her hand in her pocket, gave me a shilling, and bid me mind my work, and learn to work well, and I might be a gentlewoman for aught she knew.

All this while my good old nurse, Mrs Mayoress, and all the rest of them, did not understand me at all, for they meant one sort of thing by the word gentlewoman, and I meant quite another; for, alas! all I understood by being a gentlewoman, was to be able to work for myself, and get enough to keep me without going to service, whereas they meant to live great and high, and I know not what.

Well, after Mrs Mayoress was gone, her two daughters came in,

and they called for the gentlewoman too, and they talked a long
while to me, and I answered them in my innocent way; but
always, if they asked me whether I resolved to be a gentlewoman, I
answered, Yes. At last they asked me what a gentlewoman was?
That puzzled me much. However, I explained myself negatively,
that it was one that did not go to service, to do house-work; they
were mightily pleased, and liked my little prattle to them, which, it
seems, was agreeable enough to them, and they gave me money
too.

As for my money, I gave it all to my mistress-nurse, as I called
her, and told her she should have all I got when I was a
gentlewoman as well as now. By this and some other of my talk,
my old tutoress began to understand what I meant by being a
gentlewoman, and that it was no more than to be able to get my
bread by my own work; and at last she asked me whether it was
not so.

I told her, yes, and insisted on it, that to do so was to be a
gentlewoman; 'For,' says I, 'there is such a one,' naming a woman
that mended lace and washed the ladies' laced heads;* 'she,' says
I, 'is a gentlewoman, and they call her madam.'

'Poor child,' says my good old nurse, 'you may soon be such a
gentlewoman as that, for she is a person of ill fame, and has had
two bastards.'

I did not understand anything of that; but I answered, 'I am sure
they call her madam, and she does not go to service nor do house-
work'; and therefore I insisted that she was a gentlewoman, and I
would be such a gentlewoman as that.

The ladies were told all this again, and they made themselves
merry with it, and every now and then Mr Mayor's daughters
would come and see me, and ask where the little gentlewoman
was, which made me not a little proud of myself besides. I was
often visited by these young ladies, and sometimes they brought
others with them; so that I was known by it almost all over the
town.

I was now about ten years old, and began to look a little
womanish, for I was mighty grave, very mannerly, and as I had
often heard the ladies say I was pretty, and would be very
handsome, you may be sure it made me not a little proud.
However, that pride had no ill effect upon me yet; only, as they
often gave me money, and I gave it my old nurse, she, honest
woman, was so just as to lay it out again for me, and gave me

head-dresses, and linen, and gloves, and I went very neat, for if I had rags on, I would always be clean or else I would dabble them in water myself; but, I say, my good nurse, when I had money given me, very honestly laid it out for me, and would always tell the ladies this or that was bought with their money; and this made them give me more, till at last I was indeed called upon by the magistrates to go out to service. But then I was become so good a workwoman myself, and the ladies were so kind to me, that I was past it; for I could earn as much for my nurse as was enough to keep me; so she told them, that if they would give her leave, she would keep the gentlewoman, as she called me, to be her assistant, and teach the children, which I was very well able to do; for I was very nimble at my work, though I was yet very young.

But the kindness of the ladies did not end here, for when they understood that I was no more maintained by the town as before, they gave me money oftener; and as I grew up, they brought me work to do for them, such as linen to make, laces to mend, and heads to dress up, and not only paid me for doing them, but even taught me how to do them; so that I was a gentlewoman indeed, as I understood that word; for before I was twelve years old, I not only found myself clothes, and paid my nurse for my keeping, but got money in my pocket too.

The ladies also gave me clothes frequently of their own or their children's; some stockings, some petticoats, some gowns, some one thing, some another; and these my old woman managed for me like a mother, and kept them for me, obliged me to mend them, and turn them to the best advantage, for she was a rare housewife.

At last one of the ladies took such a fancy to me that she would have me home to her house, for a month, she said, to be among her daughters.

Now, though this was exceeding kind in her, yet, as my good woman said to her, unless she resolved to keep me for good and all, she would do the little gentlewoman more harm than good. 'Well,' says the lady, 'that's true; I'll only take her home for a week, then, that I may see how my daughters and she agree, and how I like her temper, and then I'll tell you more; and in the meantime, if anybody comes to see her as they used to do, you may only tell them you have sent her out to my house.'

This was prudently managed enough, and I went to the lady's

house; but I was so pleased there with the young ladies, and they so pleased with me, that I had enough to do to come away, and they were as unwilling to part with me.

However, I did come away, and live almost a year more with my honest old woman, and began now to be very helpful to her; for I was almost fourteen years old, was tall of my age, and looked a little womanish; but I had such a taste of genteel living at the lady's house that I was not so easy in my old quarters as I used to be, and I thought it was fine to be a gentlewoman indeed, for I had quite other notions of a gentlewoman now than I had before; and as I thought that it was fine to be a gentlewoman, so I loved to be among gentlewomen, and therefore I longed to be there again.

When I was about fourteen years and a quarter old, my good old nurse, mother I ought to call her, fell sick and died. I was then in a sad condition indeed, for as there is no great bustle in putting an end to a poor body's family when once they are carried to the grave, so the poor good woman being buried, the parish children were immediately removed by the churchwardens; the school was at an end, and the day children of it had no more to do but just stay at home till they were sent somewhere else. As for what she left, a daughter, a married woman, came and swept it all away, and removing the goods, they had no more to say to me than to jest with me, and tell me that the little gentlewoman might set up for herself if she pleased.

I was frighted out of my wits almost, and knew not what do to; for I was, as it were, turned out of doors to the wide world, and that which was still worse, the old honest woman had two-and-twenty shillings of mine in her hand, which was all the estate the little gentlewoman had in the world; and when I asked the daughter for it she huffed* me, and told me she had nothing to do with it.

It was true the good, poor woman had told her daughter of it, and that it lay in such a place, that it was the child's money, and had called once or twice for me to give it me, but I was unhappily out of the way, and when I came back she was past being in a condition to speak of it. However, the daughter was so honest afterwards as to give it me, though at first she used me cruelly about it.

Now was I a poor gentlewoman indeed, and I was just that very night to be turned into the wide world; for the daughter removed all the goods, and I had not so much as a lodging to go to, or a bit of bread to eat. But it seems some of the neighbours took so much compassion of me as to acquaint the lady in whose family I had been; and immediately she sent her maid to fetch me, and away I went with them bag and baggage, and with a glad heart, you may be sure. The fright of my condition had made such an impression upon me that I did not want now to be a gentlewoman, but was very willing to be a servant, and that any kind of servant they thought fit to have me be.

But my new generous mistress had better thoughts for me. I call her generous, for she exceeded the good woman I was with before in everything, as in estate; I say, in everthing except honesty; and for that, though this was a lady most exactly just, yet I must not forget to say on all occasions, that the first, though poor, was as uprightly honest as it was possible.

I was no sooner carried away, as I have said, by this good gentlewoman, but the first lady, that is to say, the Mayoress that was, sent her daughters to take care of me; and another family which had taken notice of me when I was the little gentlewoman sent for me after her, so that I was mightily made of; nay, and they were not a little angry, especially the Mayoress, that her friend had taken me away from her; for, as she said, I was hers by right, she having been the first that took any notice of me. But they that had me would not part with me; and as for me, I could not be better than where I was.

Here I continued till I was between seventeen and eighteen years old, and here I had all the advantages for my education that could be imagined; the lady had masters home to teach her daughters to dance, and to speak French, and to write, and others to teach them music; and as I was always with them, I learned as fast as they; and though the masters were not appointed to teach me, yet I learned by imitation and inquiry all that they learned by instruction and direction; so that, in short, I learned to dance and speak French as well as any of them, and to sing much better, for I had a better voice than any of them. I could not so readily come at playing the harpsichord or the spinet, because I had no instrument of my own to practise on, and could only come at theirs in the intervals when they left it; but yet I learned tolerably well, and the young ladies at length got two instruments, that is to say, a harpsichord and a spinet, too, and then they taught me them-selves. But as to dancing, they could hardly help my learning country-dances, because they always wanted me to make up even number; and, on the other hand, they were as heartily willing to learn me everything that they had been taught themselves as I could be to take the learning.

By this means I had, as I have said, all the advantages of education that I could have had if I had been as much a gentlewoman as they were with whom I lived; and in some things I had the advantage of my ladies, though they were my superiors, viz., that mine were all the gifts of nature, and which all their fortunes could not furnish. First, I was apparently* handsomer than any of them; secondly, I was better shaped; and, thirdly, I sang better, by which I mean I had a better voice; in all which you will, I hope, allow me to say, I do not speak my own conceit, but the opinion of all that knew the family.

I had with all these the common vanity of my sex, viz., that being really taken for very handsome, or, if you please, for a great beauty, I very well knew it, and had as good an opinion of myself as anybody else could have of me, and particularly I loved to hear anybody speak of it, which happened often, and was a great satisfaction to me.

Thus far I have had a smooth story to tell of myself, and in all this part of my life I not only had the reputation of living in a very good family, and a family noted and respected everywhere for virtue and sobriety, and for every valuable thing, but I had the character too of a very sober, modest, and virtuous young woman, and such I had always been; neither had I yet any occasion to think of anything else, or to know what a temptation to wickedness meant.

But that which I was too vain of was my ruin, or rather my vanity was the cause of it. The lady in the house where I was had two sons, young gentlemen of extraordinary parts* and behaviour, and it was my misfortune to be very well with them both, but they managed themselves with me in a quite different manner.

The eldest, a gay gentleman, that knew the town as well as the country, and though he had levity enough to do an ill-natured thing, yet had too much judgment of things to pay too dear for his pleasures; he began with that unhappy snare to all women, viz., taking notice upon all occasions how pretty I was, as he called it, how agreeable, how well-carriaged, and the like; and this he contrived so subtly, as if he had known as well how to catch a woman in his net as a partridge when he went a-setting, for he would contrive to be talking this to his sisters, when, though I was not by, yet he knew I was not so far off but that I should be sure to hear him. His sisters would return softly to him, 'Hush, brother, she will hear you; she is but in the next room.' Then he would put it off and talk softlier, as if he had not known it, and begin to acknowledge he was wrong; and then, as if he had forgot himself, he would speak aloud again, and I, that was so well pleased to hear it, was sure to listen for it upon all occasions.

After he had thus baited his hook, and found easily enough the method how to lay it in my way, he played an open game; and one day, going by his sister's chamber when I was there, he comes in with an air of gaiety. 'Oh, Mrs Betty,'* said he to me, 'how do you do, Mrs Betty? Don't your cheeks burn, Mrs Betty?' I made a curtsey and blushed, but said nothing. 'What makes you talk so, brother?' said the lady. 'Why,' says he, 'we have been talking of her below-stairs this half-hour.' 'Well,' says his sister, 'you can say no harm of her, that I am sure, so 'tis no matter what you have been talking about.' 'Nay,' says he, ''tis so far from talking harm of her, that we have been talking a great deal of good, and a great many fine things have been said of Mrs Betty, I assure you; and particularly, that she is the handsomest young woman in Colchester; and, in short, they begin to toast her health in the town.'

'I wonder at you, brother,' says the sister. 'Betty wants but one thing, but she had as good want everything, for the market is against our sex just now; and if a young woman has beauty, birth, breeding, wit, sense, manners, modesty, and all to an extreme, yet if she has not money she's nobody, she had as good want them all; nothing but money now recommends a woman; the men play the game all into their own hands.'

Her younger brother, who was by, cried, 'Hold, sister, you run too fast; I am an exception to your rule. I assure you, if I find a woman so accomplished as you talk of, I won't trouble myself about the money.' 'Oh,' says the sister, 'but you will take care not to fancy one then without the money.'

'You don't know that neither,' says the brother.

'But why, sister,' says the elder brother, 'why do you exclaim so about the fortune? You are none of them that want a fortune, whatever else you want.'

'I understand you, brother,' replies the lady very smartly; 'you suppose I have the money and want the beauty; but as times go now, the first will do, so I have the better of my neighbours.'

'Well,' says the younger brother, 'but your neighbours may be even with you, for beauty will steal a husband sometimes in spite of money, and when the maid chances to be handsomer than the mistress, she often times makes as good a market, and rides in a coach before her.'

I thought it was time for me to withdraw, and I did so, but not so far but that I heard all their discourse, in which I heard abundance of fine things said of myself, which prompted my vanity, but, as I soon found, was not the way to increase my interest in the family, for the sister and the younger brother fell grievously out about it; and as he said some very disobliging things to her, upon my account, so I could easily see that she resented them by her future conduct to me, which indeed was very unjust, for I had never had the least thought of what she suspected as to her younger brother; indeed, the elder brother, in his distant, remote way, had said a great many things as in jest, which I had the folly to believe were in earnest, or to flatter myself with the hopes of what I ought to have supposed he never intended.

It happened one day that he came running upstairs, towards the room where his sisters used to sit and work, as he often used to do; and calling to them before he came in, as was his way too, I being there alone, stepped to the door, and said, 'Sir, the ladies are not here; they are walked down the garden.' As I stepped forward to say this, he was just got to the door, and clasping me in his arms, as if it had been by chance, 'Oh, Mrs Betty,' says he, 'are you here? That's better still; I want to speak with you, more than I do with them'; and then, having me in his arms, he kissed me three or four times.

I struggled to get away, and yet did it but faintly neither, and he held me fast, and still kissed me, till he was out of breath, and, sitting down, says he, 'Dear Betty, I am in love with you.'

His words, I must confess, fired my blood; all my spirits flew about my heart, and put me into disorder enough. He repeated it afterwards several times, that he was in love with me, and my heart spoke as plain as a voice that I liked it; nay, whenever he said, 'I am in love with you,' my blushes plainly replied, 'Would you were, sir.' However, nothing else passed at that time; it was but a surprise, and I soon recovered myself. He had stayed longer with me, but he happened to look out at the window and see his sisters coming up the garden, so he took his leave, kissed me again, told me he was very serious, and I should hear more of him very quickly, and away he went infinitely pleased and had there not been one misfortune in it, I had been in the right, but the mistake lay here, that Mrs Betty was in earnest, and the gentleman was not.

From this time my head ran upon strange things, and I may truly say I was not myself, to have such a gentleman talk to me of being in love with me, and of my being such a charming creature, as he told me I was. These were things I knew not how to bear; my vanity was elevated to the last degree. It is true I had my head full of pride, but, knowing nothing of the wickedness of the times, I had not one thought of my virtue about me; and had my young master offered it at first sight, he might have taken any liberty he thought fit with me; but he did not see his advantage, which was my happiness for that time.

It was not long but he found an opportunity to catch me again, and almost in the same posture; indeed, it had more of design in it on his part, though not on my part. It was thus: the young ladies were gone a-visiting with their mother; his brother was out of town; and as for his father, he had been at London for a week before. He had so well watched me that he knew where I was, though I did not so much as know that he was in the house, and he briskly comes up the stairs, and seeing me at work, comes into the room to me directly, and began just as he did before, with taking me in his arms, and kissing me for almost a quarter of an hour together.

It was his younger sister's chamber that I was in, and as there was nobody in the house but the maid below-stairs, he was, it may be, the ruder; in short, he began to be in earnest with me indeed. Perhaps he found me a little too easy, for I made no resistance to him while he only held me in his arms and kissed me; indeed, I was too well pleased with it to resist him much.

Well, tired with that kind of work, we sat down and there he talked with me a great while; he said he was charmed with me, and that he could not rest till he had told me how he was in love with me, and, if I could love him again, and would make him happy, I should be the saving of his life and many such fine things. I said little to him again, but easily discovered* that I was a fool, and that I did not in the least perceive what he meant.

Then he walked about the room, and taking me by the hand, I walked with him; and by-and-by, taking his advantage, he threw me down upon the bed, and kissed me there most violently; but, to give him his due, offered no manner of rudeness to me, only kissed me a great while. After this he thought he had heard somebody come upstairs, so he got off from the bed, lifted me up, professing a great deal of love for me; but told me it was all an honest affection, and that he meant no ill to me, and with that put five guineas into my hand, and went downstairs.

I was more confounded with the money than I was before with the love, and began to be so elevated that I scarce knew the ground I stood on. I am the more particular in this, that if it comes to be read by any innocent young body, they may learn from it to guard themselves against the mischiefs which attend an early knowledge of their own beauty. If a young woman once thinks herself handsome, she never doubts the truth of any man that tells her he is in love with her; for if she believes herself charming enough to captivate him, 'tis natural to expect the effects of it.

This gentleman had now fired his inclination as much as he had my vanity, and, as if he had found that he had an opportunity, and was sorry he did not take hold of it, he comes up again in about half an hour, and falls to work with me again just as he did before, only with a little less introduction.

And first, when he entered the room, he turned about and shut the door. 'Mrs Betty,' said he, 'I fancied before somebody was coming upstairs, but it was not so; however,' adds he, 'if they find me in the room with you, they shan't catch me a-kissing of you.' I told him I did not know who should be coming upstairs, for I believed there was nobody in the house but the cook and the other maid, and they never came up those stairs. 'Well, my dear,' says he, ''tis good to be sure, however'; and so he sits down and we began to talk. And now though I was still on fire with his first visit, and said little, he did as it were put words in my mouth, telling me how passionately he loved me, and that though he could not till he came to his estate, yet he was resolved to make me happy then, and himself too; that is to say, to marry me, and abundance of such things, which I, poor thing, did not understand the drift of, but acted as if there was no kind of love but that which tended to matrimony; and if he had spoke of that, I had no room, as well as no power, to have said no; but we were not come to that length yet.

We had not sat long, but he got up, and, stopping my very breath with kisses, threw me upon the bed again; but then he went further with me than decency permits me to mention, nor had it been in my power to have denied him at that moment had he offered much more than he did.

However, though he took these freedoms with me, it did not go to that which they call the last favour, which, to do him justice, he did not attempt; and he made that self-denial of his a plea for all his freedoms with me upon other occasions after this. When this was over he stayed but a little while, but he put almost a handful of gold in my hand, and left me a thousand protestations of his passion for me, and of his loving me above all the women in the world.

It will not be strange if I now began to think; but, alas! it was but with very little solid reflection. I had a most unbounded stock of vanity and pride, and but a very little stock of virtue. I did indeed cast sometimes with myself* what my young master aimed at, but thought of nothing but the fine words and the gold; whether he intended to marry me or not, seemed a matter of no great consequence to me; nor did I so much as think of making any capitulation* for myself, till he made a kind of formal proposal to me, as you shall hear presently.

Thus I gave up myself to ruin without the least concern, and am a fair memento to all young women whose vanity prevails over their virtue. Nothing was ever so stupid on both sides. Had I acted as became me, and resisted as virtue and honour required, he had either desisted his attacks, finding no room to expect the end of his design, or had made fair and honourable proposals of marriage; in which case, whoever blamed him, nobody could have blamed me. In short, if he had known me, and how easy the trifle he aimed at was to be had, he would have troubled his head no further, but have given me four or five guineas, and have lain with me the next time he had come at me. On the other hand, if I had known his thoughts, and how hard he supposed I would be to be gained, I might have made my own terms, and if I had not capitulated for an immediate marriage, I might for a maintenance till marriage, and might have had what I would; for he was rich to excess, besides what he had in expectation; but I had wholly abandoned all such thoughts, and was taken up only with the pride of my beauty, and of being loved by such a gentleman. As for the gold, I spent whole hours in looking upon it; I told* the guineas over a thousand times a day. Never poor vain creature was so wrapt up with every part of the story as I was, not considering what was before me, and how near my ruin was at the door; and indeed I think I rather wished for that ruin than studied to avoid it.

In the meantime, however, I was cunning enough not to give the least room to any in the family to imagine that I had the least correspondence* with him. I scarce ever looked towards him in public, or answered if he spoke to me; when, but for all that, we had every now and then a little encounter, where we had room for a word or two; and now and then a kiss but no fair opportunity for the mischief intended; and especially considering that he made more circumlocution than he had occasion for; and the work appearing difficult to him, he really made it so.

But as the devil is an unwearied tempter, so he never fails to find an opportunity for the wickedness he invites to. It was one evening that I was in the garden, with his two younger sisters and himself, when he found means to convey a note into my hand, by which he told me that he would to-morrow desire me publicly to go on an errand for him, and that I should see him somewhere by the way.

Accordingly, after dinner, he very gravely says to me, his sisters being all by, 'Mrs Betty, I must ask a favour of you.' 'What's that?' says the second sister. 'Nay, sister,' says he very gravely, 'if you can't spare Mrs Betty to-day, any other time will do.' Yes, they said, they could spare her well enough; and the sister begged pardon for asking. 'Well, but,' says the eldest sister, 'you must tell Mrs Betty what it is; if it be any private business that we must not hear, you may call her out. There she is.' 'Why, sister,' says the gentleman very gravely, 'what do you mean? I only desire her to go into the High Street' (and then he pulls out a turnover), 'to such a shop'; and then he tells them a long story of two fine neckcloths he had bid money for, and he wanted to have me go and make an errand to buy a neck to that turnover* that he showed, and if they would not take my money for the neckcloths, to bid a shilling more, and haggle with them; and then he made more errands, and so continued to have such petty business to do, that I should be sure to stay a good while.

When he had given me my errands, he told them a long story of a visit he was going to make to a family they all knew, and where was to be such-and-such gentlemen, and very formally asked his sisters to go with him, and they as formally excused themselves, because of company that they had notice was to come and visit them that afternoon; all which, by the way, he had contrived on purpose.

He had scarce done speaking but his man came up to tell him that Sir W— H—'s coach stopped at the door; he runs down, and comes up again immediately. 'Alas!' says he aloud, 'there's all my mirth spoiled at once; Sir W— has sent his coach for me, and desires to speak with me.' It seems this Sir W— was a gentleman who lived about three miles off, to whom he had spoke on purpose to lend him his chariot for a particular occasion, and had appointed it to call for him, as it did, about three o'clock.

Immediately he calls for his best wig, hat, and sword, and ordering his man to go to the other place to make his excuse – that was to say, he made an excuse to send his man away – he prepares to go into the coach. As he was going, he stopped awhile, and speaks mighty earnestly to me about his business, and finds an opportunity to say very softly, 'Come away, my dear, as soon as ever you can.' I said nothing, but made a curtsey, as if I had done so to what he said in public. In about a quarter of an hour I went out too; I had no dress other than before, except that I had a hood, a mask, a fan, and a pair of gloves in my pocket; so that there was not the least suspicion in the house. He waited for me in a back-lane which he knew I must pass by, and the coachman knew whither to go, which was to a certain place, called Mile End,* where lived a confidant of his, where we went in, and where was all the convenience in the world to be as wicked as we pleased.

When we were together he began to talk very gravely to me, and to tell me he did not bring me there to betray me; that his passion for me would not suffer him to abuse me; that he resolved to marry me as soon as he came to his estate; that in the meantime, if I would grant his request, he would maintain me very honourably; and made me a thousand protestations of his sincerity and of his affection to me; and that he would never abandon me, and, as I may say, made a thousand more preambles than he need to have done.

However, as he pressed me to speak, I told him I had no reason to question the sincerity of his love to me after so many protestations, but—, and there I stopped, as if I left him to guess the rest. 'But what, my dear?' says he. 'I guess what you mean: what if you should be with child? Is not that it? Why, then,' says he, 'I'll take care of you, and provide for you, and the child too; and that you may see I am not in jest,' says he, 'here's an earnest for you,' and with that he pulls out a silk purse with a hundred guineas in it, and gave it me; 'and I'll give you such another,' says he, 'every year till I marry you.'

My colour came and went at the sight of the purse, and with the fire of his proposal together, so that I could not say a word, and he easily perceived it; so putting the purse into my bosom, I made no more resistance to him, but let him do just what he pleased, and as often as he pleased; and thus I finished my own destruction at once, for from this day, being forsaken of my virtue and my modesty, I had nothing of value left to recommend me, either to God's blessing or man's assistance.

But things did not end here. I went back to the town, did the business he directed me to, and was at home before anybody thought me long. As for my gentleman, he stayed out till late at night, and there was not the least suspicion in the family either on his account or on mine.

We had after this frequent opportunities to repeat our crime, and especially at home, when his mother and the young ladies went abroad a-visiting, which he watched so narrowly as never to miss; knowing always beforehand when they went out, and then failed not to catch me all alone, and securely enough; so that we took our fill of our wicked pleasures for near half a year; and yet, which was the most to my satisfaction, I was not with child.

But before this half-year was expired, his younger brother, of whom I have made some mention in the beginning of the story, falls to work with me; and he finding me alone in the garden one evening, begins a story of the same kind to me, made good, honest professions of being in love with me, and, in short, proposes fairly and honourably to marry me.

I was now confounded, and driven to such an extremity as the like was never known to me. I resisted the proposal with obstinacy, and began to arm myself with arguments. I laid before him the inequality of the match, the treatment I should meet with in the family, the ingratitude it would be to his good father and mother, who had taken me into their house upon such generous principles, and when I was in such a low condition; and, in short, I said everything to dissuade him that I could imagine except telling him the truth, which would indeed have put an end to it all, but that I durst not think of mentioning.

But here happened a circumstance that I did not expect indeed, which put me to my shifts; for this young gentleman, as he was plain and honest, so he pretended to nothing but what was so too; and, knowing his own innocence, he was not so careful to make his having a kindness for Mrs Betty a secret in the house as his brother was. And though he did not let them know that he had talked to me about it, yet he said enough to let his sisters perceive he loved me, and his mother saw it too, which, though they took no notice of to me, yet they did to him, and immediately I found their carriage to me altered more than ever before.

I saw the cloud, though I did not foresee the storm. It was easy, I say, to see their carriage was altered, and that it grew worse and worse every day, till at last I got information that I should in a very little while be desired to remove.

I was not alarmed at the news, having a full satisfaction that I should be provided for; and especially considering that I had reason every day to expect I should be with child, and that then I should be obliged to remove without any pretences for it.

After some time the younger gentleman took an opportunity to tell me that the kindness he had for me had got vent* in the family. He did not charge me with it, he said, for he knew well enough which way it came out. He told me his way of talking had been the occasion of it, for that he did not make his respect for me so much a secret as he might have done, and the reason was, that he was at a point,* that if I would consent to have him, he would tell them all openly that he loved me, and that he intended to marry me; that it was true his father and mother might resent it, and be unkind, but he was now in a way to live, being bred to the law, and he did not fear maintaining me; and that, in short, as he believed I would not be ashamed of him, so he was resolved not to be ashamed of me, and that he scorned to be afraid to own me now, whom he resolved to own after I was his wife, and therefore I had nothing to do but to give him my hand, and he would answer for all the rest.

I was now in a dreadful condition indeed, and now I repented heartily my easiness with the eldest brother; not from any reflection of conscience, for I was a stranger to those things, but I could not think of being a whore to one brother and a wife to the other. It came also into my thoughts that the first brother had promised to make me his wife when he came to his estate; but I presently remembered, what I had often thought of, that he had never spoken a word of having me for a wife after he had conquered me for a mistress; and indeed, till now, though I said I thought of it often, yet it gave no disturbance at all, for as he did not seem in the least to lessen his affection to me, so neither did he lessen his bounty, though he had the discretion himself to desire me not to lay out a penny in clothes, or to make the least show extraordinary, because it would necessarily give jealousy* in the family, since everybody knew I could come at such things no manner of ordinary way, but by some private friendship, which they would presently have suspected.

I was now in a great strait, and knew not what to do; the main difficulty was this: the younger brother not only laid close siege to me, but suffered it to be seen. He would come into his sister's room, and his mother's room, and sit down, and talk a thousand kind things to me even before their faces; so that the whole house talked of it, and his mother reproved him for it, and their carriage to me appeared quite altered. In short, his mother had let fall some speeches, as if she intended to put me out of the family; that is, in English, to turn me out of doors. Now I was sure this could not be a secret to his brother, only that he might think, as indeed nobody else yet did, that the youngest brother had made any proposal to me about it; but as I could easily see that it would go further, so I saw likewise there was an absolute necessity to speak of it to him, or that he would speak of it to me, but knew not whether I should break it to him or let it alone till he should break it to me.

Upon serious consideration, for indeed now I began to consider things very seriously, and never till now, I resolved to tell him of it first; and it was not long before I had an opportunity, for the very next day his brother went to London upon some business, and the family being out a-visiting, just as it happened before, and as indeed was often the case, he came according to his custom to spend an hour or two with Mrs Betty.

When he had sat down awhile he easily perceived there was an alteration in my countenance, that I was not so free and pleasant with him as I used to be, and particularly, that I had been a-crying; he was not long before he took notice of it, and asked me in very kind terms what was the matter, and if anything troubled me. I would have put it off if I could, but it was not to be concealed; so after suffering many importunities to draw that out of me, which I longed as much as possible to disclose, I told him that it was true something did trouble me, and something of such a nature that I could hardly conceal from him, and yet that I could not tell how to tell him of it neither; that it was a thing that not only surprised me, but greatly perplexed me, and that I knew not what course to take, unless he would direct me. He told me with great tenderness, that let it be what it would, I should not let it trouble me, for he would protect me from all the world.

I then began at a distance, and told him I was afraid the ladies had got some secret information of our correspondence – for that it was easy to see that their conduct was very much changed towards me, and that now it was come to pass that they frequently found fault with me, and sometimes fell quite out with me, though I never gave them the least occasion; that whereas I used always to lie with the elder sister, I was lately put to lie by myself, or with one of the maids; and that I had overheard them several times talking very unkindly about me; but that which confirmed it all was, that one of the servants had told me that she had heard I was to be turned out, and that it was not safe for the family that I should be any longer in the house.

He smiled when he heard of this, and I asked him how he could make so light of it, when he must needs know that if there was any discovery I was undone, and that it would hurt him, though not ruin him, as it would me. I upbraided him, that he was like the rest of his sex; that, when they had the character of a woman at their mercy, oftentimes made it their jest, and at least looked upon it as a trifle, and counted the ruin of those they had had their will of as a thing of no value.

He saw me warm and serious, and he changed his style immediately; he told me he was sorry I should have such a thought of him; that he had never given me the least occasion for it, but had been as tender of my reputation as he could be of his own; that he was sure our correspondence had been managed with so much address, that not one creature in the family had so much as a suspicion of it; that if he smiled when I told him my thoughts, it was at the assurance he lately received, that our understanding one another was not so much as guessed at, and that when he had told me how much reason he had to be easy, I should smile as he did, for he was very certain it would give me a full satisfaction.

'This is a mystery I cannot understand,' says I, 'or how it should be to my satisfaction that I am to be turned out of doors; for if our correspondence is not discoverd, I know not what else I have done to change the faces of the whole family to me, who formerly used me with so much tenderness, as if I had been one of their own children.'

'Why, look you, child,' says he, 'that they are uneasy about you, that is true; but that they have the least suspicion of the case as it is, and as it respects you and I, is so far from being true, that they suspect my brother Robin; and, in short, they are fully persuaded he makes love to you; nay, the fool has put it into their heads too himself, for he is continually bantering them about it, and making a jest of himself. I confess I think he is wrong to do so, because he cannot but see it vexes them, and makes them unkind to you; but it is a satisfaction to me, because of the assurance it gives me, that they do not suspect me in the least, and I hope this will be to your satisfaction too.'

'So it is,' says I, 'one way; but this does not reach my case at all, nor is this the chief thing that troubles me, though I have been concerned about that too.' 'What is it, then?' says he. With which, I fell into tears, and could say nothing to him at all. He strove to pacify me all he could, but began at last to be very pressing upon me to tell what it was. At last I answered, that I thought I ought to tell him too, and that he had some right to know it; besides, that I wanted his direction in the case, for I was in such perplexity that I knew not what course to take, and then I related the whole affair to him. I told him how imprudently his brother had managed himself, in making himself so public; for that if he had kept it a secret, I could but have denied him positively, without giving any reason for it, and he would in time have ceased his solicitations; but that he had the vanity, first, to depend upon it that I would not deny him, and then had taken the freedom to tell his design to the whole house.

I told him how far I had resisted him, and how sincere and honourable his offers were; 'but,' says I, 'my case will be doubly hard; for as they carry it ill to me now, because he desires to have me, they'll carry it worse when they shall find I have denied him; and they will presently say, there's something else in it, and that I am married already to somebody else, or that I would never refuse a match so much above me as this was.'

This discourse surprised him indeed very much. He told me that it was a critical point indeed for me to manage, and he did not see which way I should get out of it; but he would consider of it, and let me know next time we met, what resolution he was come to about it; and in the meantime desired I would not give my consent to his brother, nor yet give him a flat denial, but that I would hold him in suspense awhile.

I seemed to start at his saying, I should not give him my consent. I told him, he knew very well I had no consent to give; that he had engaged himself to marry me, and that I was thereby engaged to him; that he had all along told me I was his wife, and I looked upon myself as effectually so as if the ceremony had passed; and that it was from his own mouth that I did so, he having all along persuaded me to call myself his wife.

'Well, my dear,' says he, 'don't be concerned at that now; if I am not your husband, I'll be as good as a husband to you; and do not let those things trouble you now, but let me look a little further into this affair, and I shall be able to say more next time we meet.'

He pacified me as well as he could with this, but I found he was very thoughtful, and that though he was very kind to me, and kissed me a thousand times, and more I believe, and gave me money too, yet he offered no more all the while we were together, which was above two hours, and which I much wondered at, considering how it used to be, and what opportunity we had.

His brother did not come from London for five or six days, and it was two days more before he got an opportunity to talk with him; but then getting him by himself, he talked very close to him about it, and the same evening found means (for we had a long conference together) to repeat all their discourse to me, which, as near as I can remember, was to the purpose following. He told him he heard strange news of him since he went, viz., that he made love to Mrs Betty. 'Well,' says his brother, a little angrily, 'and what then? What has anybody to do with that?' 'Nay, ' says his brother, 'don't be angry, Robin; I don't pretend to have anything to do with it, but I find they do concern themselves about it, and that they have used the poor girl ill about it, which I should take as done to myself.' 'Whom do you mean by THEY?' says Robin. 'I mean my mother and the girls,' says the elder brother.

'But hark ye,' says his brother, 'are you in earnest? Do you really love the girl?' 'Why, then,' says Robin, 'I will be free with you; I do love her above all the women in the world, and I will have her, let them say and do what they will. I believe the girl will not deny me.'

It stuck me to the heart when he told me this, for though it was most rational to think I would not deny him, yet I knew in my own conscience I must, and I saw my ruin in my being obliged to do so; but I knew it was my business to talk otherwise then, so I interrupted him in his story thus: 'Ay!' said I, 'Does he think I

cannot deny him? But he shall find I can deny him for all that.'
'Well, my dear,' says he, 'But let me give you the whole story as it
went on between us, and then say what you will.'

Then he went on and told me that he replied thus: 'But,
brother, you know she has nothing, and you may have several
ladies with good fortunes.' ''Tis no matter for that,' said Robin;
'I love the girl, and I will never please my pocket in marrying,
and not please my fancy.' 'And so, my dear,' adds he, 'there is no
opposing him.'

'Yes, yes,' says I, 'I can oppose him; I have learned to say No,
now, though I had not learnt it before; if the best lord in the land
offered me marriage now, I could very cheerfully say No to him.'

'Well, but, my dear,' says he, 'what can you say to him? You
know, as you said before, he will ask you many questions about it,
and all the house will wonder what the meaning of it should be.'

'Why,' says I, smiling, 'I can stop all their mouths at one clap by
telling him, and them too, that I am married already to his elder
brother.'

He smiled a little too at the word, but I could see it startled him,
and he could not hide the disorder it put him into. However, he
returned, 'Why, though that may be true in some sense, yet I
suppose you are but in jest when you talk of giving such an answer
as that; it may not be convenient on many accounts.'

'No, no,' says I pleasantly, 'I am not so fond of letting that
secret come out, without your consent.'

'But what, then, can you say to them,' says he, 'when they find
you positive against a match which would be apparently so much
to your advantage?' 'Why,' says I, 'should I be at a loss? First, I am
not obliged to give them any reason; on the other hand, I may tell
them I am married already, and stop there, and that will be a full
stop too to him, for he can have no reason to ask one question
after it.'

'Ay,' says he; 'but the whole house will tease you about that,
and if you deny them positively, they will be disobliged at you,
and suspicious besides.'

'Why,' says I, 'what can I do? What would you have me do? I
was in strait enough before, as I told you, and acquainted you
with the circumstances, that I might have your advice.'

'My dear,' says he, 'I have been considering very much upon it,
you may be sure, and though the advice has many mortifications
in it to me, and may at first seem strange to you, yet, all things

considered, I see no better way for you than to let him go on, and if you find him hearty and in earnest, marry him.'

I gave him a look full of horror at those words, and turning pale as death, was at the very point of sinking down out of the chair I sat in; when, giving a start, 'My dear,' says he aloud, 'what's the matter with you? Where are you a-going?' and a great many such things; and with jogging and calling to me, fetched me a little to myself, though it was a good while before I fully recovered my senses, and was not able to speak for several minutes.

When I was fully recovered he began again. 'My dear,' says he, 'I would have you consider seriously of it. You may see plainly how the family stand in this case, and they would be stark mad if it was my case, as it is my brother's; and for aught I see, it would be my ruin and yours too.'

'Ay!' says I, still speaking angrily; 'are all your protestations and vows to be shaken by the dislike of the family? Did I not always object that to you, and you made a light thing of it, as what you were above, and would not value; and is it come to this now? Is this your faith and honour, your love, and the solidity of your promises?'

He continued perfectly calm, notwithstanding all my reproaches, and I was not sparing of them at all; but he replied at last, 'My dear, I have not broken one promise with you yet; I did tell you I would marry you when I was come to my estate; but you see my father is a hale, healthy man, and may live these thirty years still, and not be older than several are round us in the town; and you never proposed my marrying you sooner, because you know it might be my ruin; and as to the rest, I have not failed you in anything.'

I could not deny a word of this. 'But why, then,' says I, 'can you persuade me to such a horrid step as leaving you, since you have not left me? Will you allow no affection, no love on my side, where there has been so much on your side? Have I made you no returns? Have I given no testimony of my sincerity and of my passion? Are the sacrifices I have made of honour and modesty to you no proof of my being tied to you in bonds too strong to be broken?'

'But here, my dear,' says he, 'you may come into a safe station, and appear with honour, and the remembrance of what we have done may be wrapped up in an eternal silence, as if it had never happened; you shall always have my sincere affection, only then it shall be honest, and perfectly just to my brother; you shall be my dear sister, as now you are my dear—' and there he stopped.

'Your dear whore,' says I, 'you would have said, and you might as well have said it; but I understand you. However, I desire you to remember the long discourses you have had with me, and the many hours' pain you have taken to persuade me to believe myself an honest woman; that I was your wife intentionally, and that it was as effectual a marriage that had passed between us as if we had been publicly wedded by the parson of the parish. You know these have been your own words to me.'

I found this was a little too close* upon him, but I made it up in what follows. He stood stock-still for a while, and said nothing, and I went on thus: 'You cannot,' says I, 'without the highest injustice, believe that I yielded upon all these persuasions without a love not to be questioned, not to be shaken again by anything that could happen afterward. If you have such dishonourable thoughts of me, I must ask you what foundation have I given for such a suggestion? If, then, I have yielded to the importunities of my affection, and if I have been persuaded to believe that I am really your wife, shall I now give the lie to all those arguments, and call myself your whore, or mistress, which is the same thing? And will you transfer me to your brother? Can you transfer my affection? Can you bid me cease loving you, and bid me love him? Is it in my power, think you, to make such a change at demand? No, sir,' said I, 'depend upon it 'tis impossible, and whatever the change on your side may be, I will ever be true; and I had much rather, since it is come that unhappy length, be your whore than your brother's wife.'

He appeared pleased and touched with the impression of this last discourse, and told me that he stood where he did before; that he had not been unfaithful to me in any one promise he had ever made yet, but that there were so many terrible things presented themselves to his view in the affair before me, that he had thought of the other as a remedy, only that he thought this would not be an entire parting us, but we might love as friends all our days, and perhaps with more satisfaction than we should in the station we were now in; that he durst say, I could not apprehend anything from him as to betraying a secret,which could not but be the destruction of us both, if it came out; that he had but one question to ask to me that could lie in the way of it, and if that question was answered, he could not but think still it was the only step I could take.

I guessed at his question presently, viz., whether I was not with child. As to that, I told him he need not be concerned about it, for I was not with child. 'Why, then, my dear,' says he, 'we have no time to talk further now. Consider of it; I cannot but be of the opinion still, that it will be the best course you can take.' And with this he took his leave, and the more hastily too, his mother and sisters ringing at the gate just at the moment he had risen up to go.

He left me in the utmost confusion of thought; and he easily perceived it the next day, and all the rest of the week, but he had no opportunity to come at me all that week, till the Sunday after, when I, being indisposed, did not go to church, and he, making some excuse, stayed at home.

And now he had me an hour and half again by myself, and we fell into the same arguments all over again; at last I asked him warmly, what opinion he must have of my modesty, that he could suppose I should so much as entertain a thought of lying with two brothers, and assured him it could never be. I added, if he was to tell me that he would never see me more, than which nothing but death could be more terrible, yet I could never entertain a thought so dishonourable to myself, and so base to him; and therefore, I entreated him, if he had one grain of respect or affection left for me, that he would speak no more of it to me, or that he would pull his sword out and kill me. He appeared surprised at my obstinacy, as he called it; told me I was unkind to myself, and unkind to him in it; that it was a crisis unlooked for upon us both, but that he did not see any other way to save us both from ruin, and therefore he thought it the more unkind; but that if he must say no more of it to me, he added with an unusual coldness, that he did not know anything else we had to talk of; and so he rose up to take his leave. I rose up too, as if with the same indifference; but when he came to give me as it were a parting kiss, I burst out into such a passion of crying, that though I would have spoke, I could not, and only pressing his hand, seemed to give him the adièu, but cried vehemently.

He was sensibly moved with this; so he sat down again, and said a great many kind things to me, but still urged the necessity of what he had proposed; all the while insisting that if I did refuse, he would notwithstanding provide for me; but letting me plainly see that he would decline me in the main point — nay, even as a mistress; making it a point of honour not to lie with the woman that, for aught he knew, might one time or other come to be his brother's wife.

The bare loss of him as a gallant was not so much my affliction as the loss of his person, whom indeed I loved to distraction; and the loss of all the expectations I had, and which I always built my hopes upon, of having him one day for my husband. These things oppressed my mind so much, that, in short, the agonies of my mind threw me into a high fever, and long it was, that none of the family expected my life.

I was reduced very low indeed, and was often delirious; but nothing lay so near me, as the fear that when I was light-headed, I should say something or other to his prejudice. I was distressed in my mind also to see him, and so he was to see me, for he really loved me most passionately; but it could not be; there was not the least room to desire it on one side or other.

It was near five weeks that I kept my bed; and though the violence of my fever abated in three weeks, yet it several times returned; and the physicians said two or three times, they could do no more for me, but that they must leave nature and the distemper to fight it out. After the end of five weeks I grew better, but was so weak, so altered, and recovered so slowly, that the physicians apprehended I should go into a consumption; and which vexed me most, they gave their opinion that my mind was oppressed, that something troubled me, and, in short, that I was in love. Upon this, the whole house set upon me to press me to tell whether I was in love or not, and with whom; but as I well might, I denied my being in love at all.

They had on this occasion a squabble one day about me at table, that had like to put the whole family in an uproar. They happened to be all at table but the father; as for me, I was ill, and in my chamber. At the beginning of the talk, the old gentlewoman, who had sent me somewhat to eat, bid her maid go up and ask me if I would have any more; but the maid brought down word I had not eaten half what she had sent me already. 'Alas,' says the old lady, 'that poor girl! I am afraid she will never be well.' 'Well!' says the elder brother; 'how should Mrs Betty be well? They say she is in love.' 'I believe nothing of it,' says the old gentlewoman. 'I don't know,' says the elder sister, 'what to say to it; they have made such a rout* about her being so handsome, and so charming, and I know not what, and that in her hearing too, that has turned the creature's head, I believe, and who knows what possessions may follow such doings? For my part, I don't know what to make of it.'

'Why, sister, you must acknowledge she is very handsome,' says the elder brother. 'Ay, and a great deal handsomer than you, sister,' says Robin, 'and that's your mortification.' 'Well, well, that is not the question,' says his sister; 'the girl is well enough, and she knows it; she need not be told of it to make her vain.'

'We don't talk of her being vain,' says the elder brother, 'but of her being in love; maybe she is in love with herself; it seems my sisters think so.'

'I would she was in love with me,' says Robin; 'I'd quickly put her out of her pain.' 'What d'ye mean by that, son?' says the old lady; 'how can you talk so?' 'Why, madam,' says Robin again, very honestly, 'do you think I'd let the poor girl die for love, and of me, too, that is so near at hand to be had?' 'Fie, brother!' says the second sister, 'how can you talk so? Would you take a creature that has not a groat* in the world?' 'Prithee, child,' says Robin, 'beauty's a portion, and good humour with it is a double portion; I wish thou hadst half her stock of both for the portion.' So there was her mouth stopped.

'I find,' says the eldest sister, 'if Betty is not in love, my brother is. I wonder he has not broke his mind to Betty; I warrant she won't say No.' 'They that yield when they are asked,' says Robin, 'are one step before them that were never asked to yield, and two steps before them that yield before they are asked; and that's an answer to you, sister.'

This fired the sister, and she flew into a passion, and said, things were come to that pass that it was time the wench, meaning me, was out of the family; and but that she was not fit to be turned out, she hoped her father and mother would consider of it, as soon as she could be removed.

Robin replied, that was for the master and mistress of the family, who were not to be taught by one that had so little judgment as his eldest sister.

It ran up a great deal further; the sister scolded, Robin rallied* and bantered, but poor Betty lost ground by it extremely in the family. I heard of it, and cried heartily, and the old lady came up to me, somebody having told her that I was so much concerned about it. I complained to her that it was very hard the doctors should pass such a censure* upon me, for which they had no

ground; and that it was still harder, considering the circumstances
I was under in the family; that I hoped I had done nothing to lessen
her esteem for me, or given any occasion for the bickering
between her sons and daughters, and had more need to think of a
coffin than of being in love, and begged she would not let me
suffer in her opinion for anybody's mistakes but my own.

She was sensible of the justice of what I said, but told me, since
there had been such a clamour among them, and that her younger
son talked after such a rattling way as he did, she desired I would
be so faithful to her as to answer her but one question sincerely. I
told her I would, and with the utmost plainness and sincerity.
Why, then, the question was, whether there was anything
between her son Robert and me. I told her with all the
protestations of sincerity that I was able to make, and as I might
well do, that there was not, nor ever had been; I told her that Mr
Robert had rattled and jested, as she knew it was his way, and that
I took it always as I supposed he meant it, to be a wild airy way of
discourse that had no signification in it; and assured her that there
was not the least tittle of what she understood by it between us;
and that those who had suggested it had done me a great deal of
wrong, and Mr Robert no service at all.

The old lady was fully satisfied, and kissed me, spoke cheerfully
to me, and bid me take care of my health and want for nothing,
and so took her leave. But when she came down she found the
brother and all his sisters together by the ears; they were angry,
even to passion, at his upbraiding them with their being homely,
and having never had any sweethearts, never having been asked
the question, their being so forward as almost to ask first, and the
like. He rallied them with Mrs Betty; how pretty, how good-
humoured, how she sung better than they did, and danced better,
and how much handsomer she was; and in doing this he omitted
no ill-natured thing that could vex them. The old lady came down
in the height of it, and to stop it, told them the discourse she had
had with me, and how I answered, that there was nothing between
Mr Robert and I.

'She's wrong there,' says Robin, 'for if there was not a great deal
between us, we should be closer together than we are. I told her I
loved her hugely,' says he, 'but I could never make the jade believe
I was in earnest.' 'I do not know how you should,' says his
mother; 'nobody in their senses could believe you were in earnest,
to talk so to a poor girl, whose circumstances you know so well.'

'But prithee, son,' adds she, 'since you tell us you could not make her believe you were in earnest, what must we believe about it? For you ramble so in your discourse that nobody knows whether you are in earnest or in jest; but as I find the girl, by your own confession, has answered truly, I wish you would do so too, and tell me seriously, so that I may depend upon it, is there anything in it or no? Are you in earnest or no? Are you distracted, indeed, or are you not? 'Tis a weighty question; I wish you would make us easy about it.'

'By my faith, madam,' says Robin, ''tis in vain to mince the matter, or tell any more lies about it; I am in earnest, as much as a man that's going to be hanged. If Mrs Betty would say she loved me, and that she would marry me, I'd have her to-morrow morning fasting, and say, "To have and to hold," instead of eating my breakfast.'

'Well,' says the mother, 'then there's one son lost'; and she said it in a very mournful tone, as one greatly concerned at it. 'I hope not, madam,' says Robin; 'no man is lost when a good wife has found him.' 'Why, but, child,' says the old lady, 'she is a beggar.' 'Why, then, madam, she has the more need of charity,' says Robin; 'I'll take her off the hands of the parish, and she and I'll beg together.' 'It's bad jesting with such things,' says the mother. 'I don't jest, madam,' says Robin; 'we'll come and beg your pardon, madam, and your blessing, madam, and my father's.' 'This is all out of the way, son,' says the mother. 'If you are in earnest you are undone.' 'I am afraid not,' says he, 'for I am really afraid she won't have me. After all my sister's huffing, I believe I shall never be able to persuade her to it.'

'That's a fine tale, indeed. She is not so far gone neither. Mrs Betty is no fool,' says the youngest sister. 'Do you think she has learned to say No, any more than other people?' 'No, Mrs Mirthwit,' says Robin, 'Mrs Betty's no fool, but Mrs Betty may be engaged some other way, and what then?' 'Nay,' says the eldest sister, 'we can say nothing to that. Who must it be to, then? She is never out of the doors; it must be between you.' 'I have nothing to say to that,' says Robin. 'I have been examined enough; there's my brother. If it must be between us, go to work with him.'

This stung the elder brother to the quick, and he concluded that Robin had discovered something. However, he kept himself from appearing disturbed. 'Prithee,' says he, 'don't go to sham your stories off upon me; I tell you I deal in no such ware; I have nothing to say to no Mrs Bettys in the parish'; and with that he rose up and brushed off.* 'No,' says the eldest sister, 'I dare answer for my brother; he knows the world better.'

Thus the discourse ended; but it left the eldest brother quite confounded. He concluded his brother had made a full discovery, and he began to doubt whether I had been concerned in it or not; but with all his management, he could not bring it about to get at me. At last, he was so perplexed that he was quite desperate, and resolved he would see me whatever came of it. In order to this, he contrived it so, that one day after dinner, watching his eldest sister, till he could see her go upstairs, he runs after her. 'Hark ye, sister,' says he, 'where is this sick woman? May not a body see her?' 'Yes,' says the sister, 'I believe you may; but let me go in first a little, and I'll tell you.' So she ran up to the door, and gave me notice, and presently called to him again. 'Brother,' says she, 'you may come in if you please.' So in he came, just in the same kind of rant. 'Well,' says he at the door, as he came in, 'where's this sick body that's in love? How do ye do, Mrs Betty?' I would have got up out of my chair, but was so weak I could not for a good while; and he saw it, and his sister too; and she said, 'Come, do not strive to stand up; my brother desires no ceremony, especially now you are so weak.' 'No, no, Mrs Betty, pray sit still,' says he, and so sits himself down in a chair over against me, and appeared as if he was mighty merry.

He talked a deal of rambling stuff to his sister and to me; sometimes of one thing, sometimes another, on purpose to amuse* her, and every now and then would turn it upon the old story. 'Poor Mrs Betty,' says he, 'it is a sad thing to be in love; why, it has reduced you sadly.' At last I spoke a little. 'I am glad to see you so merry, sir,' says I; 'but I think the doctor might have found something better to do than to make his game of his patients. If I had been ill of no other distemper, I know the proverb too well to have let him come to me.' 'What proverb?' says he. 'What—

> Where love is the case,
> The doctor's an ass. *

Is not that it, Mrs Betty?' I smiled, and said nothing. 'Nay,' says he, 'I think the effect has proved it to be love; for it seems the doctor has done you little service; you mend very slowly, they say. I doubt there's somewhat in it, Mrs Betty; I doubt you are sick of the incurables. I smiled, and said, 'No, indeed, sir, that's none of my distemper.'

We had a deal of such discourse, and sometimes others that signified as little. By and by he asked me to sing them a song, at which I smiled, and said my singing days were over. At last he asked me if he should play upon his flute to me; his sister said, she believed my head could not bear it. I bowed, and said, 'Pray, madam, do not hinder it; I love the flute very much.' Then his sister said, 'Well, do, then, brother.' With that he pulled out the key of his closet. 'Dear sister,' says he, 'I am very lazy; do step and fetch my flute; it lies in such a drawer,' naming a place where he was sure it was not, that she might be a little while a-looking for it.

As soon as she was gone, he related the whole story to me of the discourse his brother had about me, and his concern about it, which was the reason of his contriving this visit. I assured him I had never opened my mouth either to his brother or to anybody else. I told him the dreadful exigence I was in; that my love to him, and his offering to have me forget that affection, and remove it to another, had thrown me down; and that I had a thousand times wished I might die rather than recover, and to have the same circumstances to struggle with as I had before. I added that I foresaw that as soon as I was well I must quit the family, and that as for marrying his brother, I abhorred the thoughts of it after what had been my case with him, and that he might depend upon it I would never see his brother again upon that subject; that if he would break all his vows, and oaths, and engagements with me, be that between his conscience and himself; but he should never be able to say that I, whom he had persuaded to call myself his wife, and who had given him the liberty to use me as a wife, was not as faithful to him as a wife ought to be, whatever he might be to me.

He was going to reply, and had said that he was sorry I could not be persuaded, and was a-going to say more, but he heard his sister a-coming, and so did I; and yet I forced out these few words as a reply, that I could never be persuaded to love one brother and marry the other. He shook his head, and said, 'Then I am ruined,' meaning himself; and that moment his sister entered the room, and told him she could not find the flute. 'Well,' says he merrily, 'this laziness won't do'; so he gets up, and goes himself to look for it, but comes back without it too; not but that he could have found it, but he had no mind to play; and, besides, the errand he sent his sister on was answered another way; for he only wanted to speak to me, which he had done, though not much to his satisfaction.

I had, however, a great deal of satisfaction in having spoken my mind to him in freedom, and with such an honest plainness, as I have related; and though it did not at all work the way I desired, that is to say, to oblige the person to me the more, yet it took from him all possibility of quitting me but by a downright breach of honour, and giving up all the faith of a gentleman, which he had so often engaged by, never to abandon me, but to make me his wife as soon as he came to his estate.

It was not many weeks after this before I was about the house again, and began to grow well; but I continued melancholy and retired, which amazed the whole family, except he that knew the reason of it; yet it was a great while before he took any notice of it, and I, as backward to speak as he, carried* as respectfully to him, but never offered to speak a word that was particular of any kind whatsoever; and this continued for sixteen or seventeen weeks; so that, as I expected every day to be dismissed the family, on account of what distaste they had taken another way, in which I had no guilt, I expected to hear no more of this gentleman, after all his solemn vows, but to be ruined and abandoned.

At last I broke* the way myself in the family for my removing; for being talking seriously with the old lady one day, about my own circumstances, and how my distemper had left a heaviness upon my spirits, the old lady said, 'I am afraid, Betty, what I have said to you about my son has had some influence upon you, and that you are melancholy on his account; pray, will you let me know how the matter stands with you both, if it may not be improper? For, as for Robin, he does nothing but rally and banter when I speak of it to him.' 'Why, truly, madam,' said I, 'that matter stands as I wish it did not, and I shall be very sincere with you in it, whatever befalls me. Mr Robert has several times proposed marriage to me, which is what I had no reason to expect, my poor circumstances considered; but I have always resisted him, and that perhaps in terms more positive than became me, considering the regard that I ought to have for every branch of your family; but,' said I, 'madam, I could never so far forget my obligations to you and all your house, to offer to consent to a thing which I knew must needs be disobliging to you, and have positively told him that I would never entertain a thought of that kind unless I had your consent, and his father's also, to whom I was bound by so many invincible obligations.'

'And is this possible, Mrs Betty?' says the old lady. 'Then you have been much juster to us than we have been to you; for we have all looked upon you as a kind of a snare to my son, and I had a proposal to make for your removing, for fear of it; but I had not yet mentioned it to you, because I was afraid of grieving you too much, lest it should throw you down again; for we have a respect for you still, though not so much as to have it be the ruin of my son; but if it be as you say, we have all wronged you very much.'

'As to the truth of what I say, madam,' said I, 'I refer to your son himself; if he will do me any justice, he must tell you the story just as I have told it.'

Away goes the old lady to her daughters and tells them the whole story, just as I had told it to her; and they were surprised at it, you may be sure, as I believed they would be. One said she could never have thought it; another said Robin was a fool; a third said she would not believe a word of it, and she would warrant that Robin would tell the story another way. But the old lady, who was resolved to go to the bottom of it before I could have the least opportunity of acquainting her son with what had passed, resolved, too, that she would talk with her son immediately, and to that purpose sent for him, for he was gone but to a lawyer's house in the town, and upon her sending he returned immediately.

Upon his coming up to them, for they were all together, 'Sit down, Robin,' says the old lady; 'I must have some talk with you.' 'With all my heart, madam,' says Robin, looking very merry. 'I hope it is about a good wife, for I am at a great loss in that affair.' 'How can that be?' says his mother. 'Did not you say you resolved to have Mrs Betty?' 'Ay, madam,' says Robin; 'but there is one that has forbid the banns.' 'Forbid the banns! Who can that be?' 'Even Mrs Betty herself,' says Robin. 'How so?' says his mother. 'Have you asked her the question, then?' 'Yes, indeed, madam,' says Robin; 'I have attacked her in form* five times since she was sick, and am beaten off; the jade is so stout she won't capitulate nor yield upon any terms, except such as I can't effectually grant.' 'Explain yourself,' says the mother, 'for I am surprised; I do not understand you. I hope you are not in earnest.'

'Why, madam,' says he, 'the case is plain enough upon me, it explains itself; she won't have me, she says; is not that plain enough? I think 'tis plain, and pretty rough too.' 'Well, but,' says the mother, 'you talk of conditions that you cannot grant; what does she want – a settlement? Her jointure* ought to be according to her portion; what does she bring?' 'Nay, as to fortune,' says Robin, 'she is rich enough; I am satisfied in that point; but 'tis I that am not able to come up to her terms, and she is positive she. will not have me without.'

Here the sisters put in. 'Madam,' says the second sister, "tis impossible to be serious with him; he will never give a direct answer to anything; you had better let him alone, and talk no more of it; you know how to dispose of her out of his way.' Robin was a little warmed with his sister's rudeness, but he was even with her presently. 'There are two sorts of people, madam,' says he, turning to his mother, 'that there is no contending with; that is, a wise body and a fool; 'tis a little hard I should engage with both of them together.'

The younger sister then put in. 'We must be fools indeed,' says she, 'in my brother's opinion, that he should make us believe he has seriously asked Mrs Betty to marry him, and she has refused him.'

'Answer, and answer not, says Solomon,'* replied her brother. 'When your brother had said that he had asked her no less than five times, and that she positively denied him, methinks a younger sister need not question the truth of it, when her mother did not.' 'My mother, you see, did not understand it,' says the second sister. 'There's some difference,' says Robin, 'between desiring me to explain it, and telling me she did not believe it.'

'Well, but, son,' says the old lady, 'if you are disposed to let us into the mystery of it, what were those hard conditions?' 'Yes, madam,' says Robin, 'I had done it before now, if the teasers here had not worried me by way of interruption. The conditions are, that I bring my father and you to consent to it, and without that she protests she will never see me more upon that head; and the conditions, as I said, I suppose I shall never be able to grant. I hope my warm sisters will be answered now, and blush a little.'

This answer was surprising to them all, though less to the mother, because of what I had said to her. As to the daughters, they stood mute a great while; but the mother said, with some passion, 'Well, I heard this before, but I could not believe it; but if it is so, then we have all done Betty wrong, and she has behaved better than I expected.' 'Nay,' says the eldest sister, 'if it is so, she has acted handsomely indeed.' 'I confess,' says the mother, 'it was none of her fault, if he was enough fool to take a fancy to her; but to give such an answer to him, shows more respect to us than I can tell how to express; I shall value the girl the better for it, as long as I know her.' 'But I shall not,' says Robin, 'unless you will give your consent.' 'I'll consider of that awhile,' says the mother; 'I assure you, if there were not some other objections, this conduct of hers would go a great way to bring me to consent.' 'I wish it would go quite through with it,' says Robin; 'if you had as much thought about making me easy as you have about making me rich, you would soon consent to it.'

'Why, Robin,' says the mother again, 'are you really in earnest? Would you fain have her?' 'Really, madam,' says Robin, 'I think 'tis hard you should question me again upon that head. I won't say that I will have her. How can I solve that point, when you see I cannot have her without your consent? But this I will say, I am earnest, that I will never have anybody else, if I can help it. Betty or nobody is the word, and the question which of the two shall be in your breast to decide, madam, provided only, that my good-humoured sisters here may have no vote in it.'

All this was dreadful to me, for the mother began to yield, and Robin pressed her home in it. On the other hand, she advised with the eldest son, and he used all the arguments in the world to persuade her to consent; alleging his brother's passionate love for me, and my generous regard to the family, in refusing my own advantages upon such a nice point of honour, and a thousand such things. And as to the father, he was a man in a hurry of public affairs and getting money, seldom at home, thoughtful of the main chance, but left all those things to his wife.

You may easily believe, that when the plot was thus, as they thought, broke out, it was not so difficult or so dangerous for the elder brother, whom nobody suspected of anything, to have a freer access than before; nay, the mother, which was just as he wished, proposed it to him to talk with Mrs Betty. 'It may be, son,' said she, 'you may see farther into the thing than I, and see if she has been so positive as Robin says she has been, or no.' This was as well as he could wish, and he, as it were, yielding to talk with me at his mother's request, she brought me to him into her own chamber, told me her son had some business with me at her request, and then she left us together, and he shut the door after her.

He came back to me and took me in his arms, and kissed me very tenderly; but told me it was now come to that crisis, that I should make myself happy or miserable as long as I lived; that if I could not comply to his desire, we should both be ruined. Then he told me the whole story between Robin, as he called him, and his mother, and his sisters, and himself, as above. 'And now, dear child,' says he, 'consider what it will be to marry a gentlemen of a good family, in good circumstances, and with the consent of the whole house, and to enjoy all that the world can give you; and what, on the other hand, to be sunk into the dark circumstances of a woman that has lost her reputation; and that though I shall be a private friend to you while I live, yet as I shall be suspected always, so you will be afraid to see me, and I shall be afraid to own you.

He gave me no time to reply, but went on with me thus: 'What has happened between us, child, so long as we both agree to do so, may be buried and forgotten. I shall always be your sincere friend, without any inclination to nearer intimacy when you become my sister; and we shall have all the honest part of conversation* without any reproaches between us of having done amiss. I beg of you to consider it, and do not stand in the way of your own safety and prosperity; and to satisfy you that I am sincere,' added he, 'I here offer you five hundred pounds to make you some amends for the freedoms I have taken with you, which we shall look upon as some of the follies of our lives, which 'tis hoped we may repent of.'

He spoke this in so much more moving terms than it is possible for me to express, that you may suppose as he held me above an hour and a half in this discourse; so he answered all my objections and fortified his discourse with all the arguments that human wit and art could devise.

I cannot say, however, that anything he said made impression enough upon me so as to give me any thought of the matter, till he told me at last very plainly, that if I refused, he was sorry to add that he could never go on with me in that station as we stood before; that though he loved me as well as ever, and that I was as agreeable to him, yet the sense of virtue had not so forsaken him as to suffer him to lie with a woman that his brother courted to make his wife; that if he took his leave of me, with a denial from me in this affair, whatever he might do for me in the point of support, grounded on his first engagement of maintaining me, yet he would not have me be surprised that he was obliged to tell me he could not allow himself to see me any more; and that, indeed, I could not expect it of him.

I received this last part with some tokens of surprise and disorder, and had much ado to avoid sinking down, for indeed I loved him to an extravagance not easy to imagine; but he perceived my disorder, and entreated me to consider seriously of it; assured me that it was the only way to preserve our mutual affection; that in this station we might love as friends, with the utmost passion, and with a love of relation untainted, free from our own just reproaches, and free from other people's suspicions; that he should ever acknowledge his happiness owing to me; that he would be debtor to me as long as he lived, and would be paying that debt as long as he had breath. Thus he wrought me up, in short, to a kind of hesitation in the matter; having the dangers on one side represented in lively figures, and, indeed, heightened by my imagination of being turned out to the wide world a mere cast-off whore, for it was no less, and perhaps exposed as such, with little to provide for myself, with no friend, no acquaintance in the whole world, out of that town, and there I could not pretend to stay. All this terrified me to the last degree, and he took care upon all occasions to lay it home to me in the worst colours. On the other hand, he failed not to set forth the easy, prosperous life which I was going to live.

He answered all that I could object from affection, and from former engagements, with telling me the necessity that was before us of taking other measures now; and as to his promises of marriage, the nature of things, he said, had put an end to that, by the probability of my being his brother's wife, before the time to which his promises all referred.

Thus, in a word, I may say, he reasoned me out of my reason; he conquered all my arguments, and I began to see a danger that I was in, which I had not considered of before, and that was, of being dropped by both of them, and left alone in the world to shift for myself.

This, and his persuasion, at length prevailed with me to consent, though with so much reluctance, that it was easy to see I should go to church like a bear to the stake.* I had some little apprehensions about me, too, lest my new spouse, who, by the way, I had not the least affection for, should be skilful enough to challenge me on another account, upon our first coming to bed together; but whether he did it with design or not, I know not, but his elder brother took care to make him very much fuddled before he went to bed, so that I had the satisfaction of a drunken bedfellow the first night. How he did it I know not, but I concluded that he certainly contrived it, that his brother might be able to make no judgment of the difference between a maid and a married woman; nor did he ever entertain any notions of it, or disturb his thoughts about it.

I should go back a little here, to where I left off. The elder brother having thus managed me, his next business was to manage his mother, and he never left till he had brought her to acquiesce and be passive, even without acquainting the father, other than by post letters; so that she consented to our marrying privately, leaving her to manage the father afterwards.

Then he cajoled with his brother, and persuaded him what service he had done him, and how he had brought his mother to consent, which, though true, was not indeed done to serve him, but to serve himself; but thus diligently did he cheat him, and had the thanks of a faithful friend for shifting off his whore into his brother's arms for a wife. So naturally do men give up honour and justice, and even Christianity, to secure themselves.

I must now come back to brother Robin, as we always called him, who having got his mother's consent, as above, came big with the news to me, and told me the whole story of it, with a sincerity so visible, that I must confess it grieved me that I must be the instrument to abuse so honest a gentleman. But there was no remedy; he would have me, and I was not obliged to tell him that I was his brother's whore, though I had no other way to put him off; so I came gradually into it, and behold we were married.

Modesty forbids me to reveal the secrets of the marriage-bed, but nothing could have happened more suitable to my circumstances than that, as above, my husband was so fuddled when he came to bed, that he could not remember in the morning whether he had had any conversation* with me or no, and I was obliged to tell him he had, though, in reality, he had not, that I might be sure he could make no inquiry about anything else.

It concerns the story in hand very little to enter into the further particulars of the family, or of myself, for the five years that I lived with this husband, only to observe that I had two children by him, and that at the end of the five years he died. He had been really a very good husband to me, and we lived very agreeably together;

but as he had not received much from them, and had in the little time he lived acquired no great matters, so my circumstances were not great, nor was I much mended by the match. Indeed, I had preserved the elder brother's bonds to me to pay me £500, which he offered me for my consent to marry his brother; and it is, with what I had saved of the money he formerly gave me and about as much more by my husband, left me a widow with about £1200 in my pocket.

My two children were, indeed, taken happily* off of my hands by my husband's father and mother, and that was all they got by Mrs Betty.

I confess I was not suitably affected with the loss of my husband; nor can I say that I ever loved him as I ought to have done, or was suitable to the good usage I had from him, for he was a tender, kind, good-humoured man as any woman could desire; but his brother being so always in my sight, at least while we were in the country* was a continual snare to me; and I never was in bed with my husband, but I wished myself in the arms of his brother. And though his brother never offered me the least kindness that way after our marriage, but carried it just as a brother ought to do, yet it was impossible for me to do so to him; in short, I committed adultery and incest with him every day in my desires, which, without doubt, was as effectually criminal.

Before my husband died his elder brother was married, and we being then removed to London, were written to by the old lady to come and be at the wedding. My husband went, but I pretended indisposition, so I stayed behind; for, in short, I could not bear the sight of his being given to another woman, though I knew I was never to have him myself.

I was now, as above, left loose to the world, and being still young and handsome, as everybody said of me, and I assure you I thought myself so, and with a tolerable fortune in my pocket, I put no small value upon myself. I was courted by several very considerable tradesmen, and particularly very warmly by one, a linen-draper, at whose house, after my husband's death, I took a lodging, his sister being my acquaintance. Here I had all the liberty and opportunity to be gay and appear in company that I could desire, my landlord's sister being one of the maddest, gayest things alive, and not so much mistress of her virtue as I thought at first she had been. She brought me into a world of wild company, and even brought home several persons, such as she liked well enough to gratify, to see her pretty widow. Now, as fame and fools make an assembly, I was here wonderfully caressed, had abundance of admirers, and such as called themselves lovers; but I found not one fair proposal among them all. As for their common design, that I understood too well to be drawn into any more snares of that kind. The case was altered with me; I had money in my pocket, and had nothing to say to them. I had been tricked once by that cheat called love, but the game was over; I was resolved now to be married or nothing, and to be well married or not at all.

I loved the company, indeed, of men of mirth and wit, and was often entertained with such, as I was also with others; but I found by just observation, that the brightest men came upon the dullest errand; that is to say, the dullest as to what I aimed at. On the other hand, those who came with the best proposals were the dullest and most disagreeable part of the world. I was not averse to a tradesman; but then I would have a tradesman, forsooth, that was something of a gentlemen too; that when my husband had a mind to carry me to the court, or to the play, he might become a sword, and look as like a gentlemen as another man; and not like one that had the mark of his apron-strings upon his coat, or the mark of his hat upon his periwig; that should look as if he was set on to his sword, when his sword was put on to him, and that carried his trade in his countenance.

Well, at last I found this amphibious creature, this land-water thing, called a gentleman-tradesman; and as a just plague upon my folly, I was catched in the very snare* which, as I might say, I laid for myself.

This was a draper too, for though my comrade would have bargained for me with her brother, yet when they came to the point, it was, it seems, for a mistress, and I kept true to this notion, that a woman should never be kept for a mistress that had money to make herself a wife.

Thus my pride, not my principle, my money, not my virtue, kept me honest; though, as it proved, I found I had much better have been sold by my she-comrade to her brother than have sold myself as I did to a tradesman, that was a rake, gentleman, shopkeeper, and beggar, all together.

But I was hurried on (by my fancy to a gentleman) to ruin myself in the grossest manner that ever woman did; for my new husband coming to a lump of money at once, fell into such a profusion of expense, that all I had, and all he had, would not have held it out above one year.

He was very fond of me for about a quarter of a year, and what I got by that was, that I had the pleasure of seeing a great deal of my money spent upon myself. 'Come, my dear,' says he to me one day, 'shall we go and take a turn into the country for a week?' 'Ay, my dear,' says I; 'whither would you go?' 'I care not whither,' says he, 'but I have a mind to look like quality for a week; we'll go to Oxford,' says he. 'How,' says I, 'shall we go? I am no horse-woman, and 'tis too far for a coach.' 'Too far!' says he; 'no place is too far for a coach-and-six. If I carry you out, you shall travel like a duchess.' 'Hum,' says I, 'my dear, 'tis a frolic; but if you have a mind to it, I don't care.' Well, the time was appointed; we had a rich coach, very good horses, a coachman, postilion, and two footmen in very good liveries; a gentleman on horseback, and a page with a feather in his hat upon another horse. The servants all called him my lord, and I was her honour the Countess, and thus we travelled to Oxford, and a pleasant journey we had; for, give him his due, not a beggar alive knew better how to be a lord than my husband. We saw all the rarities at Oxford; talked with two or three fellows of colleges about putting a nephew, that was left to his lordship's care, to the university, and of their being his tutors. We diverted ourselves with bantering several other poor scholars, with the hopes of being at least his lordship's chaplain and putting on a scarf; and thus having lived like quality indeed, as to expense, we went away for Northampton, and, in a word, in about twelve days' ramble came home again, to the tune of about £93 expense.

Vanity is the perfection of a fop. My husband had this excellence, that he valued nothing of expense. As his history, you may be sure, has very little weight in it, 'tis enough to tell you that in about two years and a quarter he broke,* got into a sponging-house, being arrested in an action too heavy for him to give bail to, so he sent for me to come to him.

It was no surprise to me, for I had foreseen some time before that all was going to wreck, and had been taking care to reserve something, if I could, for myself; but when he sent for me, he behaved much better than I expected. He told me plainly he had played the fool, and suffered himself to be surprised, which he might have prevented; that now he foresaw he could not stand it, and therefore he would have me go home, and in the night take away everything I had in the house of any value, and secure it; and

after that, he told me that if I could get away £100 or £200 in
goods out of the shop, I should do it; 'only,' says he, 'let me
know nothing of it, neither what you take or whether you carry
it; for as for me,' says he, 'I am resolved to get out of this house
and be gone; and if you never hear of me more, my dear,' says
he, 'I wish you well; I am only sorry for the injury I have done
you.' He said some very handsome things to me indeed at
parting; for I told you he was a gentleman, and that was all the
benefit I had of his being so; that he used me very handsomely,
even to the last, only spent all I had, and left me to rob the
creditors for something to subsist on.

However, I did as he bade me, that you may be sure; and
having thus taken my leave of him, I never saw him more, for he
found means to break out of the bailiff's house that night, or the
next; how, I knew not, for I could come at no knowledge of
anything, more than this, that he came home about three o'clock
in the morning, caused the rest of his goods to be removed into
the Mint,* and the shop to be shut up; and having raised what
money he could, he got over to France, from whence I had one or
two letters from him, and no more.

I did not see him when he came home, for he having given me
such instructions as above, and I having made the best of my
time, I had no more business back again at the house, not
knowing but I might have been stopped there by the creditors;
for a commission of bankrupt being soon after issued, they
might have stopped me by orders from the commissioners. But
my husband, having desperately got out from the bailiff's by
letting himself down from almost the top of the house to the top
of another building, and leaping from thence, which was almost
two stories, and which was enough indeed to have broken his
neck, he came home and got away his goods before the creditors
could come to seize; that is to say, before they could get out the
commission, and be ready to send their officers to take possession.

My husband was so civil to me, for still I say he was much of a
gentleman, that in the first letter he wrote me, he let me know
where he had pawned twenty pieces of fine holland for £30,
which were worth above £90, and enclosed me the token for the
taking them up, paying the money, which I did, and made in
time above £100 of them, having leisure to cut them, and sell
them to private families, as opportunities offered.

However, with all this, and all that I had secured before, I found, upon casting things up, my case was very much altered, and my fortune much lessened; for, including the hollands and a parcel of fine muslins, which I carried off before, and some plate and other things, I found I could hardly muster up £500; and my condition was very odd, for though I had no child (I had had one by my gentleman draper, but it was buried), yet I was a widow bewitched, I had a husband and no husband, and I could not pretend to marry again, though I knew well enough my husband would never see England any more, if he lived fifty years. Thus, I say, I was limited from marriage, what offer soever might be made me; and I had not one friend to advise with in the condition I was in, at least not one whom I could trust the secret of my circumstances to; for if the commissioners were to have been informed where I was, I should have been fetched up, and all I had saved be taken away.

Upon these apprehensions, the first thing I did was to go quite out of my knowledge,* and go by another name. This I did effectually, for I went into the Mint too, took lodgings in a very private place, dressed me up in the habit of a widow, and called myself Mrs Flanders.

Here, however, I concealed myself, and though my new acquaintance knew nothing of me, yet I soon got a great deal of company about me; and whether it be that women are scarce among the people that generally are to be found there, or that some consolations in the miseries of that place are more requisite than on other occasions, I soon found that an agreeable woman was exceedingly valuable among the sons of affliction there; and that those that could not pay half a crown in the pound to their creditors, and run in debt at the sign of the bull for their dinners, would yet find money for a supper, if they liked the woman.

However, I kept myself safe yet, though I began, like my Lord Rochester's mistress,* that loved his company, but would not admit him further, to have the scandal of a whore without the joy; and upon this score, tired with the place, and with the company too, I began to think of removing.

It was indeed a subject of strange reflection to me, to see men in the most perplexed circumstances, who were reduced some degrees below being ruined, whose families were objects of their own terror and other people's charity, yet while a penny lasted, nay, even beyond it, endeavouring to drown their sorrow in their wickedness; heaping up more guilt upon themselves, labouring to forget former things, which now it was the proper time to remember, making more work for repentance, and sinning on, as a remedy for sin past.

But it is none of my talent to preach; these men were too wicked even for me. There was something horrid and absurd in their way of sinning, for it was all a force even upon themselves; they did not only act against conscience, but against nature, and nothing was more easy than to see how sighs would interrupt their songs, and paleness and anguish sit upon their brows, in spite of the forced smiles they put on; nay, sometimes it would break out at their very mouths, when they had parted with their money for a lewd treat or a wicked embrace. I have heard them, turning about, fetch a deep sigh, and cry, 'What a dog am I! Well, Betty, my dear, I'll drink thy health, though'; meaning the honest wife, that perhaps had not a half-crown for herself and three or four children. The next morning they were at their penitentials again, and perhaps the poor weeping wife comes over to him, either brings him some account of what his creditors are doing, and how she and the children are turned out of doors, or some other dreadful news; and this adds to his self-reproaches; but when he has thought and pored on it till he is almost mad, having no principles to support him, nothing within him or above him to comfort him, but finding it all darkness on every side, he flies to the same relief again, viz. to drink it away, debauch it away, and falling into company of men in just the same condition with himself, he repeats the crime, and thus he goes every day one step onward of his way to destruction.

I was not wicked enough for such fellows as these. Yet, on the contrary, I began to consider here very seriously what I had to do; how things stood with me, and what course I ought to take. I knew I had no friends, no, not one friend or relation in the world; and that little I had left apparently wasted, which when it was gone, I saw nothing but misery and starving was before me. Upon these considerations, I say, and filled with horror at the place I was in, I resolved to be gone.

I had made an acquaintance with a sober, good sort of a woman, who was a widow, too, like me, but in better circumstances. Her husband had been a captain of a ship, and having had the misfortune to be cast away coming home from the West Indies, was so reduced by the loss, that though he had saved his life then, it broke his heart, and killed him afterwards; and his widow being pursued by the creditors, was forced to take shelter in the Mint. She soon made things up with the help of friends, and was at liberty again; and finding that I rather was there to be concealed, than by any particular prosecutions, and finding also that I agreed with her, or rather she with me, in a just abhorrence of the place and of the company, she invited me to go home with her, till I could put myself in some posture of settling in the world to my mind; withal telling me, that it was ten to one but some good captain of a ship might take a fancy to me, and court me, in that part of the town where she lived.

I accepted of her offer, and was with her half a year, and should have been longer, but in that interval what she proposed to me happened to herself, and she married very much to her advantage. But whose fortune soever was upon the increase, mine seemed to be upon the wane, and I found nothing present, except two or three boatswains, or such fellows, but as for the commanders, they were generally of two sorts. 1. Such as, having good business, that is to say, a good ship, resolved not to marry, but with advantage. 2. Such as, being out of employ, wanted a wife to help them to a ship; I mean (1) a wife who, having some money, could enable them to hold a good part of a ship themselves, so to encourage owners to come in; or (2) a wife who, if she had not money, had friends who were concerned in shipping, and so could help to put the young man into a good ship; and neither of these was my case, so I looked like one that was to lie on hand. *

This knowledge I soon learned by experience, viz., that the state of things was altered as to matrimony, that marriages were here the consequence of politic schemes, for forming interests, carrying on business, and that love had no share, or but very little, in the matter.

That as my sister-in-law at Colchester had said, beauty, wit, manners, sense, good humour, good behaviour, education, virtue, piety, or any other qualification, whether of body or mind, had no power to recommend; that money only made a woman agreeable; that men chose mistresses indeed by the gust of their affection, and it was requisite for a whore to be handsome, well shaped, have a good mien, and a graceful behaviour; but that for a wife, no deformity would shock the fancy, no ill qualities the judgment; the money was the thing; the portion was neither crooked, or monstrous, but the money was always agreeable, whatever the wife was.

On the other hand, as the market ran all on the men's side, I found the women had lost the privilege of saying no; that it was a favour now for a woman to have the question asked, and if any young lady had so much arrogance as to counterfeit a negative, she never had the opportunity of denying twice, much less of recovering that false step, and accepting what she had seemed to decline. The men had such choice everywhere, that the case of the women was very unhappy; for they seemed to ply at every door, and if the man was by great chance refused at one house, he was sure to be received at the next.

Besides this, I observed that the men made no scruple to set themselves out and to go a-fortune-hunting, as they call it, when they had really no fortune themselves to demand it, or merit to deserve it; and they carried it so high, that a woman was scarce allowed to inquire after the character or estate of the person that pretended to her. This I had an example of in a young lady at the next house to me, and with whom I had contracted an intimacy; she was courted by a young captain, and though she had near £2000 to her fortune, she did but inquire of some of his neighbours about his character, his morals, or substance, and he took occasion at the next visit to let her know, truly, that he took it very ill, and that he should not give her the trouble of his visits any more. I heard of it, and I had begun my acquaintance with her. I went to see her upon it; she entered into a close conversation with me about it, and unbosomed herself very freely. I perceived presently that though she thought herself very ill used, yet she had no power to resent it; that she was exceedingly piqued she had lost him, and particularly that another of less fortune had gained him.

I fortified her mind against such a meanness, as I called it; I told her, that as low as I was in the world, I would have despised a man that should think I ought to take him upon his own recommendation only; also I told her, that as she had a good fortune, she had no need to stoop to the disaster of the times; that it was enough that the men could insult us that had but little money, but if she suffered such an affront to pass upon her without resenting it, she would be rendered low prized upon all occasions; that a woman can never want an opportunity to be revenged of a man that has used her ill, and that there were ways enough to humble such a fellow as that, or else certainly women were the most unhappy creatures in the world.

She was very well pleased with the discourse, and told me seriously that she would be very glad to make him sensible of her resentment, and either to bring him on again or have the satisfaction of her revenge being as public as possible.

I told her, that if she would take my advice, I would tell her how she should obtain her wishes in both those things; and that I would engage I would bring the man to her door again, and make him beg to be let in. She smiled at that, and soon let me see, that if he came to her door, her resentment was not so great to let him stand long there.

However, she listened very willingly to my offer of advice; so I told her that the first thing she ought to do was a piece of justice to herself, namely, that whereas he had reported among the ladies that he had left her, and pretended to give the advantage of the negative to himself, she should take care to have it well spread among the women, which she could not fail of an opportunity to do that she had inquired into his circumstances, and found he was not the man he pretended to be. 'Let them be told, too, madam,' said I, 'that he was not the man you expected, and that you thought it was not safe to meddle with him; that you heard he was of an ill temper, and that he boasted how he had used the women ill upon many occasions, and that particularly he was debauched in his morals,' etc. The last of which, indeed, had some truth in it; but I did not find that she seemed to like him much the worse for that part.

She came most readily into all this, and immediately she went to work to find instruments. She had very little difficulty in the search, for telling her story in general to a couple of her gossips, it was the chat of the tea-table all over that part of the town, and I met with it wherever I visited; also, as it was known that I was acquainted with the young lady herself, my opinion was asked very often, and I confirmed it with all the necessary aggravations, and set out his character in the blackest colours; and as a piece of secret intelligence, I added what the gossips knew nothing of, viz., that I had heard he was in very bad circumstances; that he was under a necessity of a fortune to support his interest with the owners of the ship he commanded; that his own part was not paid for, and if it was not paid quickly, his owners would put him out of the ship, and his chief mate was likely to command it, who offered to buy that part which the captain had promised to take.

I added, for I was heartily piqued at the rogue, as I called him, that I had heard a rumour too, that he had a wife alive at Plymouth, and another in the West Indies, a thing which they all knew was not very uncommon for such kind of gentlemen.

This worked as we both desired it, for presently the young lady at the next door, who had a father and mother that governed both her and her fortune, was shut up, and her father forbid him the house. Also in one place more the woman had the courage, however strange it was, to say no; and he could try nowhere but he was reproached with his pride, and that he pretended not to give the women leave to inquire into his character, and the like.

By this time he began to be sensible of his mistake; and seeing all the women on that side of the water alarmed, he went over to Ratcliff,* and got access to some of the ladies there; but though the young women there too were, according to the fate of the day, pretty willing to be asked, yet such was his ill luck, that his character followed him over the water; so that though he might have had wives enough, yet it did not happen among the women that had good fortunes, which was what he wanted.

But this was not all; she very ingeniously managed another thing herself, for she got a young gentleman, who was a relation, to come and visit her two or three times a week in a very fine chariot and good liveries, and her two agents, and I also, presently spread a report all over that this gentleman came to court her; that he was a gentleman of a thousand pounds a year, and that he was fallen in love with her, and that she was going to her aunt's in the city, because it was inconvenient for the gentleman to come to her with his coach to Rotherhithe,* the streets being so narrow and difficult.

This took immediately. The captain was laughed at in all companies, and was ready to hang himself; he tried all the ways possible to come at her again, and wrote the most passionate letters to her in the world; and in short, by great application, obtained leave to wait on her again, as he said, only to clear his reputation.

At this meeting she had her full revenge of him; for she told him, she wondered what he took her to be, that she should admit any man to a treaty of so much consequence as that of marriage without inquiring into his circumstances; that if he thought she was to be huffed into wedlock, and that she was in the same circumstances which her neighbours might be in, viz., to take up the first good Christian that came, he was mistaken; that, in a word, his character was really bad, or he was very ill beholden to his neighbours; and that unless he could clear up some points, in which she had justly been prejudiced, she had no more to say to him, but give him the satisfaction of knowing that she was not afraid to say no, either to him, or any man else.

With that she told him what she had heard, or rather raised herself by my means, of his character; his not having paid for the part he pretended to own of the ship he commanded; of the resolution of his owners to put him out of the command, and to put his mate in his stead; and of the scandal raised on his morals; his having a wife at Plymouth, and another in the West Indies, and the like; and she asked him whether she had not good reason, if these things were not cleared up, to refuse him, and to insist upon having satisfaction in points so significant as they were.

He was so confounded at her discourse that he could not answer a word, and she began to believe that all was true, by his disorder, though she knew that she had been the raiser of these reports herself.

After some time he recovered a little, and from that time was the most humble, modest, and importunate man alive in his courtship.

She asked him if he thought she was so at her last shift that she could or ought to bear such treatment, and if he did not see that she did not want those who thought it worth their while to come farther to her than he did; meaning the gentleman whom she had brought to visit her by way of sham.

She brought him by these tricks to submit to all possible measures to satisfy her, as well of his circumstances as of his behaviour. He brought her undeniable evidence of his having paid for his part of the ship; he brought her certificates from his owners, that the report of their intending to remove him from the command of the ship was false and groundless; in short, he was quite the reverse of what he was before.

Thus I convinced her, that if the men made their advantage of our sex in the affair of marriage, upon the supposition of there being such a choice to be had, and of the women being so easy, it was only owing to this, that the women wanted courage to maintain their ground, and that, according to my Lord Roch-ester:*

> A woman's ne'er so ruined but she can
> Revenge herself on her undoer, man.

After these things this young lady played her part so well, that though she resolved to have him, and that indeed having him was the main bent of her design, yet she made his obtaining her to be to him the most difficult thing in the world; and this she did, not by a haughty, reserved carriage, but by a just policy, playing back upon him his own game; for as he pretended, by a kind of lofty carriage, to place himself above the occasion of a character,* she broke with him upon that subject, and at the same time that she made him submit to all possible inquiry after his affairs, she apparently shut the door against his looking into her own.

It was enough to him to obtain her for a wife. As to what she had, she told him plainly, that as he knew her circumstances, it was but just she should know his; and though at the same time he had only known her circumstances by common fame, yet he had made so many protestations of his passion for her, that he could ask no more but her hand to his grand request, and the like ramble* according to the custom of lovers. In short, he left himself no room to ask any more questions about her estate, and she took the advantage of it, for she placed part of her fortune so in trustees, without letting him know anything of it, that it was quite out of his reach, and made him be very well contented with the rest.

It is true she was pretty well besides, that is to say, she had about £1400 in money, which she gave him; and the other, after some time, she brought to light as a perquisite to herself, which he was to accept as a mighty favour, seeing, though it was not to be his, it might ease him in the article of her particular expenses; and I must add, that by this conduct, the gentleman himself became not only more humble in his applications to her to obtain her, but also was much the more an obliging husband when he had her. I cannot but remind the ladies how much they place themselves below the common station of a wife, which, if I may be allowed not to be partial, is low enough already; I say, they place themselves below their common station, and prepare their own mortifications, by their submitting so to be insulted by the men beforehand, which I confess I see no necessity of.

This relation may serve, therefore, to let the ladies see, that the advantage is not so much on the other side as the men think it is;

and that though it may be true, the men have but too much choice among us, and that some women may be found who will dishonour themselves, be cheap, and too easy to come at, yet if they will have women worth having, they may find them as uncomeatable* as ever, and that those that are otherwise have often such deficiencies, when had, as rather recommend the ladies that are difficult, than encourage the men to go on with their easy courtship, and expect wives equally valuable that will come at first call.

Nothing is more certain than that the ladies always gain of the men by keeping their ground, and letting their pretended lovers see they can resent being slighted, and that they are not afraid of saying no. They insult us mightily, with telling us of the number of women; that the wars, and the sea, and trade, and other incidents have carried the men so much away, that there is no proportion between the numbers of the sexes; but I am far from granting that the number of the women is so great, or the number of the men so small; but if they will have me tell the truth, the disadvantage of the women is a terrible scandal upon the men, and it lies here only; namely, that the age is so wicked, and the sex so debauched, that, in short, the number of such men as an honest woman ought to meddle with is small indeed, and it is but here and there that a man is to be found who is fit for an honest woman to venture upon.

But the consequence even of that too amounts to no more than this, that women ought to be the more nice,* for how do we know the just character of the man that makes the offer? To say that the woman should be the more easy on this occasion, is to say we should be the forwarder to venture because of the greatness of the danger, which is very absurd.

On the contrary, the women have ten thousand times the more reason to be wary and backward, by how much the hazard of being betrayed is the greater; and would the ladies act the wary part, they would discover every cheat that offered; for, in short, the lives of very few men nowadays will bear a character; and if the ladies do but make a little inquiry, they would soon be able to distinguish the men and deliver themselves. As for women that do not think their own safety worth their own thought, that, impatient of their present state, run into matrimony as a horse rushes into the battle, I can say nothing to them but this, that they are a sort of ladies that are to be prayed for among the rest of distempered people, and they look like people that venture their

estates in a lottery where there is a hundred thousand blanks to
one prize.

No man of common sense will value a woman the less for not
giving up herself at the first attack, or for not accepting his
proposal without inquiring into his person or character; on the
contrary, he must think her the weakest of all creatures, as the rate
of men now goes; in short, he must have a very comtemptible
opinion of her capacities, that having but one cast for her life,
shall cast that life away at once, and make matrimony, like death,
be a leap in the dark. *

I would fain have the conduct of my sex a little regulated in this
particular, which is the same thing in which, of all the parts of life,
I think at this time we suffer most in; 'tis nothing but lack of
courage, the fear of not being married at all, and of that frightful
state of life called an old maid. This, I say, is the woman's snare;
but would the ladies once but get above that fear, and manage
rightly, they would more certainly avoid it by standing their
ground, in a case so absolutely necessary to their felicity, than by
exposing themselves as they do; and if they did not marry so soon,
they would make themselves amends by marrying safer. She is
always married too soon who gets a bad husband, and she is never
married too late who gets a good one; in a word, there is no
woman, deformity or lost reputation excepted, but if she manages
well may be married safely one time or other; but if she
precipitates herself, it is ten thousand to one but she is undone.

But I come now to my own case, in which there was at this time
no little nicety. The circumstances I was in made the offer of a
good husband the most necessary thing in the world to me, but I
found soon that to be made cheap and easy was not the way. It
soon began to be found that the widow had no fortune, and to say
this was to say all that was ill of me, being well-bred, handsome,
witty, modest, and agreeable; all which I had allowed to my
character, whether justly or no is not the purpose; I say, all these
would not do without the dross. In short, the widow, they said,
had no money.

I resolved, therefore, that it was necessary to change my station,
and make a new appearance in some other place, and even to pass
by another name if I found occasion.

I communicated my thoughts to my intimate friend, the
captain's lady, whom I had so faithfully served in her case with the
captain, and who was as ready to serve me in the same kind as I

could desire. I made no scruple to lay my circumstances open to her; my stock was but low, for I had made but about £540 at the close of my last affair, and I had wasted some of that; however, I had about £460 left, a great many very rich clothes, a gold watch, and some jewels, though of no extraordinary value, and about £30 or £40 left in linen not disposed of.

My dear and faithful friend, the captain's wife, was so sensible of the service I had done her in the affair above, that she was not only a steady friend to me, but, knowing my circumstances, she frequently made me presents as money came into her hands, such as fully amounted to a maintenance, so that I spent none of my own; and at last she made this unhappy proposal to me, viz., that as we had observed, as above, how the men made no scruple to set themselves out as persons meriting a woman of fortune of their own, it was but just to deal with them in their own way, and if it was possible to deceive the deceiver.*

The captain's lady, in short, put this project into my head, and told me if I would be ruled by her I should certainly get a husband of fortune, without leaving him any room to reproach me with want of my own. I told her that I would give up myself wholly to her directions, and that I would have neither tongue to speak or feet to step in that affair but as she should direct me, depending that she would extricate me out of every difficulty that she brought me into, which she said she would answer for.

The first step she put me upon was to call her cousin, and go to a relation's house of hers in the country, where she directed me, and where she brought her husband to visit me; and calling me cousin, she worked matters so about, that her husband and she together invited me most passionately to come to town and live with them, for they now lived in a quite different place from where they were before. In the next place, she tells her husband that I had at least £1500 fortune, and that I was like to have a great deal more.

It was enough to tell her husband this; there needed nothing on my side. I was but to sit still and wait the event, for it presently went all over the neighbourhood that the young widow at Captain—'s was a fortune, that she had at least £1500, and perhaps a great deal more, and that the captain said so; and if the captain was asked at any time about me, he made no scruple to affirm it, though he knew not one word of the matter other than that his wife had told him so; and in this he thought no harm, for he really believed it to be so. With the reputation of this fortune, I presently found myself blessed with admirers enough (and that I had my choice of men), as they said they were, which, by the way, confirms what I was saying before. This being my case, I, who had a subtle game to play, had nothing now to do but to single out from them all the properest man that might be for my pupose; that is to say, the man who was most likely to depend upon the hearsay of fortune, and not inquire too far into the particulars; and unless I did this I did nothing, for my case would not bear much inquiry.

I picked out my man without much difficulty, by the judgment I made of his way of courting me. I had let him run on with his protestations that he loved me above all the world; that if I would make him happy, that was enough; all which I knew was upon supposition that I was very rich, though I never told him a word of it myself.

This was my man; but I was to try him to the bottom; and indeed in that consisted my safety, for if he balked, I knew I was undone, as surely as he was undone if he took me; and if I did not make some scruple about his fortune, it was the way to lead him to raise some about mine; and first, therefore, I pretended on all occasions to doubt his sincerity, and told him perhaps he only courted me for my fortune. He stopped my mouth in that part with the thunder of his protestations as above, but still I pretended to doubt.

One morning he pulls off his diamond ring, and writes upon the glass of the sash in my chamber this line:

> You I love, and you alone.

I read it, and asked him to lend me the ring, with which I wrote under it, thus:

> And so in love says every one.

He takes his ring again, and writes another line thus:

> Virtue alone is an estate.

I borrowed it again, and I wrote under it:

> But money's virtue, gold is fate.

He coloured as red as fire to see me turn so quick upon him, and in a kind of rage told me he would conquer me, and wrote again thus:

> I scorn your gold, and yet I love.

I ventured all upon the last cast of poetry, as you'll see, for I wrote boldly under his last:

> I'm poor; let's see how kind you'll prove.

This was a sad truth to me; whether he believed me or no I could not tell; I supposed then that he did not. However, he flew to me, took me in his arms, and, kissing me very eagerly, and with the greatest passion imaginable, he held me fast till he called for a pen and ink, and told me he could not wait the tedious writing on a glass, but pulling out a piece of paper, he began and wrote again:

> Be mine with all your poverty.

I took his pen, and followed immediately, thus:

> Yet secretly you hope I lie.

He told me that was unkind, because it was not just, and that I put him upon contradicting me, which did not consist with good manners, and, therefore, since I had insensibly drawn him into this poetical scribble, he begged I would not oblige him to break it off. So he writes again:

> Let love alone be our debate.

I wrote again:

> She loves enough that does not hate.

This he took for a favour, and so laid down the cudgels, that is to say, the pen; I say, he took it for a favour, and a mighty one it was, if he had known all. However, he took it as I meant it, that is, to let him think I was inclined to go on with him, as indeed I had reason to do, for he was the best-humoured merry sort of a fellow that I ever met with; and I often reflected how doubly criminal it was to deceive such a man; but that necessity, which pressed me to a settlement suitable to my condition, was my authority for it; and certainly his affection to me, and the goodness of his temper, however they might argue against using him ill, yet they strongly argued to me that he would better take the disappointment than some fiery-tempered wretch, who might have nothing to recommend him but those passions which would serve only to make a woman miserable.

Besides, though I had jested with him (as he supposed it) so often about my poverty, yet when he found it to be true, he had foreclosed all manner of objection, seeing, whether he was in jest or in earnest, he had declared he took me without any regard to my portion, and, whether I was in jest or in earnest, I had declared myself to be very poor; so that, in a word, I had him fast both ways; and though he might say afterwards he was cheated, yet he could never say that I had cheated him.

He pursued me close after this, and as I saw there was no need to fear losing him, I played the indifferent part with him longer than prudence might otherwise have dictated to me; but I considered how much this caution and indifference would give me the advantage over him when I should come to own my circumstances to him; and I managed it the more warily, because I found he inferred from thence that I either had the more money or the more judgment, and would not venture at all.

I took the freedom one day to tell him that it was true I had received the compliment of a lover from him, namely, that he would take me without inquiring into my fortune, and I would make him a suitable return in this, viz., that I would make as little inquiry into his as consisted with reason, but I hoped he would allow me to ask some questions, which he should answer or not as he thought fit; one of these questions related to our manner of living, and the place where, because I had heard he had a great plantation in Virginia, and I told him I did not care to be transported.

He began from this discourse to let me voluntarily into all his affairs, and to tell me in a frank, open way all his circumstances, by which I found he was very well to pass in the world; but that great part of his estate consisted of three plantations, which he had in Virginia, which brought him in a very good income of about £300 a year, but that if he was to live upon them, would bring him in four times as much. 'Very well,' thought I; 'you shall carry me thither, then, as soon as you please, though I won't tell you so beforehand.'

I jested with him about the figure he would make in Virginia; but I found he would do anything I desired, so I turned my tale. I told him I had good reason not to desire to go there to live; because if his plantations were worth so much there, I had not a fortune suitable to a gentleman of £1200 a year, as he said his estate would be.

He replied, he did not ask what my fortune was; he had told me from the beginning he would not, and he would be as good as his word; but whatever it was, he assured me he would never desire me to go to Virginia with him, or go thither himself without me, unless I made it my choice.

All this, you may be sure, was as I wished, and indeed nothing could have happened more perfectly agreeable. I carried it on as far as this with a sort of indifferency that he often wondered at, and I mention it the rather to intimate again to the ladies that nothing but want of courage for such an indifferency makes our sex so cheap, and prepares them to be ill used as they are; would they venture the loss of a pretending fop now and then, who carries it high upon the point of his own merit, they would certainly be slighted less and courted more. Had I discovered really what my great fortune was, and that in all I had not full £500 when he expected £1500, yet I hooked him so fast, and played him so long, that I was satisfied he would have had me in my worst circumstances; and indeed it was less a surprise to him when he learnt the truth than it would have been, because having not the least blame to lay on me, who had carried it with an air of indifference to the last, he could not say one word, except that indeed he thought it had been more, but that, if it had been less, he did not repent his bargain; only that he should not be able to maintain me so well as he intended.

In short, we were married, and very happily married on my side, I assure you, as to the man; for he was the best-humoured man that ever woman had, but his circumstances were not so good as I imagined, as, on the other hand, he had not bettered himself so much as he expected.

When we were married, I was shrewdly put to it* to bring him that little stock I had, and to let him see it was no more; but there was a necessity for it, so I took my opportunity one day when we were alone, to enter into a short dialogue with him about it. 'My dear,' said I, 'we have been married a fortnight; is it not time to let you know whether you have got a wife with something or with nothing?' 'Your own time for that, my dear,' says he; 'I am satisfied I have got the wife I love; I have not troubled you much,' says he, 'with my inquiry after it.'

'That's true,' said I, 'but I have a great difficulty about it, which I scarce know how to manage.' 'What's that, my dear?' says he. 'Why,' says I, ''tis a little hard upon me, and 'tis harder upon you;

I am told that Captain —' (meaning my friend's husband) 'has told you I had a great deal more than ever I pretended to have, and I am sure I never employed him so to do.'

'Well,' says he, 'Captain — may have told me so, but what then? If you have not so much, that may lie at his door, but you never told me what you had, so I have no reason to blame you if you have nothing at all.'

'That is so just,' said I, 'and so generous, that it makes my having but a little a double affliction to me.'

'The less you have, my dear,' says he, 'the worse for us both; but I hope your affliction is not caused for fear I should be unkind to you for want of a portion. No, no, if you have nothing, tell me plainly; I may perhaps tell the captain he has cheated me, but I can never say you have, for did not you give it under your hand that you was poor? and so I ought to expect you to be.'

'Well,' said I, 'my dear, I am glad I have not been concerned in deceiving you before marriage. If I deceive you since, 'tis ne'er the worse; that I am poor, 'tis too true, but not so poor as to have nothing neither'; so I pulled out some bank bills and gave him about £160. 'There is something, my dear,' says I, 'and not quite all neither.'

I had brought him so near to expecting nothing, by what I had said before, that the money, though the sum was small in itself, was doubly welcome; he owned it was more than he looked for, and that he did not question by my discourse to him, but that my fine clothes, gold watch, and a diamond ring or two, had been all my fortune.

I let him please himself with that £160 two or three days, and then having been abroad that day, and as if I had been to fetch it, I brought him £100 more home in gold, and told him there was a little more portion for him; and, in short, in about a week more, I brought him £180 more, and about £60 in linen, which I made him believe I had been obliged to take with the £100 which I gave him in gold, as a composition* for a debt of £600, being little more than five shillings in the pound, and overvalued too.

'And now, my dear,' says I to him, 'I am very sorry to tell you that I have given you my whole fortune.' I added, that if the person who had my £600 had not abused me, I had been worth £1000 to him, but that as it was, I had been faithful, and reserved nothing to myself, but if it had been more he should have had it.

He was so obliged by the manner, and so pleased with the sum, for he had been in a terrible fright lest it had been nothing at all, that he accepted it very thankfully. And thus I got over the fraud of passing for a fortune without money, and cheating a man into marrying me on pretence of it; which, by the way, I take to be one of the most dangerous steps a woman can take, and in which she runs the most hazards of being ill-used afterwards.

My husband, to give him his due, was a man of infinite good nature, but he was no fool; and finding his income not suited to the manner of living which he had intended, if I had brought him what he expected, and being under a disappointment in his return of his plantations in Virginia, he discovered many times his inclination of going over to Virginia, to live upon his own; and often would be magnifying the way of living there, how cheap, how plentiful, how pleasant, and the like.

I began presently to understand his meaning, and I took him up very plainly one morning, and told him that I did so; that I found his estate turned to no account at this distance, compared to what it would do if he lived upon the spot, and that I found he had a mind to go and live there; that I was sensible he had been disappointed in a wife, and that finding his expectations not answered that way, I could do no less, to make him amends, than tell him that I was very willing to go to Virginia with him and live there.

He said a thousand kind things to me upon the subject of my making such a proposal to him. He told me that though he was disappointed in his expectations of a fortune, he was not disappointed in a wife, and that I was all to him that a wife could be, but that this offer was so kind, that it was more than he could express.

To bring the story short, we agreed to go. He told me that he had a very good house there, well furnished; that his mother lived in it, and one sister, which was all the relations he had; that as soon as he came there, they would remove to another house, which was her own for life, and his after her decease; so that I should have all the house to myself; and I found it all exactly as he said.

We put on board the ship which we went in a large quantity of good furniture for our house, with stores of linen and other necessaries, and a good cargo for sale, and away we went.

To give an account of the manner of our voyage, which was long and full of dangers, is out of my way; I kept no journal, neither did my husband. All that I can say is, that after a terrible passage, frighted twice with dreadful storms, and once with what was still more terrible, I mean a pirate, who came on board, and took away almost all our provisions; and which would have been beyond all to me, they had once taken my husband, but by entreaties were prevailed with to leave him; – I say, after all these terrible things, we arrived in York River in Virginia, and coming to our plantation, we were received with all the tenderness and affection, by my husband's mother, that could be expressed.

We lived here all together, my mother-in-law, at my entreaty, continuing in the house, for she was too kind a mother to be parted with; my husband likewise continued the same at first, and I thought myself the happiest creature alive, when an odd and surprising event put an end to all the felicity in a moment, and rendered my condition the most uncomfortable in the world.

My mother was a mighty cheerful, good-humoured old woman – I may call her so, for her son was above thirty; I say she was very pleasant, good company, and used to entertain me, in particular, with abundance of stories to divert me, as well of the country we were in as of the people.

Among the rest, she often told me how the greatest part of the inhabitants of that colony came thither in very indifferent circumstances from England; that, generally speaking, they were of two sorts; either, first, such as were brought over by masters of ships to be sold as servants; or, second, such as are transported after having been found guilty of crimes punishable with death.

'When they come here,' says she, 'we make no difference; the planters buy them, and they work together in the field, till their time is out. When 'tis expired,' said she, 'they have encouragement given them to plant for themselves; for they have a certain number of acres of land allotted them by the country, and they go to work to clear and cure the land, and then to plant it with tobacco and corn for their own use; and as the merchants will trust them with tools and necessaries, upon the credit of their crop before it is grown, so they again plant every year a little more than the year before, and so buy whatever they want with the crop that is before them. Hence, child,' says she, 'many a Newgate-bird becomes a great man, and we have,' continued she, 'several justices of the peace, officers of the trained bands,* and magistrates of the towns they live in, that have been burnt in the hand.'*

She was going on with that part of the story, when her own part in it interrupted her, and with a great deal of good-humoured confidence, she told me she was one of the second sort of inhabitants herself; that she came away openly, having ventured too far in a particular case, so that she was become a criminal; 'And here's the mark of it, child,' says she, and showed me a very fine white arm and hand, but branded in the inside of the hand, as in such cases it must be.

This story was very moving to me, but my mother, smiling, said, 'You need not think such a thing strange, daughter, for some of the best men in the country are burnt in the hand, and they are not ashamed to own it. There's Major –,' says she, 'he was an eminent pickpocket; there's Justice Ba—r, was a shoplifter, and both of them were burnt in the hand; and I could name you several such as they are.'

We had frequent discourses of this kind, and abundance of instances she gave me of the like. After some time, as she was telling some stories of one that was transported but a few weeks ago, I began in an intimate kind of way to ask her to tell me something of her own story, which she did with the utmost plainness and sincerity; how she had fallen into very ill company in London in her young days, occasioned by her mother sending her frequently to carry victuals to a kinswoman of hers who was a prisoner in Newgate, in a miserable starving condition, who was afterwards condemned to die, but having got respite by pleading her belly, perished afterwards in the prison.

Here my mother-in-law ran out in a long account of the wicked practices in that dreadful place. 'And, child,' says my mother, 'perhaps you may know little of it, or, it may be, have heard nothing about it; but depend upon it,' says she, 'we all know here that there are more thieves and rogues made by that one prison of Newgate than by all the clubs and societies of villains in the nation; 'tis that cursed place,' says my mother, 'that half peoples this colony.'

Here she went on with her own story so long, and in so particular a manner, that I began to be very uneasy; but coming to one particular that required telling her name, I thought I should have sunk down in the place. She perceived I was out of order, and asked me if I was not well, and what ailed me. I told her I was so affected with the melancholy story she had told that it had overcome me, and I begged of her to talk no more of it. 'Why, my dear,' says she very kindly, 'what need these things trouble you? These passages were long before your time, and they give me no trouble at all now; nay, I look back on them with a particular satisfaction, as they have been a means to bring me to this place.' Then she went on to tell me how she fell into a good family, where behaving herself well, and her mistress dying, her master married her, by whom she had my husband and his sister, and that by her diligence and good management after her husband's death, she had improved the plantations to such a degree as they then were, so that most of the estate was of her getting, not of her husband's, for she had been a widow upwards of sixteen years.

I heard this part of the story with very little attention, because I wanted much to retire and give vent to my passions; and let any one judge what must be the anguish of my mind when I came to reflect that this was certainly no more or less than my own mother, and that I had now had two children, and was big with another by my own brother, and lay with him still every night.

I was now the most unhappy of all women in the world. Oh! had the story never been told me, all had been well; it had been no crime to have lain with my husband, if I had known nothing of it.

I had now such a load on my mind that it kept me perpetually waking; to reveal it I could not find would be to any purpose, and yet to conceal it would be next to impossible; nay, I did not doubt but I should talk in my sleep, and tell my husband of it whether I would or no. If I discovered it, the least thing I could expect was to lose my husband, for he was too nice and too honest a man to have continued my husband after he had known I had been his sister; so that I was perplexed to the last degree.

I leave it to any man to judge what difficulties presented to my view. I was away from my native country, at a distance prodigious, and the return to me unpassable. I lived very well, but in a circumstance insufferable in itself. If I had discovered myself to my mother, it might be difficult to convince her of the particulars, and I had no way to prove them. On the other hand, if she had questioned or doubted me, I had been undone, for the bare suggestion would have immediately separated me from my husband, without gaining my mother or him; so that between the surprise on one hand, and the uncertainty on the other, I had been sure to be undone.

In the meantime, as I was but too sure of the fact, I lived therefore in open avowed incest and whoredom, and all under the appearance of an honest wife; and though I was not much touched with the crime of it, yet the action had something in it shocking to nature, and made my husband even nauseous to me. However, upon the most sedate consideration, I resolved that it was absolutely necessary to conceal it all, and not make the least discovery of it either to mother or husband; and thus I lived with the greatest pressure imaginable for three years more.

During this time my mother used to be frequently telling me old stories of her former adventures, which, however, were no ways pleasant to me; for by it, though she did not tell it me in plain terms, yet I could understand, joined with what I heard myself, of my first tutors, that in her younger days she had been whore and thief; but I verily believe she had lived to repent sincerely of both, and that she was then a very pious, sober, and religious woman.

Well, let her life have been what it would then, it was certain that my life was very uneasy to me; for I lived, as I have said, but in the worst sort of whoredom, and as I could expect no good of it, so really no good issue came of it, and all my seeming prosperity wore off, and ended in misery and destruction. It was some time, indeed, before it came to this, for everything went wrong with us afterwards, and that which was worse, my husband grew strangely altered, froward,* jealous, and unkind, and I was as impatient of bearing his carriage, as the carriage was unreasonable and unjust. These things proceeded so far, and we came at last to be in such ill terms with one another, that I claimed a promise of him, which he entered willingly into with me when I consented to come from England with him, viz. that if I did not like to live there, I should come away to England again when I pleased, giving him a year's warning to settle his affairs.

I say, I now claimed this promise of him, and I must confess I did it not in the most obliging terms that could be neither; but I insisted that he treated me ill, that I was remote from my friends, and could do myself no justice, and that he was jealous without cause, my conversation* having been unblamable, and he having no pretence for it, and that to remove to England would take away all occasion from him.

I insisted so peremptorily upon it, that he could not avoid coming to a point, either to keep his word with me or to break it; and this, notwithstanding he used all the skill he was master of, and employed his mother and other agents to prevail with me to alter my resolutions; indeed, the bottom of the thing lay at my heart, and that made all his endeavours fruitless, for my heart was alienated from him. I loathed the thoughts of bedding with him, and used a thousand pretences of illness and humour to prevent his touching me, fearing nothing more than to be with child again, which to be sure would have prevented, or at least delayed, my going over to England.

However, at last I put him so out of humour that he took up a rash and fatal resolution, that, in short, I should not go to England; that though he had promised me, yet it was an unreasonable thing; that it would be ruinous to his affairs, would unhinge his whole family, and be next to an undoing him in the world; that therefore I ought not to desire it of him, and that no wife in the world that valued her family and her husband's prosperity, would insist upon such a thing.

This plunged* me again, for when I considered the thing calmly, and took my husband as he really was, a diligent, careful man in the main, and that he knew nothing of the dreadful circumstances that he was in, I could not but confess to myself that my proposal was very unreasonable, and what no wife that had the good of her family at heart would have desired.

But my discontents were of another nature; I looked upon him no longer as a husband, but as a near relation, the son of my own mother, and I resolved somehow or other to be clear of him, but which way I did not know.

It is said by the ill-natured world, of our sex, that if we are set on a thing, it is impossible to turn us from our resolutions; in short, I never ceased poring upon the means to bring to pass my voyage, and came that length with my husband at last, as to propose going without him. This provoked him to the last degree, and he called me not only an unkind wife, but an unnatural mother, and asked me how I could entertain such a thought without horror, as that of leaving my two children (for one was dead) without a mother, and never to see them more. It was true, had things been right, I should not have done it, but now, it was my real desire never to see them, or him either, any more; and as to the charge of unnatural, I could easily answer it to myself, while I knew that the whole relation was unnatural in the highest degree.

However, there was no bringing my husband to anything; he would neither go with me, or let me go without him, and it was out of my power to stir without his consent, as any one that is acquainted with the constitution of that country knows very well.

We had many family quarrels about it, and they began to grow up to a dangerous height; for as I was quite estranged from him in affection, so I took no heed to my words, but sometimes gave him language that was provoking; in short, I strove all I could to bring him to a parting with me, which was what above all things I desired most.

He took my carriage very ill, and indeed he might well do so for at last I refused to bed with him, and carrying on the breach upon all occasions to extremity, he told me once he thought I was mad, and if I did not alter my conduct, he would put me under cure; that is to say, into a madhouse. I told him he should find I was far enough from mad, and that it was not in his power, or any other villain's, to murder me. I confess at the same time I was heartily frighted at his thoughts of putting me into a madhouse, which would at once have destroyed all the possibility of bringing the truth out; for that then no one would have given credit to a word of it.

This therefore brought me to a resolution whatever came of it, to lay open my whole case; but which way to do it, or to whom, was an inextricable difficulty, when another quarrel with my husband happened, which came up to such an extreme as almost pushed me on to tell it him all to his face; but though I kept it in so as not to come to the particulars, I spoke so much as put him into the utmost confusion, and in the end brought out the whole story.

He began with a calm expostulation upon my being so resolute to go to England; I defended it, and one hard word bringing on another, as is usual in all family strife, he told me I did not treat him as if he was my husband, or talk of my children as if I was a mother; and, in short, that I did not deserve to be used as a wife; that he had used all the fair means possible with me; that he had argued with all the kindness and calmness that a husband or a Christian ought to do, and that I made him such a vile return, that I treated him rather like a dog than a man, and rather like the most contemptible stranger than a husband; that he was very loath to use violence with me, but that, in short, he saw a necessity of it now, and that for the future he should be obliged to take such measures as should reduce me to my duty.

My blood was now fired to the utmost, and nothing could appear more provoked. I told him, for his fair means and his foul, they were equally contemned by me; that for my going to England, I was resolved on it, come what would; and that as to treating him not like a husband, and not showing myself a mother to my children, there might be something more in it than he understood at present; but I thought fit to tell him thus much, that he neither was my lawful husband, nor they lawful children, and that I had reason to regard neither of them more than I did.

I confess I was moved to pity him when I spoke it, for he turned pale as death, and stood mute as one thunderstruck, and once or twice I thought he would have fainted; in short, it put him in a fit something like an apoplex; he trembled, a sweat or dew ran off his face, and yet he was cold as a clod, so that I was forced to fetch something to keep life in him. When he recovered of that, he grew sick and vomited, and in a little after was put to bed, and the next morning was in a violent fever.

However, it went off again, and he recovered, though but slowly, and when he came to be a little better, he told me I had given him a mortal wound with my tongue, and he had only one thing to ask before he desired an explanation. I interrupted him, and told him I was sorry I had gone so far, since I saw what disorder it put him into, but I desired him not to talk to me of explanations, for that would but make things worse.

This heightened his impatience, and, indeed, perplexed him beyond all bearing; for now he began to suspect that there was some mystery yet unfolded, but could not make the least guess at it; all that ran in his brain was, that I had another husband alive, but I assured him there was not the least of that in it; indeed, as to my other husband, he was effectually dead to me, and had told me I should look on him as such, so I had not the least uneasiness on that score.

But now I found the thing too far gone to conceal it much longer, and my husband himself gave me an opportunity to ease myself of the secret, much to my satisfaction. He had laboured with me three or four weeks, but to no purpose, only to tell him whether I had spoken those words only to put him in a passion, or whether there was anything of truth in the bottom of them. But I continued inflexible, and would explain nothing, unless he would first consent to my going to England, which he would never do, he said, while he lived; on the other hand, I said it was in my power to make him willing when I pleased – nay, to make him entreat me to go; and this increased his curiosity, and made him importunate to the highest degree.

At length he tells all this story to his mother, and sets her upon me to get it out of me, and she used her utmost skill indeed; but I put her to a full stop at once, by telling her that the mystery of the whole matter lay in herself; that it was my respect to her had made me conceal it; and that, in short, I could go no farther, and therefore conjured her not to insist upon it.

She was struck dumb at this suggestion, and could not tell what to say or to think; but laying aside the supposition as a policy* of mine, continued her importunity on account of her son, and, if possible, to make up the breach between us two. As to that, I told her that it was indeed a good design in her, but that it was impossible to be done; and that if I should reveal to her the truth of what she desired, she would grant it to be impossible, and cease to desire it. At last I seemed to be prevailed on by her importunity, and told her I dare trust her with a secret of the greatest importance, and she would soon see that this was so, and that I would consent to lodge it in her breast, if she would engage solemnly not to acquaint her son with it without my consent.

She was long in promising this part, but rather than not come at the main secret she agreed to that too, and after a great many other preliminaries, I began, and told her the whole story. First I told her how much she was concerned in all the unhappy breach which had happened between her son and me, by telling me her own story and her London name; and that the surprise she saw I was in was upon that occasion. Then I told her my own story, and my name, and assured her, by such other tokens as she could not deny, that I was no other, nor more or less, than her own child, her daughter, born of her body in Newgate; the same that had saved her from the gallows by being in her belly, and that she left in such-and-such hands when she was transported.

It is impossible to express the astonishment she was in; she was not inclined to believe the story, or to remember the particulars; for she immediately foresaw the confusion that must follow in the family upon it; but everything concurred so exactly with the stories she had told me of herself, and which, if she had not told me, she would perhaps have been content to have denied, that she had stopped her own mouth, and she had nothing to do but take me about the neck and kiss me, and cry most vehemently over me, without speaking one word for a long time together. At last she broke out: 'Unhappy child!' says she, 'what miserable chance could bring thee hither? and in the arms of my son, too! Dreadful girl!' says she, 'why, we are all undone! Married to thy own brother! three children, and two alive, all of the same flesh and blood! My son and my daughter lying together as husband and wife! all confusion and distraction! Miserable family! what will become of us? what is to be said? what is to be done?' And thus she ran on a great while; nor had I any power to speak, or if I had, did I know what to say, for every word wounded me to the soul. With this kind of amazement* we parted for the first time, though my mother was more surprised than I was, because it was more news to her than to me. However, she promised again that she would say nothing of it to her son till we had talked of it again.

It was not long, you may be sure, before we had a second conference upon the same subject; when, as if she had been willing to forget the story she had told me of herself, or to suppose that I had forgot some of the particulars, she began to tell them with alterations and omissions; but I refreshed her memory in many things which I supposed she had forgot, and then came in so opportunely with the whole history, that it was impossible for her to go from it; and then she fell into her rhapsodies again, and exclamations at the severity of her misfortunes. When these things were a little over with her, we fell into a close debate about what should be first done before we gave an account of the matter to my husband. But to what purpose could be all our consultations? We could neither of us see our way through it, or how it could be safe to open such a scene to him. It was impossible to make any judgment, or give any guess at what temper he would receive it in, or what measures he would take upon it; and if he should have so little government of himself as to make it public, we easily foresaw that it would be the ruin of the whole family; and if at last he should take the advantage the law would give him, he might put me away with disdain, and leave me to sue for the little portion that I had, and perhaps waste it all in the suit, and then be a beggar; and thus I should see him, perhaps, in the arms of another wife in a few months, and be myself the most miserable creature alive.

My mother was as sensible of this as I; and, upon the whole, we knew not what to do. After some time we came to more sober resolutions, but then it was with this misfortune too, that my mother's opinion and mine were quite different from one another, and indeed inconsistent with one another; for my mother's opinion was, that I should bury the whole thing entirely, and continue to live with him as my husband, till some other event should make the discovery of it more convenient; and that in the meantime she would endeavour to reconcile us together again, and restore our mutual comfort and family peace; that we might lie as we used to do together, and so let the whole matter remain a secret as close as death; 'for, child,' says she, 'we are both undone if it comes out.'

To encourage me to this, she promised to make me easy in my circumstances, and to leave me what she could at her death, secured for me separately from my husband; so that if it should come out afterwards, I should be able to stand on my own feet, and procure justice too from him.

This proposal did not agree with my judgment, though it was very fair and kind in my mother; but my thoughts ran quite another way.

As to keeping the thing in our own breasts, and letting it all remain as it was, I told her it was impossible; and I asked her how she could think I could bear the thoughts of lying with my own brother. In the next place I told her that her being alive was the only support of the discovery, and that while she owned me for her child, and saw reason to be satisfied that I was so, nobody else would doubt it; but that if she should die before the discovery, I should be taken for an impudent creature that had forged such a thing to go away from my husband, or should be counted crazed and distracted. Then I told her how he had threatened already to put me into a madhouse, and what concern I had been in about it, and how that was the thing that drove me to the necessity of discovering it to her as I had done.

From all which I told her, that I had, on the most serious reflections I was able to make in the case, come to this resolution, which I hoped she would like, as a medium between both, viz., that she should use her endeavours with her son to give me leave to go for England, as I had desired, and to furnish me with a sufficient sum of money, either in goods along with me, or in bills for my support there, all along suggesting that he might one time or other think it proper to come over to me.

That when I was gone, she should then, in cold blood, discover the case to him gradually, and as her own discretion should guide;

so that he might not be surprised with it, and fly out into any passions and excesses; and that she should concern herself to prevent his slighting the children, or marrying again, unless he had a certain account of my being dead.

This was my scheme, and my reasons were good; I was really alienated from him in the consequence of these things; indeed I mortally hated him as a husband, and it was impossible to remove that riveted aversion I had to him; at the same time, it being an unlawful, incestuous living, added to that aversion, and everything added to make cohabiting with him the most nauseous thing to me in the world; and I think verily it was come to such a height, that I could almost as willingly have embraced a dog, as have let him offer anything of that kind to me, for which reason I could not bear the thoughts of coming between the sheets with him. I cannot say that I was right in carrying it such a length, while at the same time I did not resolve to discover the thing to him; but I am giving an account of what was, not of what ought or ought not to be.

In this directly opposite opinion to one another my mother and I continued a long time, and it was impossible to reconcile our judgments; many disputes we had about it, but we could never either of us yield our own, or bring over the other.

I insisted on my aversion to lying with my own brother, and she insisted upon its being impossible to bring him to consent to my going to England; and in this uncertainty we continued, not differing so as to quarrel, or anything like it, but so as not to be able to resolve what we should do to make up that terrible breach.

At last I resolved on a desperate course, and told my mother my resolution, viz., that, in short, I would tell him of it myself. My mother was frighted to the last degree at the very thoughts of it; but I bid her be easy, told her I would do it gradually and softly, and with all the art and good humour I was mistress of, and time it also as well as I could, taking him in good humour too. I told her I did not question but if I could be hypocrite enough to feign more affection to him than I really had, I should succeed in all my design, and we might part by consent, and with a good agreement, for I might love him well enough for a brother, though I could not for a husband.

All this while he lay at my mother to find out, if possible, what was the meaning of that dreadful expression of mine, as he called it, which I mentioned before; namely, that I was not his lawful wife, nor my children his legal children. My mother put him off, told him she could bring me to no explanations, but found there was something that disturbed me very much, and she hoped she should get it out of me in time, and in the meantime recommended to him earnestly to use me more tenderly, and win me with his usual good carriage; told him of his terrifying and affrighting me with his threats of sending me to a madhouse and the like, and advised him not to make a woman desperate on any account whatever.

He promised her to soften his behaviour, and bid her assure me that he loved me as well as ever, and that he had no such design as that of sending me to a madhouse, whatever he might say in his passion; also he desired my mother to use the same persuasions to me too, and we might live together as we used to do.

I found the effects of this treaty presently. My husband's conduct was immediately altered, and he was quite another man to me; nothing could be kinder and more obliging than he was to me upon all occasions; and I could do no less than make some return to it, which I did as well as I could, but it was but in an awkward manner at best, for nothing was more frightful to me than his caresses, and the apprehensions of being with child again by him was ready to throw me into fits; and this made me see that there was an absolute necessity of breaking the case to him without any more delay, which, however, I did with all the caution and reserve imaginable.

He had continued his altered carriage to me near a month, and we began to live a new kind of life with one another, and could I have satisfied myself to have gone on with it, I believe it might have continued as long as we had continued alive together. One evening, as we were sitting and talking together under a little awning, which served as an arbour at the entrance into the garden, he was in a very pleasant agreeable humour, and said abundance of kind things to me relating to the pleasure of our present good agreement, and the disorders of our past breach, and what a satisfaction it was to him that we had room to hope we should never have any more of it.

I fetched a deep sigh, and told him there was nobody in the world could be more delighted than I was in the good agreement we had always kept up, or more afflicted with the breach of it; but I was sorry to tell him that there was an unhappy circumstance in our case, which lay too close to my heart, and which I knew not how to break to him, that rendered my part of it very miserable, and took from me all the comfort of the rest.

He importuned me to tell him what it was. I told him I could not tell how to do it; that while it was concealed from him, I alone was unhappy, but if he knew it also, we should be both so; and that, therefore, to keep him in the dark about it was the kindest thing that I could do, and it was on that account alone that I kept a secret from him, the very keeping of which, I thought, would first or last be my destruction.

It is impossible to express his surprise at this relation, and the double importunity which he used with me to discover it to him. He told me I could not be called kind to him, nay, I could not be faithful to him, if I concealed it from him. I told him I thought so too, and yet I could not do it. He went back to what I had said before to him, and told me he hoped it did not relate to what I said in my passion, and that he had resolved to forget all that as the effect of a rash, provoked spirit. I told him I wished I could forget it all too, but that it was not to be done, the impression was too deep and it was impossible.

He then told me he was resolved not to differ with me in anything, and that therefore he would acquiesce in whatever I did or said; only begged I would then agree, that whatever it was, it should no more interrupt our quiet and our mutual kindness.

This was the most provoking thing he could have said to me, for I really wanted his further importunities, that I might be prevailed with to bring out that which indeed was like death to me to conceal. So I answered him plainly that I could not say I was glad not to be importuned, though I could not tell how to comply. 'But come, my dear,' said I, 'what conditions will you make with me upon the opening this affair to you?'

'Any conditions in the world,' said he, 'that you can in reason desire of me.' 'Well,' said I, 'come, give it me under your hand,* that if you do not find I am in any fault, or that I am willingly concerned in the causes of the misfortunes that is to follow, you will not blame me, use me the worse, do me any injury, or make me be the sufferer for that which is not my fault.'

'That,' says he, 'is the most reasonable demand in the world; not to blame you for that which is not your fault. Give me a pen and ink,' says he; so I ran in and fetched pen, ink, and paper, and he wrote the condition down in the very words I had proposed it, and signed it with his name. 'Well,' says he, 'what is next, my dear?' 'Why,' says I, 'the next is, that you will not blame me for not discovering the secret to you before I knew it.' 'Very just again,' says he; 'with all my heart'; so he wrote down that also, and signed it.

'Well, my dear,' says I, 'then I have but one condition more to make with you, and that is, that as there is nobody concerned in it but you and I, you shall not discover it to any person in the world, except your own mother; and that in all the measures you shall take upon the discovery, as I am equally concerned in it with you, though as innocent as yourself, you shall do nothing in a passion, nothing to my prejudice, or to your mother's prejudice without my knowledge and consent.'

This a little amazed him, and he wrote down the words distinctly, but read them over and over before he signed them, hesitating at them several times, and repeating them: 'My mother's prejudice! and your prejudice! What mysterious thing can this be?' However, at last he signed it.

'Well,' says I, 'my dear, I'll ask you no more under your hand; but as you are to hear the most unexpected and surprising thing that perhaps ever befell any family in the world, I beg you to promise me you will receive it with composure and a presence of mind suitable to a man of sense.'

'I'll do my utmost,' says he, 'upon condition you will keep me no longer in suspense, for you terrify me with all these preliminaries.'

'Well, then,' says I, 'it is this: As I told you before in a heat, that I was not your lawful wife, and that our children were not legal children, so I must let you know now in calmness, and in kindness, but with affliction enough, that I am your own sister, and you my own brother, and that we are both the children of our mother now alive, and in the house, who is convinced of the truth of it, in a manner not to be denied or contradicted.'

I saw him turn pale and look wild; and I said, 'Now remember your promise, and receive it with presence of mind; for who could have said more to prepare you for it than I have done?' However, I called a servant, and got him a little glass of rum (which is the usual dram of the country), for he was fainting away.

When he was a little recovered I said to him, 'This story, you may be sure, requires a long explanation, and, therefore, have patience and compose your mind to hear it out, and I'll make it as short as I can'; and with this, I told him what I thought was needful of the fact, and particularly how my mother came to discover it to me, as above. 'And now, my dear,' says I, 'you will see reason for my capitulations, and that I neither have been the cause of this matter, nor could be so, and that I could know nothing of it before now.'

'I am fully satisfied of that,' says he, 'but 'tis a dreadful surprise to me; however, I know a remedy for it all, and a remedy that shall put an end to all your difficulties, without your going to England.' 'That would be strange,' said I, 'as all the rest.' 'No, no,' says he, 'I'll make it easy; there's nobody in the way of it all but myself.' He looked a little disordered when he said this, but I did not apprehend anything from it at that time, believing, as it used to be said, that they who do those things never talk of them, or that they who talk of such things never do them.

But things were not come to their height with him, and I observed he became pensive and melancholy; and in a word, as I thought, a little distempered in his head. I endeavoured to talk him into temper, and into a kind of scheme for our government in the affair, and sometimes he would be well, and talk with some courage about it; but the weight of it lay too heavy upon his thoughts, and went so far that he made two attempts upon himself, and in one of them had actually strangled himself,* and had not his mother come into the room in the very moment, he had died; but with the help of a negro servant, she cut him down and recovered him.

Things were now come to a lamentable height. My pity for him now began to revive that affection which at first I really had for him, and I endeavoured sincerely, by all the kind carriage I could, to make up the breach; but, in short, it had gotten too great a head,* it preyed upon his spirits, and it threw him into a lingering consumption, though it happened not to be mortal. In this distress I did not know what to do, as his life was apparently declining, and I might perhaps have married again there, very much to my advantage, had it been my business to have stayed in the country; but my mind was restless too; I hankered after coming to England, and nothing would satisfy me without it.

In short, by an unwearied importunity, my husband, who was apparently decaying, as I observed, was at last prevailed with; and so my fate pushing me on, the way was made clear for me, and my mother concurring, I obtained a very good cargo for my coming to England.

When I parted with my brother (for such I am now to call him), we agreed that after I arrived, he should pretend to have an account that I was dead in England, and so might marry again when he would. He promised, and engaged to me to correspond with me as a sister, and to assist and support me as long as I lived; and that if he died before me, he would leave sufficient to his mother to take care of me still, in the name of a sister, and he was in some respects just to this; but it was so oddly managed that I felt the disappointments very sensibly afterwards, as you shall hear in its time.

I came away in the month of August, after I had been eight years in that country; and now a new scene of misfortunes attended me, which perhaps few women have gone through the like.

We had an indifferent good voyage till we came just upon the coast of England, and where we arrived in two-and-thirty days, but were then ruffled with two or three storms, one of which drove us away to the coast of Ireland, and we put in at Kinsale. We remained there about thirteen days, got some refreshment on shore, and put to sea again, though we met with very bad weather again, in which the ship sprung her mainmast, as they called it. But we got at last into Milford Haven, in Wales, where, though it was remote from our port, yet having my foot safe upon the firm ground of the isle of Britain, I resolved to venture it no more upon the waters, which had been so terrible to me; so getting my clothes and money on shore, with my bills of loading and other papers, I resolved to come for London, and leave the ship to get to her port as she could; the port whither she was bound was to Bristol, where my brother's chief correspondent lived.

I got to London in about three weeks, where I heard a little while after that the ship was arrived at Bristol, but at the same time had the misfortune to know that by the violent weather she had been in, and the breaking of her mainmast, she had great damage on board, and that a great part of her cargo was spoiled.

I had now a new scene of life upon my hands, and a dreadful appearance it had. I was come away with a kind of final farewell. What I brought with me was indeed considerable, had it come safe, and by the help of it I might have married again tolerably well; but as it was, I was reduced to between two and three hundred pounds in the whole, and this without any hope of recruit.* I was entirely without friends, nay, even so much as without acquaintances, for I found it was absolutely necessary not to revive former acquaintance; and as for my subtle friend that set me up formerly for a fortune, she was dead, and her husband also.

The looking after my cargo of goods soon after obliged me to take a journey to Bristol, and during my attendance upon that affair I took the diversion of going to Bath,* for as I was still far from being old, so my humour, which was always gay, continued so to an extreme; and being now, as it were, a woman of fortune, though I was a woman without a fortune, I expected something or other might happen in the way that might mend my circumstances, as had been my case before.

Bath is a place of gallantry* enough; expensive, and full of snares. I went thither, indeed, in the view of taking what might offer; but I must do myself that justice as to protest I meant nothing but in an honest way, nor had any thoughts about me at first that looked the way which afterwards I suffered them to be guided.

Here I stayed the whole latter season, as it is called there, and contracted some unhappy acquaintance, which rather prompted the follies I fell afterwards into than fortified me against them. I lived pleasantly enough, kept good company, that is to say, gay, fine company; but had the discouragement to find this way of living sunk me exceedingly, and that as I had no settled income, so spending upon the main stock was but a certain kind of bleeding to death; and this gave me many sad reflections. However, I shook them off, and still flattered myself that something or other might offer for my advantage.

But I was in the wrong place for it. I was not now at Redriff, where if I had set myself tolerably up, some honest sea captain or other might have talked with me upon the honourable terms of matrimony; but I was at Bath, where men find a mistress sometimes, but very rarely look for a wife; and consequently all the particular acquaintances a woman can expect there must have some tendency that way.

I had spent the first season well enough; for though I had contracted some acquaintance with a gentleman who came to Bath for his diversion, yet I had entered into no felonious treaty. I had resisted some casual offers of gallantry, and had managed that way well enough. I was not wicked enough to come into the crime for the mere vice of it, and I had no extraordinary offers that tempted me with the main thing which I wanted.

However, I went this length the first season, viz., I contracted an acquaintance with a woman in whose house I lodged, who, though she did not keep an ill house,* yet had none of the best principles in herself. I had on all occasions behaved myself so well as not to get the least slur upon my reputation, and all the men that I had conversed with were of so good reputation that I had not gotten the least reflection by conversing with them; nor did any of them seem to think there was room for a wicked correspondence if they had offered it; yet there was one gentlemen, as above, who always singled me out for the diversion of my company, as he called it, which, as he was pleased to say, was very agreeable to him, but at that time there was no more in it.

I had many melancholy hours at Bath after all the company was gone; for though I went to Bristol sometimes for the disposing of my effects, and for recruits of money, yet I chose to come back to Bath for my residence, because, being on good terms with the woman in whose house I lodged in the summer, I found that during the winter I lived rather cheaper there than I could do anywhere else. Here, I say, I passed the winter as heavily as I had passed the autumn cheerfully; but having contracted a nearer intimacy with the said woman, in whose house I lodged, I could not avoid communicating something of what lay hardest upon my mind, and particularly the narrowness of my circumstances. I told her also, that I had a mother and a brother in Virginia in good circumstances; and as I had really written back to my mother in particular to represent my condition, and the great loss I had received, so I did not fail to let my new friend know that I expected a supply from thence, and so indeed I did; and as the ships went from Bristol to York River, in Virginia, and back again generally in less time than from London, and that my brother corresponded chiefly at Bristol, I thought it was much better for me to wait here for my returns than to go to London.

My new friend appeared sensibly affected with my condition, and indeed was so very kind as to reduce the rate of my living with her to so low a price during the winter, that she convinced me she got nothing by me; and as for lodging, during the winter I paid nothing at all.

When the spring season came on, she continued to be as kind to me as she could, and I lodged with her for a time, till it was found necessary to do otherwise. She had some persons of character that frequently lodged in her house, and in particular the gentleman who, as I said, singled me out for his companion in the winter before; and he came down again with another gentleman in his company and two servants, and lodged in the same house. I suspected that my landlady had invited him thither, letting him know that I was still with her; but she denied it.

In a word, this gentlemen came down and continued to single me out for his peculiar confidence. He was a complete gentleman, that must be confessed, and his company was agreeable to me, as mine, if I might believe him, was to him. He made no professions to me but of an extraordinary respect, and he had such an opinion of my virtue, that, as he often professed, he believed, if he should offer anything else, I should reject him with contempt. He soon understood from me that I was a widow; that I had arrived at Bristol from Virginia by the last ships; and that I waited at Bath till the next Virginia fleet should arrive, by which I expected considerable effects. I understood by him that he had a wife, but that the lady was distempered in her head, and was under the conduct of her own relations, which he consented to, to avoid any reflection that might be cast upon him for mismanaging her cure; and in the meantime he came to Bath to divert his thoughts under such a melancholy circumstance.

My landlady, who of her own accord encouraged the correspondence on all occasions, gave me an advantageous character of him, as of a man of honour, and of virtue, as well as of a great estate. And indeed I had reason to say so of him too; for though we lodged both on a floor, and he had frequently come into my chamber, even when I was in bed, and I also into his, yet he never offered anything to me further than a kiss, or so much as solicited me to anything till long after, as you shall hear.

I frequently took notice to my landlady of his exceeding modesty, and she again used to tell me she believed it was so from the beginning; however, she used to tell me that she thought I ought to expect some gratifications from him for my company, for indeed he did as it were engross me. I told her I had not given him the least occasion to think I wanted it, or that I would accept of it from him. She told me she would take that part upon her, and she managed it so dexterously, that the first time we were together alone, after she had talked with him, he began to inquire a little into my circumstances, as how I had subsisted myself since I came on shore, and whether I did not want money. I stood off very boldly. I told him that though my cargo of tobacco was damaged, yet that it was not quite lost; that the merchant that I had been consigned to had so honestly managed for me that I had not wanted, and that I hoped with frugal management, I should make it hold out till more would come, which I expected by the next fleet; that in the meantime I had retrenched my expenses, and whereas I kept a maid last season, now I lived without; and whereas I kept a chamber and a dining-room then on the first floor, I now had but one room two pair of stairs,* and the like; 'but I live,' said I, 'as well satisfied now as then'; adding, that his company had made me live much more cheerfully than otherwise I should have done, for which I was much obliged to him; and so I put off all room for any offer at the present. It was not long before he attacked me again, and told me he found that I was backward to trust him with the secret of my circumstances, which he was sorry for; assuring me that he inquired into it with no design to satisfy his own curiosity, but merely to assist me if there was any occasion; but since I would not own myself to stand in need of any assistance, he had but one thing more to desire of me, and that was, that I would promise him that when I was any way straitened, I would frankly tell him of it, and that I would make use of him with the same freedom that he made the offer; adding, that I should always find I had a true friend, though perhaps I was afraid to trust him.

I omitted nothing that was fit to be said by one infinitely obliged, to let him know that I had a due sense of his kindness; and indeed from that time I did not appear so much reserved to him as I had done before, though still within the bounds of the strictest virtue on both sides; but how free soever our conversation was, I could not arrive to that freedom which he desired, viz., to tell him I wanted money, though I was secretly very glad of his offer.

Some weeks passed after this, and still I never asked him for money; when my landlady, a cunning creature, who had often pressed me to it, but found that I could not do it, makes a story of her own inventing, and comes in bluntly to me when we were together, 'Oh, widow!' says she, 'I have bad news to tell you this morning.' 'What is that?' said I. 'Are the Virginia ships taken by the French?' for that was my fear. 'No, no,' says she, 'but the man you sent to Bristol yesterday for money is come back, and says he has brought none.'

I could by no means like her project; I thought it looked too much like prompting him, which he did not want, and I saw that I

should lose nothing by being backward, so took her up short. 'I
can't imagine why he should say so,' said I, 'for I assure you he
brought me all the money I sent him for, and here it is,' said I
(pulling out my purse with about twelve guineas in it); and added,
'I intend you shall have most of it by and by.'

He seemed distasted* a little at her talking as she did, as well as
I, taking it, as I fancied he would, as something forward of her;
but when he saw me give such an answer, he came immediately to
himself. The next morning we talked of it again, when I found he
was fully satisfied; and, smiling, said he hoped I would not want
money, and not tell him of it, and that I had promised him
otherwise. I told him I had been very much dissatisfied at my
landlady's talking so publicly the day before of what she had
nothing to do with; but I supposed she wanted what I owed her,
which was about eight guineas, which I had resolved to give her,
and had given it her the same night.

He was in a mighty good humour when he heard me say I had
paid her, and it went off into some other discourse at that time.
But the next morning, he having heard me up before him, he called
to me, and I answered. He asked me to come into his bedchamber;
he was in bed when I came in, and he made me come and sit down
on his bedside, for he said he had something to say to me. After
some very kind expressions, he asked me if I would be very honest
to him, and give a sincere answer to one thing he would desire of
me. After some little cavil with him at the word 'sincere', and
asking him if I had ever given him any answers which were not
sincere, I promised him I would. Why, then, his request was, he
said, to let him see my purse. I immediately put my hand into my
pocket, and laughing at him, pulled it out, and there was in it three
guineas and a half. Then he asked me if there was all the money I
had. I told him no, laughing again, not by a great deal.

Well, then, he said, he would have me promise to go and fetch
him all the money I had, every farthing. I told him I would, and
went into my chamber, and fetched him a little private drawer,
where I had about six guineas more, and some silver, and threw it
all down upon the bed, and told him there was all my wealth,
honestly to a shilling. He looked a little at it, but did not tell* it,
and huddled it all into the drawer again, and then reaching his
pocket, pulled out a key, and bade me open a little walnut-tree
box he had upon this table, and bring him such a drawer, which I
did. In this drawer there was a great deal of money in gold, I

believe near two hundred guineas, but I knew not how much. He took the drawer, and taking me by the hand, made me put it in and take a whole handful; I was backward at that, but he held my hand hard in his hand, and put it into the drawer, and made me take out as many guineas almost as I could well take up at once.

When I had done so, he made me put them into my lap, and took my little drawer, and poured out all my own money among his, and bade me get me gone, and carry it all into my own chamber.

I relate this story the more particularly, because of the good-humour of it, and to show the temper with which we conversed. It was not long after this, but he began every day to find fault with my clothes, with my laces, and head-dresses, and, in a word, pressed me to buy better, which, by the way, I was willing enough to do, though I did not seem to be so. I loved nothing in the world better than fine clothes; but I told him I must house-wife* the money he had lent me, or else I should not be able to pay him again. He then told me, in a few words, that as he had a sincere respect for me, and knew my circumstances, he had not lent me that money, but given it me, and that he thought I had merited it from him, by giving him my company so entirely as I had done. After this he made me take a maid, and keep house, and his friend being gone, he obliged me to diet* him, which I did very willingly, believing, as it appeared, that I should lose nothing by it, nor did the woman of the house fail to find her account in it too.

We had lived thus near three months, when the company beginning to wear away at Bath, he talked of going away, and fain he would have me to go to London with him. I was not very easy in that proposal, not knowing what posture I was to live in there, or how he might use me. But while this was in debate, he fell very sick; he had gone out to a place in Somersetshire, called Shepton,* and was there taken very ill, and so ill that he could not travel; so he sent his man back to Bath, to beg me that I would hire a coach and come over to him. Before he went, he had left his money and other things of value with me, and what to do with them I did not know, but I secured them as well as I could, and locked up the lodgings and went to him, where I found him very ill indeed, so I persuaded him to be carried in a litter to Bath, where was more help and better advice to be had.

He consented, and I brought him to Bath, which was about fifteen miles, as I remember. Here he continued very ill of a fever, and kept his bed five weeks, all which time I nursed him and tended him as carefully as if I had been his wife; indeed, if I had been his wife I could not have done more. I sat up with him so much and so often, that at last, indeed, he would not let me sit up any longer, and then I got a pallet-bed into his room, and lay in it just at his bed's feet.

I was indeed sensibly affected with his condition, and with the apprehension of losing such a friend as he was, and was like to be to me, and I used to sit and cry by him many hours together. At last he grew better, and gave hopes that he would recover, as indeed he did, though very slowly.

Were it otherwise than what I am going to say, I should not be backward to disclose it, as it is apparent I have done in other cases; but I affirm, through all this conversation, abating the coming into the chamber when I or he was in bed, and the necessary offices of attending him night and day when he was sick, there had not passed the least immodest word or action between us. Oh that it had been so to the last!

After some time he gathered strength and grew well apace, and I would have removed my pallet-bed, but he would not let me, till he was able to venture himself without anybody to sit up with him, when I removed to my own chamber.

He took many occasions to express his sense of my tenderness for him; and when he grew well he made me a present of fifty guineas for my care, and, as he called it, hazarding my life to save his.

And now he made deep protestations of a sincere inviolable affection for me, but with the utmost reserve for my virtue and his own. I told him I was fully satisfied of it. He carried it that length that he protested to me, that if he was naked in bed with me, he would as sacredly preserve my virtue as he would defend it, if I was assaulted by a ravisher. I believed him, and told him I did so; but this did not satisfy him; he would, he said, wait for some opportunity to give me an undoubted testimony of it.

It was a great while after this that I had occasion, on my business, to go to Bristol, upon which he hired me a coach, and would go with me; and now indeed our intimacy increased. From Bristol he carried me to Gloucester, which was merely a journey of pleasure, to take the air; and here it was our hap to have no lodgings in the inn, but in one large chamber with two beds in it. The master of the house going with us to show his rooms, and coming into that room, said very frankly to him, 'Sir, it is none of my business to inquire whether the lady be your spouse or no, but if not, you may lie as honestly in these two beds as if you were in two chambers,' and with that he pulls a great curtain which drew quite across the room, and effectually divided the beds. 'Well,' says my friend, very readily, 'these beds will do; and as for the rest, we are too near akin to lie together, though we may lodge near one another'; and this put an honest face on the thing too. When we came to go to bed, he decently went out of the room till I was in bed, and then went to bed in the other bed, but lay there talking to me a great while.

At last, repeating his usual saying, that he could lie naked in the bed with me, and not offer me the least injury, he starts out of his bed. 'And now, my dear,' says he, 'you shall see how just I will be to you, and that I can keep my word,' and away he comes to my bed.

I resisted a little, but I must confess I should not have resisted him much, if he had not made those promises at all; so after a little struggle, I lay still and let him come to bed. When he was there he took me in his arms, and so I lay all night with him, but he had no more to do with me, or offered anything to me, other than embracing me, as I say, in his arms, no, not the whole night, but rose up and dressed him in the morning, and left me as innocent for him as I was the day I was born.

This was a surprising thing to me, and perhaps may be so to others, who know how the laws of nature work; for he was a vigorous, brisk person. Nor did he act thus on a principle of religion at all, but of mere affection; insisting on it, that though I was to him the most agreeable woman in the world, yet, because he loved me, he could not injure me.

I own it was a noble principle, but as it was what I never saw before, so it was perfectly amazing. We travelled the rest of the journey as we did before, and came back to Bath, where, as he had opportunity to come to me when he would, he often repeated the same moderation, and I frequently lay with him, and although all the familiarities of man and wife were common to us, yet he never once offered to go any farther, and he valued himself much upon it. I do not say that I was so wholly pleased with it as he thought I was, for I own I was much wickeder than he.

We lived thus near two years, only with this exception, that he went three times to London in that time, and once he continued there four months; but to do him justice, he always supplied me with money to subsist on very handsomely.

Had we continued thus, I confess we had had much to boast of; but, as wise men say, it is ill venturing too near the brink of a command.* So we found it; and here again I must do him the justice to own that the first breach was not on his part. It was one night that we were in bed together warm and merry, and having drunk, I think, a little more both of us than usual, though not in the least to disorder us, when, after some other follies which I cannot name, and being clasped close in his arms, I told him (I repeat it with shame and horror of soul) that I could find in my heart to discharge him of his engagement for one night and no more.

He took me at my word immediately, and after that there was no resisting him; neither indeed had I any mind to resist him any more.

Thus the government of our virtue was broken, and I exchanged the place of friend for that unmusical, harsh-sounding title of whore. In the morning we were both at our penitentials; I cried very heartily, he expressed himself very sorry; but that was all either of us could do at that time, and the way being thus cleared, and the bars of virtue and conscience thus removed, we had the less to struggle with.

It was but a dull kind of conversation that we had together for all the rest of that week; I looked on him with blushes, and every now and then started that melancholy objection, 'What if I should be with child now? What will become of me then?' He encouraged me by telling me, that as long as I was true to him, he would be so to me; and since it was gone such a length (which indeed he never intended), yet if I was with child, he would take care of that and me too. This hardened us both. I assured him if I was with child, I would die for want of a midwife rather than name him as the father of it; and he assured me I should never want if I should be with child. These mutual assurances hardened us in the thing, and after this we repeated the crime as often as we pleased, till at length, as I feared, so it came to pass, and I was indeed with child.

After I was sure it was so, and I had satisfied him of it too, we began to think of taking measures for the managing it, and I proposed trusting the secret to my landlady, and asking her advice, which he agreed to. My landlady, a woman (as I found) used to such things, made light of it; she said she knew it would come to that at last, and made us very merry about it. As I said above, we found her an experienced old lady at such work; she undertook everything, engaged to procure a midwife and a nurse, to satisfy all inquiries, and bring us off with reputation, and she did so very dexterously indeed.

When I grew near my time, she desired my gentlemen to go away to London, or make as if he did so. When he was gone, she acquainted the parish officers that there was a lady ready to lie in at her house, but that she knew her husband very well, and gave them, as she pretended, an account of his name, which she called Sir Walter Cleave;* telling them he was a worthy gentleman, and that she would answer for all inquiries, and the like. This satisfied the parish officers presently, and I lay in in as much credit as I could have done if I had really been my Lady Cleave; and was assisted in my travail by three or four of the best citizens' wives of Bath, which, however, made me a little the more expensive to him. I often expressed my concern to him about that part, but he bid me not be concerned at it.

As he had furnished me very sufficiently with money for the extraordinary expenses of my lying in, I had everything very handsome about me, but did not affect to be so gay or extravagant neither; besides, knowing the world, as I had done, and that such kind of things do not often last long, I took care to lay up as much money as I could for a wet day, as I called it; making him believe it was all spent upon the extraordinary appearance of things in my lying in.

By this means, with what he had given me as above, I had at the end of my lying in two hundred guineas by me, including also what was left of my own.

I was brought to bed of a fine boy indeed, and a charming child it was; and when he heard of it, he wrote me a very kind, obliging letter about it, and then told me he thought it would look better for me to come away for London as soon as I was up and well; that he had provided apartments for me at Hammersmith,* as if I came only from London; and that after a while I should go back to Bath, and he would go with me.

I liked his offer very well, and hired a coach on purpose, and taking my child and a wet-nurse to tend and suckle it, and a maid-servant with me, away I went for London.

He met me at Reading in his own chariot, and taking me into that, left the servant and the child in the hired coach, and so he brought me to my new lodgings at Hammersmith; with which I had abundance of reason to be very well pleased, for they were very handsome rooms.

And now I was indeed in the height of what I might call prosperity, and I wanted nothing but to be a wife, which, however, could not be in this case, and therefore on all occasions I studied to save what I could, as I said above, against the time of scarcity; knowing well enough that such things as these do not always continue; that men that keep mistresses often change them, grow weary of them, or jealous of them, or something or other; and sometimes the ladies that are thus well used, are not careful by a prudent conduct to preserve the esteem of their persons, or the nice article of their fidelity, and then they are justly cast off with contempt.

But I was secured in this point, for as I had no inclination to change, so I had no manner of acquaintance, so no temptation to look any farther. I kept no company but in the family where I lodged, and with a clergyman's lady at next door; so that when he was absent I visited nobody, nor did he ever find me out of my chamber or parlour whenever he came down; if I went anywhere to take the air, it was always with him.

The living in this manner with him, and his with me, was certainly the most undesigned thing in the world; he often protested to me that when he became first acquainted with me, and even to the very night when we first broke in upon our rules, he never had the least design of lying with me; that he always had a sincere affection for me, but not the least real inclination to do what he had done. I assured him I never suspected him; that if I had I should not so easily have yielded to the freedoms which brought it on, but that it was all a surprise, and was owing to our having yielded too far to our mutual inclinations that night; and indeed I have often observed since, and leave it as a caution to the readers of this story, that we ought to be cautious of gratifying our inclinations in loose and lewd freedoms, lest we find our resolutions of virtue fail us in the juncture when their assistance should be most necessary.

It is true that from the first hour I began to converse with him, I resolved to let him lie with me, if he offered it; but it was because I wanted his help, and knew of no other way of securing him. But when we were that night together, and, as I have said, had gone such a length, I found my weakness; the inclination was not to be resisted, but I was obliged to yield up all even before he asked it.

However, he was so just to me that he never upbraided me with that; nor did he ever express the least dislike of my conduct on any other occasion, but always protested he was as much delighted with my company as he was the first hour we came together.

It is true that he had no wife, that is to say, she was no wife to him, but the reflections of conscience oftentimes snatch a man, especially a man of sense, from the arms of a mistress, as it did him at last, though on another occasion.

On the other hand, though I was not without secret reproaches of my own conscience for the life I led, and that even in the greatest height of the satisfaction I ever took, yet I had the terrible prospect of poverty and starving, which lay on me as a frightful spectre, so that there was no looking behind me; but as poverty brought me into it, so fear of poverty kept me in it, and I frequently resolved to leave it quite off, if I could but come to lay up money enough to maintain me. But these were thoughts of no weight, and whenever he came to me they vanished; for his company was so delightful, that there was no being melancholy when he was there; the reflections were all the subject of those hours when I was alone.

I lived six years in this happy but unhappy condition, in which time I brought him three children, but only the first of them lived; and though I removed twice in that six years, yet I came back the sixth year to my first lodgings at Hammersmith. Here it was that I was one morning surprised with a kind but melancholy letter from my gentlemen, intimating that he was very ill, and was afraid he should have another fit of sickness, but that his wife's relations being in the house with him, it would not be practicable to have me with him, which, however, he expressed his great dissatisfaction in, and that he wished I could be allowed to tend and nurse him as I did before.

I was very much concerned at this account, and was very impatient to know how it was with him. I waited a fortnight or thereabouts, and heard nothing, which surprised me, and I began to be very uneasy indeed. I think, I may say, that for the next fortnight I was near to distracted. It was my particular difficulty, that I did not know directly where he was; for I understood at first he was in the lodgings of his wife's mother; but having removed myself to London, I soon found, by the help of the direction I had for writing my letters to him, how to inquire after him, and there I found that he was at a house in Bloomsbury, whither he had removed his whole family; and that his wife and wife's mother were in the same house, though the wife was not suffered to know that she was in the same house with her husband.

Here I also soon understood that he was at the last extremity, which made me almost at the last extremity too, to have a true account. One night I had the curiosity to disguise myself like a servant-maid, in a round cap and straw hat, and went to the door, as sent by a lady of his neighbourhood, where he lived before, and giving master and mistress's service, I said I was sent to know how Mr— did, and how he had rested that night. In delivering this message I got the opportunity I desired; for, speaking with one of the maids, I held a long gossip's tale with her, and had all the particulars of his illness, which I found was a pleurisy, attended with a cough and fever. She told me also who was in the house, and how his wife was, who, by her relation, they were in some hopes might recover her understanding; but as to the gentlemen himself, the doctors said there was very little hopes of him, that in the morning they thought he had been dying, and that he was but little better then, for they did not expect that he could live over the next night.

This was heavy news for me, and I began now to see an end of my prosperity, and to see that it was well I had played the good housewife, and saved something while he was alive, for now I had no view of my own living before me.

It lay very heavy upon my mind, too, that I had a son, a fine lovely boy, about five years old, and no provision made for it, at least that I knew of. With these considerations, and a sad heart, I went home that evening, and began to cast with myself how I should live, and in what manner to bestow myself, for the residue of my life.

You may be sure I could not rest without inquiring again very quickly what was become of him; and not venturing to go myself, I sent several sham messengers, till after a fortnight's waiting longer, I found that there was hopes of his life, though he was still very ill; then I abated my sending to the house, and in some time after, I learnt in the neighbourhood that he was about house, and then that he was abroad* again.

I made no doubt then but that I should soon hear of him, and began to comfort myself with my circumstances being, as I thought, recovered. I waited a week, and two weeks, and with much surprise near two months, and heard nothing, but that, being recovered, he was gone into the country for the air after his distemper. After this it was yet two months more, and then I understood he was come to his city house again, but still I heard nothing from him.

I had written several letters for him, and directed them as usual, and found two or three of them had been called for, but not the rest. I wrote again in a more pressing manner than ever, and in one of them let him know that I must be forced to wait on him myself, representing my circumstances, the rent of lodgings to pay, and the provision for the child wanting, and my own deplorable condition, destitute of subsistence after his most solemn engagement to take care of and provide for me. I took a copy of this letter, and finding it lay at the house near a month, and was not called for, I found means to have the copy of it put into his hands at a coffee-house where I had found he had used to go.

This letter forced an answer from him, by which, though I found I was to be abandoned, yet I found he had sent a letter to me some time before, desiring me to go down to Bath again. Its contents I shall come to presently.

It is true that sick-beds are the times when such correspondences as this are looked on with different countenances, and seen with other eyes than we saw them with before: my lover had been at the gates of death, and at the very brink of eternity; and, it seems, struck with a due remorse, and with sad reflections upon his past life of gallantry and levity; and among the rest, his criminal correspondence with me, which was indeed neither more or less than a long-continued life of adultery, had represented itself as it really was, not as it had been formerly thought by him to be, and he looked upon it now with a just abhorrence.

I cannot but observe also, and leave it for the direction of my sex in such cases of pleasure, that whenever sincere repentance succeeds such a crime as this, there never fails to attend a hatred of the object; and the more the affection might seem to be before, the hatred will be more in proportion. It will always be so; indeed it cannot be otherwise; for there cannot be a true and sincere abhorrence of the offence, and the love to the cause of it remain; there will, with an abhorrence of the sin, be found a detestation of the fellow-sinner; you can expect no other.

I found it so here, though good manners, and justice in this gentleman, kept him from carrying it on to any extreme; but the short history of his part in this affair was thus; he perceived by my last letter, and by the rest, which he went for after, that I was not gone to Bath, and that his first letter had not come to my hand, upon which he writes me this following:

MADAM:—I am surprised that my letter, dated the 8th of last month, did not come to your hand; I give you my word it was delivered at your lodgings, and to the hands of your maid.

I need not acquaint you with what has been my condition for some time past; and how, having been at the edge of the grave, I am, by the unexpected and undeserved mercy of Heaven, restored again. In the condition I have been in, it cannot be strange to you that our unhappy correspondence has not been the least of the burthens which lay upon my conscience. I need say no more; those things that must be repented of, must also be reformed.

I wish you would think of going back to Bath. I enclose you here a bill of £50 for clearing yourself at your lodgings, and carrying you down, and hope it will be no surprise to you to add, that on this account only, and not for any offence given me on your side, I can *see you no more*. I will take due care of the child; leave him where he is, or take him with you, as you please. I wish you the like reflections, and that they may be to your advantage. – I am, etc.

I was struck with this letter, as with a thousand wounds; the reproaches of my own conscience were such as I cannot express, for I was not blind to my own crime; and I reflected that I might with less offence have continued with my brother, since there was no crime in our marriage on that score, neither of us knowing it.

But I never once reflected that I was all this while a married woman, a wife to Mr—, the linen-draper, who, though he had left me by the necessity of his circumstances, had no power to discharge me from the marriage contract which was between us, or to give me a legal liberty to marry again; so that I had been no less than a whore and an adulteress all this while. I then reproached myself with the liberties I had taken, and how I had been a snare to this gentlemen, and that indeed I was principal in the crime; that now he was mercifully snatched out of the gulf by a convincing work upon his mind,* but that I was left as if I was abandoned by Heaven to a continuing in my wickedness.

Under these reflections I continued very pensive and sad for near a month, and did not go down to Bath, having no inclination to be with the woman whom I was with before, lest, as I thought, she should prompt me to some wicked course of life again, as she had done; and besides, I was loth she should know I was cast off as above.

And now I was greatly perplexed about my little boy. It was death to me to part with the child, and yet when I considered the danger of being one time or other left with him to keep without being able to support him, I then resolved to leave him; but then I concluded to be near him myself too, that I might have the satisfaction of seeing him, without the care of providing for him. So I sent my gentleman a short letter that I had obeyed his orders in all things but that of going back to Bath; that however parting from him was a wound to me that I could never recover, yet that I was fully satisfied his reflections were just, and would be very far from desiring to obstruct his reformation.

Then I represented my own circumstances to him in the most moving terms. I told him that those unhappy distresses which first moved him to a generous friendship for me, would, I hoped, move him to a little concern for me now, though the criminal part of our correspondence, which I believe neither of us intended to fall into at that time, was broken off; that I desired to repent as sincerely as he had done, but entreated him to put me in some condition that I might not be exposed to temptations from the frightful prospect of poverty and distress; and if he had the least apprehensions of my being troublesome to him, I begged he would put me in a posture to go back to my mother in Virginia, from whence he knew I came, and that would put an end to all his fears on that account. I concluded, that if he would send me £50 more to facilitate my going away, I would send him back a general release, and would promise never to disturb him more with any importunities; unless it were to hear of the well-doing of the child, who, if I found my mother living, and my circumstances able, I would send for, and take him also off his hands.

This was indeed all a cheat thus far, viz., that I had no intention to go to Virginia, as the account of my former affairs there may convince anybody of; but the business was to get this last £50 of him, if possible, knowing well enough it would be the last penny I was ever to expect.

However, the argument I used, namely, of giving him a general release, and never troubling him any more, prevailed effectually, and he sent me a bill for the money by a person who brought with him a general release for me to sign, and which I frankly* signed; and thus, though full sore against my will, a final end was put to this affair.

And here I cannot but reflect upon the unhappy consequence of too great freedoms between persons stated* as we were, upon the pretence of innocent intentions, love of friendship, and the like; for the flesh has generally so great a share in those friendships, that it is great odds but inclination prevails at last over the most solemn resolutions; and that vice breaks in at the breaches of decency, which really innocent friendship ought to preserve with the greatest strictness. But I leave the readers of these things to their own just reflections, which they will be more able to make effectual than I, who so soon forgot myself, and am therefore but a very indifferent monitor.

I was now a single person again, as I may call myself; I was loosed from all the obligations either of wedlock or mistress-ship in the world, except my husband the linen-draper, whom I having not now heard from in almost fifteen years, nobody could blame me for thinking myself entirely freed from; seeing also he had at his going away told me, that if I did not hear frequently from him, I should conclude he was dead, and I might freely marry again to whom I pleased.

I now began to cast up my accounts. I had by many letters, and much importunity, and with the intercession of my mother too, had a second return of some goods from my brother, as I now call him, in Virginia, to make up the damage of the cargo I brought away with me, and this too was upon the condition of my sealing a general release to him, which, though I thought hard, yet I was obliged to promise. I managed so well in this case, that I got my goods away before the release was signed, and then I always found something or other to say to evade the thing, and to put off the signing it at all; till at length I pretended I must write to my brother before I could do it.

Including this recruit, and before I got the last £50, I found my strength to amount, put all together, to about £400, so that with that I had above £450. I had saved £100 more, but I met with a disaster with that, which was this — that a goldsmith in whose hands I had trusted it broke, so I lost £70 of my money, the man's composition not making above £30 out of his £100. I had a little plate,* but not much, and was well enough stocked with clothes and linen.

With this stock I had the world to begin again; but you are to consider that I was not now the same woman as when I lived at Rotherhithe; for, first of all, I was near twenty years older, and did not look the better for my age, nor for my rambles to Virginia and back again; and though I omitted nothing that might set me out to advantage, except painting,* for that I never stooped to, yet there would always be some difference seen between five-and-twenty and two-and-forty.

I cast about innumerable ways for my future state of life, and began to consider very seriously what I should do, but nothing offered. I took care to make the world take me for something more than I was, and had it given out that I was a fortune, and that my estate was in my own hands, the last of which was very true, the first of it was as above. I had no acquaintance, which was one of my worst misfortunes, and the consequence of that was, I had no adviser, and, above all, I had nobody to whom I could in confidence commit the secret of my circumstances; and I found by experience, that to be friendless is the worst condition, next to being in want, that a woman can be reduced to: I say a woman, because 'tis evident men can be their own advisers and their own directors, and know how to work themselves out of difficulties and into business better than women; but if a woman has no friend to communicate her affairs to, and to advise and assist her, 'tis ten to one but she is undone; nay, and the more money she has, the more danger she is in of being wronged and deceived; and this was my case in the affair of the £100 which I left in the hands of the goldsmith, as above, whose credit, it seems, was upon the ebb before, but I, that had nobody to consult with, knew nothing of it, and so lost my money.

When a woman is thus left desolate and void of counsel, she is just like a bag of money or a jewel dropt on the highway, which is a prey to the next comer; if a man of virtue and upright principles happens to find it, he will have it cried, and the owner may come to hear of it again; but how many times shall such a thing fall into hands that will make no scruple of seizing it for their own, to once that it shall come into good hands?

This was evidently my case, for I was now a loose, unguided creature, and had no help, no assistance, no guide for my conduct; I knew what I aimed at, and what I wanted, but knew nothing how to pursue the end by direct means. I wanted to be placed in a settled state of living, and had I happened to meet with a sober, good husband, I should have been as true a wife to him as virtue itself could have formed. If I had been otherwise, the vice came in always at the door of necessity, not at the door of inclination; and I understood too well, by the want of it, what the value of a settled life was, to do anything to forfeit the felicity of it; nay, I should have made the better wife for all the difficulties I had passed through, by a great deal; nor did I in any of the times that I had been a wife give my husbands the least uneasiness on account of my behaviour.

But all this was nothing; I found no encouraging prospect. I waited; I lived regularly, and with as much frugality as became my circumstances; but nothing offered, nothing presented, and the main stock wasted apace. What to do I knew not; the terror of approaching poverty lay hard upon my spirits. I had some money, but where to place it I knew not, nor would the interest of it maintain me, at least not in London.

At length a new scene opened. There was in the house where I lodged a north-country gentlewoman, and nothing was more frequent in her discourse than her account of the cheapness of provisions, and the easy way of living in her country; how plentiful and how cheap everything was, what good company they kept, and the like; till at last I told her she almost tempted me to go and live in her country; for I that was a widow, though I had sufficient to live on, yet had no way of increasing it; and that London was an extravagant place; that I found I could not live here under £100 a year, unless I kept no company, no servant, made no appearance, and buried myself in privacy, as if I was obliged to it by necessity.

I should have observed, that she was always made to believe, as everybody else was, that I was a great fortune, or at least that I had three or four thousand pounds, if not more, and all in my own hands; and she was mighty sweet upon me when she thought me inclined in the least to go into her country. She said she had a sister lived near Liverpool; that her brother was a considerable gentleman there, and had a great estate also in Ireland; that she would go down there in about two months, and if I would give her my company thither, I should be as welcome as herself for a month or more as I pleased, till I should see how I liked the country; and if I thought fit to live there, she would undertake they would take care, though they did not entertain lodgers themselves, they would recommend me to some agreeable family, where I should be placed to my content.

If this woman had known my real circumstances, she would never have laid so many snares, and taken so many weary steps, to catch a poor desolate creature that was good for little when it was caught; and indeed I, whose case was almost desperate, and thought I could not be much worse, was not very anxious about what might befall me, provided they did me no personal injury; so I suffered myself, though not without a great deal if invitation, and great professions of sincere friendship and real kindness — I say, I suffered myself to be prevailed upon to go with her, and accordingly I put myself in a posture for a journey, though I did not absolutely know whither I was to go.

And now I found myself in great distress; what little I had in the world was all in money, except, as before, a little plate, some linen, and my clothes; as for household stuff I had little or none, for I had lived always in lodgings; but I had not one friend in the world with whom to trust that little I had, or to direct me how to dispose of it. I thought of the bank, and of the other companies in London, but I had no friend to commit the management of it to, and to keep and carry about me bank bills, tallies, orders, and such things, I looked upon as unsafe; that if they were lost, my money was lost, and then I was undone; and, on the other hand, I might be robbed, and perhaps murdered in a strange place for them; and what to do I knew not.

It came into my thoughts one morning that I would go to the bank myself, where I had often been to receive the interest of some bills I had, and where I had found the clerk to whom I applied myself, very honest to me, and particularly so fair one time, that when I had mistold my money, and taken less than my due, and was coming away, he set me to rights and gave me the rest, which he might have put into his own pocket.

I went to him and asked if he would trouble himself to be my adviser, who was a poor friendless widow, and knew not what to do. He told me, if I desired his opinion of anything within the reach of his business, he would do his endeavour that I should not be wronged, but that he would also help me to a good, sober person of his acquaintance, who was a clerk in such business too, though not in their house, whose judgment was good, and whose honesty I might depend upon; 'for,' added he, 'I will answer for him, and for every step he takes; if he wrongs you, madam, of one farthing, it shall lie at my door; and he delights to assist people in such cases – he does it as an act of charity.'

I was a little at a stand at this discourse; but after some pause I told him I had rather have depended upon him, because I had found him honest, but if that could not be, I would take his recommendation sooner than any one's else. 'I dare say, madam,' says he, 'that you will be as well satisfied with my friend as with me, and he is thoroughly able to assist you, which I am not.' It seems he had his hands full of the business of the bank, and had engaged to meddle with no other business than that of his office: he added, that his friend should take nothing of me for his advice or assistance, and this indeed encouraged me.

He appointed the same evening, after the bank was shut, for me to meet him and his friend. As soon as I saw his friend, and he began but to talk of the affair, I was fully satisfied I had a very honest man to deal with; his countenance spoke it; and his character, as I heard afterwards, was everywhere so good, that I had no room for any more doubts upon me.

After the first meeting, in which I only said what I had said before, he appointed me to come the next day, telling me I might in the meantime satisfy myself of him by inquiry, which, however, I knew not how to do, having no acquaintance myself.

Accordingly I met him the next day, when I entered more freely with him into my case. I told him my circumstances at large; that I was a widow come over from America, perfectly desolate and friendless; that I had a little money, and but a little, and was almost distracted for fear of losing it, having no friend in the world to trust with the management of it; that I was going into the north of England to live cheap, that my stock might not waste; that I would willingly lodge my money in the bank, but that I durst not carry the bills about me; and how to correspond about it, or with whom, I knew not.

He told me I might lodge the money in the bank as an account and its being entered in the books would entitle me to the money at any time; and if I was in the north I might draw bills on the cashier, and receive it when I would; but that then it would be esteemed as running cash, and the bank would give no interest for it; that I might buy stock with it, and so it would lie in store for me, but that then if I wanted to dispose of it, I must come up to town to transfer it, and even it would be with some difficulty I should receive the half-yearly dividend, unless I was here in person, or had some friend I could trust with having the stock in his name to do it for me, and that would have the same difficulty in it as before; and with that he looked hard at me and smiled a little. At last says he, 'Why do you not get a head-steward, madam, that may take you and your money together, and then you would have the trouble taken off of your hands?' 'Ay, sir, and the money too, it may be,' said I; 'for truly I find the hazard that way is as much as 'tis t'other way'; but I remember I said secretly to myself, 'I wish you would ask me the question fairly; I would consider very seriously on it before I said No.'

He went on a good way with me, and I thought once or twice he was in earnest, but, to my real affliction, I found at last he had a wife; but when he owned he had a wife he shook his head, and said with some concern, that indeed he had a wife, and no wife. I began to think he had been in the condition of my late lover, and that his wife had been lunatic, or some such thing. However, we had not much more discourse at that time, but he told me he was in too much hurry of business then, but that if I would come home to his house after their business was over, he would consider what might be done for me, to put my affairs in a posture of security. I told him I would come, and desired to know where he lived. He gave me a direction in writing, and when he gave it me he read it to me, and said, 'There 'tis, madam, if you dare trust yourself with me.' 'Yes, sir,' said I, 'I believe I may venture to trust you with myself, for you have a wife, you say, and I don't want a husband; besides, I dare trust you with my money, which is all I have in the world, and if that were gone, I may trust myself anywhere.'

He said some things in jest that were very handsome and mannerly, and would have pleased me very well if they had been in earnest; but that passed over, I took the directions, and appointed to be at this house at seven o'clock the same evening.

When I came he made several proposals for my placing my money in the bank, in order to my having interest for it; but still some difficulty or other came in the way, which he objected as not safe; and I found such a sincere disinterested honesty in him, that I began to think I had certainly found the honest man I wanted, and that I could never put myself into better hands; so I told him with a great deal of frankness that I had never met with a man or woman yet that I could trust, or in whom I could think myself safe, but that I saw he was so disinterestedly concerned for my safety, that I would freely trust him with the management of that little I had, if he would accept to be steward for a poor widow that could give him no salary.

He smiled, and, standing up, with great respect saluted me. He told me he could not but take it very kindly that I had so good an opinion of him; that he would not deceive me; that he would do anything in his power to serve me, and expect no salary; but that he could not by any means accept of a trust that might bring him to be suspected of self-interest, and that if I should die he might have disputes with my executors, which he should be very loath to encumber himself with.

I told him if those were all his objections I would soon remove them, and convince him that there was not the least room for any difficulty; for that, first, as for suspecting him, if ever, now was the time to suspect him, and not to put the trust into his hands; and whenever I did suspect him, he could but throw it up then, and refuse to go on. Then, as to executors, I assured him I had no heirs, nor any relations in England, and I would have neither heirs or executors but himself, unless I should alter my condition, and then his trust and trouble should cease together, which, however I had no prospect of yet; but I told him if I died as I was, it should be all his own, and he would deserve it by being so faithful to me, as I was satisfied he would be.

He changed his countenance at this discourse, and asked me how I came to have so much goodwill for him; and looking very much pleased, said he might very lawfully wish he was single for my sake. I smiled, and told him, that as he was not, my offer could have no design upon him, and to wish was not to be allowed, 'twas criminal to his wife.

He told me I was wrong; 'for,' says he, 'as I said before, I have a wife and no wife, and 'twould be no sin to wish her hanged.' 'I know nothing of your circumstances that way, sir,' said I; 'but it cannot be innocent to wish your wife dead.' 'I tell you,' says he again, 'she is a wife and no wife; you don't know what I am, or what she is.'

'That's true,' said I, 'sir, I don't know what you are; but I believe you to be an honest man, and that's the cause of all my confidence in you.'

'Well, well,' says he, 'and so I am; but I am something else too, madam; for,' says he, 'to be plain with you, I am a cuckold, and she is a whore.' He spoke it in a kind of jest, but it was with such an awkward smile, that I perceived it stuck very close to him, and he looked dismally when he said it.

'That alters the case indeed, sir,' said I, 'as to that part you were speaking of; but a cuckold, you know, may be an honest man; it does not alter that case at all. Besides, I think,' said I, 'since your wife is so dishonest to you, you are too honest to her to own her for your wife; but that,' said I, 'is what I have nothing to do with.' 'Nay,' says he, 'I do think to clear my hands of her; for, to be plain with you, madam,' added he, 'I am no contented cuckold neither: on the other hand, I assure you it provokes me to the highest degree, but I can't help myself; she that will be a whore, will be a whore.'

I waived the discourse, and began to talk of my business; but I found he could not have done with it, so I let him alone, and he went on to tell me all the circumstances of his case, too long to relate here; particularly, that having been out of England some time before he came to the post he was in, she had had two children in the meantime by an officer in the army; and that when he came to England, and, upon her submission took her again, and maintained her very well, yet she ran away from him with a linen-draper's apprentice, robbed him of what she could come at, and continued to live from him still; 'so that, madam,' says he, 'she is a whore not by necessity, which is the common bait, but by inclination, and for the sake of the vice.'

Well, I pitied him, and wished him well rid of her, and still would have talked of my business, but it would not do. At last he looked steadily at me. 'Look you, madam,' says he, 'you came to ask advice of me, and I will serve you as faithfully as if you were my own sister; but I must turn the tables, since you oblige me to do it, and are so friendly to me, and I think I must ask advice of you. Tell me, what must a poor abused fellow do with a whore? What can I do to do myself justice upon her?'

'Alas! sir,' says I, ''tis a case too nice for me to advise in, but it seems to me she has run away from you, so you are rid of her fairly; what can you desire more?' 'Ay, she is gone indeed,' said he, 'but I am not clear of her for all that.' 'That's true,' says I; 'she may indeed run you into debt, but the law has furnished you with methods to prevent that also; you may cry her down* as they call it.'

'No, no,' says he, 'that is not the case; I have taken care of all that; 'tis not that part that I speak of, but I would be rid of her that I might marry again.'

'Well, sir,' says I, 'then you must divorce her; if you can prove what you say, you may certainly get that done, and then you are free.

'That's very tedious and expensive,' says he.

'Why,' says I, 'if you can get any woman you like to take your word, I suppose your wife would not dispute the liberty with you that she takes herself.'

'Ay,' says he, 'but it would be hard to bring an honest woman to do that; and for the other sort,' says he, 'I have had enough of her to meddle with any more whores.'

It occurred to me presently, 'I would have taken your word with all my heart, if you had but asked me the question'; but that was to myself. To him I replied, 'Why, you shut the door against any honest woman accepting you, for you condemn all that should venture upon you, and conclude that a woman that takes you now can't be honest.'

'Why,' says he, 'I wish you would satisfy me that an honest woman would take me; I'd venture it'; and then turns short upon me, 'Will you take me, madam?'

'That's not a fair question,' says I, 'after what you have said; however, lest you should think I wait only a recantation of it, I shall answer you plainly, No, not I; my business is of another kind with you; and I did not expect you would have turned my serious application to you, in my distracted case, into a comedy.'

'Why, madam,' says he, 'my case is as distracted as yours can be, and I stand in as much need of advice as you do, for I think if I have not relief somewhere I shall be mad myself, and I know not what course to take, I protest to you.'

'Why, sir,' says I, ''tis easier to give advice in your case than mine.' 'Speak, then,' says he, 'I beg of you, for now you encourage me.'

'Why,' says I, 'if your case is so plain, you may be legally divorced, and then you may find honest women enough to ask the question of fairly; the sex is not so scarce that you can want a wife.'

'Well, then,' said he, 'I am in earnest; I'll take your advice; but shall I ask you one question seriously beforehand?'

'Any question,' said I; 'but that you did before.'

'No, that answer will not do,' said he, 'for, in short, that is the question I shall ask.'

'You may ask what questions you please, but you have my answer to that already,' said I; 'besides, sir,' said I, 'can you think so ill of me as that I would give any answer to such a question beforehand? Can any woman alive believe you in earnest, or think you design anything but to banter her?'

'Well, well,' says he, 'I do not banter you, I am in earnest; consider of it.'

'But, sir,' says I, a little gravely, 'I came to you about my own business; I beg of you to let me know what you will advise me to do?'

'I will be prepared,' says he, 'against you come again.'

'Nay,' said I, 'you have forbid my coming any more.'

'Why so?' said he, and looked a little surprised.

'Because,' said I, 'you can't expect I should visit you on the account you talk of.'

'Well,' says he, 'you shall promise to come again, however, and I will not say any more of it till I have the divorce. But I desire you'll prepare to be better conditioned* when that's done, for you shall be the woman, or I will not be divorced at all; I owe it to your unlooked-for kindness, if to nothing else, but I have other reasons too.'

He could not have said anything in the world that pleased me better; however, I knew that the way to secure him was to stand off while the thing was so remote, as it appeared to be, and that it was time enough to accept of it when he was able to perform it. So I said very respectfully to him, it was time enough to consider of these things when he was in a condition to talk of them; in the meantime, I told him, I was going a great way from him, and he would find objects enough to please him better. We broke off here for the present, and he made me promise him to come again the next day, for my own business, which after some pressing I did; though had he seen farther into me, I wanted no pressing on that account.

I came the next evening accordingly, and brought my maid with me, to let him see that I kept a maid. He would have had me let the maid have stayed, but I would not, but ordered her aloud to come for me again about nine o'clock. But he forbid that, and told me he would see me safe home, which I was not very well pleased with, supposing he might do that to know where I lived, and inquire into my character and circumstances. However, I ventured that, for all the people there knew of me was to my advantage; and all the character he had of me was, that I was a woman of fortune, and that I was a very modest, sober body; which, whether true or not in the main yet you may see how necessary it is for all women who expect anything in the world, to preserve the character of their virtue, even when perhaps they may have sacrificed the thing itself.

I found, and was not a little pleased with it, that he had provided a supper for me. I found also he lived very handsomely, and had a house very handsomely furnished, and which I was rejoiced at indeed, for I looked upon it as all my own.

We had now a second conference upon the subject matter of the last. He laid his business very home indeed; he protested his affection to me, and indeed I had no room to doubt it; he declared that it began from the first moment I talked with him, and long before I had mentioned leaving my effects with him. ''Tis no matter when it began,' thought I; 'if it will but hold, 'twill be well enough.' He then told me how much the offer I had made of trusting him with my effects had engaged him. 'So I intended it should,' thought I, 'but then I thought you had been a single man too.' After we had supped, I observed he pressed me very hard to drink two or three glasses of wine, which, however, I declined, but drank one glass or two. He then told me he had a proposal to make to me, which I should promise him I would not take ill if I should not grant it. I told him I hoped he would make no dishonourable proposal to me, especially in his own house, and that if it was such, I desired he would not mention it, that I might not be obliged to offer any resentment to him that did not become the respect I professed for him, and the trust I had placed in him, in coming to his house; and begged of him he would give me leave to go away, and accordingly began to put on my gloves and prepare to be gone, though at the same time I no more intended it than he intended to let me.

Well, he importuned me not to talk of going; he assured me he was very far from offering any such thing to me that was dishonourable, and if I thought so, he would choose to say no more of it.

That part I did not relish at all. I told him I was ready to hear anything that he had to say, depending that he would say nothing unworthy of himself, or unfit for me to hear. Upon this, he told me his proposal was this: that I would marry him, though he had not yet obtained the divorce from the whore his wife; and to satisfy me that he meant honourably, he would promise not to desire me to live with him, or go to bed to him till the divorce was obtained. My heart said yes to this offer at first word, but it was necessary to play the hypocrite a little more with him; so I seemed to decline the motion with some warmth as unfair, told him that such a proposal could be of no signification, but to entangle us both in great difficulties; for if he should not at last obtain the divorce, yet we could not dissolve the marriage, neither could we proceed in it; so that if he was disappointed in the divorce, I left him to consider what a condition we should both be in.

In short, I carried on the argument against this so far, that I convinced him it was not a proposal that had any sense in it; then he went from it to another, viz., that I would sign and seal a contract with him, conditioning to marry him as soon as the divorce was obtained, and to be void if he could not get it.

I told him that was more rational than the other; but as this was the first time that ever I could imagine him weak enough to be in earnest, I did not use to say yes at first asking; I would consider of it. I played with this lover as an angler does with a trout: I found I had him fast on the hook; so I jested with his new proposal, and put him off. I told him he knew little of me, and bade him inquire about me; I let him also go home with me to my lodging, though I would not ask him to go in, for I told him it was not decent.

In short, I ventured to avoid signing a contract, and the reason why I did it was because the lady that had invited me to go with her into Lancashire insisted so positively upon it, and promised me such great fortunes, and fine things there, that I was tempted to go and try. 'Perhaps,' said I, 'I may mend myself very much'; and then I made no scruple of quitting my honest citizen, whom I was not so much in love with as not to leave him for a richer.

In a word, I avoided a contract; but told him I would go into the north, that he would know where to write to me by the business I had entrusted him with; that I would give him a sufficient pledge of my respect for him, for I would leave almost all I had in the world in his hands; and I would thus far give him my word, that as soon as he had sued out the divorce, if he would send me an account of it, I would come up to London, and that then we would talk seriously of the matter.

It was a base design I went with, that I must confess, though I was invited thither with a design much worse, as the sequel will discover. Well, I went with my friend, as I called her, into Lancashire. All the way we went she caressed me with the utmost appearance of a sincere, undissembled affection; treated me, except my coach-hire, all the way; and her brother brought a gentleman's coach to Warrington to receive us, and we were carried from thence to Liverpool with as much ceremony as I could desire.

We were also entertained at a merchant's house in Liverpool three or four days very handsomely; I forbear to tell his name, because of what followed. Then she told me she would carry me to an uncle's house of hers where we should be nobly entertained; and her uncle, as she called him, sent a coach and four horses for us, and we were carried near forty miles I know not whither.

We came, however, to a gentlemen's seat, where was a numerous family, a large park, extraordinary company indeed, and where she was called cousin. I told her, if she had resolved to bring me into such company as this, she should have let me have furnished myself with better clothes. The ladies took notice of that, and told me very genteelly they did not value people in their own country so much by their clothes as they did in London; that their cousin had fully informed them of my quality, and that I did not want clothes to set me off; in short, they entertained me not like what I was, but like what they thought I had been, namely, a widow lady of a great fortune.

The first discovery I made here was, that the family were all Roman Catholics, and the cousin too; however, nobody in the world could behave better to me, and I had all the civility shown that I could have had if I had been of their opinion. The truth is, I had not so much principle of any kind as to be nice in point of religion; and I presently learned to speak favourably of the Romish Church; particularly, I told them I saw little but the prejudice of education in all the differences that were among Christians about religion, and if it had so happened that my father had been a Roman Catholic, I doubted not but I should have been as well pleased with their religion as my own.

This obliged them in the highest degree, and as I was besieged day and night with good company and pleasant discourse, so I had two or three old ladies that lay at me upon the subject of religion too. I was so complaisant that I made no scruple to be present at their mass, and to conform to all their gestures as they

showed me the pattern, but I would not come too cheap;* so that I
only in the main encouraged them to expect that I would turn
Roman Catholic if I was instructed in the Catholic doctrine, as
they called it; and so the matter rested.

I stayed here about six weeks; and then my conductor led me
back to a country village, about six miles from Liverpool, where
her brother, as she called him, came to visit me in his own chariot,
with two footmen in a good livery; and the next thing was to make
love to me. As it happened to me, one would think I could not
have been cheated, and indeed I thought so myself, having a safe
card at home, which I resolved not to quit unless I could mend
myself very much. However, in all appearance this brother was a
match worth my listening to, and the least his estate was valued at
was £1000 a year, but the sister said it was worth £1500 a year,
and lay most of it in Ireland.

I that was a great fortune, and passed for such, was above being
asked how much my estate was; and my false friend, taking it
upon a foolish hearsay, had raised it from £500 to £5000, and by
the time she came into the country she called it £15,000. The
Irishman, for such I understood him to be, was stark mad at this
bait; in short, he courted me, made me presents, and ran in debt
like a madman for the expenses of his courtship. He had, to give
him his due, the appearance of an extraordinary fine gentleman;
he was tall, well-shaped, and had an extraordinary address;
talked as naturally of his park and his stables, of his horses, his
gamekeepers, his woods, his tenants, and his servants, as if he had
been in a mansion-house, and I had seen them all about me.

He never so much as asked me about my fortune or estate, but
assured me that when we came to Dublin he would jointure me in
£600 a year in good land, and that he would enter into a deed of
settlement, or contract, here for the performance of it.

This was such language indeed as I had not been used to, and I
was here beaten out of all my measures; I had a she-devil in my
bosom, every hour telling me how great her brother lived. One
time she would come for my orders, how I would have my coach
painted, and how lined; and another time, what clothes my page
should wear: in short, my eyes were dazzled, I had now lost my
power of saying no, and, to cut the story short, I consented to be
married; but to be more private, we were carried farther into the
country, and married by a priest, which I was assured would
marry us as effectually as a Church of England parson.

I cannot say but I had some reflections in this affair upon the dishonourable forsaking my faithful citizen, who loved me sincerely, and who was endeavouring to quit himself of a scandalous whore by whom he had been barbarously used, and promised himself infinite happiness in his new choice; which choice was now giving up herself to another in a manner almost as scandalous as hers could be.

But the glittering show of a great estate and of fine things which the deceived creature that was not my deceiver represented every hour to my imagination hurried me away, and gave me no time to think of London, or of anything there, much less of the obligation I had to a person of infinitely more real merit than what was now before me.

But the thing was done; I was now in the arms of my new spouse, who appeared still the same as before; great even to magnificence, and nothing less than a thousand pounds a year could support the ordinary equipage he appeared in.

After we had been married about a month, he began to talk of my going to West Chester* in order to embark for Ireland. However, he did not hurry me, for we stayed near three weeks longer, and then he sent to Chester for a coach to meet us at the Black Rock,* as they call it, over against Liverpool. Thither we went in a fine boat they call a pinnace, with six oars; his servants, and horses, and baggage going in a ferry-boat. He made his excuse to me, that he had no acquaintance at Chester, but he would go before and get some handsome apartments for me at a private house. I asked him how long we should stay at Chester. He said, not at all, any longer than one night or two, but he would immediately hire a coach to go to Holyhead. Then I told him he should by no means give himself the trouble to get private lodgings for one night or two, for that Chester being a great place, I made no doubt but there would be very good inns and accommodation enough; so we lodged at an inn not far from the Cathedral; I forget what sign it was at.

Here my spouse, talking of my going to Ireland, asked me if I had no affairs to settle at London before we went off. I told him no, not of any great consequence, but what might be done as well by letter from Dublin. 'Madam,' says he very respectfully, 'I suppose the greatest part of your estate, which my sister tells me is most of it in money in the Bank of England, lies secure enough; but in case it required transferring, or any way altering its property, it might be necessary to go up to London and settle those things before we went over.

I seemed to look strange at it, and told him I knew not what he meant; that I had no effects in the Bank of England that I knew of, and I hoped he could not say that I had ever told him I had. No, he said, I had not told him so, but his sister had said the greatest part of my estate lay there; 'and I only mentioned it, my dear,' said he, 'that if there was any occasion to settle it, or order anything about it, we might not be obliged to the hazard and trouble of another voyage back again'; for he added, that he did not care to venture me too much upon the sea.

I was surprised at this talk, and began to consider what the meaning of it must be; and it presently occurred to me that my friend, who called him brother, had represented me in colours which were not my due; and I thought that I would know the bottom of it before I went out of England, and before I should put myself into I know not whose hands in a strange country.

Upon this I called his sister into my chamber the next morning, and letting her know the discourse her brother and I had been upon, I conjured her to tell me what she had said to him, and upon what foot it was that she had made this marriage. She owned that she had told him that I was a great fortune, and said that she was told so at London. 'Told so?' says I warmly; 'did I ever tell you so?' No, she said, it was true I never did tell her so, but I had said several times that what I had was in my own disposal. 'I did so,' returned I very quick, 'but I never told you I had anything called a fortune; no, that I had £100, or the value of £100 in the world. And how did it consist with my being a fortune,' said I, 'that I should come here into the north of England with you, only upon the account of living cheap?' At these words, which I spoke warm and high, my husband came into the room, and I desired him to come in and sit down, for I had something of moment to say before them both, which it was absolutely necessary he should hear.

He looked a little disturbed at the assurance with which I seemed to speak it, and came and sat down by me, having first shut the door; upon which I began, for I was very much provoked, and turning myself to him, 'I am afraid,' says I, 'my dear' (for I spoke with kindness on his side), 'that you have a very great abuse put upon you, and an injury done you never to be repaired in your marrying me, which, however, as I have had no hand in it, I desire

I may be fairly acquitted of it, and that the blame may lie where it ought and nowhere else, for I wash my hands of every part of it.' 'What injury can be done me, my dear,' says he, 'in marrying you? I hope it is to my honour and advantage every way.' 'I will soon explain it to you,' says I, 'and I fear there will be no reason to think yourself well used; but I will convince you, my dear,' says I again, 'that I have had no hand in it.'

He looked now scared and wild, and began, I believed, to suspect what followed; however, looking towards me, and saying only, 'Go on,' he sat silent, as if to hear what I had more to say; so I went on. 'I asked you last night,' said I, speaking to him, 'if ever I made any boast to you of my estate, or ever told you I had any estate in the Bank of England or anywhere else, and you owned I had not, as is most true; and I desire you will tell me here, before your sister, if ever I gave you any reason from me to think so, or that ever we had any discourse about it'; and he owned again I had not, but said I had appeared always as a woman of fortune, and he depended on it that I was so, and hoped he was not deceived. 'I am not inquiring whether you have been deceived,' said I; 'I fear you have, and I too; but I am clearing myself from being concerned in deceiving you.

'I have been now asking your sister if ever I told her of any fortune or estate I had, or gave her any particulars of it; and she owns I never did. And pray, madam,' said I, 'be so just to me, to charge me if you can, if ever I pretended to you that I had an estate; and why, if I had, should I ever come down into this country with you on purpose to spare that little I had, and live cheap?' She could not deny one word, but said she had been told in London that I had a very great fortune, and that it lay in the Bank of England.

'And now, dear sir,' said I, turning myself to my new spouse again, 'be so just to me as to tell me who has abused both you and me so much as to make you believe I was a fortune, and prompt you to court me to this marriage?' He could not speak a word, but pointed to her; and, after some more pause, flew out in the most furious passion that ever I saw a man in my life, cursing her, and calling her all the whores and hard names he could think of; and that she had ruined him, declaring that she had told him I had £15,000, and that she was to have £500 of him for procuring this match for him. He then added, directing his speech to me, that she was none of his sister, but had been his whore for two years before; that she had had £100 of him in part of this bargain, and that he was utterly undone if things were as I said; and in his raving he swore he would let her heart's blood out immediately, which frightened her and me too. She cried, said she had been told so in the house where I lodged. But this aggravated him more than before, that she should put so far upon him, and run things such a length upon no other authority than a hearsay; and then turning to me again, said very honestly, he was afraid we were both undone; 'for, to be plain, my dear, I have no estate,' says he; 'what little I had, this devil has made me run out in putting me into this equipage.' She took the opportunity of his being earnest in talking with me, and got out of the room, and I never saw her more.

I was confounded now as much as he, and knew not what to say. I thought many ways that I had the worst of it; but his saying he was undone, and that he had no estate neither, put me into a mere* distraction. 'Why,' says I to him, 'this has been a hellish juggle, for we are married here upon the foot of a double fraud: you are undone by the disappointmnt, it seems; and if I had had a fortune I had been cheated too, for you say you have nothing.'

'You would indeed have been cheated, my dear,' says he, 'but you would not have been undone, for £15,000 would have maintained us both very handsomely in this country; and I had resolved to have dedicated every groat of it to you; I would not have wronged you of a shilling, and the rest I would have made up in my affection to you, and tenderness of you, as long as I lived.'

This was very honest indeed, and I really believe he spoke as he intended, and that he was a man that was as well qualified to make me happy, as to his temper and behaviour, as any man ever was; but his having no estate, and being run into debt on this ridiculous account in the country, made all the prospect dismal and dreadful, and I knew not what to say or what to think.

I told him it was very unhappy that so much love and so much good nature as I discovered in him should be thus precipitated into misery; that I saw nothing before us but ruin; for as to me, it was my unhappiness, that what little I had was not able to relieve us a week, and with that I pulled out a bank-bill of £20 and eleven guineas, which I told him I had saved out of my little income, and that by the account that creature had given me of the way of living in that country, I expected it would maintain me three or four years; that if it was taken from me, I was left destitute, and he knew what the condition of a woman must be if she had no money in her pocket; however, I told him, if he would take it, there it was.

He told me with great concern, and I thought I saw tears in his eyes, that he would not touch it; that he abhorred the thoughts of stripping me and making me miserable; that he had fifty guineas left, which was all he had in the world, and he pulled it out and threw it down on the table, bidding me take it, though he were to starve for want of it.

I returned, with the same concern for him, that I could not bear to hear him talk so; that, on the contrary, if he could propose any probable method of living, I would do anything that became me, and that I would live as narrow as he could desire.

He begged of me to talk no more at that rate, for it would make him distracted; he said he was bred a gentleman, though he was reduced to a low fortune, and that there was but one way left which he could think of, and that would not do, unless I could answer him one question, which, however, he said he would not press me to. I told him I would answer it honestly; whether it would be to his satisfaction or no, that I could not tell.

'Why, then, my dear, tell me plainly,' says he, 'will the little you have keep us together in any figure, or in any station or place, or will it not?'

It was my happiness that I had not discovered myself or my circumstances at all – no, not so much as my name; and seeing there was nothing to be expected from him, however good-humoured and however honest he seemed to be, but to live on what I knew would soon be wasted, I resolved to conceal everything but the bank bill and eleven guineas; and I would have been very glad to have lost that and have been set down where he took me up. I had indeed another bank bill about me of £30, which was the whole of what I brought with me, as well to subsist on in the country, as not knowing what might offer; because this creature, the go-between that had thus betrayed us both, had made me believe strange things of marrying to my advantage, and I was not willing to be without money, whatever might happen. This bill I concealed, and that made me the freer of the rest, in consideration of his circumstances, for I really pitied him heartily.

But to return to this question, I told him I never willingly deceived him, and I never would. I was very sorry to tell him that the little I had would not subsist us; that it was not sufficient to subsist me alone in the south country, and that this was the reason that made me put myself into the hands of that woman who called him brother, she having assured me that I might board very handsomely at a town called Manchester* where I had not yet been, for about £6 a year; and my whole income not being above £15 a year, I thought I might live easy upon it, and wait for better things.

He shook his head and remained silent, and a very melancholy evening we had; however, we supped together, and lay together that night, and when we had almost supped he looked a little better and more cheerful, and called for a bottle of wine. 'Come, my dear,' says he, 'though the case is bad, it is to no purpose to be dejected. Come, be as easy as you can; I will endeavour to find out some way or other to live; if you can but subsist yourself, that is better than nothing. I must try the world again; a man ought to think like a man; to be discouraged is to yield to the misfortune.' With this he filled a glass, and drank to me, holding my hand all the while the wine went down, and protesting his main concern was for me.

It was really a true, gallant spirit he was of, and it was the more grievous to me. 'Tis something of relief even to be undone by a man of honour, rather than by a scoundrel; but here the greatest disappointment was on his side, for he had really spent a great deal of money, and it was very remarkable on what poor terms she proceeded. First, the baseness of the creature herself is to be observed, who, for the getting £100 herself, could be content to let him spend three or four more, though perhaps it was all he had in the world, and more than all; when she had not the least ground more than a little tea-table chat, to say that I had any estate, or was a fortune, or the like. It is true the design of deluding a woman of fortune, if I had been so, was base enough; the putting the face of great things upon poor circumstances was a fraud, and bad enough; but the case a little differed too, and that in his favour, for he was not a rake that made a trade to delude women, and, as some have done, get six or seven fortunes after one another, and then rifle* and run away from them; but he was already a gentleman, unfortunate and low, but had lived well; and though, if I had had a fortune, I should have been enraged at the slut for betraying me, yet really for the man, a fortune would not have been ill bestowed on him, for he was a lovely person indeed, of generous principles, good sense, and of abundance of good humour.

We had a great deal of close conversation that night, for we neither of us slept much; he was as penitent, for having put all those cheats upon me, as if it had been felony, and that he was going to execution; he offered me again every shilling of the money he had about him, and said he would go into the army and seek for more.

I asked him why he would be so unkind to carry me into Ireland, when I might suppose he could not have subsisted me there. He took me in his arms. 'My dear,' said he, 'I never designed to go to Ireland at all, much less to have carried you thither, but came hither to be out of the observation of the people, who had heard what I pretended to, and that nobody might ask me for money before I was furnished to supply them.'

'But, where then,' said I, 'were we to have gone next?'

'Why, my dear,' said he, 'I'll confess the whole scheme to you as I had laid it; I purposed here to ask you something about your estate, as you see I did, and when you, as I expected you would, had entered into some account of the particulars, I would have made an excuse to have put off our voyage to Ireland for some time, and so have gone for London. Then, my dear,' says he, 'I resolved to have confessed all the circumstances of my own affairs to you, and let you know I had indeed made use of these artifices to obtain your consent to marry me, but had now nothing to do but to ask your pardon, and to tell you how abundantly I would endeavour to make you forget what was past, by the felicity of the days to come.'

'Truly,' said I to him, 'I find you would soon have conquered me; and it is my affliction now, that I am not in a condition to let you see how easily I should have been reconciled to you, and have passed by all the tricks you had put upon me, in recompense of so much good humour. But, my dear, ' said I, 'what can we do now? We are both undone; and what better are we for our being reconciled, seeing we have nothing to live on?'

We proposed a great many things, but nothing could offer where there was nothing to begin with. He begged me at last to talk no more of it, for, he said, I would break his heart; so we talked of other things a little, till at last he took a husband's leave of me, and so went to sleep.

He rose before me in the morning; and indeed having lain awake almost all night, I was very sleepy, and lay till near eleven o'clock. In this time he took his horses, and three servants, and all his linen and baggage, and away he went, leaving a short but moving letter for me on the table, as follows:

My Dear, – I am a dog; I have abused you; but I have been drawn in to do it by a base creature, contrary to my principle and the general practice of my life. Forgive me, my dear! I ask you pardon with the greatest sincerity; I am the most miserable of men, in having deluded you. I have been so happy to possess you, and am now so wretched as to be forced to fly from you. Forgive me, my dear; once more I say, forgive me! I am not able to see you ruined by me, and myself unable to support you. Our marriage is nothing; I shall never be able to see you again; I here discharge you from it; if you can marry to your advantage, do not decline it on my account. I here swear to you on my faith, and on the word of a man of honour, I will never disturb your repose if I should know of it, which, however, is not likely. On the other hand, if you should not marry, and if good fortune should befall me, it shall be all yours, wherever you are.

I have put some of the stock of money I have left into your pocket; take places for yourself and your maid in the stage-coach, and go for London. I hope it will bear your charges thither, without breaking into your own. Again I sincerely ask your pardon, and will do so as often as I shall ever think of you. Adieu, my dear, for ever! – I am, yours most affectionately.

J. E.

Nothing that ever befell me in my life sank so deep into my heart as this farewell. I reproached him a thousand times in my thoughts for leaving me, for I would have gone with him through the world, if I had begged my bread. I felt in my pocket, and there I found ten guineas, his gold watch, and two little rings, one a small diamond ring, worth only about £6, and the other a plain gold ring.

I sat down and looked upon these things two hours together, and scarce spoke a word, till my maid interrupted me by telling me my dinner was ready. I ate but little, and after dinner I fell into a violent fit of crying, every now and then calling him by his name, which was James. 'O Jemmy!' said I, 'come back, come back. I'll give you all I have; I'll beg, I'll starve with you.' And thus I ran raving about the room several times, and then sat down between whiles, and then walked about again, called upon him to come back, and then cried again; and thus I passed the afternoon, till about seven o'clock, when it was near dusk in the evening, being August, when, to my unspeakable surprise, he comes back into the inn, and comes directly up into my chamber.

I was in the greatest confusion imaginable, and so was he too. I could not imagine what should be the occasion of it, and began to be at odds with myself whether to be glad or sorry; but my affection biased all the rest, and it was impossible to conceal my joy, which was too great for smiles, for it burst out into tears. He was no sooner entered the room, but he ran to me and took me in his arms, holding me fast, and almost stopping my breath with his kisses, but spoke not a word. At length I began. 'My dear,' said I, 'how could you go away from me?' to which he gave no answer, for it was impossible for him to speak.

When our ecstasies were a little over, he told me he was gone above fifteen miles, but it was not in his power to go any farther without coming back to see me again and to take his leave of me once more.

I told him how I had passed my time, and how loud I had called him to come back again. He told me he heard me very plain upon Delamere Forest,* at a place about twelve miles off. I smiled. 'Nay,' says he, 'do not think I am in jest, for if ever I heard your voice in my life, I heard you call me aloud, and sometimes I thought I saw you running after me.' 'Why,' said I, 'what did I say?' for I had not named the words to him. 'You called aloud,' says he, 'and said, O Jemmy; O Jemmy! come back, come back.'

I laughed at him. 'My dear,' says he, 'do not laugh, for, depend upon it, I heard your voice as plain as you hear mine now; if you please, I'll go before a magistrate and make oath of it.' I then began to be amazed and surprised, and indeed frighted, and told him what I had really done, and how I had called after him, as above. When we had amused* ourselves a while about this, I said to him, 'Well, you shall go away from me no more; I'll go all over the world with you rather.' He told me it would be a very difficult thing for him to leave me, but since it must be, he hoped I would make it as easy to me as I could; but as for him, it would be his destruction, that he foresaw.

However, he told me that he had considered he had left me to travel to London alone, which was a long journey; and that as he might as well go that way as any way else, he was resolved to see me hither, or near it; and if he did go away then without taking his leave, I should not take it ill of him; and this he made me promise.

He told me how he had dismissed his three servants, sold their horses, and sent the fellows away to seek their fortunes, and all in a little time, at a town on the road, I know not where; 'and,' says he, 'it cost me some tears all alone by myself, to think how much happier they were than their master, for they could go to the next gentleman's house to see for a service,* whereas,' said he, 'I knew not whither to go, or what to do with myself.'

I told him I was so completely miserable in parting with him, that I could not be worse; and that now he was come again, I would not go from him, if he would take me with him, let him go whither he would. And in the meantime I agreed that we would go together to London; but I could not be brought to consent he should go away at last and not take his leave of me, but told him, jesting, that if he did, I would call him back again as loud as I did before. Then I pulled out his watch, and gave it him back, and his two rings, and his ten guineas; but he would not take them, which made me very much suspect that he resolved to go off upon the road, and leave me.

The truth is, the circumstances he was in, the passionate expressions of his letter, the kind, gentlemanly treatment I had from him in all the affair, with the concern he showed for me in it, his manner of parting with that large share which he gave me of his little stock left – all these had joined to make such impressions on me, that I could not bear the thoughts of parting with him.

Two days after this we quitted Chester, I in the stage-coach, and he on horseback. I dismissed my maid at Chester. He was very much against my being without a maid, but she being hired in the country (keeping no servant at London), I told him it would have been barbarous to have taken the poor wench, and have turned her away as soon as I came to town; and it would also have been a needless charge on the road; so I satisfied him, and he was easy on that score.

He came with me as far as Dunstable,* within thirty miles of London, and then he told me fate and his own misfortunes obliged him to leave me, and that it was not convenient for him to go to London, for reasons which it was of no value to me to know, and I saw him preparing to go. The stage-coach we were in did not usually stop at Dunstable, but I desiring it for a quarter of an hour, they were content to stand at an inn-door a while, and we went into the house.

Being in the inn, I told him I had but one favour more to ask him, and that was, that since he could not go any farther, he would give me leave to stay a week or two in the town with him, that we might in that time think of something to prevent such a ruinous thing to us both as a final separation would be; and that I had something of moment to offer to him, which perhaps he might find practicable to our advantage.

This was too reasonable a proposal to be denied, so he called the landlady of the house, and told her his wife was taken ill, and so ill that she could not think of going any farther in a stage-coach, which had tired her almost to death, and asked if she could not get us a lodging for two or three days in a private house, where I might rest me a little, for the journey had been too much for me. The landlady, a good sort of a woman, well-bred, and very obliging, came immediately to see me; told me she had two or three very good rooms in a part of the house quite out of the noise, and if I saw them she did not doubt but I would like them, and I should have one of her maids, that should do nothing else but wait on me. This was so very kind, that I could not but accept of it; so I went to look on the rooms, and liked them very well, and indeed they were extraordinarily furnished, and very pleasant lodgings; so we paid the stage-coach, took out our baggage, and resolved to stay here a while.

Here I told him I would live with him now till all my money was spent, but would not let him spend a shilling of his own. We had some kind squabble about that, but I told him it was the last time I was like to enjoy his company, and I desired that he would let me be master in that thing only, and he should govern in everything else; so he acquiesced.

Here one evening, taking a walk into the fields, I told him I would now make the proposal to him I had told him of; accordingly I related to him how I had lived in Virginia, that I had a mother I believed was alive there still, though my husband was dead some years. I told him that had not my effects miscarried, which, by the way, I magnified pretty much, I might have been fortune good enough to him to have kept us from being parted in this manner. Then I entered into the manner of people's settling in those countries, how they had a quantity of land given them by the constitution of the place; and if not, that it might be purchased at so easy a rate that it was not worth naming.

I then gave him a full and distinct account of the nature of planting; how with carrying over but two or three hundred pounds' value in English goods, with some servants and tools, a man of application would presently lay a foundation for a family, and in a few years would raise an estate.

I let him into the nature of the product of the earth, how the ground was cured and prepared, and what the usual increase of it was; and demonstrated to him, that in a very few years, with such a beginning, we should be as certain of being rich as we were now certain of being poor.

He was surprised at my discourse; for we made it the whole subject of our conversation for near a week together, in which time I laid it down in black and white, as we say, that it was morally impossible, with a supposition of any reasonable good conduct, but that we must thrive there and do very well.

Then I told him what measures I would take to raise such a sum as £300, or thereabouts; and I argued with him how good a method it would be to put an end to our misfortunes, and restore our circumstances in the world, to what we had both expected; and I added, that after seven years we might be in a posture to leave our plantation in good hands, and come over again and receive the income of it, and live here and enjoy it; and I gave him examples of some that had done so, and lived now in very good figure in London.

In short, I pressed him so to it, that he almost agreed to it, but still something or other broke it off; till at last he turned the tables, and began to talk almost to the same purpose of Ireland.

He told me that a man that could confine himself to a country life, and that could but find stock to enter upon any land, should have farms there for £50 a year, as good as were let for £200 a year; that the produce was such, and so rich the land, that if much was not laid up, we were sure to live as handsomely upon it as a gentlemen of £3000 a year could do in England; and that he had laid a scheme to leave me in London, and go over and try; and if he found he could lay a handsome foundation of living, suitable to the respect he had for me, as he doubted not he should do, he would come over and fetch me.

I was dreadfully afraid that upon such a proposal he would have taken me at my word, viz., to turn my little income into money, and let him carry it over into Ireland and try his experiment with it; but he was too just to desire it, or to have accepted it if I had offered it; and he anticipated me in that, for he added, that he would go and try his fortune that way, and if he found he could do anything at it to live, then by adding mine to it when I went over, we should live like ourselves; but that he would not hazard a shilling of mine till he had made the experiment with a little, and he assured me that if he found nothing to be done in Ireland, he would then come to me and join in my project for Virginia.

He was so earnest upon his project being to be tried first, that I could not withstand him; however, he promised to let me hear from him in a very little time after his arriving there, to let me know whether his prospect answered his design, that if there was not a probability of success, I might take the occasion to prepare for our other voyage, and then, he assured me, he would go with me to America with all his heart.

I could bring him to nothing further than this, and which entertained us near a month, during which I enjoyed his company, which the most entertaining that ever I met with in my life before. In this time he let me into part of the story of his own life, which was indeed surprising, and full of an infinite variety, sufficient to fill up a much brighter history, for its adventures and incidents, than any I ever saw in print; but I shall have occasion to say more of him hereafter.

We parted at last, though with the utmost reluctance on my side; and indeed he took his leave very unwillingly too, but necessity obliged him for his reasons were very good why he would not come to London, as I understood more fully afterwards.

I gave him a direction how to write to me, though still I reserved the grand secret, which was not to let him ever know my true name, who I was, or where to be found; he likewise let me know how to write a letter to him, so that he said he would be sure to receive it.

I came to London the next day after we parted, but did not go directly to my old lodgings, but for another nameless reason took a private lodging in St John's Street, or, as it is vulgarly called, St Jones's, near Clerkenwell,* and here being perfectly alone, I had leisure to sit down and reflect seriously upon the last seven months' ramble I had made, for I had been abroad no less. The pleasant hours I had with my last husband I looked back on with an infinite deal of pleasure; but that pleasure was very much lessened when I found some time after that I was really with child.

This was a perplexing thing, because of the difficulty which was before me where I should get leave to lie in, it being one of the nicest things in the world at that time of day for a woman that was a stranger, and had no friends, to be entertained in that circumstance without security, which I had not, neither could I procure any.

I had taken care all this while to preserve a correspondence with my friend at the bank, or rather he took care to correspond with me, for he wrote to me once a week; and though I had not spent my money so fast as to want any from him, yet I often wrote also to let him know I was alive. I had left directions in Lancashire, so that I had these letters conveyed to me; and during my recess at St Jones's I received a very obliging letter from him, assuring me that his process for a divorce went on with success, though he met with some difficulties in it that he did not expect.

I was not displeased with the news that his process was more tedious than he expected; for though I was in no condition to have had him yet, not being so foolish to marry him when I knew myself to be with child by another man, as some I know have ventured to do, yet I was not willing to lose him, and, in a word, resolved to have him, if he continued in the same mind, as soon as I was up again; for I saw apparently I should hear no more from my other husband; and as he had all along pressed me to marry, and had assured me he would not be at all disgusted at it, or ever offer to claim me again, so I made no scruple to resolve to do it if I could, and if my other friend stood to his bargain; and I had a great deal of reason to be assured that he would, by the letters he wrote to me, which were the kindest and most obliging that could be.

I now grew big, and the people where I lodged perceived it, and began to take notice of it to me, and as far as civility would allow, intimated that I must think of removing. This put me to extreme perplexity, and I grew very melancholy, for indeed I knew not what course to take; I had money, but no friends, and was like now to have a child upon my hands to keep, which was a difficulty I had never had upon me yet, as my story hitherto makes appear.

In the course of this affair I fell very ill, and my melancholy really increased my distemper. My illness proved at length to be only an ague, but my apprehensions were really that I should miscarry. I should not say apprehensions, for indeed I would have been glad to miscarry, but I could never entertain so much as a thought of taking anything to make me miscarry; I abhorred, I say, so much as the thought of it.

However, speaking of it, the gentlewoman who kept the house proposed to me to send for a midwife. I scrupled it at first, but after some time consented, but told her I had no acquaintance with any midwife, and so left it to her.

It seems the mistress of the house was not so great a stranger to such cases as mine was as I thought at first she had been, as will appear presently; and she sent for a midwife of the right sort – that is to say, the right sort for me.

The woman appeared to be an experienced woman in her business, I mean as a midwife; but she had another calling too, in which she was as expert as most women, if not more. My landlady had told her I was very melancholy, and that she believed that had done me harm; and once, before me, said to her, 'Mrs B——, I believe this lady's trouble is of a kind that is pretty much in your way, and therefore if you can do anything for her, pray do, for she is a very civil gentlewoman'; and so she went out of the room.

I really did not understand her, but my Mother Midnight* began very seriously to explain what she meant, as soon as she was gone. 'Madam,' says she, 'you seem not to understand what your landlady means; and when you do, you need not let her know all at that you do so.

'She means that you are under some circumstances that may render your lying in difficult to you, and that you are not willing to be exposed. I need say no more, but to tell you, that if you think fit to communicate so much of your case to me as is necessary, for I do not desire to pry into those things, I perhaps may be in a condition to assist you, and to make you easy, and remove all your dull thoughts upon that subject.'

Every word this creature said was a cordial to me, and put new life and new spirit into my very heart; my blood began to circulate immediately, and I was quite another body; I ate my victuals again, and grew better presently after it. She said a great deal more to the same purpose, and then having pressed me to be free with her, and promised in the solemnest manner to be secret, she stopped a little, as if waiting to see what impression it made on me, and what I would say.

I was too sensible of the want I was in of such a woman not to accept her offer; I told her my case was partly as she guessed, and partly not, for I was really married, and had a husband, though he was so remote at that time as that he could not appear publicly.

She took me short, and told me that was none of her business; all the ladies that came under her care were married women to her. 'Every woman,' says she, 'that is with child has a father for it,' and whether that father was a husband or no husband was no business of hers; her business was to assist me in my present circumstances, whether I had a husband or no; 'For, madam,' says she, 'to have a husband that cannot appear is to have no husband, and therefore whether you are a wife or a mistress is all one to me.'

I found presently, that whether I was a whore or a wife, I was to pass for a whore here, so I let that go. I told her it was true, as she said, but that, however, if I must tell her my case, I must tell it her as it was; so I related it as short as I could, and I concluded it to her. 'I trouble you with this, madam,' said I, 'not that, as you said before, it is much to the purpose in your affair; but this is to the purpose, namely, that I am not in any pain about being seen, or being concealed, for 'tis perfectly indifferent to me; but my difficulty is, that I have no acquaintance in this part of the nation.'

'I understand you, madam,' says she; 'you have no security to bring to prevent the parish impertinence* usual in such cases, and perhaps,' says she, 'do not know very well how to dispose of the child when it comes.' 'The last,' says I, 'is not so much my concern as the first.' 'Well, madam,' answers the midwife, 'dare you put yourself into my hands? I live in such a place; though I do not inquire after you, you may inquire after me. My name is B—; I live in such a street' – naming the street – 'at the sign of the cradle.* My profession is a midwife, and I have many ladies that come to my house to lie in. I have given security to the parish in general to secure them from any charge from what shall come into the world under my roof. I have but one question to ask in the whole affair, madam,' says she, 'and if that be answered, you shall be entirely easy of the rest.'

I presently understood what she meant, and told her, 'Madam, I believe I understand you. I thank God, though I want friends in this part of the world, I do not want money, so far as may be necessary, though I do not abound in that neither': this I added, because I would not make her expect great things. 'Well, madam,' says she, 'that is the thing, indeed, without which nothing can be done in these cases; and yet,' says she, 'you shall see that I will not impose upon you, or offer anything that is unkind to you, and you shall know everything beforehand, that you may suit yourself to the occasion, and be either costly or sparing as you see fit.'

I told her she seemed to be so perfectly sensible of my condition, that I had nothing to ask of her but this, that as I had money sufficient, but not a great quantity, she would order it so that I might be at as little superfluous charge as possible.

She replied, that she should bring in an account of the expenses of it in two or three shapes; I should choose as I pleased; and I desired her to do so.

The next day she brought it, and the copy of her three bills was as follows:

		£	s	d
1	For three months' lodging in her house, including my diet, at 10s. a week	6	0	0
2	For a nurse for the month, and use of child-bed linen	1	10	0
3	For a minister to christen the child, and to the godfathers and clerk	1	10	0
4	For a supper at the christening if I had five friends at it	1	0	0
	For her fees as a midwife, and the taking off the trouble of the parish	3	3	0
	To her maidservant attending	0	10	0
		£13	13	0

This was the first bill; the second was in the same terms:

		£	s	d
1	For three months' lodging and diet, etc., at 20s. per week	12	0	0
2	For a nurse for the month, and the use of linen and lace	2	10	0
3	For the minister to christen the child, etc., as above	2	0	0
4	For a supper, and for sweetmeats	3	3	0
	For her fees as above	5	5	0
	For a servant maid	1	0	0
		£25	18	0

This was the second-rate bill; the third, she said, was for a degree higher, and when the father or friends appeared:

		£	s	d
1	For three months' lodging and diet, having two rooms and a garret for a servant	30	0	0

2	For a nurse for the month, and the finest suit of child-bed linen	4	0	0
3	For the minister to christen the child, etc.	2	10	0
4	For a supper, the gentlemen to send in the wine	6	0	0
	The maid, besides their own maid, only	0	10	0

£53 14 0

I looked upon all the three bills, and smiled, and told her I did not see but that she was very reasonable in her demands, all things considered, and I did not doubt but her accommodations were good.

She told me I should be a judge of that when I saw them. I told her I was sorry to tell her that I feared I must be her lowest-rated customer; 'and perhaps, madam,' said I, 'you will make me the less welcome upon that account.' 'No, not at all,' said she; 'for where I have one of the third sort, I have two of the second and four of the first, and I get as much by them in proportion as by any; but if you doubt my care of you, I will allow any friend you have to see if you are well waited on or no.'

Then she explained the particulars of her bill. 'In the first place, madam,' said she, 'I would have you observe that here is three months keeping you at but 10s. a week; I undertake to say you will not complain of my table. I suppose,' says she, 'you do not live cheaper where you are now?' 'No, indeed,' said I, 'nor so cheap, for I give 6s. per week for my chamber, and find my own diet, which costs me a great deal more.'

'Then, madam,' says she, 'if the child should not live, as it sometimes happens, there is the minister's article saved; and if you have no friends to come, you may save the expense of a supper; so that take those articles out, madam,' says she, 'your lying in will not cost you above £5 3s. more than your ordinary charge of living.'

This was the most reasonable thing that I ever heard of; so I smiled, and told her I would come and be a customer; but I told her also, that as I had two months and more to go, I might perhaps be obliged to stay longer with her than three months, and desired to know if she would not be obliged to remove me before it was proper. No, she said; her house was large, and besides, she never put anybody to remove, that had lain in, till they were willing to go; and if she had more ladies offered, she was not so ill-beloved among her neighbours but she could provide accommodation for twenty, if there was occasion.

I found she was an eminent lady in her way, and, in short, I agreed to put myself into her hands. She then talked of other things, looked about into my accommodations where I was, found fault with my wanting attendance and conveniences, and that I should not be used so at her house. I told her I was shy of speaking, for the woman of the house looked stranger, or at least I thought so, since I had been ill, because I was with child; and I was afraid she would put some affront or other upon me, supposing that I had been able to give but a slight account of myself.

'O dear,' says she, 'her ladyship is no stranger to these things; she has tried to entertain ladies in your condition, but could not secure the parish; and besides, such a nice lady, as you take her to be. However, since you are agoing, you shall not meddle with her, but I'll see you are a little better looked after while you are here, and it shall not cost you the more neither.'

I did not understand her; however, I thanked her, so we parted. The next morning she sent me a chicken roasted and hot, and a bottle of sherry, and ordered the maid to tell me that she was to wait on me every day as long as I stayed there.

This was surprisingly good and kind, and I accepted it very willingly. At night she sent to me again, to know if I wanted anything, and to order the maid to come to her in the morning for dinner. The maid had orders to make me some chocolate in the morning before she came away, and at noon she brought me the sweetbread of a breast of veal, whole, and a dish of soup for my dinner; and after this manner she nursed me up at a distance, so that I was mightily well pleased, and quickly well, for indeed my dejections before were the principal part of my illness.

I expected, as is usually the case among such people, that the servant she sent me would have been some impudent brazen wench of Drury Lane* breeding, and I was very uneasy upon that account; so I would not let her lie in the house the first night, but had my eyes about me as narrowly as if she had been a public thief.

My gentlewoman guessed presently what was the matter, and sent her back with a short note, that I might depend upon the honesty of her maid; that she would be answerable for her upon all accounts; and that she took no servants without very good security. I was then perfectly easy; and indeed the maid's behaviour spoke for itself, for a modester, quieter, soberer girl never came into anybody's family, and I found her so afterwards.

As soon as I was well enough to go abroad, I went with the maid to see the house, and to see the apartment I was to have; and everything was so handsome and so clean, that, in short, I had nothing to say, but was wonderfully pleased with what I had met with, which, considering the melancholy circumstances I was in, was beyond what I looked for.

It might be expected that I should give some account of the nature of the wicked practices of this woman, in whose hands I was now fallen; but it would be but too much encouragement to the vice, to let the world see what easy measures were here taken to rid the women's burthen of a child clandestinely gotten. This grave matron had several sorts of practice, and this was one, that if a child was born, though not in her house (for she had the occasion to be called to many private labours), she had people always ready, who for a piece of money would take the child off their hands, and off from the hands of the parish too; and those children, as she said, were honestly taken care of. What should become of them all, considering so many, as by her account she was concerned with, I cannot conceive.

I had many times discourses upon that subject with her; but she was full of this argument, that she saved the life of many an innocent lamb, as she called them, which would perhaps have been murdered; and of many a woman, who, made desperate by the misfortune, would otherwise be tempted to destroy their children. I granted her that this was true, and a very commendable thing, provided the poor children fell into good hands afterwards, and were not abused and neglected by the nurses. She answered, that she always took care of that, and had no nurses in her business but what were very good people, and such as might be depended upon.

I could say nothing to the contrary, and so was obliged to say, 'Madam, I do not question but you do your part, but what those people do is the main question'; and she stopped my mouth again with saying she took the utmost care about it.

The only thing I found in all her conversation on these subjects, that gave me any distaste, was, that one time in discoursing about my being so far gone with child, she said something that looked as if she could help me off with my burthen sooner, if I was willing; or, in English, that she could give me something to make me miscarry, if I had a desire to put an end to my troubles that way;

but I soon let her see that I abhorred the thoughts of it; and, to do her justice, she put it off so cleverly, that I could not say she really intended it, or whether she only mentioned the practice as a horrible thing; for she couched her words so well, and took my meaning so quickly, that she gave her negative before I could explain myself.

To bring this part into as narrow a compass as possible, I quitted my lodging at St Jones's, and went to my new governess, for so they called her in the house, and there I was indeed treated with so much courtesy, so carefully looked to, and everything so well, that I was surprised at it, and could not at first see what advantage my governess made of it; but I found afterwards that she professed to make no profit of the lodgers' diet, nor indeed could she get much by it, but that her profit lay in the other articles of her management, and she made enough that way, I assure you; for 'tis scarce credible what practice she had, as well abroad as at home, and yet all upon the private account, or, in plain English, the whoring account.

While I was in her house, which was near four months, she had no less than twelve ladies of pleasure brought to bed within doors, and I think she had two-and-thirty, or thereabouts, under her conduct without doors; whereof one, as nice as she was with me, was lodged with my old landlady at St Jones's.

This was a strange testimony of the growing vice of the age, and as bad as I had been myself, it shocked my very sense; I began to nauseate* the place I was in, and, above all, the practice; and yet I must say that I never saw, nor do I believe there was to be seen, the least indecency in the house the whole time I was there.

Not a man was ever seen to come upstairs, except to visit the lying-in ladies within their month, nor then without the old lady with them, who made it a piece of the honour of her management that no man should touch a woman, no, not his own wife, within the month; nor would she permit any man to lie in the house upon any pretence whatever, no, not though it was with his own wife; and her saying for it was, that she cared not how many children were born in her house, but she would have none got there if she could help it.

It might perhaps be carried farther than was needful, but it was an error of the right hand* if it was an error, for by this she kept up the reputation, such as it was, of her business, and obtained this character, that though she did take care of the women when they were debauched, yet she was not instrumental to their being debauched at all; and yet it was a wicked trade she drove too.

While I was here, and before I was brought to bed, I received a letter from my trustee at the bank, full of kind, obliging things, and earnestly pressing me to return to London; it was near a fortnight old when it came to me, because it had first been sent into Lancashire, and then returned to me. He concluded with telling me that he had obtained a decree against his wife, and that he would be ready to make good his engagement to me, if I would accept of him, adding a great many protestations of kindness and affection, such as he would have been far from offering if he had known the circumstances I had been in, and which, as it was, I had been very far from deserving.

I returned an answer to this letter, and dated it at Liverpool, but sent it by a messenger, alleging that it came in cover to a friend in town. I gave him joy of his deliverance, but raised some scruples at the lawfulness of his marrying again, and told him I supposed he would consider very seriously upon that point before he resolved on it, the consequence being too great for a man of his judgment to venture rashly upon; so concluded wishing him very well in whatever he resolved, without letting him into anything of my own mind, or giving any answer to his proposal of my coming to London to him, but mentioned at a distance my intention to return the latter end of the year, this being dated in April.

I was brought to bed about the middle of May, and had another brave boy, and myself in as good condition as usual on such occasions. My governess did her part as a midwife with the greatest art and dexterity imaginable, and far beyond all that ever I had had any experience of before.

Her care of me in my travail, and after in my lying in, was such, that if she had been my own mother it could not have been better. Let none be encouraged in their loose practices from this dexterous lady's management, for she has gone to her place, and I dare say has left nothing behind her that can or will come up to it.

I think I had been brought to bed about twenty days when I received another letter from my friend at the bank, with the surprising news that he had obtained a final sentence of divorce against his wife, and had served her with it on such a day, and that he had such an answer to give to all my scruples about his marrying again as I could not expect, and as he had no desire of; for that his wife, who had been under some remorse before for her usage of him, as soon as she heard that he had gained his point, had very unhappily destroyed herself that same evening.

He expressed himself very handsomely as to his being concerned at her disaster, but cleared himself of having any hand in it, and that he had only done himself justice in a case in which he was notoriously injured and abused. However, he said that he was extremely afflicted at it, and had no view of any satisfaction left in this world, but only in the hope that I would come and relieve him by my company; and then he pressed me violently indeed to give him some hopes, that I would at least come up to town and let him see me, when he would further enter into discourse about it.

I was exceedingly surprised at the news, and began now seriously to reflect on my circumstances, and the inexpressible misfortune it was to have a child upon my hands; and what to do in it I knew not. At last I opened my case at a distance to my governess; I appeared melancholy for several days, and she lay at me continually to know what troubled me. I could not for my life tell her that I had an offer of marriage, after I had so often told her that I had a husband, so that I really knew not what to say to her. I owned I had something which very much troubled me, but at the same time told her I could not speak of it to any one alive.

She continued importuning me several days, but it was impossible, I told her, for me to commit the secret to anybody. This, instead of being an answer to her, increased her importunities; she urged her having been trusted with the greatest secrets of this nature, that it was her business to conceal everything, and that to discover things of that nature would be her ruin. She asked me if ever I had found her tattling of other people's affairs, and how could I suspect her? She told me, to unfold myself to her was telling it to nobody; that she was silent as death; that it must be a very strange case indeed, that she could not help me out of; but to conceal it was to deprive myself of all possible help, or means of help, and to deprive her of the opportunity of serving me. In short, she had such a bewitching eloquence, and so great a power of persuasion, that there was no concealing anything from her.

So I resolved to unbosom myself to her. I told her the history of my Lancashire marriage, and how both of us had been disappointed; how we came together, and how we parted; how he discharged me, as far as lay in him, and gave me free liberty to marry again, protesting that if he knew it he would never claim me, or disturb or expose me; that I thought I was free, but was dreadfully afraid to venture, for fear of the consequences that might follow in case of a discovery.

Then I told her what a good offer I had; showed her my friend's letters, inviting me to London, and with what affection they were written, but blotted out the name, and also the story about the disaster of his wife, only that she was dead.

She fell a-laughing at my scruples about marrying, and told me the other was no marriage, but a cheat on both sides; and that, as we were parted by mutual consent, the nature of the contract was destroyed, and the obligation was mutually discharged. She had arguments for this at the tip of her tongue; and, in short, reasoned me out of my reason; not but that it was too by the help of my own inclination.

But then came the great and main difficulty, and that was the child; this, she told me, must be removed, and that so as that it should never be possible for any one to discover it. I knew there was no marrying without concealing that I had had a child, for he would soon have discovered by the age of it that it was born, nay, and gotten too, since my parley with him, and that would have destroyed all the affair.

But it touched my heart so forcibly to think of parting entirely with the child, and, for aught I knew, of having it murdered, or starved by neglect and ill-usage, which was much the same, that I could not think of it without horror. I wish all those women who consent to the disposing their children out of the way, as it is called, for decency sake, would consider that 'tis only a contrived method for murder; that is to say, killing their children with safety.

It is manifest to all that understand anything of children, that we are born into the world helpless, and uncapable either to supply our own wants or so much as make them known; and that without help we must perish; and this help requires not only an assisting hand, whether of the mother or somebody else, but there are two things necessary in that assisting hand, that is, care and skill; without both which, half the children that are born would die, nay, though they were not to be denied food, and one-half more of those that remained would be cripples or fools, lose their limbs, and perhaps their sense. I question not but that these are partly the reasons why affection was placed by nature in the hearts of mothers to their children; without which they would never be able to give themselves up, as 'tis necessary they should, to the care and waking pains needful to the support of children.

Since this care is needful to the life of children, to neglect them is to murder them; again, to give them up to be managed by those people who have none of that needful affection placed by nature in them, is to neglect them in the highest degree; nay, in some it goes farther, and is in order to their being lost; so that 'tis an intentional murder, whether the child lives or dies.

All those things represented themselves to my view, and that in the blackest and most frightful form; and, as I was very free with my governess, whom I had now learned to call mother, I represented to her all the dark thoughts which I had about it, and told her what distress I was in. She seemed graver by much at this part than at the other; but as she was hardened in these things beyond all possibility of being touched with the religious part, and the scruples about the murder, so she was equally impenetrable in that part which related to affection. She asked me if she had not been careful and tender of me in my lying in, as if I had been her own child. I told her I owned she had. 'Well, my dear,' says she, 'and when you are gone, what are you to me? And what would it be to me if you were to be hanged? Do you think there are not women who, as it is their trade, and they get their bread by it, value themselves upon their being as careful of children as their own mothers? Yes, yes, child,' says she, 'fear it not; how were we nursed ourselves? Are you sure you were nursed up by your own mother? and yet you look fat and fair, child,' says the old beldam; and with that she stroked me over the face. 'Never be concerned, child,' says she, going on in her drolling way; 'I have no murderers about me; I employ the best nurses that can be had, and have as few children miscarry under their hands as there would if they were all nursed by mothers; we want neither care nor skill.'

She touched me to the quick when she asked if I was sure that I was nursed by my own mother; on the contrary, I was sure I was not; and I trembled and looked pale at the very expression. Sure, said I to myself, this creature cannot be a witch, or have any conversation with a spirit, that can inform her what I was, before I was able to know it myself; and I looked at her as if I had been frighted; but reflecting that it could not be possible for her to know anything about me, that went off, and I began to be easy, but it was not presently.

She perceived the disorder I was in, but did not know the meaning of it; so she ran on in her wild talk upon the weakness of my supposing that children were murdered because they were not all nursed by the mother, and to persuade me that the children she disposed of were as well used as if the mothers had the nursing of them themselves.

'It may be true, mother,' says I, 'for aught I know, but my doubts are very strongly grounded.' 'Come, then,' says she, 'let's hear some of them.' 'Why, first,' says I, 'you give a piece of money to these people to take the child off the parent's hands, and to take care of it as long as it lives. Now we know, mother,' said I, 'that those are poor people, and their gain consists in being quit of the charge as soon as they can; how can I doubt but that, as it is best for them to have the child die, they are not over solicitous about its life?'

'This is all vapours* and fancy,' says she; 'I tell you their credit depends upon the child's life, and they are as careful as any mother of you all.'

'O mother,' says I, 'if I was but sure my little baby would be carefully looked to, and have justice done it, I should be happy; but it is impossible I can be satisfied in that point unless I saw it, and to see it would be ruin and destruction, as my case now stands; so what to do I know not.'

'A fine story!' says the governess. 'You would see the child, and you would not see the child; you would be concealed and discovered both together. These are things impossible, my dear, and so you must e'en do as other conscientious mothers have done before you, and be contented with things as they must be, though not as you wish them to be.'

I understood what she meant by conscientious mothers; she would have said conscientious whores, but she was not willing to disoblige me, for really in this case I was not a whore, because legally married, the force of my former marriage excepted.

However, let me be what I would, I was not come up to that pitch of hardness common to the profession; I mean, to be unnatural, and regardless of the safety of my child; and I preserved this honest affection so long, that I was upon the point of giving up my friend at the bank, who lay so hard at me to come to him, and marry him, that there was hardly any room to deny him.

At last my old governess came to me, with her usual assurance.

'Come, my dear,' says she, 'I have found out a way how you shall be at a certainty that your child shall be used well, and yet the people that take care of it shall never know you.'

'O mother,' says I, 'if you can do so, you will engage me to you for ever.' 'Well,' says she, 'are you willing to be at some small annual expense, more than what we usually give to the people we contract with?' 'Ay,' says I, 'with all my heart, provided I may be concealed.' 'As to that,' says she, 'you shall be secure, for the nurse shall never dare to inquire about you; and you shall once or twice a year go with me and see your child, and see how 'tis used, and be satisfied that it is in good hands, nobody knowing who you are.'

'Why,' said I, 'do you think that when I come to see my child, I shall be able to conceal my being the mother of it? Do you think that possible?'

'Well,' says she, 'if you discover it, the nurse shall be never the wiser; she shall be forbid to take any notice. If she offers it, she shall lose the money which you are to be supposed to give her, and the child shall be taken from her too.'

I was very well pleased with this. So the next week a countrywoman was brought from Hertford, or thereabouts, who was to take the child off our hands entirely, for £10 in money. But if I would allow £5 a year more to her, she would be obliged to bring the child to my governess's house as often as we desired, or we should come down and look at it, and see how well she used it.

The woman was a very wholesome-looked, likely woman, a cottager's wife, but she had very good clothes and linen, and everything well about her; and with a heavy heart and many a tear, I let her have my child. I had been down at Hertford, and looked at her and at her dwelling, which I liked well enough; and I promised her great things if she would be kind to the child, so she knew at first word that I was the child's mother. But she seemed to be so much out of the way, and to have no room to inquire after me, that I thought I was safe enough. So, in short, I consented to let her have the child, and I gave her £10; that is to say, I gave it to my governess, who gave it the poor woman before my face, she agreeing never to return the child to me, or to claim anything more for its keeping, or bringing up; only that I promised, if she took a great deal of care of it, I would give her something more as often as I came to see it; so that I was not bound to pay the £5, only that I promised my governess I would do it. And thus my great care was over, after a manner, which, though it did not at all satisfy my mind, yet was the most convenient for me, as my affairs then stood, of any that could be thought of at that time.

I then began to write to my friend at the bank in a more kindly style, and particularly about the beginning of July I sent him a letter, that I purposed to be in town some time in August. He returned me an answer in the most passionate terms imaginable, and desired me to let him have timely notice, and he would come and meet me two days' journey. This puzzled me scurvily, and I did not know what answer to make to it. Once I was resolved to take the stage-coach to West Chester, on purpose only to have the satisfaction of coming back, that he might see me really come in the same coach; for I had a jealous* thought, though I had no ground for it at all, lest he should think I was not really in the country.

I endeavoured to reason myself out of it, but it was in vain; the impression lay so strong on my mind, that it was not to be resisted. At last it came as an addition to my new design of going into the country, that it would be an excellent blind to my old governess, and would cover entirely all my other affairs, for she did not know in the least whether my new lover lived in London or in Lancashire; and when I told her my resolution, she was fully persuaded it was in Lancashire.

Having taken my measures for this journey, I let her know it, and sent the maid which tended me from the beginning to take a place for me in the coach. She would have had me let the maid have waited on me down to the last stage, and come up again in the wagon, but I convinced her it would not be convenient. When I went away, she told me she would enter into no measures for correspondence, for she saw evidently that my affection to my child would cause me to write to her, and to visit her too, when I came to town again. I assured her it would, and so took my leave, well satisfied to have been freed from such a house, however good my accommodations there had been.

I took the place in the coach not to its full extent, but to a place called Stone* in Cheshire, where I not only had no manner of business, but not the least acquaintance with any person in the town. But I knew that with money in the pocket one is at home anywhere; so I lodged there two or three days, till, watching my opportunity, I found room in another stage-coach, and took passage back again for London, sending a letter to my gentleman that I should be such a certain day at Stony-Stratford, where the coachman told me he was to lodge.

It happened to be a chance coach that I had taken up, which, having been hired on purpose to carry some gentlemen to West Chester, who were going for Ireland, was now returning, and did not tie itself up to exact times or places, as the stages did; so that, having been obliged to lie still on Sunday, he had time to get himself ready to come out, which otherwise he could not have done.

His warning was so short, tnat he could not reach Stony-Stratford time enough to be with me at night, but he met me at a place called Brickhill* the next morning, just as we were coming into the town.

I confess I was very glad to see him, for I thought myself a little disappointed over-night. He pleased me doubly too by the figure he came in, for he brought a very handsome gentleman's coach and four horses, with a servant to attend him.

He took me out of the stage-coach immediately, which stopped at an inn in Brickhill; and putting into the same inn, he set up his own coach, and bespoke his dinner. I asked him what he meant by that, for I was for going forward with the journey. He said, No, I had need of a little rest upon the road, and that was a very good sort of a house, though it was but a little town; so we would go no farther that night, whatever came of it.

I did not press him much, for since he had come so far to meet me, and put himself to so much expense, it was but reasonable I should oblige him a little too; so I was easy as to that point.

After dinner we walked to see the town, to see the church, and to view the fields and the country, as is usual for strangers to do; and our landlord was our guide in going to see the church. I observed my gentleman inquired pretty much about the parson, and I took the hint immediately, that he certainly would propose to be married; and it followed presently, that, in short, I would not refuse him; for, to be plain with my circumstances I was in no condition now to say no; I had no reason now to run any more such hazards.

But while these thoughts ran round in my head, which was the work of a few moments, I observed my landlord took him aside and whispered to him, though not very softly neither, for so much I overheard: 'Sir, if you shall have occasion—' the rest I could not hear, but it seems it was to this purpose: 'Sir, if you shall have occasion for a minister, I have a friend a little way off that will serve you, and be as private as you please.' My gentleman answered loud enough for me to hear, 'Very well, I believe I shall.'

I was no sooner come back to the inn, but he fell upon me with irresistible words, that since he had had the good fortune to meet me, and everything concurred, it would be hastening his felicitiy if I would put an end to the matter just there. 'What do you mean?' says I, colouring a little. 'What, in an inn, and on the road! Bless us all,' said I, 'how can you talk so?' 'Oh, I can talk so very well,' says he; 'I came on purpose to talk so, and I'll show you that I did'; and with that he pulls out a great bundle of papers. 'You fright me,' said I; 'what are all these?' 'Don't be frighted, my dear, ' said he, and kissed me. This was the first time that he had been so free to call me my dear; then he repeated it, 'Don't be frighted; you shall see what it is all'; then he laid them all abroad.* There was first the deed or sentence of divorce from his wife, and the full evidence of her playing the whore; then there was the certificates of the minister and churchwardens of the parish where she lived, proving that she was buried, and intimating the manner of her death; the copy of the coroner's warrant for a jury to sit upon her, and the verdict of the jury, who brought it in *Non compos mentis*.* All this was to give me satisfaction, though, by the way, I was not so scrupulous, had he known all, but that I might have taken him without it; however, I looked them all over as well as I could, and told him that this was all very clear indeed, but that he need not have brought them out with him, for it was time enough. Well, he said, it might be time enough for me, but no time but the present time was time enough for him.

There were other papers rolled up, and I asked him what they were. 'Why, ay,' says he, 'that's the question I wanted to have you ask me'; so he takes out a little shagreen* case, and gives me out of it a very fine diamond ring. I could not refuse it, if I had a mind to do so, for he put it upon my finger; so I only made him a curtsey. Then he takes out another ring: 'And this,' says he, 'is for another occasion,' and puts that into his pocket. 'Well, but let me see it, though,' says I, and smiled; 'I guess what it is; I think you are mad.' 'I should have been mad if I had done less,' says he; and still he did not show it me, and I had a great mind to see it; so says I, 'Well, but let me see it.' 'Hold,' says he; 'first look here'; then he took up the roll again, and read it, and behold! it was a licence for us to be married. 'Why,' says I, 'are you distracted? You were fully satisfied, sure, that I would yield at first word, or resolved to take no denial.' 'The last is certainly the case,' said he. 'But you may be mistaken,' said I. 'No, no,' says he, 'I must not be denied, I can't be denied'; and with that he fell to kissing me so violently, I could not get rid of him.

There was a bed in the room, and we were walking to and again, eager in the discourse; at last, he takes me by surprise in his arms, and threw me on the bed, and himself with me, and holding me still fast in his arms, but without the least offer of any indecency, courted me to consent with such repeated entreaties and arguments, protesting his affection, and vowing he would not let me go till I had promised him, that at last I said, 'Why, you resolve not to be denied indeed, I think.' 'No, no,' says he, 'I must not be denied, I won't be denied, I can't be denied.' 'Well, well,' said I, and giving him a slight kiss, 'then you shan't be denied; let me get up.'

He was so transported with my consent, and the kind manner of it, that I began to think once he took it for a marriage, and would not stay for the form; but I wronged him, for he took me by the hand, pulled me up again, and then giving me two or three kisses, thanked me for my kind yielding to him; and was so overcome with the satisfaction of it, that I saw tears stand in his eyes.

I turned from him, for it filled my eyes with tears too, and asked him leave to retire a little to my chamber. If I had a grain of true repentance for an abominable life of twenty-four years past, it was then. Oh, what a felicity is it to mankind, said I to myself, that they cannot see into the hearts of one another! How happy had it been if I had been wife to a man of so much honesty and so much affection from the beginning!

Then it occurred to me, 'What an abominable creature am I! and how is this innocent gentleman going to be abused by me! How little does he think, that having divorced a whore, he is throwing himself into the arms of another! that he is going to marry one that has lain with two brothers, and has had three children by her own brother! one that was born in Newgate, whose mother was a whore, and is now a transported thief! one that has lain with thirteen men, and has had a child since he saw me! Poor gentleman!' said I, 'what is he going to do?' After this reproaching myself was over, it followed thus: 'Well, if I must be his wife, if it please God to give me grace, I'll be a true wife to him, and love him suitably to the strange excess of his passion for me; I will make amends, by what he shall see, for the abuses I put upon him, which he does not see.'

He was impatient for my coming out of my chamber, but finding me long, he went downstairs and talked with my landlord about the parson.

My landlord, an officious though well-meaning fellow, had sent away for the clergyman; and when my gentleman began to speak to him of sending for him, 'Sir,' says he to him, 'my friend is in the house'; so without any more words he brought them together. When he came to the minister, he asked him if he would venture to marry a couple of strangers that were both willing. The parson said that Mr— had said something to him of it; that he hoped it was no clandestine business; that he seemed to be a grave gentleman, and he supposed madam was not a girl, so that the consent of friends* should be wanted. 'To put you out of doubt of that,' says my gentleman, 'read this paper'; and out he pulls the licence. 'I am satisfied,' says the minister; 'where is the lady?' 'You shall see her presently,' says my gentleman.

When he had said thus he comes upstairs, and I was by that time come out of my room; so he tells me the minister was below, and that upon showing him the licence, he was free to marry us with all his heart, 'but he asks to see you'; so he asked if I would let him come up.

''Tis time enough,' said I, 'in the morning, is it not?' 'Why,' said he, 'my dear, he seemed to scruple whether it was not some young girl stolen from her parents, and I assured him we were both of age to command our own consent; and that made him ask to see you.' 'Well,' said I, 'do as you please'; so up they brings the parson, and a merry, good sort of gentleman he was. He had been told, it seems, that we had met there by accident; that I came in a Chester coach, and my gentleman in his own coach to meet me; that we were to have met last night at Stony-Stratford, but that he could not reach so far. 'Well, sir,' says the parson, 'every ill turn has some good in it. The disappointment, sir,' says he to my gentleman, 'was yours, and the good turn is mine, for if you had met at Stony-Stratford I had not the honour to marry you. Landlord, have you a Common Prayer Book?'

I started as if I had been frighted. 'Sir,' says I, 'what do you mean? What, to marry in an inn, and at night too!' 'Madam,' says the minister, 'if you will have it be in the church, you shall; but I assure you your marriage will be as firm here as in the church; we are not tied by the canons to marry nowhere but in the church; and as for the time of day, it does not at all weigh in this case; our princes are married in their chambers, and at eight or ten o'clock at night.'

I was a great while before I could be persuaded, and pretended not to be willing at all to be married but in the church. But it was all grimace,* so I seemed at last to be prevailed on, and my landlord, and his wife and daughter, were called up. My landlord was father and clerk and all together, and we were married, and very merry we were; though I confess the self-reproaches which I had upon me before lay close to me, and extorted every now and then a deep sigh from me, which my bridegroom took notice of, and endeavoured to encourage me, thinking, poor man, that I had some little hesitations at the step I had taken so hastily.

We enjoyed ourselves that evening completely, and yet all was kept so private in the inn that not a servant in the house knew of it, for my landlady and her daughter waited on me, and would not let any of the maids come upstairs. My landlady's daughter I called my bridesmaid; and sending for a shopkeeper the next morning, I gave the young woman a good suit of knots,* as good as the town would afford, and finding it was a lacemaking town, I gave her mother a piece of bone-lace* for a head.

One reason that my landlord was so close was, that he was unwilling that the minister of the parish should hear of it; but for all that somebody heard of it, so as that we had the bells set a-ringing the next morning early, and the music,* such as the town would afford, under our window. But my landlord brazened it out, that we were married before we came thither, only that, being his former guests, we would have our wedding-supper at his house.

We could not find in our hearts to stir the next day; for, in short, having been disturbed by the bells in the morning, and having perhaps not slept overmuch before, we were so sleepy afterwards that we lay in bed till almost twelve o'clock.

I begged my landlady that we might have no more music in the town, nor ringing of bells, and she managed it so well that we were very quiet; but an odd passage interrupted all my mirth for a good while. The great room of the house looked into the street, and I had walked to the end of the room, and it being a pleasant, warm day, I had opened the window, and was standing at it for some air, when I saw three gentlemen ride by, and go into an inn just against us.

It was not to be concealed, nor did it leave me any room to question it, but the second of the three was my Lancashire husband. I was frighted to death; I never was in such a consternation in my life; I thought I should have sunk into the ground; my blood ran chill in my veins, and I trembled as if I had been in a cold fit of an ague. I say, there was no room to question the truth of it; I knew his clothes, I knew his horse, and I knew his face.

The first reflection I made was, that my husband was not by to see my disorder, and that I was very glad of. The gentlemen had not been long in the house but they came to the window of their room, as is usual; but my window was shut, you may be sure. However, I could not keep from peeping at them, and there I saw him again, heard him call to one of the servants for something he wanted, and received all the terrifying confirmations of its being the same person that were possible to be had.

My next concern was, to know what was his business there; but that was impossible. Sometimes my imagination formed an idea of one frightful thing, sometimes of another; sometimes I thought he had discovered me, and was come to upbraid me with ingratitude and breach of honour; then I fancied he was coming upstairs to insult me; and innumerable thoughts came into my head, of what was never in his head, nor ever could be, unless the devil had revealed it to him.

I remained in the fright near two hours, and scarce ever kept my eye from the window or door of the inn where they were. At last, hearing a great clutter in the passage of their inn, I ran to the window, and, to my great satisfaction, I saw them all three go out again and travel on westward. Had they gone towards London, I should have been still in a fright, lest I should meet him again, and that he should know me; but he went the contrary way, and so I was eased of that disorder.

We we resolved to be going the next day, but about six o'clock at night we were alarmed with a great uproar in the street, and people riding as if they had been out of their wits; and what was it but a hue-and-cry* after three highwaymen, that had robbed two coaches and some travellers near Dunstable Hill, and notice had, it seems, been given that they had been seen at Brickhill, at such a house, meaning the house where those gentlemen had been.

The house was immediately beset and searched, but there were witnesses enough that the gentlemen had been gone above three hours. The crowd having gathered about, we had the news presently; and I was heartily concerned now another way. I presently told the people of the house, that I durst say those were honest persons, for that I knew one of the gentlemen to be a very honest person, and of a good estate in Lancashire.

The constable who came with the hue-and-cry was immediately informed of this, and came over to me to be satisfied from my own mouth; and I assured him that I saw the three gentlemen as I was at the window; that I saw them afterwards at the windows of the room they dined in; that I saw them take horse, and I would assure him I knew one of them to be such a man, that he was a gentleman of a very good estate, and an undoubted character in Lancashire, from whence I was just now upon my journey.

The assurance with which I delivered this gave the mob gentry a check, and gave the constable such satisfaction, that he immediately sounded a retreat, told his people these were not the men, but that he had an account they were very honest gentlemen; and so they went all back again. What the truth of the matter was I knew not, but certain it was that the coaches were robbed at Dunstable Hill, and £560 in money taken; besides, some of the lace merchants that always travel that way had been visited too. As to the three gentlemen, that remains to be explained hereafter.

Well, this alarm stopped us another day, though my spouse told me it was always safest travelling after a robbery, for that the thieves were sure to be gone far enough off when they had alarmed the country; but I was uneasy, and indeed principally lest my old acquaintance should be upon the road still, and should chance to see me.

I never lived four pleasanter days together in my life. I was a mere* bride all this while, and my new spouse strove to make me easy in everything. O could this state of life have continued! how had all my past troubles been forgot, and my future sorrows been avoided! But I had a past life of a most wretched kind to account for, some of it in this world as well as in another.

We came away the fifth day; and my landlord, because he saw me uneasy, mounted himself, his son, and three honest country fellows with good fire-arms, and, without telling us of it, followed the coach, and would see us safe into Dunstable.

We could do no less than treat them very handsomely at

Dunstable, which cost my spouse about ten or twelve shillings, and something he gave the men for their time too, but my landlord would take nothing for himself.

This was the most happy contrivance for me that could have fallen out; for had I come to London unmarried, I must either have come to him for the first night's entertainment, or have discovered to him that I had not one acquaintance in the whole city of London, that could receive a poor bride for the first night's lodging with her spouse. But now I made no scruple of going directly home with him, and there I took possession at once of a house well furnished, and a husband in very good circumstances, so that I had a prospect of a very happy life, if I knew how to manage it; and I had leisure to consider of the real value of the life I was likely to live. How different it was to be from the loose part I had acted before, and how much happier a life of virtue and sobriety is, than that which we call a life of pleasure!

O had this particular scene of life lasted, or had I learnt from that time I enjoyed it, to have tasted the true sweetness of it, and had I not fallen into that poverty which is the sure bane of virtue, how happy had I been, not only here, but perhaps for ever! for while I lived thus, I was really a penitent for all my life past. I looked back on it with abhorrence, and might truly be said to hate myself for it. I often reflected how my lover at Bath, struck by the hand of God, repented and abandoned me, and refused to see me any more, though he loved me to an extreme; but I, prompted by that worst of devils, poverty, returned to the vile practice, and made the advantage of what they call a handsome face be the relief to my necessities, and beauty be a pimp to vice.

Now I seemed landed in a safe harbour, after the stormy voyage of life past was at an end, and I began to be thankful for my deliverance. I sat many an hour by myself, and wept over the remembrance of past follies, and the dreadful extravagances of a wicked life, and sometimes I flattered myself that I had sincerely repented.

But there are temptations which it is not in the power of human nature to resist, and few know what would be their case, if driven to the same exigencies. As covetousness is the root of all evil,* so poverty is the worst of all snares. But I waive that discourse till I come to the experiment.

I lived with this husband in the utmost tranquillity; he was a quiet, sensible, sober man; virtuous, modest, sincere, and in his business diligent and just. His business was in a narrow compass, and his income sufficient to a plentiful way of living in the ordinary way. I do not say to keep an equipage, and make a figure, as the world calls it, nor did I expect it, or desire it; for as I abhorred the levity and extravagance of my former life, so I chose now to live retired, frugal, and within ourselves. I kept no company, made no visits; minded my family, and obliged my husband; and this kind of life became a pleasure to me.

We lived in an uninterrupted course of ease and content for five years, when a sudden blow from an almost invisible hand blasted all my happiness, and turned me out into the world in a condition the reverse of all that had been before it.

My husband having trusted one of his fellow-clerks with a sum of money, too much for our fortunes to bear the loss of, the clerk failed, and the loss fell very heavy on my husband; yet it was not so great but that, if he had had courage to have looked his misfortunes in the face, his credit was so good that, as I told him, he would easily recover it; for to sink under trouble is to double the weight, and he that will die in it, shall die in it.

It was in vain to speak comfortably to him; the wound had sunk too deep; it was a stab that touched the vitals; he grew melancholy and disconsolate, and from thence lethargic,* and died. I foresaw the blow, and extremely oppressed in my mind, for I saw evidently that if he died I was undone.

I had had two children by him, and no more, for it began to be time for me to leave bearing children, for I was now eight-and-forty, and I suppose if he had lived I should have had no more.

I was now left in a dismal and disconsolate case indeed, and in several things worse than ever. First, it was past the flourishing time with me, when I might expect to be courted for a mistress; that agreeable part had declined some time, and the ruins only appeared of what had been; and that which was worse than all was this, that I was the most dejected, disconsolate creature alive. I that had encouraged my husband, and endeavoured to support his spirits under his trouble, could not support my own; I wanted that spirit in trouble which I told him was so necessary for bearing the burthen.

But my case was indeed deplorable, for I was left perfectly friendless and helpless, and the loss my husband had sustained had reduced his circumstances so low, that though indeed I was not in debt, yet I could easily foresee that what was left would not support me long; that it wasted daily for subsistence, so that it would be soon all spent, and then I saw nothing before me but the utmost distress; and this represented itself so lively to my thoughts, that it seemed as if it was come, before it was really very near; also my very apprehensions doubled the misery, for I fancied every sixpence that I paid for a loaf of bread was the last I had in the world, and that to-morrow I was to fast, and be starved to death.

In this distress I had no assistant, no friend to comfort or advise me; I sat and cried and tormented myself night and day, wringing my hands, and sometimes raving like a distracted woman; and indeed I have often wondered it had not affected my reason, for I had the vapours* to such a degree, that my understanding was sometimes quite lost in fancies and imaginations.

I lived two years in this dismal condition, wasting that little I had, weeping continually over my dismal circumstances, and, as it were, only bleeding to death, without the least hope or prospect of help; and now I had cried so long, and so often, that tears were exhausted, and I began to be desperate, for I grew poor apace.

For a little relief, I had put off my house and took lodgings; and as I was reducing my living, so I sold off most of my goods, which put a little money in my pocket, and I lived near a year upon that, spending very sparingly, and eking things out to the utmost; but still when I looked before me, my heart would sink within me at the inevitable approach of misery and want. O let none read this part without seriously reflecting on the circumstances of a desolate state, and how they would grapple with want of friends and want of bread; it will certainly make them think not of sparing what they have only, but of looking up to heaven for support, and of the wise man's prayer,* 'Give me not poverty, lest I steal.'

Let them remember that a time of distress is a time of dreadful temptation, and all the strength to resist is taken away; poverty presses, the soul is made desperate by distress, and what can be done? It was one evening, when being brought, as I may say, to the last gasp, I think I may truly say I was distracted and raving, when prompted by I know not what spirit, and, as it were, doing I did not know what, or why, I dressed me (for I had still pretty good clothes), and went out. I am very sure I had no manner of design in my head when I went out; I neither knew or considered where to go, or on what business; but as the devil carried me out, and laid his bait for me, so he brought me, to be sure, to the place, for I knew not whither I was going, or what I did.

Wandering thus about, I knew not whither. I passed by an apothecary's shop in Leadenhall Street,* where I saw lie on a stool just before the counter a little bundle wrapped in a white cloth; beyond it stood a maid-servant with her back to it, looking up towards the top of the shop, where the apothecary's apprentice, as I suppose, was standing upon the counter, with his back also to the door, and a candle in his hand, looking and reaching up to the upper shelf, for something he wanted, so that both were engaged, and nobody else in the shop.

This was the bait; and the devil who laid the snare prompted me, as if he had spoke, for I remember, and shall never forget it, 'twas like a voice spoken over my shoulder, 'Take the bundle; be quick; do it this moment.' It was no sooner said but I stepped into the shop, and with my back to the wench, as if I had stood up for a cart that was going by, I put my hand behind me and took the bundle, and went off with it, the maid or fellow not perceiving me, or any one else.

It is impossible to express the horror of my soul all the while I did it. When I went away I had no heart to run, or scarce to mend my pace. I crossed the street indeed, and went down the first turning I came to, and I think it was a street that went through into Fenchurch Street;* from thence I crossed and turned through so many ways and turnings, that I could never tell which way it was, nor where I went; I felt not the ground I stepped on, and the farther I was out of danger, the faster I went, till, tired and out of breath, I was forced to sit down on a little bench at a door, and then found I was got into Thames Street,* near Billingsgate. I rested me a little and went on; my blood was all in a fire; my heart beat as if I was in a sudden fright. In short, I was under such a surprise that I knew not whither I was agoing, or what to do.

After I had tired myself thus with walking a long way about, and so eagerly, I began to consider, and make home to my lodging, where I came about nine o'clock at night.

What the bundle was made up for, or on what occasion laid where I found it, I knew not, but when I came to open it, I found there was a suit of childbed-linen in it, very good, and almost new, the lace very fine; there was a silver porringer of a pint, a small silver mug, and six spoons, with some other linen, a good smock, and three silk handkerchiefs, and in the mug a paper, 18s.6d. in money.

All the while I was opening these things I was under such dreadful impressions of fear, and in such terror of mind, though I was perfectly safe, that I cannot express the manner of it. I sat me down, and cried most vehemently. 'Lord,' said I, 'what am I now? a thief! Why, I shall be taken next time, and be carried to Newgate, and be tried for my life!'* And with that I cried again a long time, and I am sure, as poor as I ws, if I had durst for fear, I would certainly have carried the things back again; but that went off after a while. Well, I went to bed for that night, but slept little; the horror of the fact was upon my mind, and I knew not what I said or did all night, and all the next day. Then I was impatient to hear some news of the loss; and would fain know how it was, whether they were a poor body's goods, or a rich. 'Perhaps,' said I, 'it may be some poor widow like me, that had packed up these goods to go and sell them for a little bread for herself and a poor child, and are now starving and breaking their hearts for want of that little they would have fetched.' And this thought tormented me worse than all the rest, for three or four days.

But my own distresses silenced all these reflections, and the prospect of my own starving, which grew every day more frightful to me, hardened my heart by degrees. It was then particularly heavy upon my mind, that I had been reformed, and had, as I hoped, repented of all my past wickedness; that I had lived a sober, grave, retired life for several years, but now I should be driven by the dreadful necessity of my circumstances to the gates of destruction, soul and body; and two or three times I fell upon my knees, praying to God, as well as I could, for deliverance; but I cannot but say, my prayers had no hope in them. I knew not what to do; it was all fear without, and dark within; and I reflected on my past life as not repented of, that Heaven was now beginning to punish me, and would make me as miserable as I had been wicked.

Had I gone on here I had perhaps been a true penitent; but I had an evil counsellor within, and he was continually prompting me to relieve myself by the worst means; so one evening he tempted me again by the same wicked impulse that had said, 'Take that bundle,' to go out again and seek for what might happen.

I went out now by daylight, and wandered about I knew not whither, and in search of I knew not what, when the devil put a snare in my way of a dreadful nature indeed, and such a one as I have never had before or since. Going through Aldersgate Street,* there was a pretty little child had been at a dancing-school, and was agoing home all alone; and my prompter, like a true devil, set me upon this innocent creature. I talked to it, and it prattled to me again, and I took it by the hand and led it along till I came to a paved alley that goes into Bartholomew Close, and I led it in there. The child said, that was not its way home. I said, 'Yes, my dear, it is; I'll show you the way home.' The child had a little necklace on of gold beads, and I had my eye upon that, and in the dark of the alley I stooped, pretending to mend the child's clog that was loose, and took off her necklace, and the child never felt it, and so led the child on again. Here, I say, the devil put me upon killing the child in the dark alley, that it might not cry, but the very thought frighted me so that I was ready to drop down; but I turned the child about and bade it go back again, for that was not its way home; the child said, so she would; and I went through into Bartholomew Close,* and then turned round to another passage that goes into Long Lane, so away into Charterhouse Yard, and out into St John's Street; then crossing into Smithfield, went down Chick Lane, and into Field Lane, to Holborn Bridge, when, mixing with the crowd of people usually passing there, it was not possible to have been found out; and thus I made my second sally into the world.

The thoughts of this booty put out all the thoughts of the first, and the reflections I had made wore quickly off; poverty hardened my heart, and my own necessities made me regardless of anything. The last affair left no great concern upon me, for as I did the poor child no harm, I only thought I had given the parents a just reproof for their negligence, in leaving the poor lamb to come home by itself, and it would teach them to take more care another time.

This string of beads was worth about £12 or £14. I suppose it might have been formerly the mother's, for it was too big for the child's wear, but that, perhaps, the vanity of the mother to have her child look fine at the dancing-school, had made her let the child wear it; and no doubt the child had a maid sent to take care of it, but she, like a careless jade, was taken up perhaps with some fellow that had met her, and so the poor baby wandered till it fell into my hands.

However, I did the child no harm; I did not so much as fright it, for I had a great many tender thoughts about me yet, and did nothing but what, as I may say, mere necessity drove me to.

I had a great many adventures after this, but I was young in the business, and did not know how to manage, otherwise than as the devil put things into my head; and, indeed, he was seldom backward to me. One adventure I had which was very lucky to me. I was going through Lombard Street* in the dusk of the evening, just by the end of Three King Court, when on a sudden comes a fellow running by me as swift as lightning, and throws a bundle that was in his hand just behind me, as I stood up against the corner of the house at the turning into the alley. Just as he threw it in, he said, 'God bless you, mistress, let it lie there a little,' and away he runs. After him comes two more, and immediately a young fellow without his hat, crying, 'Stop thief!' They pursued the two last fellows so close, that they were forced to drop what they had got, and one of them was taken into the bargain; the other got off free.

I stood stock-still all this while, till they came back, dragging the poor fellow they had taken, and lugging the things they had found, extremely well satisfied that they had recovered the booty and taken the thief; and thus they passed by me, for I looked only like one who stood up while the crowd was gone.

Once or twice I asked what was the matter, but the people neglected answering me, and I was not very importunate; but after the crowd was wholly passed, I took my opportunity to turn about and take up what was behind me and walk away. This, indeed, I did with less disturbance than I had done formerly, for these things I did not steal, but they were stolen to my hand. I got safe to my lodgings with this cargo, which was a piece of fine black lustring* silk, and a piece of velvet; the latter was but part of a piece of about eleven yards; the former was a whole piece of near fifty yards. It seems it was a mercer's shop that they had rifled. I say rifled, because the goods were so considerable that they had lost; for the goods that they recovered were pretty many, and I believe came to about six or seven several pieces of silk. How they came to get so many I could not tell; but as I had only robbed the thief, I made no scruple at taking these goods, and being very glad of them too.

I had pretty good luck thus far, and I made several adventures more, though with but small purchase, yet with good success, but I went in daily dread that some mischief would befall me, and that I should certainly come to be hanged at last. The impression this made on me was too strong to be slighted, and it kept me from making attempts that, for aught I knew, might have been very safely performed; but one thing I cannot omit, which was a bait to me many a day. I walked frequently out into the villages round the town to see if nothing would fall in my way there; and going by a house near Stepney, I saw on the windowboard two rings, one a small diamond ring, and the other a plain gold ring, to be sure laid there by some thoughtless lady, that had more money than forecast,* perhaps only till she washed her hands.

I walked several times by the window to observe if I could see whether there was anybody in the room or no, and I could see nobody, but still I was not sure. It came presently into my thoughts to rap at the glass, as if I wanted to speak with somebody, and if anybody was there they would be sure to come to the window, and then I would tell them to remove those rings, for that I had seen two suspicious fellows take notice of them. This was a ready thought. I rapped once or twice, and nobody came, when I thrust hard against the square of glass, and broke it with little noise, and took out the two rings, and walked away; the diamond ring was worth about £3, and the other about 9s.

I was now at a loss for a market for my goods, and especially for my two pieces of silk. I was very loath to dispose of them for a trifle as the poor unhappy thieves in general do, who, after they have ventured their lives for perhaps a thing of value, are forced to sell it for a song when they have done; but I was resolved I would not do thus, whatever shift I made; however, I did not well know what course to take. At last I resolved to go to my old governess, and acquaint myself with her again. I had punctually supplied the £5 a year to her for my little boy as long as I was able, but at last was obliged to put a stop to it. However, I had written a letter to her, wherein I had told her that my circumstances were reduced; that I had lost my husband, and that I was not able to do it any longer, and begged the poor child might not suffer too much for its mother's misfortunes.

I now made her a visit, and I found that she drove something of the old trade still, but that she was not in such flourishing circumstances as before; for she had been sued by a certain gentleman who had had his daughter stolen from him, and who, it seems, she had helped to convey away; and it was very narrowly that she escaped the gallows. The expense also had ravaged her, so that her house was but meanly furnished, and she was not in such repute for her practice as before; however, she stood upon her legs*, as they say, and as she was a bustling woman, and had some stock left, she was turned pawnbroker, and lived pretty well.

She received me very civilly, and with her usual obliging manner told me she would not have the less respect for me for my being reduced; that she had taken care my boy was very well looked after, though I could not pay for him, and that the woman that had him was easy, so that I needed not to trouble myself about him till I might be better able to do it effectually.

I told her I had not much money left, but that I had some things that were money's worth, if she could tell me how I might turn them into money. She asked what it was I had. I pulled out the string of gold beads, and told her it was one of my husband's presents to me; then I showed her the two parcels of silk, which I told her I had from Ireland, and brought up to town with me, and the little diamond ring. As to the small parcel of plate and spoons, I had found means to dispose of them myself before; and as for the childbed-linen I had, she offered me to take it herself, believing it to have been my own. She told me that she was turned pawn-broker, and that she would sell those things for me as pawned to her; and so she sent presently for proper agents that bought them, being in her hands, without any scruple, and gave good prices too.

I now began to think this necessary woman might help me a little in my low condition to some business, for I would gladly have turned my hand to any honest employment if I could have got it; but honest business did not come within her reach. If I had been younger perhaps she might have helped me, but my thoughts were off of that kind of livelihood, as being quite out of the way after fifty, which was my case, and so I told her.

She invited me at last to come, and be at her house till I could find something to do, and it should cost me very little, and this I gladly accepted of; and now living a little easier, I entered into some measures to have my little son by my last husband taken off; and this she made easy too, reserving a payment only of £5 a year, if I could pay it. This was such a help to me, that for a good while I left off the wicked trade that I had so newly taken up; and gladly I would have got work, but that was very hard to do for one that had no acquaintance.

However, at last I got some quilting work for ladies' beds, petticoats, and the like; and this I liked very well, and worked very hard, and with this I began to live; but the diligent devil, who resolved I should continue in his service, continually prompted me to go out and take a walk, that is to say, to see if anything would offer in the old way.

One evening I blindly obeyed his summons, and fetched a long circuit through the streets, but met with no purchase; but not content with that, I went out the next evening too, when going by an alehouse I saw the door of a little room open, next the very street, and on the table a silver tankard, things much in use in public-houses at that time. It seems some company had been drinking there, and the careless boys had forgot to take it away.

I went into the box frankly, and setting the silver tankard on the corner of the bench, I sat down before it, and knocked with my foot; a boy came presently, and I bade him fetch me a pint of warm ale, for it was cold weather; the boy ran, and I heard him go down the cellar to draw the ale. While the boy was gone, another boy came, and cried, 'D'ye call?' I spoke with a melancholy air, and said, 'No; the boy is gone for a pint of ale for me.'

While I sat here, I heard the woman in the bar say, 'Are they all gone in the five?' which was the box I sat in, and the boy said, 'Yes.' 'Who fetched the tankard away?' says the woman. 'I did,' says another boy; 'that's it,' pointing, it seems, to another tankard, which he had fetched from another box by mistake; or else it must be, that the rogue forgot that he had not brought it in, which certainly he had not.

I heard all this much to my satisfaction, for I found plainly that the tankard was not missed, and yet they concluded it was fetched away; so I drank my ale, called to pay, and as I went away I said, 'Take care of your plate, child,' meaning a silver pint mug which he brought me to drink in. The boy said, 'Yes, madam, very welcome,' and away I came.

I came home to my governess, and now I thought it was a time to try her, that if I might be put to the necessity of being exposed she might offer me some assistance. When I had been at home some time, and had an opportunity of talking to her I told her I had a secret of the greatest consequence in the world to commit to her, if she had respect enough for me to keep it a secret. She told me she had kept one of my secrets faithfully; why should I doubt her keeping another? I told her the strangest thing in the world had befallen me, even without any design, and so told her the whole story of the tankard. 'And have you brought it away with you, my dear?' says she. 'To be sure I have,' says I, and showed it to her. 'But what shall I do now?' says I; 'must not I carry it again?'

'Carry it again!' says she. 'Ay, if you want to go to Newgate.' 'Why,' says I, 'they can't be so base to stop me, when I carry it to them again?' 'You don't know those sort of people, child,' says she; 'they'll not only carry you to Newgate, but hang you too, without any regard to the honesty of returning it; or bring in an account of all the other tankards as they have lost, for you to pay for.' 'What must I do, then?' says I. 'Nay,' says she, 'as you have played the cunning part and stole it, you must e'en keep it; there's no going back now. Besides, child,' says she, 'don't you want it more than they do? I wish you could light of such a bargain once a week.'

This gave me a new notion of my governess, and that since she was turned pawnbroker, she had a sort of people about her that were none of the honest ones that I had met with there before.

I had not been long there but I discovered it more plainly than before, for every now and then I saw hilts of swords, spoons, forks, tankards, and all such kind of ware brought in, not to be pawned, but to be sold downright; and she bought them all without asking any questions, but had good bargains, as I found by her discourse.

I found also that in following this trade she always melted down the plate she bought, that it might not be challenged; and she came to me and told me one morning that she was going to melt, and if I would, she would put my tankard in, that it might not be seen by anybody. I told her, with all my heart; so she weighed it, and allowed me the full value in silver again; but I found she did not do so to the rest of her customers.

Some time after this, as I was at work, and very melancholy, she begins to ask me what the matter was. I told her my heart was very heavy; I had little work and nothing to live on, and knew not what course to take. She laughed, and told me I must go out again and try my fortune; it might be that I might meet with another piece of plate. 'O mother!' says I, 'that is a trade that I have no skill in, and if I should be taken I am undone at once.' Says she, 'I could help you to a schoolmistress that shall make you as dexterous as herself.' I trembled at that proposal, for hitherto I had had no confederates nor any acquaintance among that tribe. But she conquered all my modesty, and all my fears; and in a little time, by the help of this confederate, I grew as impudent a thief, and as dexterous, as ever Moll Cutpurse* was, though, if fame does not belie her, not half so handsome.

The comrade she helped me to dealt in three sorts of craft, viz. shoplifting, stealing of shop-books and pocket-books, and taking off gold watches from the ladies' sides; and this last she did so dexterously that no woman ever arrived to the perfection of that art, like her. I liked the first and the last of these things very well, and I attended her some time in the practice, just as a deputy attends a midwife, without any pay.

At length she put me to practice. She had shown me her art, and I had several times unhooked a watch from her own side with great dexterity. At last she showed me a prize, and this was a young lady with child, who had a charming watch. The thing was to be done as she came out of the church. She goes on one side of the lady, and pretends, just as she came to the steps, to fall, and fell against the lady with so much violence as put her into a great fright, and both cried out terribly. In the very moment that she jostled the lady, I had hold of the watch, and holding it the right way, the start she gave drew the hook out, and she never felt it. I made off immediately, and left my schoolmistress to come out of her fright gradually, and the lady too; and presently the watch was missed. 'Ay,' says my comrade, 'then it was those rogues that thrust me down, I warrant ye; I wonder the gentlewoman did not miss her watch before, then we might have taken them.'

She humoured the thing so well that nobody suspected her, and I was got home a full hour before her. This was my first adventure in company. The watch was indeed a very fine one, and had many trinkets about it, and my governess allowed us £20 for it, of which I had half. And thus I was entered a complete thief, hardened to a pitch above all the reflections of conscience or modesty, and to a degree which I never thought possible in me.

Thus the devil, who began, by the help of an irresistible poverty, to push me into this wickedness, brought me to a height beyond the common rate, even when my necessities were not so terrifying; for I had now got into a little vein of work, and as I was not at a loss to handle my needle, it was very probable I might have got my bread honestly enough.

I must say, that if such a prospect of work had presented itself at first, when I began to feel the approach of my miserable circumstances – I say, had such a prospect of getting bread by working presented itself then, I had never fallen into this wicked trade, or into such a wicked gang as I was now embarked with; but practice had hardened me, and I grew audacious to the last degree; and the more so, because I had carried it on so long, and had never been taken; for, in a word, my new partner in wickedness and I went on together so long, without being ever detected, that we not only grew bold, but we grew rich, and we had at one time one-and-twenty gold watches in our hands.

I remember that one day being a little more serious than ordinary, and finding I had so good a stock beforehand as I had, for I had near £200 in money for my share, it came strongly into my mind, no doubt from some kind spirit, if such there be, that as at first poverty excited me, and my distresses drove me to these dreadful shifts, so seeing those distresses were now relieved, and I could also get something towards a maintenance by working, and had so good a bank to support me, why should I not now leave off, while I was well? that I could not expect to go always free; and if I was once surprised, I was undone.

This was doubtless the happy minute, when, if I had hearkened to the blessed hint, from whatsoever hand it came, I had still a cast for an easy life. But my fate was otherwise determined; the busy devil that drew me in had too fast hold of me to let me go back; but as poverty brought me in, so avarice kept me in, till there was no going back. As to the arguments which my reason dictated for persuading me to lay down, avarice stepped in and said, 'Go on; you have had very good luck; go on till you have gotten four or five hundred pounds, and then you shall leave off, and then you may live easy without working at all.'

Thus I, that was once in the devil's clutches, was held fast there as with a charm, and had no power to go without the circle, till I was engulfed in labyrinths of trouble too great to get out at all.

However, these thoughts left some impression upon me, and made me act with some more caution than before, and more than my directors used for themselves. My comrade, as I called her (she should have been called my teacher), with another of her scholars, was the first in the misfortune; for, happening to be upon the hunt for purchase, they made an attempt upon a linen-draper in Cheapside,* but were snapped by a hawk's-eyed journeyman, and seized with two pieces of cambric, which were taken also upon them.

This was enough to lodge them both in Newgate, where they

had the misfortune to have some of their former sins brought to remembrance. Two other indictments being brought against them, and the facts being proved upon them, they were both condemned to die. They both pleaded their bellies, and were both voted quick with child,* though my tutoress was no more with child than I was.

I went frequently to see them, and condole with them, expecting that it would be my turn next; but the place gave me so much horror, reflecting that it was the place of my unhappy birth, and of my mother's misfortunes, that I could not bear it, so I left off going to see them.

And oh! could I but have taken warning by their disasters, I had been happy still for I was yet free, and had nothing brought against me; but it could not be, my measure was not yet filled up.

My comrade, having the brand of an old offender,* was executed; the young offender was spared, having obtained a reprieve, but lay starving a long while in prison, till at last she got her name into what they call a circuit pardon, and so came off.

This terrible example of my comrade frighted me heartily, and for a good while I made no excursions; but one night, in the neighbourhood of my governess's house, they cried 'Fire.' My governess looked out, for we were all up, and cried immediately that such a gentlewoman's house was all of a light fire atop and so indeed it was. Here she gives me a jog. 'Now, child,' says she, 'there is a rare opportunity, the fire being so near that you may go to it before the street is blocked up with the crowd.' She presently gave me my cue. 'Go, child,' says she, 'to the house, and run in and tell the lady, or anybody you see, that you come to help them, and that you came from such a gentlewoman'; that is, one of her acquaintance farther up the street.

Away I went, and, coming to the house, I found them all in confusion, you may be sure. I ran in, and finding one of the maids, 'Alas! sweetheart,' said I, 'how came this dismal accident? Where is your mistress? Is she safe? And where are the children? I come from Madam— to help you.' Away runs the maid. 'Madam, madam,' says she, screaming as loud as she could yell, 'here is a gentlewoman come from Madam— to help us.' The poor woman, half out of her wits, with a bundle under her arm, and two little children, comes towards me. 'Madam,' says I, 'let me carry the poor children to Madam— ; she desires you to send them; she'll take care of the poor lambs'; and so I takes one of them out of her hand, and she lifts the other up into my arms. 'Ay, do, for God's sake,' says she, 'carry them. Oh! thank her for her kindness.' 'Have you anything else to secure, madam?' says I; 'she will take care of it.' 'Oh dear!' says she, 'God bless her; take this bundle of plate and carry it to her too. Oh, she is a good woman! Oh, we are utterly ruined, undone!' And away she runs from me out of her wits, and the maids after her, and away comes I with the two children and the bundle.

I was no sooner got into the street but I saw another woman come to me. 'Oh!' says she, 'mistress,' in a piteous tone, 'you will let fall the child. Come, come, this is a sad time; let me help you'; and immediately lays hold of my bundle to carry it for me. 'No,' says I; 'if you will help me, take the child by the hand, and lead it for me but to the upper end of the street; I'll go with you and satisfy you for your pains.'

She could not avoid going, after what I said; but the creature, in short, was one of the same business with me, and wanted nothing but the bundle; however, she went with me to the door, for she could not help it. When we were come there I whispered her, 'Go, child,' said I, 'I understand your trade; you may meet with purchase enough.'

She understood me and walked off. I thundered at the door with the children, and as the people were raised before by the noise of the fire, I was soon let in, and I said, 'Is madam awake? Pray tell her Mrs— desires the favour of her to take the two children in; poor lady, she will be undone, their house is all of a flame.' They took the children in very civilly, pitied the family in distress, and away came I with my bundle. One of the maids asked me if I was not to leave the bundle too. I said, 'No, sweetheart, 'tis to go to another place; it does not belong to them.'

I was a great way out of the hurry now, and so I went on and brought the bundle of plate, which was very considerable, straight home to my old governess. She told me she would not look into it, but bade me go again and look for more.

She gave me the like cue to the gentlewoman of the next house to that which was on fire, and I did my endeavour to go, but by this time the alarm of fire was so great, and so many engines playing,* and the street so thronged with people, that I could not get near the house whatever I could do; so I came back again to my governess's, and taking the bundle up into my chamber, I began to examine it. It is with horror that I tell what a treasure I found there; 'tis enough to say, that besides most of the family plate, which was considerable, I found a gold chain, an old-fashioned thing, the locket of which was broken, so that I suppose it had not been used some years, but the gold was not the worse for that; also a little box of burying rings, the lady's wedding-ring, and some broken bits of old lockets of gold, a gold watch, and a purse with about £24 value in old pieces of gold coin, and several other things of value.

This was the greatest and the worst prize that ever I was concerned in; for indeed, though, as I have said above, I was hardened now beyond the power of all reflection in other cases, yet it really touched me to the very soul when I looked into this treasure, to think of the poor disconsolate gentlewoman who had lost so much besides, and who would think, to be sure, that she had saved her plate and best things; how she would be surprised when she should find that she had been deceived, and that the person that took her children and her goods had come, as was pretended, from the gentlewoman in the next street, but that the children had been put upon her without her own knowledge.

I say, I confess the inhumanity of this action moved me very much, and made me relent exceedingly, and tears stood in my eyes upon that subject; but with all my sense of its being cruel and inhuman, I could never find in my heart to make any restitution. The reflection wore off, and I quickly forgot the circumstances that attended it.

Nor was this all; for though by this job I was become considerably richer than before, yet the resolution I had formerly taken of leaving off this horrid trade when I had gotten a little more, did not return, but I must still get more; and the avarice had such success, that I had no more thoughts of coming to a timely alteration of life, though without it I could expect no safety, no tranquillity in the possession of what I had gained; a little more, and a little more, was the case still.

At length, yielding to the importunities of my crime, I cast off all remorse, and all the reflections on that head turned to no more than this, that I might perhaps come to have one booty more that might complete all; but though I certainly had that one booty, yet every hit looked towards another, and was so encouraging to me to go on with the trade, that I had no gust to the laying it down.

In this condition, hardened by success, and resolving to go on, I fell into the snare in which I was appointed to meet with my last reward for this kind of life. But even this was not yet, for I met with several successful adventures more in this way.

My governess was for a while really concerned for the misfortune of my comrade that had been hanged, for she knew enough of my governess to have sent her the same way, and which made her very uneasy; indeed she was in a very great fright.

It is true that when she was gone, and had not told what she knew, my governess was easy as to that point, and perhaps glad she was hanged, for it was in her power to have obtained a pardon* at the expense of her friends; but the loss of her, and the sense of her kindness in not making her market of what she knew,* moved my governess to mourn very sincerely for her. I comforted her as well as I could, and she in return hardened me to merit more completely the same fate.

However, as I have said, it made me the more wary, and particularly I was very shy of shoplifting, especially among the mercers and drapers, who are a set of fellows that have their eyes very much about them. I made a venture or two among the lace folks and the milliners, and particularly at one shop where two young women were newly set up, and had not been bred to the trade. There I carried off a piece of bone-lace, worth six or seven pounds, and a paper of thread. But this was but once; it was a trick that would not serve again.

It was always reckoned a safe job when we heard of a new shop, and especially when the people were such as were not bred to shops. Such may depend upon it that they will be visited once or twice at their beginning, and they must be very sharp indeed if they can prevent it.

I made another adventure or two after this, but they were but trifles. Nothing considerable offering for a good while, I began to think that I must give over trade in earnest; but my governess, who was not willing to lose me, and expected great things of me, brought me one day into company with a young woman and a fellow that went for her husband, though, as it appeared afterwards, she was not his wife, but they were partners in the trade they carried on, and in something else too. In short, they robbed together, lay together, were taken together, and at last were hanged together.

I came into a kind of league with these two by the help of my governess, and they carried me out into three or four adventures, where I rather saw them commit some coarse and unhandy robberies, in which nothing but a great stock of impudence on their side, and gross negligence on the people's side who were robbed, could have made them successful. So I resolved from that time forward to be very cautious how I adventured with them; and, indeed, when two or three unlucky projects were proposed by them, I declined the offer, and persuaded them against it. One time they particularly proposed robbing a watchmaker of three gold watches, which they had eyed in the daytime, and found the place where he laid them. One of them had so many keys of all kinds that he made no question to open the place where the watchmaker had laid them; and so we made a kind of an appointment; but when I came to look narrowly into the thing, I found they proposed breaking open the house, and this I would not embark in, so they went without me. They did get into the house by main force, and broke up the locked place where the watches were, but found but one of the gold watches, and a silver one, which they took, and got out of the house again very clear. But the family being alarmed, cried out, 'Thieves,' and the man was pursued and taken; the young woman had got off too, but unhappily was stopped at a distance, and the watches found upon her. And thus I had a second escape, for they were convicted, and both hanged, being old offenders, though but young people; and as I said before that they robbed together, so now they hanged together, and there ended my new partnership.

I began now to be very wary, having so narrowly escaped a scouring,* and having such an example before me; but I had a new tempter, who prompted me every day – I mean my governess; and now a prize presented, which as it came by her management, so she expected a good share of the booty. There was a good quantity of Flanders lace lodged in a private house, where she had heard of it, and Flanders lace being prohibited, it was a good booty to any custom-house officer that could come at it. I had a full account from my governess, as well of the quantity as of the very place where it was concealed; so I went to a custom-house officer, and told him I had a discovery to make to him, if he would assure me that I should have my due share of the reward. This was so just an offer, that nothing could be fairer; so he agreed, and taking a constable and me with him, we beset the house. As I told him I could go directly to the place he left it to me; and the hole being very dark, I squeezed myself into it, with a candle in my hand, and so reached the pieces out to him, taking care as I gave him some so to secure as much about myself as I could conveniently dispose of. There was near £300 worth of lace in the whole, and I secured about £50 worth of it myself. The people of the house were not owners of the lace, but a merchant who had entrusted them with it; so that they were not so surprised as I thought they would be.

I left the officer overjoyed with his prize, and fully satisfied with what he had got, and appointed to meet him at a house of his own directing, where I came after I had disposed of the cargo I had about me, of which he had not the least suspicion. When I came he began to capitulate,* believing I did not understand the right I had in the prize, and would fain have put me off with £20; but I let him know that I was not so ignorant as he supposed I was; and yet I was glad, too, that he offered to bring me to a certainty.* I asked £100, and he rose up to £30; I fell to £80, and he rose again to £40; in a word, he offered £50, and I consented, only demanding a piece of lace, which I thought came to about £8 or £9, as if it had been for my own wear, and he agreed to it. So I got £50 in money paid me that same night, and made an end of the bargain; nor did he ever know who I was, or where to inquire for me, so that if it had been discovered that part of the goods were embezzled, he could have made no challenge upon me for it.

I very punctually divided this spoil with my governess, and I passed with her from this time for a very dexterous manager in the nicest cases. I found that this last was the best and easiest sort of work that was in my way, and I made it my business to inquire out prohibited goods, and after buying some, usually betrayed them, but none of these discoveries amounted to anything considerable, not like that I related just now; but I was cautious of running the great risks which I found others did, and in which they miscarried every day.

The next thing of moment was an attempt at a gentlewoman's gold watch. It happened in a crowd, at a meeting-house, where I was in very great danger of being taken. I had full hold of her watch, but giving a great jostle as if somebody had thrust me against her, and in the juncture giving the watch a fair pull, I found it would not come, so I let it go that moment, and cried as if I had been killed, that somebody had trod upon my foot, and that there was certainly pickpockets there, for somebody or other had given a pull at my watch; for you are to observe that on these adventures we always went very well dressed, and I had very good clothes on, and a gold watch by my side, as like a lady as other folks.

I had no sooner said so but the other gentlewoman cried out, 'A pickpocket,' too, for somebody, she said, had tried to pull her watch away.

When I touched her watch I was close to her, but when I cried out I stopped as it were short, and the crowd bearing her forward a little, she made a noise too, but it was at some distance from me, so that she did not in the least suspect me; but when she cried out, 'A pickpocket,' somebody cried out, 'Ay, and here has been another; this gentlewoman has been attempted too.'

At that very instant, a little farther in the crowd, and very luckily too, they cried out, 'A pickpocket,' again, and really seized a young fellow in the very fact. This, though unhappy for the wretch, was very opportunely for my case, though I had carried it handsomely enough before; but now it was out of doubt, and all the loose part of the crowd ran that way, and the poor boy was delivered up to the rage of the street, which is a cruelty I need not describe, and which, however, they are always glad of, rather than be sent to Newgate, where they lie often a long time, and sometimes they are hanged, and the best they can look for, if they are convicted, is to be transported.

This was a narrow escape to me, and I was so frighted that I ventured no more at gold watches a great while. There were indeed many circumstances in this adventure which assisted to my escape; but the chief was, that the woman whose watch I had pulled at was a fool; that is to say, she was ignorant of the nature of the attempt, which one would have thought she should not have been, seeing she was wise enough to fasten her watch so that it could not be slipped up; but she was in such a fright that she had no thought about her; for she, when she felt the pull, screamed out, and pushed herself forward, and put all the people about her into disorder, but said not a word of her watch, or of a pickpocket, for at least two minutes, which was time enough for me, and to spare; for as I had cried out behind her, as I have said, and bore myself back in the crowd as she bore forward, there were several people, at least seven or eight, the throng being still moving on, that were got between me and her in that time, and then I crying out 'A pickpocket' rather sooner than she, she might as well be the person suspected as I, and the people were confused in their inquiry; whereas, had she, with a presence of mind needful on such an occasion, as soon as she felt the pull, not screamed out as she did, but turned immediately round and seized the next body that was behind her, she had infallibly taken me.

This is a direction not of the kindest sort to the fraternity, but 'tis certainly a key to the clue* of a pickpocket's motions; and whoever can follow it, will as certainly catch the thief as he will sure to miss if he does not.

I had another adventure, which puts this matter out of doubt, and which may be an instruction for posterity in the case of a pickpocket. My good old governess, to give a short touch at her history, though she had left off the trade, was, as I may say, born a pickpocket, and, as I understood afterward, had run through all the several degrees of that art, and yet had been taken but once, when she was so grossly detected that she was convicted, and ordered to be transported; but being a woman of a rare tongue, and withal having money in her pocket, she found means, the ship putting into Ireland for provisions, to get on shore there, where she practised her old trade some years; when falling into another sort of company, she turned midwife and procuress, and played a hundred pranks, which she gave me a little history of, in confidence between us as we grew more intimate; and it was to this wicked creature that I owed all the dexterity I arrived to, in which there were few that ever went beyond me, or that practised so long without any misfortune.

It was after those adventures in Ireland, and when she was pretty well known in that country, that she left Dublin, and came over to England, where the time of her transportation being not expired, she left her former trade, for fear of falling into bad hands again, for then she was sure to have gone to wreck. Here she set up the same trade she had followed in Ireland, in which she soon, by her admirable management and a good tongue, arrived to the height which I have already described, and indeed began to be rich, though her trade fell again afterwards.

I mention thus much of the history of this woman here, the better to account for the concern she had in the wicked life I was now leading, into all the particulars of which she led me, as it were, by the hand, and gave me such directions, and I so well followed them, that I grew the greatest artist* of my time, and worked myself out of every danger with such dexterity, that when several more of my comrades ran themselves into Newgate, by that time they had been half a year at the trade, I had now practised upwards of five years, and the people at Newgate did not so much as know me; they had heard much of me indeed, and often expected me there, but I always got off, though many times in the extremest danger.

One of the greatest dangers I was now in, was that I was too well known among the trade, and some of them, whose hatred was owing rather to envy than any injury I had done them, began to be angry that I should always escape when they were always catched and hurried to Newgate. These were they that gave me the name of Moll Flanders; for it was no more of affinity with my real name, or with any of the names I had ever gone by, than black is of kin to white, except that once, as before, I called myself Mrs Flanders,* when I sheltered myself in the Mint; but that these rogues never knew, nor could I ever learn how they came to give me the name, or what the occasion of it was.

I was soon informed that some of these who were gotten fast into Newgate had vowed to impeach me; and as I knew that two or three of them were but too able to do it, I was under a great concern, and kept within doors for a good while. But my governess, who was partner in my success, and who now played a sure game, for she had no share in the hazard, – I say, my governess was something impatient of my leading such a useless, unprofitable life, as she called it; and she laid a new contrivance for my going abroad, and this was to dress me up in men's clothes, and so put me into a new kind of practice.

I was tall and personable, but a little too smoothfaced for a man; however, as I seldom went abroad but in the night, it did well enough; but it was long before I could behave in my new clothes. It was impossible to be so nimble, so ready, so dexterous as these things in a dress contrary to nature; and as I did everything clumsily, so I had neither the success or easiness of escape that I had before, and I resolved to leave it off; but that resolution was confirmed soon after by the following accident.

As my governess had disguised me like a man, so she joined me with a man, a young fellow that was nimble enough at his business, and for about three weeks we did very well together. Our principal trade was watching shopkeepers' counters, and slipping off any kinds of goods we could see carelessly laid anywhere, and we made several good bargains, as we called them, at this work. And as we kept always together, so we grew very intimate, yet he never knew that I was not a man, nay, though I several times went home with him to his lodgings, according as our business directed, and four or five times lay with him all night. But our design lay another way, and it was absolutely necessary to me to conceal my sex from him, as appeared afterwards. The circumstances of our living, coming in late, and having such business to do as required that nobody should be trusted with coming into our lodgings, were such as made it impossible to me to refuse lying with him, unless I would have owned my sex; and as it was, I effectually concealed myself.

But his ill, and my good, fortune soon put an end to this life, which I must own I was sick of too. We had made several prizes in this new way of business, but the last would have been extraordinary. There was a shop in a certain street which had a warehouse behind it that looked into another street, the house making the corner.

Through the window of the warehouse we saw lying on the counter or showboard, which was just before it, five pieces of silks, besides other stuffs, and though it was almost dark, yet the people, being busy in the fore-shop, had not had time to shut up those windows, or else had forgot it.

This the young fellow was so overjoyed with, that he could not restrain himself. It lay within his reach, he said, and he swore violently to me that he would have it, if he broke down the house for it. I dissuaded him a little, but saw there was no remedy; so he ran rashly upon it, slipped out a square out of the sash window dexterously enough, and got four pieces of the silks, and came with them towards me, but was immediately pursued with a terrible clutter and noise. We were standing together indeed, but I had not taken any of the goods out of his hand, when I said to him hastily, 'You are undone!' He ran like lightning, and I too, but the pursuit was hotter after him, because he had the goods. He dropped two of the pieces, which stopped them a little, but the crowd increased, and pursued us both. They took him soon after with the other two pieces, and then the rest followed me. I ran for it and got into my governess's house, whither some quick-eyed people followed me so warmly as to fix me there. They did not immediately knock at the door, by which I got time to throw off my disguise and dress me in my own clothes; besides, when they came there, my governess, who had her tale ready, kept her door shut, and called out to them and told them there was no man come in there. The people affirmed there did a man come in there, and swore they would break open the door.

My governess, not at all surprised, spoke calmly to them, told them they should very freely come and search her house, if they would bring a constable, and let in none but such as the constable would admit, for it was unreasonable to let in a whole crowd. This they could not refuse, though they were a crowd. So a constable was fetched immediately, and she very freely opened the door; the constable kept the door, and the men he appointed searched the house, my governess going with them from room to room. When she came to my room she called to me, and said aloud, 'Cousin, pray open the door; here's some gentlemen that must come and look into your room.'

I had a little girl with me, which was my governess's grandchild, as she called her; and I bade her open the door, and there sat I at work with a great litter of things about me, as if I had been at work all day, being undressed, with only night-clothes on my head, and a loose morning-gown about me. My governess made a kind of excuse for their disturbing me, telling partly the occasion of it, and that she had no remedy but to open the doors to them, and let them satisfy themselves, for all she could say would not satisfy them. I sat still, and bid them search if they pleased, for if there was anybody in the house, I was sure they were not in my room; and for the rest of the house, I had nothing to say to that, I did not understand what they looked for.

Everything looked so innocent and so honest about me, that they treated me civiller than I expected; but it was not till they had searched the room to a nicety, even under the bed, and in the bed, and everywhere else, where it was possible anything could be hid. When they had done, and could find nothing, they asked my pardon and went down.

When they had thus searched the house from bottom to top, and then from top to bottom, and could find nothing, they appeased the mob pretty well; but they carried my governess before the justice. Two men swore that they saw the man whom they pursued go into her house. My governess rattled and made a great noise that her house should be insulted, and that she should be used thus for nothing; that if a man did come in, he might go out again presently for aught she knew, for she was ready to make oath that no man had been within her doors all that day as she knew of, which was very true; that it might be, that as she was above-stairs, any fellow in a fright might find the door open, and run in for shelter when he was pursued, but that she knew nothing of it; and if it had been so, he certainly went out again, perhaps at the other door, for she had another door into an alley, and so had made his escape.

This was indeed probable enough, and the justice satisfied himself with giving her an oath that she had not received or admitted any man into her house to conceal him, or protect or hide him from justice. This oath she might justly take, and did so, and so she was dismissed.

It is easy to judge what a fright I was in upon this occasion, and it was impossible for my governess ever to bring me to dress in that disguise again; for, as I told her, I should certainly betray myself.

My poor partner in this mischief was now in a bad case, for he was carried away before my Lord Mayor, and by his worship committed to Newgate, and the people that took him were so willing, as well as able, to prosecute him, that they offered themselves to enter into recognisances* to appear at the sessions, and pursue the charge against him.

However, he got his indictment deferred, upon promise to discover his accomplices, and particularly the man that was concerned with him in this robbery; and he failed not to do his endeavour, for he gave in my name, whom he called Gabriel Spencer, which was the name I went by to him; and here appeared the wisdom of my concealing myself from him, without which I had been undone.

He did all he could to discover this Gabriel Spencer; he described me; he discovered the place where he said I lodged; and, in a word, all the particulars that he could of my dwelling; but having concealed the main circumstances of my sex from him, I had a vast advantage, and he could never hear of me. He brought two or three families into trouble by his endeavouring to find me out, but they knew nothing of me, any more than that he had a fellow with him that they had seen, but knew nothing of. And as to my governess, though she was the means of his coming to me, yet it was done at second-hand, and he knew nothing of her neither.

This turned to his disadvantage; for having promised discoveries, but not being able to make it good, it was looked upon as trifling, and he was the more fiercely pursued by the shopkeeper.

I was, however, terribly uneasy all this while, and that I might be quite out of the way, I went away from my governess for a while; but not knowing whither to wander, I took a maid-servant with me, and took the stage-coach to Dunstable, to my old landlord and landlady, where I lived so handsomely with my Lancashire husband. Here I told her a formal* story, that I expected my husband every day from Ireland, and that I had sent a letter to him that I would meet him at Dunstable at her house, and that he would certainly land, if the wind was fair, in a few days; so that I was come to spend a few days with them till he could come, for he would either come post,* or in the West Chester coach, I knew not which; but whichsoever it was, he would be sure to come to that house to meet me.

My landlady was mighty glad to see me, and my landlord made such a stir with me, that if I had been a princess I could not have been better used, and here I might have been welcome a month or two if I had thought fit.

But my business was of another nature. I was very uneasy (though so well disguised that it was scarce possible to detect me); lest this fellow should find me out; and though he could not charge me with the robbery, having persuaded him not to venture, and having done nothing of it myself, yet he might have charged me with other things, and have bought his own life at the expense of mine.

This filled me with horrible apprehensions. I had no resource, no friend, no confidant but my old governess, and I knew no remedy but to put my life into her hands; and so I did, for I let her know where to send to me, and had several letters from her while I stayed here. Some of them almost scared me out of my wits; but at last she sent me the joyful news that he was hanged, which was the best news to me that I had heard a great while.

I had stayed here five weeks, and lived very comfortably indeed, the secret anxiety of my mind excepted. But when I received this letter I looked pleasantly again, and told my landlady that I had received a letter from my spouse in Ireland, that I had the good news of his being very well, but had the bad news that his business would not permit him to come away so soon as he expected, and so I was like to go back again without him.

My landlady complimented me upon the good news, however,

that I had heard he was well. 'For I have observed, madam,' says she, 'you han't been so pleasant as you used to be; you have been over head and ears in care for him, I dare say,' says the good woman; ''tis easy to be seen there's an alteration in you for the better,' says she. 'Well, I am sorry the squire can't come yet,' says my landlord; 'I should have been heartily glad to have seen him. When you have certain news of his coming, you'll take a step hither again, madam,' says he; 'you shall be very welcome whenever you please to come.'

With all these fine compliments we parted, and I came merry enough to London, and found my governess as well pleased as I was. And now she told me she would never recommend any partner to me again, for she always found, she said, that I had the best luck when I ventured by myself. And so indeed I had, for I was seldom in any danger when I was by myself, or if I was, I got out of it with more dexterity than when I was entangled with the dull measures of other people, who had perhaps less forecast, and were more impatient than I; for though I had as much courage to venture as any of them, yet I used more caution before I undertook a thing, and had more presence of mind to bring myself off.

I have often wondered even at my own hardiness another way, that when all my companions were surprised, and fell so suddenly into the hand of justice, yet I could not all this while enter into one serious resolution to leave off this trade, and especially considering that I was now very far from being poor; that the temptation of necessity, which is the general introduction of all such wickedness, was now removed; that I had near £500 by me in ready money, on which I might have lived very well, if I had thought fit to have retired; but, I say, I had not so much as the least inclination to leave off; no, not so much as I had before, when I had but £200 beforehand, and when I had no such frightful examples before my eyes as these were. From hence 'tis evident, that when once we are hardened in crime, no fear can affect us, no example give us any warning.

I had indeed one comrade, whose fate went very near me* for a good while, though I wore it off too in time. That case was indeed very unhappy. I had made a prize of a piece of very good damask in a mercer's shop, and went clear off myself, but had conveyed the piece to this companion of mine, when we went out of the shop, and she went one way, I went another. We had not been long out of the shop but the mercer missed the piece of stuff, and sent his messengers, one one way, and one another, and they presently seized her that had the piece, with the damask upon her; as for me, I had very luckily stepped into a house where there was a lace chamber, up one pair of stairs, and had the satisfaction, or the terror, indeed, of looking out of the window, and seeing the poor creature dragged away to the justice, who immediately committed her to Newgate.

I was careful to attempt nothing in the lace chamber, but tumbled their goods pretty much to spend time; then bought a few yards of edging, and paid for it, and came away very sad-hearted indeed, for the poor woman who was in tribulation for what I only had stolen.

Here again my old caution stood me in good stead; though I often robbed with these people, yet I never let them know who I was, nor could they ever find out my lodging, though they often endeavoured to watch me to it. They all knew me by the name of Moll Flanders, though even some of them rather believed I was she than knew me to be so. My name was public among them indeed, but how to find me out they knew not, nor so much as how to guess at my quarters, whether they were at the east end of the town or the west; and this wariness was my safety upon all these occasions.

I kept close a great while upon the occasion of this woman's disaster. I knew that if I should do anything that should miscarry, and should be carried to prison, she would be there, and ready to witness against me, and perhaps save her life at my expense. I considered that I began to be very well known by name at the Old Bailey, though they did not know my face, and that if I should fall into their hands, I should be treated as an old offender; and for this reason I was resolved to see what this poor creature's fate should be before I stirred, though several times in her distress I conveyed money to her for her relief.

At length she came to her trial. She pleaded she did not steal the things, but that one Mrs Flanders, as she heard her called (for she did not know her), gave the bundle to her after they came out of the shop, and bade her carry it home. They asked her where this Mrs Flanders was, but she could not produce her, neither could she give the least account of me; and the mercer's men swearing positively that she was in the shop when the goods were stolen, that they immediately missed them, and pursued her, and found them upon her, thereupon the jury brought her in guilty; but the court considering that she really was not the person that stole the goods, and that it was very possible she could not find out this Mrs Flanders, meaning me, though it would save her life, which indeed was true, they allowed her to be transported; which was the utmost favour she could obtain, only that the court told her, if she could in the meantime produce the said Mrs Flanders, they would intercede for her pardon; that is to say, if she could find me out, and hang me, she should not be transported. This I took care to make impossible to her, and so she was shipped off in pursuance of her sentence a little while after.

I must repeat it again, that the fate of this poor woman troubled me exceedingly, and I began to be very pensive, knowing that I was really the instrument of her disaster; but my own life, which was so evidently in danger, took off my tenderness; and seeing she was not put to death, I was easy at her transportation, because she was then out of the way of doing me any mischief, whatever should happen.

The disaster of this woman was some months before that of the last recited story, and was indeed partly the occasion of my governess proposing to dress me up in men's clothes, that I might go about unobserved; but I was soon tired of that disguise, as I have said, for it exposed me to too many difficulties.

I was now easy as to all fear of witnesses against me, for all those that had either been concerned with me, or that knew me by the name of Moll Flanders, were either hanged or transported; and if I should have had the misfortune to be taken, I might call myself anything else, as well as Moll Flanders, and no old sins could be placed to my account; so I began to run a-tick* again, with the more freedom, and several successful adventures I made, though not such as I had made before.

We had at that time another fire happened not a great way off from the place where my governess lived, and I made an attempt there as before; but as I was not soon enough before the crowd of people came in, and could not get to the house I aimed at, instead of a prize, I got a mischief, which had almost put a period to my life and all my wicked doings together; for the fire being very furious, and the people in a great fright in removing their goods, and throwing them out of window, a wench from out of a window threw a feather-bed just upon me. It is true, the bed being soft, it broke no bones; but as the weight was great, and made greater by the fall, it beat me down, and laid me dead for a while; nor did the people concern themselves much to deliver me from it, or to recover me at all; but I lay like one dead and neglected a good while, till somebody going to remove the bed out of the way, helped me up. It was indeed a wonder the people in the house had not thrown other goods out after it, and which might have fallen upon it, and then I had been inevitably killed; but I was reserved for further afflictions.

This accident, however, spoiled my market for that time, and I came home to my governess very much hurt and frighted, and it was a good while before she could set me upon my feet again.

It was now a merry time of the year, and Bartholomew Fair* was begun. I had never made any walks that way, nor was the fair of much advantage to me; but I took a turn this year into the cloisters,* and there I fell into one of the raffling shops.* It was a thing of no great consequence to me, but there came a gentleman extremely well dressed and very rich, and as 'tis frequent to talk to everybody in those shops, he singled me out, and was very particular with me. First he told me he would put in for me to raffle, and did so; and some small matter coming to his lot, he presented it to me – I think it was a feather muff; then he continued to keep talking to me with a more than common appearance of respect, but still very civil, and much like a gentleman.

He held me in talk so long, till at last he drew me out of the raffling place to the shop-door, and then to take a walk in the cloister, still talking of a thousand things cursorily without anything to the purpose. At last he told me that he was charmed with my company, and asked me if I durst trust myself in a coach with him; he told me he was a man of honour, and would not offer anything to me unbecoming him. I seemed to decline it a while, but suffered myself to be importuned a little, and then yielded.

I was at a loss in my thoughts to conclude at first what this gentleman designed; but I found afterward he had had some drink in his head, and that he was not very unwilling to have some more. He carried me to the Spring Garden,* at Knightsbridge, where we walked in the gardens, and he treated me very handsomely; but I found he drank freely. He pressed me also to drink, but I declined it.

Hitherto he kept his word with me, and offered me nothing amiss. We came away in the coach again, and he brought me into the streets, and by this time it was near ten o'clock at night, when he stopped the coach at a house where, it seems, he was acquainted, and where they made no scruple to show us upstairs into a room with a bed in it. At first I seemed to be unwilling to go up, but after a few words I yielded to that too, being indeed willing to see the end of it, and in hopes to make something of it at last. As for the bed, etc., I was not much concerned about that part.

Here he began to be a little freer with me than he had promised; and I by little and little yielded to everything, so that, in a word, he did what he pleased with me; I need say no more. All this while he drank freely too, and about one in the morning we went into the coach again. The air and the shaking of the coach made the drink get more up in his head, and he grew uneasy, and was for acting over again what he had been doing before; but as I thought my game now secure, I resisted, and brought him to be a little still, which had not lasted five minutes but he fell fast asleep.

I took this opportunity to search him to a nicety. I took a gold watch, with a silk purse of gold, his fine full-bottom periwig and silver-fringed gloves, his sword and fine snuff-box, and gently opening the coach-door, stood ready to jump out while the coach was going on; but the coach stopping in the narrow street beyond Temple Bar* to let another coach pass, I got softly out, fastened the door again, and gave my gentleman and the coach the slip together.

This was an adventure indeed unlooked for, and perfectly undesigned by me; though I was not so past the merry part of life as to forget how to behave, when a fop so blinded by his appetite should not know an old woman from a young. I did not indeed look so old as I was by ten or twelve years; yet I was not a young wench of seventeen, and it was easy enough to be distinguished. There is nothing so absurd, so surfeiting, so ridiculous, as a man heated by wine in his head, and a wicked gust in his inclination together; he is in the possession of two devils at once, and can no more govern himself by his reason than a mill can grind without water; vice tramples upon all that was in him that had any good in it; nay, his very sense is blinded by its own rage, and he acts absurdities even in his view; such as drinking more, when he is drunk already; picking up a common woman, without any regard to what she is or who she is; whether sound or rotten, clean or unclean; whether ugly or handsome, old or young; and so blinded as not really to distinguish. Such a man is worse than lunatic; prompted by his vicious head, he no more knows what he is doing than this wretch of mine knew when I picked his pocket of his watch and his purse of gold.

These are the men of whom Solomon says,* 'They go like an ox to the slaughter, till a dart strikes through their liver'; an admirable description, by the way, of the foul disease,* which is a poisonous deadly contagion mingling with the blood, whose centre or fountain is in the liver; from whence, by the swift circulation of the whole mass, that dreadful nauseous plague strikes immediately through his liver, and his spirits are infected, his vitals stabbed through as with a dart.

It is true this poor unguarded wretch was in no danger from me, though I was greatly apprehensive at first what danger I might be in from him; but he was really to be pitied in one respect, that he seemed to be a good sort of a man in himself: a gentleman that had no harm in his design; a man of sense, and of a fine behaviour, a comely handsome person, a sober and solid countenance, a charming beautiful face, and everything that could be agreeable; only had unhappily had some drink the night before; had not been in bed, as he told me when we were together; was hot, and his blood fired with wine, and in that condition his reason, as it were asleep, had given him up.

As for me, my business was his money, and what I could make of him; and after that, if I could have found out any way to have done it, I would have sent him safe home to his house and to his family, for 'twas ten to one but he had an honest, virtuous wife and innocent children, that were anxious for his safety, and would have been glad to have gotten him home, and taken care of him, till he was restored to himself: and when with what shame and regret would he look back upon himself! how would he reproach himself with associating himself with a whore! picked up in the worst of all holes, the cloister, among the dirt and filth of the town! how would he be trembling for fear he had got the pox, for fear a dart had struck through his liver, and hate himself every time he looked back upon the madness and brutality of his debauch! how would he, if he had any principles of honour, abhor the thought of giving any ill distemper, if he had it, as for aught he knew he might, to his modest and virtuous wife, and thereby sowing the contagion in the life-blood of his posterity!

Would such gentlemen but consider the contemptible thoughts which the very women they are concerned with, in such cases as these, have of them, it would be a surfeit to them. As I said above, they value not the pleasure, they are raised by no inclination to the man, the passive jade thinks of no pleasure but the money; and when he is, as it were, drunk in the ecstasies of his wicked pleasure, her hands are in his pockets for what she can find there, and of which he can no more be sensible in the moment of his folly than he can fore-think of it when he goes about it.

I knew a woman that was so dexterous with a fellow, who indeed deserved no better usage, that while he was busy with her another way, conveyed his purse with twenty guineas in it out of his fob-pocket, where he had put it for fear of her, and put another purse with gilded counters in it into the room of it. After he had done he says to her, 'Now han't you picked my pocket?' She jested with him, and told him she supposed he had not much to lose; he put his hand to his fob, and with fingers felt that his purse was there, which fully satisfied him, and so she brought off his money. And this was a trade with her; she kept a sham gold watch and a purse of counters in her pocket to be ready on all such occasions, and I doubt not practised it with success.

I came home with this last booty to my governess, and really when I told her the story, it so affected her that she was hardly above to forbear tears, to think how such a gentleman ran a daily risk of being undone, every time a glass of wine got into his head.

But as to the purchase I got, and how entirely I stripped him, she told me it pleased her wonderfully. 'Nay, child,' says she, 'the usage may, for aught I know, do more to reform him than all the sermons that ever he will hear in his life.' And if the remainder of the story be true, so it did.

I found the next day she was wonderful inquisitive about this gentleman; the description I gave her of him, his dress, his person, his face, all concurred to make her think of a gentleman whose character she knew. She mused a while, and I going on in the particulars, says she, 'I lay £100 I know the man.'

'I am sorry if you do,' says I, 'for I would not have him exposed on any account in the world; he has had injury enough already, and I would not be instrumental to do him any more.' 'No, no,' says she, 'I will do him no injury, but you may let me satisfy my curiosity a little, for if it is he, I warrant you I find it out.' I was a little startled at that, and I told her, with an apparent concern in my face, that by the same rule he might find me out, and then I was undone. She returned warmly, 'Why, do you think I will betray you, child? No, no,' says she, 'not for all he is worth in the world. I have kept your counsel in worse things than these; sure you may trust me in this.' So I said no more.

She laid her scheme another way, and without acquainting me with it, but she was resolved to find it out. So she goes to a certain friend of hers, who was acquainted in the family that she guessed at, and told her she had some extraordinary business with such a gentleman (who, by the way, was no less than a baronet and of a very good family), and that she knew not how to come at him without somebody to introduce her. Her friend promised her readily to do it, and accordingly goes to the house to see if the gentelman was in town.

The next day she comes to my governess and tells her that Sir— was at home, but that he had met with a disaster and was very ill, and there was no speaking to him. 'What disaster?' says my governess hastily, as if she was surprised at it. 'Why,' says her friend, 'he had been at Hampstead* to visit a gentleman of his acquaintance, and as he came back again, he was set upon and robbed; and having got a little drink too, as they suppose, the rogues abused him, and he is very ill.' 'Robbed!' says my governess, 'and what did they take from him?' 'Why,' says her friend, 'they took his gold watch and his gold snuff-box, his fine periwig, and what money he had in his pocket, which was considerable, to be sure, for Sir— never goes without a purse of guineas about him.'

'Pshaw!' says my old governess, jeering, 'I warrant you he has got drunk now, and got a whore, and she has picked his pocket, and so he comes home to his wife and tells her he has been robbed; that's an old sham; a thousand such tricks are put upon the poor women every day.'

'Fie!' says her friend, 'I find you don't know Sir—; why, he is as civil a gentleman, there is not a finer man, nor a soberer, modester person in the whole city; he abhors such things; there's nobody that knows him will think such a thing of him.' 'Well, well,' says my governess, 'that's none of my business; if it was, I warrant I should find there was something of that in it; your modest men in common opinion are sometimes no better than other people, only they keep a better character, or, if you please, are the better hypocrites.'

'No, no,' says her friend, 'I can assure you Sir— is no hypocrite; he is really an honest, sober gentleman, and he has certainly been robbed.' 'Nay,' says my governess, 'it may be he has; it is no business of mine, I tell you; I only want to speak with him; my business is of another nature.' 'But,' says her friend, 'let your business be of what nature it will, you cannot see him yet, for he is not fit to be seen, for he is very ill, and bruised very much.' 'Ay,' says my governess, 'nay, then he has fallen into bad hands, to be sure.' And then she asked gravely, 'Pray, where is he bruised?' 'Why, in his head,' says her friend, 'and one of his hands, and his face, for they used him barbarously.' 'Poor gentleman,' says my governess, 'I must wait, then, till he recovers'; and adds, 'I hope it will not be long.'

Away she comes to me, and tells me this story. 'I have found out your fine gentleman, and a fine gentleman he was,' says she; 'but, mercy on him, he is in a sad pickle now. I wonder what the d—you have done to him; why, you have almost killed him.' I looked at her with disorder enough. 'I killed him!' says I; 'you must mistake the person; I am sure I did nothing to him; he was very well when I left him,' said I, 'only drunk and fast asleep.' 'I know nothing of that,' says she, 'but he is in a sad pickle now'; and so she told me all that her friend had said. 'Well, then,' says I, 'he fell into bad hands after I left him, for I left him safe enough.'

About ten days after, my governess goes again to her friend, to introduce her to this gentleman; she had inquired other ways in the meantime, and found that he was about again, so she got leave to speak with him.

She was a woman of an admirable address, and wanted nobody to introduce her; she told her tale much better than I shall be able to tell it for her, for she was mistress of her tongue, as I said already. She told him that she came, though a stranger, with a single design of doing him a service, and he should find she had no other end in it; that as she came purely on so friendly an account, she begged a promise from him, that if he did not accept what she should officiously* propose, he would not take it ill that she meddled with what was not her business; she assured him that as what she had to say was a secret that belonged to him only, so whether he accepted her offer or not, it should remain a secret to all the world, unless he exposed it himself; nor should his refusing her service in it make her so little show her respect as to do him the least injury, so that he should be entirely at liberty to act as he thought fit.

He looked very shy at first, and said he knew nothing that related to him that required much secrecy; that he had never done any man any wrong, and cared not what anybody might say of him; that it was no part of his character to be unjust to anybody, nor could he imagine in what any man could render him any service; but that if it was as she said, he could not take it ill from any one that should endeavour to serve him; and so, as it were, left her at liberty either to tell him or not to tell him, as she thought fit.

She found him so perfectly indifferent, that she was almost afraid to enter into the point with him; but, however, after some other circumlocutions, she told him, that by a strange and unaccountable accident she came to have a particular knowledge of the late unhappy adventure he had fallen into, and that in such a manner that there was nobody in the world but herself and him that were acquainted with it, no, not the very person that was with him.

He looked a little angrily at first. 'What adventure?' said he. 'Why, sir,' said she, 'of your being robbed coming from Knightsbr—; Hampstead, sir, I should say,' says she. 'Be not surprised, sir,' says she, 'that I am able to tell you every step you took that day from the cloister in Smithfield to the Spring Garden at Knightsbridge, and thence to the— in the Strand, and how you were left asleep in the coach afterwards. I say, let not this surprise you, for, sir, I do not come to make a booty of you, I ask nothing of you, and I assure you the woman that was with you knows nothing who you are, and never shall; and yet perhaps I may serve you further still, for I did not come barely to let you know that I was informed of these things, as if I wanted a bribe to conceal them; assure yourself, sir,' said she, 'that whatever you think fit to do or say to me, it shall be all a secret, as it is, as much as if I were in my grave.'

He was astonished at her discourse, and said gravely to her, 'Madam, you are a stranger to me, but it is very unfortunate that you should be let into the secret of the worst action of my life, and a thing that I am justly ashamed of, in which the only satisfaction I had was, that I thought it was known only to God and my own conscience.' 'Pray, sir,' says she, 'do not reckon the discovery of it to me to be any part of your misfortune. It was a thing, I believe, you were surprised into, and perhaps the woman used some art to prompt you to it. However, you will never find any just cause,' said she, 'to repent that I came to hear of it; nor can your mouth be more silent in it than I have been, and ever shall be.'

'Well,' says he, 'but let me do some justice to the woman too;

whoever she is, I do assure you she prompted me to nothing, she rather declined me. It was my own folly and madness that brought me into it all; ay, and brought her into it too; I must give her her due so far. As to what she took from me, I could expect no less from her in the condition I was in, and to this hour I know not whether she robbed me or the coachman; if she did it, I forgive her. I think all gentlemen that do so should be used in the same manner; but I am more concerned for some other things than I am for all that she took from me.'

My governess now began to come into the whole matter, and he opened himself freely to her. First, she said to him, in answer to what he had said about me, 'I am glad, sir, you are so just to the person that you were with. I assure you she is a gentlewoman, and no woman of the town; and however you prevailed with her as you did, I am sure 'tis not her practice. You ran a great venture indeed, sir; but if that be part of your care, you may be perfectly easy, for I do assure you no man has touched her before you, since her husband, and he has been dead now almost eight years.'

It appeared that this was his grievance, and that he was in a very great fright about it; however, when my governess said this to him, he appeared very well pleased, and said, 'Well, madam, to be plain with you, if I was satisfied of that, I should not so much value what I lost; for, as to that, the temptation was great, and perhaps she was poor, and wanted it.' 'If she had not been poor, sir,' says she, 'I assure you she would never have yielded to you; and as her poverty first prevailed with you to let you do as you did, so the same poverty prevailed with her to pay herself at last, when she saw you was in such a condition, that if she had not done it, perhaps the next coachman or chairman* might have done it more to your hurt.'

'Well,' says he, 'much good may it do her. I say again, all the gentlemen that do so ought to be used in the same manner, and then they would be cautious of themselves. I have no concern about it, but on the score which you hinted at before.' Here he entered into some freedoms with her on the subject of what passed between us, which are not so proper for a woman to write, and the great terror that was upon his mind with relation to his wife, for fear she should have received any injury from me, and should communicate it farther; and asked her at last if she could not procure him an opportunity to speak with me. My governess gave him further assurances of my being a woman clear from any such thing, and that he was as entirely safe in that respect as he was with his own lady; but as for seeing me, she said it might be of dangerous consequence; but, however, that she would talk with me, and let him know, endeavouring at the same time to persuade him not to desire it, and that it could be of no service to him, seeing she hoped he had no desire to renew the correspondence, and that on my account it was a kind of putting my life in his hands.

He told her he had a great desire to see me, that he would give her any assurances that were in his power not to take any advantages of me, and that in the first place he would give me a general release from all demands of any kind. She insisted how it might tend to further divulging the secret, and might be injurious to him, entreating him not to press for it; so at length he desisted.

They had some discourse upon the subject of the things he had lost, and he seemed to be very desirous of his gold watch, and told her if she could procure that for him, he would willingly give as much for it as it was worth. She told him she would endeavour to procure it for him, and leave the valuing it to himself.

Accordingly the next day she carried the watch, and he gave her thirty guineas for it, which was more than I should have been able to make of it, though it seems it cost much more. He spoke something of his periwig, which it seems cost him threescore guineas, and his snuff-box; and in a few days more she carried them too, which obliged him very much, and he gave her thirty more. The next day I sent him his fine sword and cane gratis, and demanded nothing of him, but had no mind to see him, unless he might be satisfied I knew who he was, which he was not willing to.

Then he entered into a long talk with her of the manner how she came to know all this matter. She formed a long tale of that part; how she had it from one that I had told the whole story to, and that was to help me dispose of the goods; and this confidante brought things to her, she being by profession a pawn-broker; and she hearing of his worship's disaster, guessed at the thing in general; that having gotten the things into her hands, she had resolved to come and try as she had done. She then gave him repeated assurances that it should never go out of her mouth, and though she knew the woman very well, yet she had not let her know, meaning me, anything of who the person was, which, by the way, was false; but, however, it was not to his damage, for I never opened my mouth of it to anybody.

I had a great many thoughts in my head about my seeing him again, and was often sorry that I had refused it. I was persuaded that if I had seen him, and let him know that I knew him, I should have made some advantage of him, and perhaps have had some maintenance from him; and though it was a life wicked enough, yet it was not so full of danger as this I was engaged in. However, those thoughts wore off, and I declined seeing him again, for that time; but my governess saw him often, and he was very kind to her, giving her something almost every time he saw her. One time in particular she found him very merry, and as she thought he had some wine in his head then, and he pressed her again to let him see the woman that, as he said, had bewitched him so that night, my governess, who was from the beginning for my seeing him, told him he was so desirous of it that she could almost yield to it, if she could prevail upon me; adding that if he would please to come to her house in the evening, she would endeavour it, upon his repeated assurances of forgetting what was past.

Accordingly she came to me, and told me all the discourse; in short, she soon biased me to consent, in a case which I had some regret in my mind for declining before; so I prepared to see him. I dressed me to all the advantage possible, I assure you, and for the first time used a little art; I say for the first time, for I had never yielded to the baseness of paint before, having always had vanity enough to believe I had no need of it.

At the hour appointed he came; and as she observed before, so it was plain still, that he had been drinking, though very far from what we call being in drink. He appeared exceeding pleased to see me, and entered into a long discourse with me upon the whole affair. I begged his pardon very often for my share of it, protested I had not any such design when first I met him, that I had not gone out with him but that I took him for a very civil gentleman, and that he made me so many promises of offering no incivility to me.

He alleged* the wine he drank, and that he scarce knew what he did, and that if it had not been so, he should never have taken the freedom with me he had done. He protested to me that he never touched any woman but me since he was married to his wife, and it was a surprise upon him; complimented me upon being so particularly agreeable to him, and the like; and talked so much of that kind, till I found he had talked himself almost into a temper to do the thing again. But I took him up short. I protested I had never suffered any man to touch me since my husband died, which was near eight years. He said he believed it; and added that madam had intimated as much to him, and that it was his opinion of that part which made him desire to see me again; and since he had once broken in upon his virtue with me, and found no ill consequences, he could be safe in venturing again; and so, in short, he went on to what I expected, and to what will not bear relating.

My old governess had foreseen it, as well as I, and therefore led him into a room which had not a bed in it, and yet had a chamber within it which had a bed, whither we withdrew for the rest of the night; and, in short, after some time being together, he went to bed, and lay there all night. I withdrew, but came again undressed before it was day, and lay with him the rest of the time.

Thus, you see, having committed a crime once is a sad handle to the committing of it again; all the reflections wear off when the temptation renews itself. Had I not yielded to see him again, the corrupt desire in him had worn off, and 'tis very probable he had never fallen into it with anybody else, as I really believe he had not done before.

When he went away, I told him I hoped he was satisfied he had not been robbed again. He told me he was fully satisfied in that point, and putting his hand in his pocket, gave me five guineas, which was the first money I had gained that way for many years.

I had several visits of the like kind from him, but he never came into a settled way of maintenance, which was what I would have been best pleased with. Once, indeed, he asked me how I did to live. I answered him pretty quick, that I assured him I had never taken that course that I took with him, but that indeed I worked at my needle, and could just maintain myself; that sometimes it was as much as I was able to do, and I shifted hard enough.*

He seemed to reflect upon himself that he should be the first person to lead me into that which he assured me he never intended to do himself; and it touched him a little, he said, that he should be the cause of his own sin and mine too. He would often make just reflections also upon the crime itself, and upon the particular circumstances of it, with respect to himself; how wine introduced the inclinations, how the devil led him to the place, and found out an object to tempt him, and he made the moral always himself.

When these thoughts were upon him he would go away, and perhaps not come again in a month's time or longer; but then as the serious part wore off, the lewd part would wear in, and then he came prepared for the wicked part. Thus we lived for some time; though he did not keep, as they call it, yet he never failed doing things that were handsome, and sufficient to maintain me without working, and, which was better, without following my old trade.

But this affair had its end too; for after about a year, I found that he did not come so often as usual, and at last he left it off altogether without any dislike or bidding adieu; and so there was an end of that short scene of life, which added no great store to me, only to make more work for repentance.

During this interval I confined myself pretty much at home; at least, being thus provided for, I made no adventures, no, not for a quarter of a year after; but then finding the fund fail, and being loath to spend upon the main stock, I began to think of my old trade, and to look abroad into the street; and my first step was lucky enough.

I had dressed myself up in a very mean habit, for as I had several shapes* to appear in, I was now in an ordinary stuff gown, a blue apron, and a straw hat; and I placed myself at the door of the Three Cups Inn in St John's Street. There were several carriers used the inn, and the stage-coaches for Barnet,* for Totteridge, and other towns that way stood always in the street in the evening, when they prepared to set out, so that I was ready for anything that offered. The meaning was this: people came frequently with bundles and small parcels to those inns, and call for such carriers or coaches as they want, to carry them into the country; and there generally attends women, porters' wives or daughters, ready to take in such things for the people that employ them.

It happened very oddly that I was standing at the inn gate, and a woman that stood there before, and which was the porter's wife belonging to the Barnet stage-coach, having observed me, asked if I waited for any of the coaches. I told her yes, I waited for my mistress, that was coming to go to Barnet. She asked me who was my mistress, and I told her any madam's name that came next me;* but it seemed I happened upon a name a family of which name lived at Hadley, near Barnet.

I said no more to her, or she to me, a good while; but by and by, somebody calling her at a door a little way off, she desired me that if anybody called for the Barnet coach, I would step and call her at the house, which it seems was an alehouse. I said 'Yes,' very readily, and away she went.

She was no sooner gone but comes a wench and a child, puffing and sweating, and asks for the Barnet coach. I answered presently, 'Here.' 'Do you belong to the Barnet coach?' says she. 'Yes, sweetheart,' said I; 'what do you want?' 'I want room for two passengers,' says she. 'Where are they, sweetheart?' said I. 'Here's this girl; pray let her go into the coach,' says she, 'and I'll go and fetch my mistress.' 'Make haste, then, sweetheart,' says I, 'for we may be full else.' The maid had a great bundle under her arm; so she put the child into the coach, and I said, 'You had best put your bundle into the coach too.' 'No,' said she; 'I am afraid somebody should slip it away from the child.' 'Give it me, then,' said I. 'Take it, then,' says she, 'and be sure you take care of it.' 'I'll answer for it,' said I, 'if it were £20 value.' 'There, take it, then,' says she, and away she goes.

As soon as I got the bundle, and the maid was out of sight, I goes on towards the alehouse, where the porter's wife was, so that if I had met her, I had then only been going to give her the bundle and to call her to her business, as if I was going away and could stay no longer; but as I did not meet her, I walked away, and turning into Charterhouse Lane,* made off through Charterhouse Yard, into Long Lane, then into Bartholomew Close, so into Little Britain, and through the Bluecoat Hospital, to Newgate Street.

To prevent being known, I pulled off my blue apron, and wrapt the bundle in it, which was made up in a piece of painted calico; I also wrapt up my straw hat in it, and so put the bundle upon my head; and it was very well that I did thus, for coming through the Bluecoat Hospital, who should I meet but the wench that had given me the bundle to hold. It seems she was going with her mistress, whom she had been to fetch, to the Barnet coaches.

I saw she was in haste, and I had no business to stop her; so away she went, and I brought my bundle safe to my governess. There was no money, plate, or jewels in it, but a very good suit of Indian damask, a gown and petticoat, a laced head and ruffles of very good Flanders lace, and some other things, such as I knew very well the value of.

This was not indeed my own invention, but was given me by one that practised it with success, and my governess liked it extremely; and indeed I tried it again several times, though never twice near the same place; for the next time I tried in Whitechapel, just by the corner of Petticoat Lane, where the coaches stand that go out to Stratford and Bow, and that side of the country; and another time at the Flying Horse* without Bishopsgate, where the Cheston coaches then lay; and I had always the good luck to come off with some booty.

Another time I placed myself at a warehouse by the waterside, where the coasting vessels from the north come, such as Newcastle-upon-Tyne, Sunderland, and other places. Here, the warehouse being shut, comes a young fellow with a letter; and he wanted a box and a hamper that was come from Newcastle-upon-Tyne. I asked him if he had the marks of it; so he shows me the letter, by virtue of which he was to ask for it, and which gave an account of the contents, the box being full of linen and the hamper full of glass ware. I read the letter, and took care to see the name, and the marks, the name of the person that sent the goods, and the name of the person they were sent to; then I bade the messenger come in the morning, for that the warehouse-keeper would not be there any more that night.

Away went I, and wrote a letter from Mr John Richardson of Newcastle to his dear cousin, Jemmy Cole, in London, with an account that he had sent by such a vessel (for I remembered all the particulars to a tittle) so many pieces of huckaback linen,* and so many ells* of Dutch holland, and the like, in a box, and a hamper of flint glasses* from Mr Henzill's glass-house,* and that the box was marked I. C. No. 1, and the hamper was directed by a label on the cording.

About an hour after, I came to the warehouse, found the warehouse-keeper, and had the goods delivered me without any scruple; the value of the linen being about £22.

I could fill up this whole discourse with the variety of such adventures, which daily invention directed to, and which I managed with the utmost dexterity, and always with success.

At length – as when does the pitcher come safe home* that goes so often to the well? – I fell into some broils, which though they could not affect me fatally, yet made me known, which was the worst thing next to being found guilty that could befall me.

I had taken up the disguise of a widow's dress; it was without any real design in view, but only waiting for anything that might offer, as I often did. It happened that while I was going along a street in Covent Garden* there was a great cry of 'Stop thief, stop thief.' Some artists* had, it seems, put a trick upon a shopkeeper, and being pursued, some of them fled one way and some another; and one of them was, they said, dressed up in widow's weeds, upon which the mob gathered about me, and some said I was the person, others said no. Immediately came the mercer's journeyman, and he swore aloud I was the person, and so seized on me. However, when I was brought back by the mob to the mercer's shop, the master of the house said freely that I was not the woman, and would have let me go immediately, but another fellow said gravely, 'Pray stay till Mr—,' meaning the journeyman, 'comes back, for he knows her'; so they kept me near half an hour.

They had called a constable, and he stood in the shop as my jailer. In talking with the constable I inquired where he lived, and what trade he was; the man not apprehending in the least what happened afterwards, readily told me his name, and where he lived; and told me, as a jest, that I might be sure to hear of his name when I came to the Old Bailey. The servants likewise used me saucily, and had much ado to keep their hands off me; the master indeed was civiller to me than they; but he would not let me go, though he owned I was not in his shop before.

I began to be a little surly with him, and told him I hoped he would not take it ill if I made myself amends upon him another time; and desired I might send for friends to see me have right done. No, he said, he could give no such liberty; I might ask it when I came before the justice of peace; and seeing I threatened him, he would take care of me in the meantime, and would lodge me safe in Newgate. I told him it was his time now, but it would be mine by and by, and governed my passion as well as I was able. However, I spoke to the constable to call me a porter, which he did, and then I called for pen, ink, and paper, but they would let me have none. I asked the porter his name, and where he lived, and the poor man told it me very willingly. I bade him observe and remember how I was treated there; that he saw I was detained there by force. I told him I should want him in another place, and it should not be the worse for him to speak. The porter said he would serve me with all his heart. 'But, madam,' says he, 'let me hear them refuse to let you go, then I may be able to speak the plainer.'

With that, I spoke aloud to the master of the shop, and said, 'Sir, you know in your own conscience that I am not the person you look for, and that I was not in your shop before; therefore I demand that you detain me here no longer, or tell me the reason of your stopping me.' The fellow grew surlier upon this than before, and said he would do neither till he thought fit. 'Very well,' said I to the constable and to the porter; 'you will be pleased to remember this, gentlemen, another time.' The porter said, 'Yes, madam'; and the constable began not to like it, and would have persuaded the mercer to dismiss him, and let me go, since, as he said, he owned I was not the person. 'Good sir,' says the mercer to him tauntingly, 'are you a justice of peace or a constable? I charged you with her; pray do your duty.' The constable told him, a little moved, but very handsomely, 'I know my duty, and what I am, sir; I doubt you hardly know what you are doing.' They had some other hard words, and in the meantime the journeymen, impudent and unmanly to the last degree, used me barbarously, and one of them, the same that first seized upon me, pretended he would search me, and began to lay hands on me. I spit in his face, called out to the constable, and bade him take notice of my usage. 'And pray, Mr Constable,' said I, 'ask that villain's name,' pointing to the man. The constable reproved him decently, told him that he did not know what he did, for he knew that his master acknowledged I was not the person; 'and,' says the constable, 'I am afraid your master is bringing himself and me too, into trouble, if this gentlewoman comes to prove who she is, and where she was, and it appears that she is not the woman you pretend to.' 'D—n her,' says the fellow again, with an impudent, hardened face; 'she is the lady, you may depend upon it; I'll swear she is the same body that was in the shop, and that I gave the piece of satin that is lost into her own hand. You shall hear more of it when Mr William and Mr Anthony (those were other journeymen) come back; they will know her again as well as I.'

Just as the insolent rogue was talking thus to the constable, comes back Mr William and Mr Anthony, as he called them, and a great rabble with them, bringing along with them the true widow that I was pretended to be; and they came sweating and blowing into the shop, and with a great deal of triumph, dragging the poor creature in a most butcherly manner up towards their master, who was in the back shop; and they cried out aloud, 'Here's the widow, sir; we have catched her at last.' 'What do you mean by that?' says the master. 'Why, we have her already; there she sits, and Mr— says he can swear this is she.' The other man, whom they called Mr Anthony, replied, 'Mr— may say what he will and swear what he will, but this is the woman, and there's the remnant of satin she stole; I took it out of her clothes with my own hand.'

I now began to take a better heart, but smiled, and said nothing; the master looked pale; the constable turned about and looked at me. 'Let 'em alone, Mr Constable,' said I; 'let 'em go on.' The case was plain and could not be denied, so the constable was charged with the right thief, and the mercer told me very civilly he was sorry for the mistake, and hoped I would not take it ill; that they had so many things of this nature put upon them every day that they could not be blamed for being very sharp in doing themselves justice. 'Not take it ill, sir!' said I. 'How can I take it well? If you had dismissed me when your insolent fellow seized on me in the street and brought me to you, and when you yourself acknowledged I was not the person, I would have put it by, and not have taken it ill, because of the many ill things I believe you have put upon you daily; but your treatment of me since has been insufferable, and especially that of your servant; I must and will have reparation for that.'

Then he began to parley with me, said he would make me any reasonable satisfaction, and would fain have had me told him what it was I expected. I told him I should not be my own judge; the law should decide it for me; and as I was to be carried before a magistrate, I should let him hear there what I had to say. He told me there was no occasion to go before the justice now; I was at liberty to go where I pleased; and calling to the constable, told him he might let me go, for I was discharged. The constable said calmly to him, 'Sir, you asked me just now if I knew whether I was a constable or a justice, and bade me do my duty, and charged me with this gentlewoman as a prisoner. Now, sir, I find you do not understand what is my duty, for you would make me a justice indeed; but I must tell you it is not in my power; I may keep a prisoner when I am charged with him, but 'tis the law and the magistrate alone that can discharge that prisoner; therefore, 'tis a mistake, sir; I must carry her before a justice now, whether you think well of it or not.' The mercer was very high with the constable at first; but the constable happening to be not a hired officer,* but a good, substantial kind of man (I think he was a corn-chandler), and a man of good sense, stood to his business, would not discharge me without going to a justice of the peace, and I insisted upon it too. When the mercer saw that, 'Well,' says he to the constable, 'you may carry her where you please; I have nothing to say to her.' 'But, sir,' says the constable, 'you will go with us, I hope, for 'tis you that charged me with her.' 'No, not I,' says the mercer; 'I tell you I have nothing to say to her.' 'But pray, sir, do,' says the constable; 'I desire it of you for your own sake, for the justice can do nothing without you.' 'Prithee, fellow,' says the mercer, 'go about your business; I tell you I have nothing to say to the gentlewoman. I charge you in the king's name to dismiss her.' 'Sir,' says the constable, 'I find you don't know what it is to be a constable; I beg of you, don't oblige me to be rude to you.' 'I think I need not; you are rude enough already,' says the mercer. 'No, sir,' says the constable, 'I am not rude; you have broken the peace in bringing an honest woman out of the street, when she was about her lawful occasions, confining her in your shop, and ill-using her here by your servants; and now can you say I am rude to you? I think I am civil to you in not commanding you in the king's name to go with me, and charging every man I see that passes your door to aid and assist me in carrying you by force; this you know I have power to do, and yet I forbear it, and once more entreat you to go with me.' Well, he would not for all this, and gave the constable ill language. However, the constable kept his temper, and would not be provoked; and then I put in and said, 'Come, Mr Constable, let him alone; I shall find ways enough to fetch him before a magistrate, I don't fear that; but there's that fellow,' says I, 'he was the man that seized on me as I was innocently going along the street, and you are a witness of his violence with me since; give me leave to charge you with him, and carry him before a justice.' 'Yes, madam,' says the constable; and turning to the fellow, 'Come, young gentleman,' says he to the journeyman, 'you must go along with us; I hope you are not above the constable's power, though your master is.'

The fellow looked like a condemned thief, and hung back, then looked at his master, as if he could help him; and he, like a fool, encouraged the fellow to be rude, and he truly resisted the constable, and pushed him back with a good force when he went to lay hold on him, at which the constable knocked him down, and called out for help. Immediately the shop was filled with people, and the constable seized the master and man, and all his servants.

The first ill consequence of this fray was, that the woman who was really the thief made off, and got clear away in the crowd, and two others that they had stopped also; whether they were really guilty or not, that I can say nothing to.

By this time some of his neighbours having come in, and seeing how things went, had endeavoured to bring the mercer to his senses, and he began to be convinced that he was in the wrong; and so at length we went all very quietly before the justice, with a mob of about five hundred people at our heels; and all the way we went I could hear the people ask what was the matter, and others reply and say, a mercer had stopped a gentlewoman instead of a thief, and had afterwards taken the thief, and now the gentlewoman had taken the mercer, and was carrying him before the justice. This pleased the people strangely, and made the crowd increase, and they cried out as they went, 'Which is the rogue? which is the mercer?' and especially the women. Then when they saw him they cried out, 'That's he, that's he'; and every now and then came a good dab of dirt at him; and thus we marched a good while, till the mercer thought fit to desire the constable to call a coach to protect himself from the rabble; so we rode the rest of the way, the constable and I, and the mercer and his man.

When we came to the justice, which was an ancient gentleman in Bloomsbury, the constable giving first a summary account of the matter, the justice bade me speak, and tell what I had to say. And first he asked my name, which I was very loath to give, but there was no remedy; so I told him my name was Mary Flanders, that I was a widow, my husband being a sea-captain, died on a voyage to Virginia; and some other circumstances I told which he could never contradict, and that I lodged at present in town, with such a person, naming my governess; but that I was preparing to go over to America, where my husband's effects lay, and that I was going that day to buy some clothes to put myself into second mourning* but had not yet been in any shop, when that fellow, pointing to the mercer's journeyman, came rushing upon me with such fury as very much frighted me, and carried me back to his master's shop, where, though his master acknowledged I was not the person, yet he would not dismiss me, but charged a constable with me.

Then I proceeded to tell how the journeymen treated me; how they would not suffer me to send for any of my friends; how afterwards they found the real thief, and took the goods they had lost upon her, and all the particulars as before.

Then the constable related his case: his dialogue with the mercer about discharging me, and at last his servant's refusing to go with him, when I had charged him with him, and his master encouraging him to do so, and at last his striking the constable, and the like, all as I have told it already.

The justice then heard the mercer and his man. The mercer indeed made a long harangue of the great loss they have daily by the lifters and thieves; that it was easy for them to make a mistake, and that when he found it, he would have dismissed me, etc., as above. As to the journeyman, he had very little to say, but that he pretended other of the servants told him that I was really the person.

Upon the whole, the justice first of all told me very courteously I was discharged; that he was very sorry that the mercer's man should, in his eager pursuit, have so little discretion as to take up an innocent person for a guilty; that if he had not been so unjust as to detain me afterwards, he believed I would have forgiven the first affront; that, however, it was not in his power to award me any reparation, other than by openly reproving them, which he should do; but he supposed I would apply to such methods as the law directed; in the meantime he would bind him over.

But as to the breach of the peace committed by the journeyman, he told me he should give me some satisfaction for that, for he should commit him to Newgate for assaulting the constable, and for assaulting of me also.

Accordingly he sent the fellow to Newgate for that assault, and his master gave bail, and so we came away; but I had the satisfaction of seeing the mob wait upon them both, as they came out, hallooing and throwing stones and dirt at the coaches they rode in; and so I came home.

After this hustle, coming home and telling my governess the story, she falls a-laughing at me. 'Why are you so merry?' says I; 'the story has not so much laughing-room in it as you imagine. I am sure I have had a great deal of hurry and fright too, with a pack of ugly rogues.' 'Laugh!' says my governess; 'I laugh, child, to see what a lucky creature you are; why, this job will be the best bargain to you that ever you made in your life, if you manage it well. I warrant you, you shall make the mercer pay £500 for damages, besides what you shall get of the journeyman.'

I had other thoughts of the matter than she had; and especially, because I had given in my name to the justice of peace; and I knew that my name was so well known among the people at Hick's Hall,* the Old Bailey, and such places that if this cause came to be tried openly, and my name came to be inquired into, no court would give much damages, for the reputation of a person of such a character. However, I was obliged to begin a prosecution in form, and accordingly my governess found me out a very creditable sort of man to manage it, being an attorney of very good business, and of good reputation, and she was certainly in the right of this; for had she employed a pettifogging hedge solicitor,* or a man not known, I should have brought it to but little.

I met this attorney, and gave him all the particulars at large, as they are recited above; and he assured me it was a case, as he said, that he did not question but that a jury would give very considerable damages; so taking his full instructions, he began the prosecution, and the mercer being arrested, gave bail. A few days after his giving bail, he comes with his attorney to my attorney, to let him know that he desired to accommodate the matter; that it was all carried on in the heat of an unhappy passion; that his client, meaning me, had a sharp provoking tongue, and that I used them ill, gibing at them and jeering them, even while they believed me to be the very person, and that I had provoked them, and the like.

My attorney managed as well on my side; made them believe I was a widow of fortune, that I was able to do myself justice, and had great friends to stand by me too, who had all made me promise to sue to the utmost, if it cost me a thousand pounds, for that the affronts I had received were insufferable.

However, they brought my attorney to this, that he promised he would not blow the coals; that if I inclined to an accommodation, he would not hinder me, and that he would rather persuade me to peace than to war; for which they told him he should be no loser; all which he told me very honestly, and told me that if they offered him any bribe, I should certainly know it; but, upon the whole, he told me very honestly that, if I would take his opinion, he would advise me to make it up with them, for that as they were in a great fright, and were desirous above all things to make it up, and knew that, let it be what it would, they must bear all the costs, he believed they would give me freely more than any jury would give upon a trial. I asked him what he thought they would be brought to; he told me he could not tell as to that, but he would tell me more when I saw him again.

Some time after this they came again, to know if he had talked with me. He told them he had; that he found me not so averse to an accommodation as some of my friends were, who resented the disgrace offered me, and set me on; that they blowed the coals in secret, prompting me to revenge, or to do myself justice, as they called it; so that he could not tell what to say to it; he told them he would do his endeavour to persuade me, but he ought to be able to tell me what proposal they made. They pretended they could not make any proposal, because it might be made use of against them; and he told them, that by the same rule he could not make any offers, for that might be pleaded in abatement of what damages a jury might be inclined to give. However, after some discourse, and mutual promises that no advantage should be taken on either side by what was transacted then, or at any other of those meetings, they came to a kind of treaty; but so remote, and so wide from one another, that nothing could be expected from it; for my attorney demanded £500 and charges, and they offered £50 without charges; so they broke off, and the mercer proposed to have a meeting with me myself; and my attorney agreed to that very readily.

My attorney gave me notice to come to this meeting in good clothes, and with some state, that the mercer might see I was something more than I seemed to be that time they had me. Accordingly I came in a new suit of second mourning, according to what I had said at the justice's. I set myself out,* too, as well as a widow's dress would admit; my governess also furnished me with a good pearl necklace, that shut in behind with a locket of diamonds, which she had in pawn; and I had a very good gold watch by my side; so that I made a very good figure; and as I stayed till I was sure they were come, I came in a coach to the door, with my maid with me.

When I came into the room the mercer was surprised. He stood up and made his bow, which I took a little notice of, and but a little, and went and sat down where my own attorney had appointed me to sit, for it was his house. After a while the mercer said, he did not know me again, and began to make some compliments. I told him, I believed he did not know me, at first; and that if he had, he would not have treated me as he did.

He told me he was very sorry for what had happened, and that it was to testify the willingness he had to make all possible reparation that he had appointed this meeting; that he hoped I would not carry things to extremity, which might be not only too great a loss to him, but might be the ruin of his business and shop, in which case I might have the satisfaction of repaying an injury with an injury ten times greater; but that I would then get nothing, whereas he was willing to do me any justice that was in his power, without putting himself or me to the trouble or charge of a suit at law.

I told him I was glad to hear him talk so much more like a man of sense than he did before; that it was true, acknowledgment in most cases of affronts was counted reparation sufficient; but this had gone too far to be made up so; that I was not revengeful, nor did I seek his ruin, or any man's else, but that all my friends were unanimous not to let me so far neglect my character as to adjust a thing of this kind without reparation; that to be taken up for a thief was such an indignity as could not be put up with; that my character was above being treated so by any that knew me, but because in my condition of a widow I had been careless of myself, I might be taken for such a creature; but that for the particular usage I had from him afterward, – and then I repeated all as before; it was so provoking, I had scarce patience to repeat it.

He acknowledged all, and was mighty humble indeed; he came up to £100 and to pay all the law charges, and added that he would make me a present of a very good suit of clothes. I came down to £300 and demanded that I should publish an advertisement of the particulars in the common newspapers.

This was a clause he never could comply with. However, at last he came up, by good management of my attorney, to £150 and a suit of black silk clothes; and there, as it were, at my attorney's request, I complied, he paying my attorney's bill and charges, and gave us a good supper into the bargain.

When I came to receive the money, I brought my governess with me, dressed like an old duchess, and a gentleman very well dressed, who we pretended courted me, but I called him cousin, and the lawyer was only to hint privately to them that this gentleman courted the widow.

He treated us handsomely indeed, and paid the money cheerfully enough; so that it cost him £200 in all, or rather more. At our last meeting, when all was agreed, the case of the journeyman came up, and the mercer begged very hard for him; told me he was a man that had kept a shop of his own, and been in good business, had a wife and several children, and was very poor; that he had nothing to make satisfaction with, but should beg my pardon on his knees. I had no spleen at the saucy rogue, nor were his submissions anything to me, since there was nothing to be got by him, so I thought it was as good to throw that in generously as not; so I told him I did not desire the ruin of any man, and therefore at his request I would forgive the wretch, it was below me to seek any revenge.

When we were at supper he brought the poor fellow in to make his acknowledgment, which he would have done with as much mean humility as his offence was with insulting pride; in which he was an instance of complete baseness of spirit, imperious, cruel, and relentless when uppermost, abject and low-spirited when down. However, I abated his cringes, told him I forgave him, and desired he might withdraw, as if I did not care for the sight of him, though I had forgiven him.

I was now in good circumstances indeed, if I could have known my time for leaving off, and my governess often said I was the richest of the trade in England; and so I believe I was, for I had £700 by me in money, besides clothes, rings, some plate, and two gold watches, and all of them stolen; for I had innumerable jobs, besides these I have mentioned. Oh! had I even now had the grace of repentance, I had still leisure to have looked back upon my follies, and have made some reparation; but the satisfaction I was to make for the public mischiefs I had done was yet left behind; and I could not forbear going abroad again, as I called it now, any more than I could when my extremity really drove me out for bread.

It was not long after the affair with the mercer was made up, that I went out in an equipage* quite different from any I had ever appeared in before. I dressed myself like a beggar-woman, in the coarsest and most despicable rags I could get, and I walked about peering and peeping into every door and window I came near; and, indeed, I was in such a plight now that I knew as ill how to behave in as ever I did in any. I naturally abhorred dirt and rags; I had been bred up tight* and cleanly, and could be no other, whatever condition I was in, so that this was the most uneasy disguise to me that ever I put on. I said presently to myself that this would not do, for this was a dress that everybody was shy and afraid of; and I thought everybody looked at me as if they were afraid I should come near them, lest I should take something from them, or afraid to come near me, lest they should get something from me. I wandered about all the evening the first time I went out, and made nothing of it, and came home again wet, draggled, and tired. However, I went out again the next night, and then I met with a little adventure, which had like to have cost me dear. As I was standing near a tavern door, there comes a gentleman on horseback, and lights at the door, and wanting to go into the tavern, he calls one of the drawers to hold his horse. He stayed pretty long in the tavern, and the drawer heard his master call, and thought he would be angry with him. Seeing me stand by him, he called to me. 'Here, woman,' says he, 'hold this horse awhile, till I go in; if the gentleman comes, he'll give you something.' 'Yes,' says I, and takes the horse, and walks off with him soberly, and carried him to my governess.

This had been a booty to those that had undertood it; but never was poor thief more at a loss to know what to do with anything that was stolen; for when I came home, my governess was quite confounded, and what to do with the creature we neither of us knew. To send him to a stable was doing nothing, for it was certain that notice would be given in the Gazette,* and the horse described, so that we durst not go to fetch it again.

All the remedy we had for this unlucky adventure was to go and set up the horse at an inn, and send a note by a porter to the tavern, that the gentleman's horse that was lost at such a time, was left at such an inn, and that he might be had there; that the poor woman that held him, having led him about the street, not being able to lead him back again, had left him there. We might have waited till the owner had published, and offered a reward, but we did not care to venture the receiving the reward.

So this was a robbery and no robbery, for little was lost by it, and nothing was got by it, and I was quite sick of going out in a beggar's dress; it did not answer at all, and besides, I thought it ominous and threatening.

While I was in this disguise, I fell in with a parcel of folks of a worse kind than any I ever sorted* with, and I saw a little into their ways too. These were coiners of money, and they made some very good offers to me, as to profit; but the part they would have had me embark in was the most dangerous. I mean that of the very working of the die, as they call it, which, had I been taken, had been certain death, and that at a stake; I say, to be burnt to death at a stake;* so that though I was to appearance but a beggar, and they promised mountains of gold and silver to me to engage, yet it would not do. 'Tis true, if I had been really a beggar, or had been desperate as when I began, I might, perhaps, have closed with it; for what care they to die, that cannot tell how to live? But at present that was not my condition, at least, I was for no such terrible risks as those; besides, the very thought of being burnt at a stake struck terror to my very soul, chilled my blood, and gave me the vapours to such a degree, as I could not think of it without trembling.

This put an end to my disguise too, for though I did not like the proposal, yet I did not tell them so, but seemed to relish it, and promised to meet again. But I durst see them no more; for if I had seen them, and not complied, though I had declined it with the greatest assurances of secrecy in the world, they would have gone near to have murdered me, to make sure work, and make themselves easy, as they call it. What kind of easiness that is, they may best judge that understand how easy men are that can murder people to prevent danger.

This and horse-stealing were things quite out of my way, and I might easily resolve I would have no more to say to them. My business seemed to lie another way, and though it had hazard enough in it too, yet it was more suitable to me, and what had more of art in it, and more chances for a coming off if a surprise should happen.

I had several proposals made also to me about that time, to come into a gang of housebreakers; but that was a thing I had no mind to venture at neither, any more than I had at the coining trade.

I offered to go along with two men and a woman, that made it their business to get into houses by stratagem. I was willing enough to venture, but there were three of them already, and they did not care to part,* nor I to have too many in a gang; so I did not close with them, and they paid dear for their next attempt.

But at length I met with a woman that had often told me what adventures she had made, and with success, at the waterside, and I closed with her, and we drove on our business pretty well. One day we came among some Dutch people at St Catharine's,* where we went on pretence to buy goods that were privately got on shore. I was two or three times in a house where we saw a good quantity of prohibited goods, and my companion once brought away three pieces of Dutch black silk that turned to good account, and I had my share in it; but in all the journeys I made by myself, I could not get an opportunity to do anything, so I laid it aside, for I had been there so often that they began to suspect something.

This balked me a little, and I resolved to push at something or other, for I was not used to come back so often without purchase; so the next day I dressed myself up fine, and took a walk to the other end of the town. I passed through the Exchange* in the Strand, but had no notion of finding anything to do there, when on a sudden I saw a great clutter in the place, and all the people, shopkeepers as well as others, standing up and staring; and what should it be but some great duchess coming into the Exchange, and they said the queen was coming. I set myself close up to a shopside with my back to the counter, as if to let the crowd pass by, when keeping my eye on a parcel of lace which the shopkeeper was showing to some ladies that stood by me, the shopkeeper and her maid were so taken up with looking to see who was a-coming, and what shop they would go to, that I found means to slip a paper of lace into my pocket, and come clear off with it; so the lady milliner paid dear enough for her gaping after the queen.

I went off from the shop, as if driven along by the throng, and mingling myself with the crowd, went out at the other door of the Exchange, and so got away before they missed their lace; and because I would not be followed, I called a coach, and shut myself up in it. I had scarce shut the coach doors, but I saw the milliner's maid and five or six more come running out into the street, and crying out as if they were frighted. They did not cry 'Stop, thief!' because nobody ran away, but I could hear the word 'robbed' and 'lace' two or three times, and saw the wench wringing her hands, and run starting to and again, like one scared. The coachman that had taken me up was getting up into the box, but was not quite up, and the horses had not begun to move, so that I was terrible uneasy, and I took the packet of lace and laid it ready to have dropped it out at the flap of the coach, which opens before, just behind the coachman; but to my great satisfaction, in less than a minute the coach began to move, that is to say, as soon as the coachman had got up and spoken to his horses; so he drove away, and I brought off my purchase, which was worth near £20.

The next day I dressed me up again, but in quite different clothes, and walked the same way again, but nothing offered till I came into St James's Park.* I saw abundance of fine ladies in the park, walking in the Mall, and among the rest, there was a little miss, a young lady of about twelve or thirteen years old, and she had a sister, as I supposed, with her that might be about nine. I observed the biggest had a fine gold watch on, and a good necklace of pearl, and they had a footman in livery with them; but as it is not usual for the footmen to go behind the ladies in the Mall, so I observed the footman stopped at their going into the Mall, and the biggest of the sisters spoke to him, to bid him be just there when they came back.

When I heard her dismiss the footman, I stepped up to him, and asked him what little lady that was? and held a little chat with him, about what a pretty child it was with her, and how genteel and well carriaged the eldest would be: how womanish, and how grave; and the fool of a fellow told me presently who she was; that she was Sir Thomas —'s eldest daughter, of Essex, and that she was a great fortune; that her mother was not come to town yet; but she was with Sir William —'s lady at her lodgings in Suffolk Street,* and a great deal more; that they had a maid and a woman to wait on them, besides Sir Thomas's coach, the coachman, and himself; and that young lady was governess to the whole family, as well here as at home; and told me abundance of things, enough for my business.

I was well dressed, and had my gold watch as well as she; so I left the footman, and I puts myself in a rank* with this lady, having stayed till she had taken one turn in the Mall, and was going forward again; by and by I saluted her by her name, with the title of Lady Betty. I asked her when she heard from her father; when my lady her mother would be in town, and how she did.

I talked so familiarly to her of her whole family that she could not suspect but that I knew them all intimately. I asked her why she would come abroad without Mrs Chime with her (that was the name of her woman) to take care of Mrs Judith, that was her sister. Then I entered into a long chat with her about her sister; what a fine little lady she was, and asked her if she had learned French; and a thousand such little things, when on a sudden the guards came, and the crowd ran to see the king go by to the Parliament House.

The ladies ran all to the side of the Mall, and I helped my lady to stand upon the edge of the boards on the side of the Mall, that she might be high enough to see; and took the little one and lifted her quite up; during which, I took care to convey the gold watch so clean away from the Lady Betty, that she never missed it till the crowd was gone, and she was gotten into the middle of the Mall.

I took my leave in the very crowd, and said, as if in haste, 'Dear Lady Betty, take care of your little sister.' And so the crowd did as it were thrust me away, and that I was unwilling to take my leave.

The hurry in such cases is immediately over, and the place clear as soon as the king is gone by; but as there is always a great running and clutter just as the king passes, so having dropped the two little ladies, and done my business with them, without any miscarriage, I kept hurrying on among the crowd, as if I ran to see the king, and so I kept before the crowd till I came to the end of the Mall, when the king going on toward the Horse Guards,* I went forward to the passage, which went then through against the end of the Haymarket, and there I bestowed a coach upon myself, and made off; and I confess I have not yet been so good as my word, viz., to go and visit my Lady Betty.

I was once in the mind to venture staying with Lady Betty till she missed the watch, and so have made a great outcry about it with her, and have got her into her coach, and put myself in the coach with her, and have gone home with her; for she appeared so fond of me, and so perfectly deceived by my so readily talking to her of all her relations and family, that I thought it was very easy to push the thing further, and to have got at least the necklace of pearl; but when I considered that though the child would not perhaps have suspected me, other people might, and that if I was searched I should be discovered, I thought it was best to go off with what I had got.

I came accidently afterwards to hear, that when the young lady missed her watch, she made a great outcry in the park, and sent her footman up and down to see if he could find me, she having described me so perfectly that he knew it was the same person that had stood and talked so long with him, and asked him so many questions about them; but I was gone far enough out of their reach before she could come at her footman to tell him the story.

I made another adventure after this, of a nature different from all I had been concerned in yet, and this was at a gaming-house near Covent Garden.

I saw several people go in and out; and I stood in the passage a good while with another woman with me, and seeing a gentleman go up that seemed to be of more than ordinary fashion, I said to him, 'Sir, pray don't they give women leave to go up?' 'Yes, madam,' says he, 'and to play too, if they please.' 'I mean so, sir,' said I. And with that he said he would introduce me if I had a mind; so I followed him to the door, and he looking in, 'There, madam,' says he, 'are the gamesters, if you have a mind to venture.' I looked in, and said to my comrade aloud, 'Here's nothing but men; I won't venture.' At which one of the gentlemen cried out, 'You need not be afraid, madam, here's none but fair gamesters; you are very welcome to come and set* what you please.' So I went a little nearer and looked on, and some of them brought me a chair, and I sat down and saw the box and dice go round apace; then I said to my comrade, 'The gentlemen play too high for us; come, let us go.'

The people were all very civil, and one gentleman encouraged me, and said, 'Come, madam, if you please to venture, if you dare trust me, I'll answer for it you shall have nothing put upon you here.' 'No, sir,' said I, smiling, 'I hope the gentlemen would not cheat a woman.' But still I declined venturing, though I pulled out a purse with money in it, that they might see I did not want money.

After I had sat awhile, one gentleman said to me, jeering, 'Come, madam, I see you are afraid to venture for yourself; I always had good luck with the ladies, you shall set for me, if you won't set for yourself.' I told him, 'Sir, I should be very loath to lose your money,' though I added, 'I am pretty lucky too; but the gentlemen play so high, and I dare not venture my own.'

'Well, well,' says he, 'there's ten guineas, madam; set them for me'; so I took the money and set, himself looking on. I run out the guineas by one and two at a time, and then the box coming to the next man to me, my gentleman gave me ten guineas more, and made me set five of them at once, and the gentleman who had the box threw out,* so there was five guineas of his money again. He was encouraged at this, and made me take the box, which was a bold venture: however, I held the box so long that I gained him his whole money, and had a handful of guineas in my lap; and which was the better luck, when I threw out, I threw but at one or two of those that had set me, and so went off easy.

When I was come this length, I offered the gentleman all the gold, for it was his own; and so would have had him play for himself, pretending that I did not understand the game well enough. He laughed, and said if I had but good luck, it was no matter whether I understood the game or no; but I should not leave off. However, he took out the fifteen guineas that he had put in first, and bade me play with the rest. I would have him to have seen how much I had got, but he said, 'No, no, don't tell them, I believe you are very honest, and 'tis bad luck to tell them'; so I played on.

I understood the game well enough, though I pretended I did not, and played cautiously, which was to keep a good stock in my lap, out of which I every now and then conveyed some into my pocket, but in such a manner as I was sure he could not see it.

I played a great while, and had very good luck for him; but the last time I held the box they set me high, and I threw boldly at all, and held the box till I had gained near fourscore guineas, but lost above half of it back at the last throw; so I got up, for I was afraid I should lose it all back again, and said to him, 'Pray come, sir, now, and take it and play for yourself; I think I have done pretty well for you.' He would have had me play on, but it grew late, and I desired to be excused. When I gave it up to him, I told him I hoped he would give me leave to tell it now, that I might see what he had gained, and how lucky I had been for him; when I told* them, there were threescore and three guineas. 'Ay,' says I, 'if it had not been for that unlucky throw, I had got you a hundred guineas.' So I gave him all the money, but he would not take it till I had put my hand into it, and taken some for myself, and bid me please myself. I refused it, and was positive I would not take it myself; if he had a mind to do anything of that kind, it should be all his own doings.

The rest of the gentlemen seeing us striving, cried, 'Give it her all'; but I absolutely refused that. Then one of them said, 'D—n ye, Jack, halve it with her; don't you know you should be always on even terms with the ladies.' So, in short, he divided it with me, and I brought away thirty guineas, besides about forty-three which I had stole privately which I was sorry for, because he was so generous.

Thus I brought home seventy-three guineas, and let my old governess see what good luck I had at play. However, it was her advice that I should not venture again, and I took her counsel, for I never went there any more; for I knew as well as she, if the itch of play came in, I might soon lose that, and all the rest of what I had got.

Fortune had smiled upon me to that degree, and I had thriven so much, and my governess too, for she always had a share with me, that really the old gentlewoman began to talk of leaving off while we were well, and being satisfied with what we had got; but I know not what fate guided me, I was as backward to it now, as she was when I proposed it to her before, and so in an ill hour we gave over the thoughts of it for the present, and, in a word, I grew more hardened and audacious than ever, and the success I had made my name as famous as any thief of my sort ever had been.

I had sometimes taken the liberty to play the same game over again, which is not according to practice, which however succeeded not amiss; but generally I took up new figures, and contrived to appear in new shapes every time I went abroad.

It was now a rumbling* time of the year, and the gentlemen being most of them gone out of town, Tunbridge, and Epsom,* and such places, were full of people. But the city was thin, and I thought our trade felt it a little, as well as others; so that at the latter end of the year I joined myself with a gang, who usually go every year to Stourbridge Fair, and from thence to Bury Fair,* in Suffolk. We promised ourselves great things here, but when I came to see how things were, I was weary of it presently; for except mere picking of pockets, there was little worth meddling with; neither if a booty had been made, was it so easy carrying it off, nor was there such a variety of occasion for business in our way, as in London; all that I made of the whole journey was a gold watch at Bury Fair, and a small parcel of linen at Cambridge, which gave me occasion to take leave of the place. It was an old bite,* and I thought might do with a country shop-keeper, though in London it would not.

I bought at a linendraper's shop, not in the fair, but in the town of Cambridge, as much fine Holland, and other things, as came to about £7; when I had done I bade them be sent to such an inn, where I had taken up my being the same morning, as if I was to lodge there that night.

I ordered the draper to send them home to me, about such an hour, to the inn where I lay, and I would pay him his money. At the time appointed the draper sends the goods, and I placed one of our gang at the chamber door, and when the innkeeper's maid brought the messenger to the door, who was a young fellow, an apprentice, almost a man, she tells him her mistress was asleep, but if he would leave the things and call in about an hour, I should be awake, and he might have the money. He left the parcel very readily, and goes his way, and in about half an hour my maid and I walked off, and that very evening I hired a horse, and a man to ride before me, and went to Newmarket, and from thence got my passage in a coach that was not quite full to Bury St Edmunds, where, as I told you, I could make but little of my trade, only at a little country opera-house I got a gold watch from a lady's side, who was not only intolerably merry, but a little fuddled, which made my work much easier.

I made off with this little booty to Ipswich, and from thence to Harwich,* where I went into an inn, as if I had newly arrived from Holland, not doubting but I should make some purchase* among the foreigners that came on shore there; but I found them generally empty of things of value, except what was in their portmanteaus and Dutch hampers, which were always guarded by footmen; however, I fairly* got one of their portmanteaus one evening out of the chamber where the gentlemen lay, the footman being fast asleep on the bed, and I suppose very drunk.

The room in which I lodged lay next to the Dutchman's, and having dragged the heavy thing with much ado out of the chamber into mine, I went out into the street to see if I could find any possibility of carrying it off. I walked about a great while, but could see no probability either of getting out the thing, or of conveying away the goods that were in it, the town being so small, and I a perfect stranger in it; so I was returning with a resolution to carry it back again, and leave it where I found it. Just at that very moment I heard a man make a noise to some people to make haste, for the boat was going to put off and the tide would be spent. I called the fellow: 'What boat is it, friend,' said I, 'that you belong to?' 'The Ipswich wherry, madam,' says he. 'When do you go off?' says I. 'This moment, madam,' says he; 'do you want to go thither?' 'Yes,' said I, 'if you can stay till I fetch my things.' 'Where are your things, madam?' says he. 'At such an inn,' said I. 'Well, I'll go with you, madam,' says he, very civilly, 'and bring them for you.' 'Come away then,' says I, and takes him with me.

The people of the inn were in a great hurry, the packet-boat from Holland being just come in, and two coaches just come also with passengers from London for another packet-boat that was going off for Holland, which coaches were to go back next day with the passengers that were just landed. In this hurry it was that I came to the bar, and paid my reckoning telling my landlady I had gotten my passsage by sea in a wherry.

These wherries are large vessels, with good accommodation for carrying passengers from Harwich to London; and though they are called wherries, which is a word used in the Thames for a small boat, rowed with one or two men, yet these are vessels able to carry twenty passengers, and ten or fifteen tons of goods, and fitted to bear the sea. All this I had found out by inquiring the night before into the several ways of going to London.

My landlady was very courteous, took my money for the reckoning, but was called away, all the house being in a hurry. So I left her, took the fellow up into my chamber, gave him the trunk, or portmanteau, for it was like a trunk, and wrapped it about with an old apron, and he went directly to his boat with it, and I after him, nobody asking us the least question about it. As for the drunken Dutch footman, he was still asleep, and his master with other foreign gentlemen at supper, and very merry below; so I went clean off with it to Ipswich, and going in the night, the people of the house knew nothing but that I was gone to London by the Harwich wherry, as I had told my landlady.

I was plagued at Ipswich with the custom-house officers, who stopped my trunk, as I called it, and would open and search it. I was willing, I told them, that they should search it, but my husband had the key, and that he was not yet come from Harwich; this I said, that if upon searching it they should find all the things be such as properly belonged to a man rather than a woman, it should not seem strange to them. However, they being positive to open the trunk, I consented to have it broken open, that is to say, to have the lock taken off, which was not difficult.

They found nothing for their turn, for the trunk had been searched before; but they discovered several things much to my satisfaction, as particularly a parcel of money in French pistoles, and some Dutch ducatoons* or rix-dollars, and the rest was chiefly two periwigs, wearing-linen, razors, wash-balls,* perfumes, and other useful things necessary for a gentleman, which all passed for my husband's, and so I was quit of them.

It was now very early in the morning, and not light, and I knew not well what course to take; for I made no doubt but I should be pursued in the morning, and perhaps be taken with the things about me; so I resolved upon taking new measures. I went publicly to an inn in the town with my trunk, as I called it, and having taken the substance out, I did not think the lumber of it worth my concern; however, I gave it the landlady of the house with a charge to take care of it, and lay it up safe till I should come again, and away I walked into the street.

When I was got into the town a great way from the inn, I met with an ancient woman who had just opened her door, and I fell into chat with her, and asked her a great many wild questions of things all remote to my purpose and design; but in my discourse I found by her how the town was situated, that I was in a street which went out towards Hadley, but that such a street went towards the water-side, such a street went into the heart of the town, and at last, such a street went towards Colchester, and so the London road lay there.

I had soon my ends* of this old woman, for I only wanted to know which was the London road, and away I walked as fast as I could; not that I intended to go on foot, either to London or to Colchester, but I wanted to get quietly away from Ipswich.

I walked about two or three miles, and then I met a plain countryman, who was busy about some husbandry work, I did not know what, and I asked him a great many questions, first, not much to the purpose, but at last told him I was going for London, and the coach was full, and I could not get a passage, and asked him if he could not tell me where to hire a horse that could carry double, and an honest man to ride before me to Colchester, so that I might get a place there in the coaches. The honest clown looked earnestly at me, and said nothing for above half a minute, when, scratching his poll,* 'A horse, say you, and to Colchester, to carry double? why yes, mistress, alack-a-day, you may have horses enough for money.' 'Well, friend,' says I, 'that I take for granted; I don't expect it without money.' 'Why, but mistress,' says he, 'how much are you willing to give?' 'Nay,' says I again, 'friend, I don't know what your rates are in the country here, for I am a stranger; but if you can get one for me, get it as cheap as you can, and I'll give you somewhat for your pains.'

'Why, that's honestly said, too,' says the countryman. 'Not so honest, neither,' said I to myself, 'if thou knewest all.' 'Why, mistress,' says he, 'I have a horse that will carry double, and I don't much care if I go myself with you, an' you like.' 'Will you?' says I; 'well, I believe you are an honest man; if you will, I shall be glad of it; I'll pay you in reason.' 'Why, look ye, mistress,' says he, 'I won't be out of-reason with you; then if I carry you to Colchester, it will be worth five shillings for myself and my horse, for I shall hardly come back to-night.'

In short, I hired the honest man and his horse; but when we came to a town* upon the road (I do not remember the name of it, but it stands upon a river), I pretended myself very ill, and I could go no farther that night, but if he would stay there with me, because I was a stranger, I would pay him for himself and his horse with all my heart.

This I did because I knew the Dutch gentlemen and their servants would be upon the road that day, either in the stage-coaches or riding post, and I did not know but the drunken fellow, or somebody else that might have seen me at Harwich, might see me again, and I thought that in one day's stop they would be all gone by.

We lay all that night there, and the next morning it was not very early when I set out, so that it was near ten o'clock by the time I got to Colchester. It was no little pleasure that I saw the town where I had so many pleasant days, and I made many inquiries after the good old friends I had once had there, but could make little out; they were all dead or removed. The young ladies had been all married or gone to London; the old gentleman, and the old lady that had been my early benefactress, all dead; and which troubled me most, the young gentleman my first lover, and afterwards my brother-in law, was dead; but two sons, men grown, were left of him, but they too were transplanted to London.

I dismissed my old man here, and stayed incognito for three or four days in Colchester, and then took a passage in a wagon, because I would not venture being seen in the Harwich coaches. But I needed not have used so much caution, for there was nobody in Harwich but the woman of the house could have known me; nor was it rational to think that she, considering the hurry she was in, and that she never saw me but once, and that by candle-light, should have ever discovered me.

I was now returned to London, and though by the accident of the last adventure, I got something considerable, yet I was not fond of any more country rambles; nor should I have ventured abroad again if I had carried the trade on to the end of my days. I gave my governess a history of my travels; she liked the Harwich journey well enough, and in discoursing of these things between ourselves she observed that a thief being a creature that watches the advantages of other people's mistakes, 'tis impossible but that to one that is vigilant and industrious many opportunities must happen, and therefore she thought that one so exquisitely keen in the trade as I was, would scarce fail of something wherever I went.

On the other hand, every branch of my story, if duly considered, may be useful to honest people, and afford a due caution to people of some sort or other to guard against the like surprises, and to have their eyes about them when they have to do with strangers of any kind, for 'tis very seldom that some snare or other is not in their way. The moral indeed, of all my history is left to be gathered by the senses and judgment of the reader; I am not qualified to preach to them. Let the experience of one creature completely wicked, and completely miserable, be a storehouse of useful warning to those that read.

I am drawing now towards a new variety of life. Upon my return, being hardened by a long race of crime, and success unparalleled, I had, as I have said, no thoughts of laying down a trade, which, if I was to judge by the example of others, must, however, end at last in misery and sorrow.

It was on the Christmas Day following, in the evening, that, to finish a long train of wickedness, I went abroad to see what might offer in my way; when going by a working silversmith's in Forster Lane,* I saw a tempting bait indeed, and not to be resisted by one of my occupation, for the shop had nobody in it, and a great deal of loose plate lay in the window, and at the seat of the man, who, I suppose, worked at one side of the shop.

I went boldly in, and was just going to lay my hand upon a piece of plate, and might have done it, and carried it clear off, for any care that the men who belonged to the shop had taken of it; but an officious fellow in a house on the other side of the way, seeing me go in, and that there was nobody in the shop, comes running over the street, and without asking me what I was, or who, seizes upon me, and cries out for the people of the house.

I had not touched anything in the shop, and seeing a glimpse of somebody running over, I had so much presence of mind as to knock very hard with my foot on the floor of the house, and was just calling out too, when the fellow laid hands on me.

However, as I had always most courage when I was in most danger, so when he laid hands on me, I stood very high upon it, that I came in to buy half a dozen of silver spoons; and to my good fortune, it was a silversmith's that sold plate, as well as worked plate for other shops. The fellow laughed at that part, and put such a value upon the service that he had done his neighbour, that he would have it be, that I came not to buy, but to steal; and raising a great crowd, I said to the master of the shop, who by this time was fetched home from some neighbouring place, that it was in vain to make a noise, and enter into talk there of the case; the fellow had insisted that I came to steal, and he must prove it, and I desired we might go before a magistrate without any more words; for I began to see I should be too hard for the man that had seized me.

The master and mistress of the shop were really not so violent as the man from t'other side of the way; and the man said, 'Mistress, you might come into the shop with a good design for aught I know, but it seemed a dangerous thing for you to come into such a shop as mine is, when you see nobody there; and I cannot do so little justice to my neighbour, who was so kind, as not to acknowledge he had reason on his side; though, upon the whole, I do not find you attempted to take anything, and I really know not what to do in it.' I pressed him to go before a magistrate with me, and if anything could be proved on me, that was like a design, I should willingly submit, but if not, I expected reparation.

Just while we were in this debate, and a crowd of people gathered about the door, came by Sir T. B., an alderman of the city, and justice of the peace, and the goldsmith hearing of it, entreated his worship to come in and decide the case.

Give the goldsmith his due, he told his story with a great deal of justice and moderation, and the fellow that had come over, and seized upon me, told his with as much heat and foolish passion, which did me good still. It came then to my turn to speak, and I told his worship that I was a stranger in London, being newly come out of the north; that I lodged in such a place, that I was passing this street, and went into a goldsmith's shop to buy half a dozen of spoons. By great good luck I had an old silver spoon in my pocket, which I pulled out, and told him I had carried that spoon to match it with half a dozen of new ones, that it might match some I had in the country; that seeing nobody in the shop, I knocked with my foot very hard to make the people hear, and had also called aloud with my voice; 'tis true, there was loose plate in the shop, but that nobody could say I had touched any of it; that a fellow came running into the shop out of the street, and laid hands on me in a furious manner, in the very moment while I was calling for the people of the house; that if he had really had a mind to have done his neighbour any service, he should have stood at a distance, and silently watched to see whether I had touched anything or no, and then have taken me in the fact. 'That is very true,' says Mr Alderman, and turning to the fellow that stopped me, he asked him if it was true that I knocked with my foot? He said yes, I had knocked, but that might be because of his coming. 'Nay,' says the alderman, taking him short, 'now you contradict yourself, for just now you said she was in the shop with her back to you, and did not see you till you came upon her.' Now it was true that my back was partly to the street, but yet as my business was of a kind that required me to have eyes every way, so I really had a glance of him running over, as I said before, though he did not perceive it.

After a full hearing, the alderman gave it as his opinion, that his neighbour was under a mistake, and that I was innocent, and the goldsmith acquiesced in it too, and his wife, and so I was dismissed; but as I was going to depart, Mr Alderman said, 'But hold, madam, if you were designing to buy spoons, I hope you will not let my friend here lose his customer by the mistake.' I readily answered, 'No, sir, I'll buy the spoons still, if he can match my odd spoon, which I brought for a pattern,' and the goldsmith showed me some of the very same fashion. So he weighed the spoons, and they came to 35s., so I pulls out my purse to pay him, in which I had near twenty guineas, for I never went without such a sum about me, whatever might happen and I found it of use at other times as well as now.

When Mr Alderman saw my money, he said, 'Well, madam, now I am satisfied you were wronged, and it was for this reason that I moved you should buy the spoons, and stayed till you had bought them, for if you had not had money to pay for them, I should have suspected that you did not come into the shop to buy, for the sort of people who come upon these designs that you have been charged with, are seldom troubled with much gold in their pockets, as I see you are.'

I smiled, and told his worship, that then I owed something of his favour to my money, but I hoped he saw reason also in the justice he had done me before. He said, yes, he had, but this had confirmed his opinion, and he was fully satisfied now of my having been injured. So I came well off from an affair in which I was at the very brink of destruction.

It was but three days after this, that not at all made cautious by my former danger, as I used to be, and still pursuing the art which I had so long been employed in, I ventured into a house where I saw the doors open, and furnished myself, as I thought verily without being perceived, with two pieces of flowered silks, such as they call brocaded silk, very rich. It was not a mercer's shop, nor a warehouse of a mercer, but looked like a private dwelling-house, and was, it seems, inhabited by a man that sold goods for a weaver to the mercers, like a broker or factor.

That I may make short of the black part of this story, I was attacked by two wenches that came open-mouthed at me just as I was going out at the door, and one of them pulled me back into the room, while the other shut the door upon me. I would have given them good words, but there was no room for it, two fiery dragons could not have been more furious; they tore my clothes, bullied and roared, as if they would have murdererd me; the mistress of the house came next, and then the master, and all outrageous.

I gave the master very good words, told him the door was open, and things were a temptation to me, that I was poor and distressed, and poverty was what many could not resist, and begged him, with tears, to have pity on me. The mistress of the house was moved with compassion, and inclined to have let me go, and had almost persuaded her husband to it also, but the saucy wenches were run even before they were sent, and had fetched a constable, and then the master said he could not go back, I must go before a justice, and answered his wife, that he might come into trouble himself if he should let me go.

The sight of a constable, indeed, struck me, and I thought I should have sunk into the ground. I fell into faintings, and indeed the people themselves thought I would have died, when the woman argued again for me, and entreated her husband, seeing they had lost nothing, to let me go. I offered him to pay for the two pieces, whatever the value was, though I had not got them, and argued that as he had his goods, and had really lost nothing, it would be cruel to pursue me to death, and have my blood for the bare attempt of taking them. I put the constable in mind, too, that I had broken no doors, nor carried anything away; and when I came to the justice, and pleaded there that I had neither broken anything to get in, nor carried anything out, the justice was inclined to have released me; but the first saucy jade that stopped me, affirming that I was going out with the goods, but that she stopped me and pulled me back, the justice upon that point committed me, and I was carried to Newgate, that horrid place! My very blood chills at the mention of its name; the place where so many of my comrades had been locked up, and from whence they went to the fatal tree,* the place where my mother suffered so deeply, where I was brought into the world, and from whence I expected no redemption, but by an infamous death: to conclude, the place that had so long expected me, and which with so much art and success I had so long avoided.

I was now fixed indeed; 'tis impossible to describe the terror of my mind, when I was first brought in, and when I looked round upon all the horrors of that dismal place. I looked on myself as lost, and that I had nothing to think of but of going out of the world, and that with the utmost infamy: the hellish noise, the roaring, swearing, and clamour, the stench and nastiness, and all the dreadful afflicting things that I saw there, joined to make the place seem an emblem of hell itself, and a kind of an entrance into it.

Now I reproached myself with the many hints I had had, as I have mentioned above, from my own reason, from the sense of my good circumstances, and of the many dangers I had escaped, to leave off while I was well, and how I had withstood them all, and hardened my thoughts against all fear. It seemed to me that I was hurried on by an inevitable fate to this day of misery, and that now I was to expiate all my offences at the gallows; that I was now to give satisfaction to justice with my blood, and that I was to come to the last hour of my life and of my wickedness together. These things poured themselves in upon my thoughts in a confused manner, and left me overwhelmed with melancholy and despair.

Then I repented heartily of all my life past, but that repentance yielded me no satisfaction, no peace, no, not in the least, because, as I said to myself, it was repenting after the power of further sinning was taken away. I seemed not to mourn that I had committed such crimes, and for the fact, as it was an offence against God and my neighbour, but that I was to be punished for it. I was a penitent, as I thought, not that I had sinned, but that I was to suffer, and this took away all the comfort of my repentance in my own thoughts.

I got no sleep for several nights or days after I came into that wretched place, and glad I would have been for some time to have died there, though I did not consider dying as it ought to be considered neither; indeed, nothing could be filled with more horror to my imagination than the very place, nothing was more odious to me than the company that was there. Oh! if I had but been sent to any place in the world, and not to Newgate, I should have thought myself happy.

In the next place, how did the hardened wretches that were there before me triumph over me! What! Mrs Flanders come to Newgate at last? What! Mrs Mary, Mrs Molly, and after that plain Moll Flanders! They thought the devil had helped me, they said, that I had reigned so long; they expected me there many years ago, they said, and was I come at last? Then they flouted me with dejections, welcomed me to the place, wished me joy, bid me have a good heart, not be cast down, things might not be so bad as I feared, and the like; then called for brandy, and drank to me, but put it all up to my score,* for they told me I was but just come to the college, as they called it, and sure I had money in my pocket, though they had none.

I asked one of this crew how long she had been there. She said four months. I asked her how the place looked to her when she first came into it. Just as it did now to me, says she, dreadful and frightful; that she thought she was in hell; 'and I believe so still,' adds she, 'but it is natural to me now, I don't disturb myself about it.' 'I suppose,' says I, 'you are in no danger of what is to follow?' 'Nay,' says she, 'you are mistaken there, I am sure, for I am under sentence, only I pleaded my belly, but am no more with child than the judge that tried me, and I expect to be called down next session.' This 'calling down' is calling down to their former judgment, when a woman has been respited for her belly, but proves not to be with child, or if she has been with child, and has been brought to bed. 'Well,' says I, 'and are you thus easy?' 'Ay,' says she, 'I can't help myself; what signifies being sad? if I am hanged, there's an end of me.' And away she turned dancing, and sings as she goes, the following piece of Newgate wit:

> If I swing by the string,
>   I shall hear the bell* ring,[1]
> And then there's an end of poor Jenny.

I mention this because it would be worth the observation of any prisoner, who shall hereafter fall into the same misfortune, and come to that dreadful place of Newgate, how time, necessity, and conversing with the wretches that are there familiarises the place to them; how at last they become reconciled to that which at first was the greatest dread upon their spirits in the world, and are as

---

[1] The bell at St Sepulchre's, which tolls upon execution-day.

impudently cheerful and merry in their misery as they were when
out of it.

I cannot say, as some do, this devil is not so black as he is
painted; for indeed no colours can represent that place to the life,
nor any soul conceive aright of it but those who have been
sufferers there. But how hell should become by degrees so natural,
and not only tolerable, but even agreeable, is a thing unintelligible
but by those who have experienced it, as I have.

The same night that I was sent to Newgate, I sent the news of it
to my old governess, who was surprised at it, you may be sure, and
spent the night almost as ill out of Newgate, as I did in it.

The next morning she came to see me; she did what she could to
comfort me, but she saw that was to no purpose; however, as she
said, to sink under the weight was but to increase the weight; she
immediately applied herself to all the proper methods to prevent
the effects of it, which we feared, and first she found out the two
fiery jades that had surprised me. She tampered with them,
persuaded them, offered them money, and, in a word, tried all
imaginable ways to prevent a prosecution; she offered one of the
wenches £100 to go away from her mistress, and not to appear
against me, but she was so resolute, that though she was but a
servant-maid at £3 a year wages, or thereabouts, she refused it,
and would have refused, as my governess said she believed, if she
had offered her £500. Then she attacked the other maid; she was
not so hard-hearted as the other, and sometimes seemed inclined
to be merciful; but the first wench kept her up, and would not so
much as let my governess talk with her, but threatened to have her
up for tampering with the evidence.

Then she applied to the master, that is to say, the man whose
goods had been stolen, and particularly to his wife, who was
inclined at first to have some compassion for me; she found the
woman the same still, but the man alleged he was bound to
prosecute, and that he should forfeit his recognisance.

My governess offered to find friends that should get his
recognisance off of the file, as they call it, and that he should not
suffer; but it was not possible to convince him that he could be
safe any way in the world but by appearing against me; so I was to
have three witnesses of fact against me, the master and his two
maids; that is to say, I was as certain to be cast for my life* as I was
that I was alive, and I had nothing to do but to think of dying. I
had but a sad foundation to build upon for that, as I said before,

for all my repentance appeared to me to be only the effect of my fear of death; not a sincere regret for the wicked life that I had lived, and which had brought this misery upon me, or for the offending my Creator, who was now suddenly to be my judge.

I lived many days here under the utmost horror; I had death, as it were, in view, and thought of nothing night or day, but of gibbets and halters, evil spirits and devils; it is not to be expressed how I was harassed, between the dreadful apprehensions of death, and the terror of my conscience reproaching me with my past horrible life.

The ordinary* of Newgate came to me, and talked a little in his way, but all his divinity ran upon confessing my crime, as he called it (though he knew not what I was in for), making a full discovery, and the like, without which he told me God would never forgive me; and he said so little to the purpose that I had no manner of consolation from him; and then to observe the poor creature preaching confession and repentance to me in the morning, and find him drunk with brandy by noon, this had something in it so shocking, that I began to nauseate the man, and his work too by degrees, for the sake of the man; so that I desired him to trouble me no more.

I know not how it was, but by the indefatigable application of my diligent governess I had no bill preferred against me the first session, I mean to the grand jury, at Guildhall;* so I had another month or five weeks before me, and without doubt this ought to have been accepted by me as so much time given me for reflection upon what was past, and preparation for what was to come. I ought to have esteemed it as a space given me for repentance, and have employed it as such, but it was not in me. I was sorry, as before, for being in Newgate, but had few signs of repentance about me.

On the contrary, like the water in the hollows of mountains, which petrifies and turns into stone whatever they are suffered to drop upon; so the continual conversing with such a crew of hell-hounds had the same common operation upon me as upon other people. I degenerated into stone; I turned first stupid and senseless, and then brutish and thoughtless, and at last raving mad as any of them; in short, I became as naturally pleased and easy with the place as if indeed I had been born there.

It is scarce possible to imagine that our natures should be capable of so much degeneracy as to make that pleasant and agreeable, that in itself is the most complete misery. Here was a circumstance that I think it is scarce possible to mention a worse: I was as exquisitely miserable as it was possible for any one to be that had life and health, and money to help them, as I had.

I had a weight of guilt upon me, enough to sink any creature who had the least power of reflection left, and had any sense upon them of the happiness of this life, or the misery of another. I had at first some remorse indeed, but no repentance; I had now neither remorse nor repentance. I had a crime charged on me, the punishment of which was death; the proof so evident, that there was no room for me so much as to plead not guilty. I had the name of an old offender, so that I had nothing to expect but death, neither had I myself any thoughts of escaping; and yet a certain strange lethargy of soul possessed me. I had no trouble, no apprehensions, no sorrow about me; the first surprise was gone; I was, I may well say, I know not how; my senses, my reason, nay, my conscience, were all asleep; my course of life for forty years had been a horrid complication of wickedness, whoredom, adultery, incest, lying, theft; and, in a word, everything but murder and treason had been my practice, from the age of eighteen, or thereabouts, to threescore; and now I was engulfed in the misery of punishment, and had an infamous death at the door; and yet I had no sense of my condition, no thought of heaven or hell, at least that went any farther than a bare flying touch, like the stitch or pain that gives a hint and goes off. I neither had a heart to ask God's mercy, or indeed to think of it. And in this, I think, I have given a brief description of the completest misery on earth.

All my terrifying thoughts were past, the horrors of the place were become familiar, and I felt no more uneasiness at the noise and clamours of the prison, than they did who made that noise; in a word, I was become a mere Newgate-bird, as wicked and as outrageous as any of them; nay, I scarce retained the habit and custom of good breeding and manners, which all along till now ran through my conversation; so thorough a degeneracy had possessed me, that I was no more the something that I had been, than if I had never been otherwise than what I was now.

In the middle of this hardened part of my life, I had another sudden surprise, which called me back a little to that thing called sorrow, which, indeed, I began to be past the sense of before. They told me one night that there was brought into the prison late the night before three highwaymen, who had committed a robbery somewhere on Hounslow Heath, I think it was, and were pursued to Uxbridge by the country,* and there taken after a gallant resistance, in which many of the country people were wounded, and some killed.

It is not to be wondered that we prisoners were all desirous enough to see these brave, topping gentlemen, that were talked up to be such as their fellows had not been known, and especially because it was said they would in the morning be removed into the press-yard,* having given money to the head master of the prison, to be allowed the liberty of that better place. So we that were women placed ourselves in the way, that we would be sure to see them; but nothing could express the amazement and surprise I was in, when the first man that came out, I knew to be my Lancashire husband, the same with whom I lived so well at Dunstable, and the same who I afterwards saw at Brickhill, when I was married to my last husband, as has been related.

I was struck dumb at the sight, and knew neither what to say, or what to do; he did not know me, and that was all the present relief I had: I quitted my company, and retired as much as that dreadful place suffers anybody to retire, and cried vehemently for a great while. 'Dreadful creature that I am,' said I, 'how many poor people have I made miserable! how many desperate wretches have I sent to the devil!' This gentleman's misfortunes I placed all to my own account. He had told me at Chester he was ruined by that match, and that his fortunes were made desperate on my account; for that thinking I had been a fortune, he was run into debt more than he was able to pay; that he would go into the army, and carry a musket, or buy a horse and take a tour,* as he called it; and though I never told him that I was a fortune, and so did not actually deceive him myself, yet I did encourage the having it thought so, and so I was the occasion originally of his mischief.

The surprise of this thing only struck deeper in my thoughts, and gave me stronger reflections than all that had befallen me before. I grieved day and night, and the more for that they told me he was the captain of the gang, and that he had committed so many robberies; that Hind, or Whitney, or the Golden Farmer* were fools to him; that he would surely be hanged, if there were no more men left in the country; and that there would be abundance of people come in against him.

I was overwhelmed with grief for him; my own case gave me no disturbance compared to this, and I loaded myself with reproaches on his account. I bewailed my misfortunes, and the ruin he was now come to, at such a rate that I relished nothing now as I did before, and the first reflections I made upon the horrid life I had lived began to return upon me; and as these things returned, my abhorrence of the place, and of the way of living in it, returned also; in a word, I was perfectly changed and become another body.

While I was under these influences of sorrow for him, came notice to me that the next sessions there would be a bill preferred to the grand jury against me, and that I should be tried for my life. My temper was touched before,* the wretched boldness of spirit which I had acquired abated, and conscious guilt began to flow in my mind. In short, I began to think, and to think indeed is one real advance from hell to heaven. All that hardened state and temper of soul, which I said so much of before, is but a deprivation of thought; he that is restored to his thinking, is restored to himself.

As soon as I began, I say, to think, the first thing that occurred to me broke out thus: 'Lord! what will become of me? I shall be cast, to be sure, and there is nothing beyond that but death! I have no friends; what shall I do? I shall be certainly cast! Lord, have mercy upon me! What will become of me?' This was a sad thought, you will say, to be the first, after so long time, that had started in my soul of that kind, and yet even this was nothing but fright at what was to come; there was not a word of sincere repentance in it all. However, I was dreadfully dejected, and disconsolate to the last degree; and as I had no friend to communicate my distressed thoughts to, it lay so heavy upon me that it threw me into fits and swoonings several times a day. I sent for my old governess, and she, give her her due, acted the part of a true friend. She left no stone unturned to prevent the grand jury* finding the bill. She went to several of the jurymen, talked with them, and endeavoured to possess them with favourable dispositions, on account that nothing was taken away, and no house broken, etc.; but all would not do; the two wenches swore home to the fact, and the jury found the bill for robbery and housebreaking, that is, for felony and burglary.

I sank down when they brought the news of it, and after I came to myself I thought I should have died with the weight of it. My governess acted a true mother to me; she pitied me, she cried with me and for me, but she could not help me; and, to add to the terror of it, 'twas the discourse all over the house that I should die for it. I could hear them talk it among themselves very often, and see them shake their heads, and say they were sorry for it, and the like, as is usual in the place. But still nobody came to tell me their thoughts, till at last one of the keepers came to me privately, and said, with a sigh, 'Well, Mrs Flanders, you will be tried a Friday' (this was but a Wednesday); 'what do you intend to do?' I turned as white as a clout,* and said, 'God knows what I shall do; for my part, I know not what to do.' 'Why,' says he, 'I won't flatter* you; I would have you prepare for death, for I doubt you will be cast; and as you are an old offender, I doubt you will find but little mercy. They say,' added he, 'your case is very plain, and that the witnesses swear so home against you, there will be no standing it.'

This was a stab into the very vitals of one under such a burthen, and I could not speak a word, good or bad, for a great while. At last I burst out into tears, and said to him, 'Oh, sir, what must I do?' 'Do!' says he; 'send for a minister, and talk with him; for, indeed, Mrs Flanders, unless you have very good friends, you are no woman for this world.'

This was plain dealing indeed, but it was very harsh to me; at least I thought it so. He left me in the greatest confusion imaginable, and all that night I lay awake. And now I began to say my prayers, which I had scarce done before since my last husband's death, or from a little while after. And truly I may well call it saying my prayers, for I was in such a confusion, and had such horror upon my mind, that though I cried, and repeated several times the ordinary expression of 'Lord, have mercy upon me!' I never brought myself to any sense of being a miserable sinner, as indeed I was, and of confessing my sins to God, and begging pardon for the sake of Jesus Christ. I was overwhelmed with the sense of my condition, being tried for my life, and being sure to be executed, and on this account I cried out all night, 'Lord! what will become of me? Lord! what shall I do? Lord, have mercy upon me!' and the like.

My poor afflicted governess was now as much concerned as I, and a great deal more truly penitent, though she had no prospect of being brought to a sentence. Not but that she deserved it as much as I, and so she said herself; but she had not done anything for many years, other than receiving what I and others had stolen, and encouraging us to steal it. But she cried and took on, like a distracted body, wringing her hands, and crying out that she was undone, that she believed there was a curse from heaven upon her,

that she should be damned, that she had been the destruction of all
her friends, that she brought such a one, and such a one, and such
a one to the gallows; and there she reckoned up ten or eleven
people, some of which I have given an account of, that came to
untimely ends; and that now she was the occasion of my ruin, for
she had persuaded me to go on, when I would have left off. I
interrupted her there. 'No, mother, no,' said I, 'don't speak of
that, for you would have had me left off when I got the mercer's
money again, and when I came home from Harwich, and I would
not hearken to you; therefore you have not been to blame; it is I
only have ruined myself, I have brought myself to this misery';
and thus we spent many hours together.

Well, there was no remedy; the prosecution went on, and on the
Thursday I was carried down to the sessions-house, where I was
arraigned, as they called it, and the next day I was appointed to be
tried. At the arraignment I pleaded 'Not guilty,' and well I might,
for I was indicted for felony and burglary; that is, for feloniously
stealing two pieces of brocaded silk, value £46, the goods of
Anthony Johnson, and for breaking open the doors; whereas I
knew very well they could not pretend I had broken up the doors,
or so much as lifted up a latch.

On the Friday I was brought to my trial. I had exhausted my
spirits with crying for two or three days before, [so] that I slept
better the Thursday night than I expected, and had more courage
for my trial than I thought possible for me to have.

When the trial began, and the indictment was read, I would
have spoke, but they told me the witnesses must be heard first, and
then I should have time to be heard. The witnesses were the two
wenches, a couple of hard-mouthed jades indeed, for though the
thing was truth in the main, yet they aggravated it to the utmost
extremity, and swore I had the goods wholly in my possession,
that I hid them among my clothes, that I was going off with them,
that I had one foot over the threshold when they discovered*
themselves, and then I put t'other over, so that I was quite out of
the house in the street with the goods before they took me, and
then they seized me, and took the goods upon me. The fact in
general was true, but I insisted upon it, that they stopped me
before I had set my foot clear of the threshold. But that did not
argue much, for I had taken the goods, and was bringing them
away, if I had not been taken.

I pleaded that I had stole nothing, they had lost nothing, that the door was open, and I went in with design to buy. If, seeing nobody in the house, I had taken any of them up in my hand, it could not be concluded that I intended to steal them, for that I never carried them farther than the door, to look on them with the better light.

The Court would not allow that by any means, and made a kind of jest of my intending to buy the goods, that being no shop for the selling of anything; and as to carrying them to the door to look at them, the maids made their impudent mocks upon that, and spent their wit upon it very much; told the Court I had looked at them sufficiently, and approved them very well, for I had packed them up, and was a-going with them.

In short, I was found guilty of felony, but acquitted of the burglary, which was but small comfort to me, the first bringing me to a sentence of death, and the last would have done no more. The next day I was carried down to receive the dreadful sentence, and when they came to ask me what I had to say why sentence should not pass, I stood mute a while, but somebody prompted me aloud to speak to the judges, for that they could represent things favourably for me. This encouraged me, and I told them I had nothing to say to stop the sentence, but that I had much to say to bespeak the mercy of the Court; that I hoped they would allow something in such a case for the circumstances of it; that I had broken no doors, had carried nothing off; that nobody had lost anything; that the person whose goods they were was pleased to say he desired mercy might be shown (which indeed he very honestly did); that, at the worst, it was the first offence, and that I had never been before any court of justice before; and, in a word, I spoke with more courage than I thought I could have done, and in such a moving tone, and though with tears, yet not so many tears as to obstruct my speech, that I could see it moved others to tears that heard me.

The judges sat grave and mute, gave me an easy hearing, and time to say all that I would, but, saying neither yes nor no to it, pronounced the sentence of death upon me, a sentence to me like death itself, which confounded me. I had no more spirit left in me. I had no tongue to speak, or eyes to look up either to God or man.

My poor governess was utterly disconsolate; and she that was my comforter before, wanted comfort now herself; and some-times mourning, sometimes raging, was as much out of herself as any mad woman in Bedlam. Nor was she only disconsolate as to me, but she was struck with horror at the sense of her own wicked life, and began to look back upon it with a taste quite different from mine, for she was penitent to the highest degree for her sins, as well as sorrowful for the misfortune. She sent for a minister, too, a serious, pious, good man, and applied herself with such earnestness, by his assistance, to the work of sincere repentance, that I believe, and so did the minister too, that she was a true penitent; and, which is still more, she was not only so for the occasion, and at that juncture, but she continued so, as I was informed, to the day of her death.

It is rather to be thought of than expressed what was now my condition. I had nothing before me but death; and as I had no friends to assist me, I expected nothing but to find my name in the dead warrant,* which was to come for the execution, next Friday, of five more and myself.

In the meantime my poor distressed governess sent me a minister, who at her request came to visit me. He exhorted me seriously to repent of all my sins, and to dally no longer with my soul; not flattering myself with hopes of life, which, he said, he was informed there was no room to expect, but unfeignedly to look up to God with my whole soul, and to cry for pardon in the name of Jesus Christ. He backed his discourses with proper quotations of Scripture, encouraging the greatest sinner to repent, and turn from their evil way; and when he had done, he kneeled down and prayed with me.

It was now that, for the first time, I felt any real signs of repentance. I now began to look back upon my past life with abhorrence, and having a kind of view into the other side of time, the things of life, as I believe they do with everybody at such a time, began to look with a different aspect, and quite another shape, than they did before. The views of felicity, the joy, the griefs of life, were quite other things; and I had nothing in my thoughts but what was so infinitely superior to what I had known in life, that it appeared to be the greatest stupidity to lay a weight upon anything, though the most valuable in this world.

The word eternity represented itself with all its incomprehensible additions, and I had such extended notions of it that I know not how to express them. Among the rest, how absurd did every pleasant thing look! – I mean, that we had counted pleasant before – when I reflected that these sordid trifles were the things for which we forfeited eternal felicity.

With these reflections came in of mere course* severe re-proaches for my wretched behaviour in my past life; that I had forfeited all hope of happiness in the eternity that I was just going to enter into; and, on the contrary, was entitled to all that was miserable; and all this with the frightful addition of its being also eternal.

I am not capable of reading lectures of instruction to anybody, but I relate this in the very manner in which things then appeared to me, as far as I am able, but infinitely short of the lively impressions which they made on my soul at that time; indeed, those impressions are not to be explained by words, or if they are, I am not mistress of words to express them. It must be the work of every sober reader to make just reflections, as their own circum-stances may direct; and this is what every one at some time or other may feel something of; I mean, a clearer sight into things to come than they had here, and a dark view of their own concern in them.

But I go back to my own case. The minister pressed me to tell him, as far as I thought convenient, in what state I found myself as to the sight I had of things beyond life. He told me he did not come as ordinary of the place, whose business it is to extort confessions from prisoners, for the further detecting of other offenders; that his business was to move me to such freedom of discourse as might serve to disburthen my own mind, and furnish him to administer comfort to me as far as was in his power; and assured me, that whatever I said to him should remain with him, and be as much a secret as if it was known only to God and myself; and that he desired to know nothing of me, but to qualify him to give proper advice to me, and to pray to God for me.

This honest, friendly way of treating me unlocked all the sluices of my passions. He broke into my very soul by it; and I unravelled all the wickedness of my life to him. In a word, I gave him an abridgment of this whole history; I gave him the picture of my conduct for fifty years in miniature.

I hid nothing from him, and he in return exhorted me to a sincere repentance, explained to me what he meant by repentance, and then drew out such a scheme of infinite mercy, proclaimed from heaven to sinners of the greatest magnitude, that he left me nothing to say, that looked like despair, or doubting of being accepted; and in this condition he left me the first night.

He visited me again the next morning, and went on with his

method of explaining the terms of divine mercy, which according to him consisted of nothing more difficult than that of being sincerely desirous of it, and willing to accept it; only a sincere regret for, and hatred of, those things which rendered me so just an object of divine vengeance. I am not able to repeat the excellent discourses of this extraordinary man; all that I am able to do, is to say that he revived my heart, and brought me into such a condition that I never knew anything of in my life before. I was covered with shame and tears for things past, and yet had at the same time a secret surprising joy at the prospect of being a true penitent, and obtaining the comfort of a penitent – I mean the hope of being forgiven; and so swift did thoughts circulate, and so high did the impressions they had made upon me run, that I thought I could freely have gone out that minute to execution, without any uneasiness at all, casting my soul entirely into the arms of infinite mercy as a penitent.

The good gentleman was so moved with a view of the influence which he saw these things had on me, that he blessed God he had come to visit me, and resolved not to leave me till the last moment.

It was no less than twelve days after our receiving sentence before any were ordered for execution, and then the dead warrant, as they call it, came down, and I found my name was among them. A terrible blow this was to my new resolutions; indeed my heart sank within me, and I swooned away twice, one after another, but spoke not a word. The good minister was sorely afflicted for me, and did what he could to comfort me, with the same arguments and the same moving eloquence that he did before, and left me not that evening so long as the prison-keepers would suffer him to stay in the prison, unless he would be locked up with me all night, which he was not willing to be.

I wondered much that I did not see him all the next day, it being but the day before the time appointed for execution; and I was greatly discouraged and dejected, and indeed almost sank for want of that comfort which he had so often, and with such success, yielded me in his former visits. I waited with great impatience, and under the greatest oppression of spirits imaginable, till about four o'clock, when he came to my apartment; for I had obtained the favour, by the help of money, nothing being to be done in that place without it, not to be kept in the condemned hole, among the rest of the prisoners who were to die, but to have a little dirty chamber to myself.

My heart leaped within me for joy when I heard his voice at the door, even before I saw him; but let any one judge what kind of motion I found in my soul when, after having made a short excuse for his not coming, he showed me that his time had been employed on my account, that he had obtained a favourable report from the Recorder* in my case, and, in short, that he had brought me a reprieve.

He used all the caution that he was able in letting me know what it would have been double cruelty to have concealed; for as grief had overset me before, so did joy overset me now, and I fell into a more dangerous swooning than at first, and it was not without difficulty that I was recovered at all.

The good man having made a very Christian exhortation to me, not to let the joy of my reprieve put the remembrance of my past sorrow out of my mind, and told me that he must leave me, to go and enter the reprieve in the books, and show it to the sheriffs, he stood up just before his going away, and in a very earnest manner prayed to God for me, that my repentance might be made unfeigned and sincere; and that my coming back, as it were, into life again might not be a returning to the follies of life, which I had made such solemn resolutions to forsake. I joined heartily in that petition, and must needs say I had deeper impressions upon my mind all that night, of the mercy of God in sparing my life, and a greater detestation of my sins, from a sense of that goodness, than I had in all my sorrow before.

This may be thought inconsistent in itself, and wide from the business of this book; particularly, I reflect that many of those who may be pleased and diverted with the relation of the wicked part of my story may not relish this, which is really the best part of my life, the most advantageous to myself, and the most instructive to others. Such, however, will, I hope, allow me liberty to make my story complete. It would be a severe satire on such to say they do not relish the repentance as much as they do the crime; and they had rather the history were a complete tragedy, as it was very likely to have been.

But I go on with my relation. The next morning there was a sad scene indeed in the prison. The first thing I was saluted with in the morning was the tolling of the great bell at St Sepulchre's, which ushered in the day. As soon as it began to toll, a dismal groaning and crying was heard from the condemned hole, where there lay six poor souls, who were to be executed that day, some for one crime, some for another, and two for murder.

This was followed by a confused clamour in the house, among the several prisoners, expressing their awkward sorrows for the poor creatures that were to die, but in a manner extremely differing one from another. Some cried for them; some brutishly huzzaed, and wished them a good journey; some damned and cursed those that had brought them to it, many pitying them, and some few, but very few, praying for them.

There was hardly room for so much composure of mind as was required for me to bless the merciful Providence that had, as it were, snatched me out of the jaws of this destruction. I remained, as it were, dumb and silent, overcome with the sense of it, and not able to express what I had in my heart; for the passions on such occasions as these are certainly so agitated as not to be able presently to regulate their own motions.

All the while the poor condemned creatures were preparing for death, and the ordinary, as they call him, was busy with them, disposing them to submit to their sentence – I say, all this while I was seized with a fit of trembling, as much as I could have been if I had been in the same condition as I was the day before; I was so violently agitated by this surprising fit that I shook as if it had been an ague, so that I could not speak or look but like one distracted. As soon as they were all put into the carts and gone, which, however, I had not courage enough to see – I say, as soon as they were gone, I fell into a fit of crying involuntarily, as a mere distemper,* and yet so violent, and it held me so long, that I knew not what course to take, nor could I stop, or put a check to it, no, not with all the strength and courage I had.

This fit of crying held me near two hours, and as I believe, held me till they were all out of the world, and then a most humble, penitent, serious kind of joy succeeded; a real transport it was, or passion of thankfulness, and in this I continued most part of the day.

In the evening the good minister visited me again, and fell to his usual good discourses. He congratulated my having a space yet allowed me for repentance, whereas the state of those six poor creatures was determined, and they were now past the offers of salvation; he pressed me to retain the same sentiments of the things of life that I had when I had a view of eternity; and at the end of all, told me that I should not conclude that all was over, that a reprieve was not a pardon, that he could not answer for the effects of it; however, I had this mercy, that I had more time given me, and it was my business to improve that time.

This discourse left a kind of sadness on my heart, as if I might expect the affair would have a tragical issue still, which, however, he had no certainty of; yet I did not at that time question him about it, he having said he would do his utmost to bring it to a good end, and that he hoped he might, but he would not have me be secure; and the consequence showed that he had reason for what he said.

It was about a fortnight after this that I had some just apprehensions that I should be included in the dead warrant at the ensuing sessions; and it was not without great difficulty, and at last an humble petition for transportation,* that I avoided it, so ill was I beholding to fame, and so prevailing was the report of being an old offender; though in that they did not do me strict justice, for I was not in the sense of the law an old offender, whatever I was in the eye of the judge, for I had never been before them in a judicial way before; so the judges could not charge me with being an old offender, but the Recorder was pleased to represent my case as he thought fit.

I had now a certainty of life indeed, but with the hard conditions of being ordered for transportation, which was, I say, a hard condition in itself, but not when comparatively considered; and therefore I shall make no comments upon the sentence, nor upon the choice I was put to. We all shall choose anything rather than death, especially when 'tis attended with an uncomfortable prospect beyond it, which was my case.

The good minister, whose interest, though a stranger to me, had obtained me the reprieve, mourned sincerely for his part. He was in hopes, he said, that I should have ended my days under the influence of good instruction, that I might not have forgot my former distresses, and that I should not have been turned loose again among such a wretched crew as are thus sent abroad, where, he said, I must have more than ordinary secret assistance from the grace of God, if I did not turn as wicked again as ever.

I have not for a good while mentioned my governess, who had been dangerously sick, and being in as near a view of death by her disease as I was by my sentence, was a very great penitent; I say, I have not mentioned her, nor indeed did I see her in all this time; but being now recovering, and just able to come abroad, she came to see me.

I told her my condition, and what a different flux and reflux of fears and hopes I had been agitated with; I told her what I had escaped, and upon what terms, and she was present when the minister expressed his fears of my relapsing again into wickedness upon my falling into the wretched company that are generally transported. Indeed I had a melancholy reflection upon it in my own mind, for I knew what a dreadful gang was always sent away together, and said to my governess that the good minister's fears were not without cause. 'Well, well,' says she, 'but I hope you will not be tempted with such a horrid example as that.' And as soon as the minister was gone, she told me she would not have me discouraged, for perhaps ways and means might be found to dispose of me in a particular way, by myself, of which she would talk further with me afterward.

I looked earnestly at her, and thought she looked more cheerfully than she usually had done, and I entertained immediately a thousand notions of being delivered, but could not for my life imagine the methods, or think of one that was feasible; but I was too much concerned in it to let her go from me without explaining herself, which though she was very loath to do, yet, as I was still pressing, she answered me in a few words, thus: 'Why, you have money, have you not? Did you ever know one in your life that was transported and had a hundred pounds in his pocket, I'll warrant ye, child?' says she.

I understood her presently, but told her I saw no room to hope for anything but a strict execution of the order, and as it was a severity that was esteemed a mercy, there was no doubt but it would be strictly observed. She said no more but this: 'We will try what can be done,' and so we parted.

I lay in the prison near fifteen weeks after this. What the reason of it was I know not, but at the end of this time I was put on board of a ship in the Thames, and with me a gang of thirteen as hardened vile creatures as ever Newgate produced in my time; and it would really take up a history longer than mine to describe the degrees of impudence and audacious villainy that those thirteen were arrived to, and the manner of their behaviour in the voyage; of which I have a very diverting account by me, which the captain of the ship who carried them over gave me, and which he caused his mate to write down at large.

It may, perhaps, be thought trifling to enter here into a relation of all the little incidents which attended me in this interval of my circumstances; I mean, between the final order for my transportation and the time of going on board the ship; and I am too near the end of my story to allow room for it; but something relating to me and my Lancashire husband I must not omit.

He had, as I have observed already, been carried from the master's side* of the ordinary prison into the press-yard, with three of his comrades, for they found another to add to them after some time; here, for what reason I knew not, they were kept without being brought to a trial almost three months. It seems they found means to bribe or buy off some who were to come in against them, and they wanted evidence to convict them. After some puzzle on this account, they made shift to get proof enough against two of them to carry them off;* but the other two, of which my Lancashire husband was one, lay still in suspense. They had, I think, one positive evidence against each of them, but the law obliging them to have two witnesses, they could make nothing of it. Yet they were resolved not to part with the men neither, not doubting but evidence would at last come in; and in order to this, I think publication was made that such prisoners were taken, and any one might come to the prison and see them.

I took this opportunity to satisfy my curiosity, pretending I had been robbed in the Dunstable coach, and that I would go to see the two highwaymen. But when I came into the press-yard, I was so disguised myself, and muffled my face up so that he could see little of me, and knew nothing of who I was; but when I came back, I said publicly that I knew them very well.

Immediately it was all over the prison that Moll Flanders would turn evidence against one of the highwaymen, and that I was to come off by it from the sentence of transportation.

They heard of it, and immediately my husband desired to see this Mrs Flanders that knew him so well, and was to be an evidence against him; and accordingly I had leave to go to him. I dressed myself up as well as the best clothes that I suffered myself ever to appear in there would allow me, and went to the press-yard, but had a hood over my face. He said little to me at first, but asked me if I knew him. I told him, 'Yes, very well'; but as I concealed my face, so I counterfeited my voice too, that he had no guess at who I was. He asked me where I had seen him. I told him between Dunstable and Brickhill; but turning to the keeper that stood by, I asked if I might not be admitted to talk with him alone. He said, 'Yes, yes,' and so very civilly withdrew.

As soon as he was gone, and I had shut the door, I threw off my hood, and bursting out into tears, 'My dear,' said I, 'do you not know me?' He turned pale, and stood speechless, like one thunderstruck, and, not able to conquer the surprise, said no more but this, 'Let me sit down'; and sitting down by the table, leaning his head on his hand, fixed his eyes on the ground as one stupid.* I cried so vehemently, on the other hand, that it was a good while ere I could speak any more; but after I had given vent to my passion, I repeated the same words, 'My dear, do you not know me?' At which he answered, 'Yes,' and said no more a good while.

After some time continuing in the surprise, as above, he cast up his eyes towards me, and said, 'How could you be so cruel?' I did not really understand what he meant; and I answered, 'How can you call me cruel?' 'To come to me,' says he, 'in such a place as this, is it not to insult me? I have not robbed you, at least not on the highway.'

I perceived by this, that he knew nothing of the miserable circumstances I was in, and thought that, having got intelligence of his being there, I had come to upbraid him with his leaving me. But I had too much to say to him to be affronted, and told him in a few words, that I was far from coming to insult him, but at best I came to condole mutually; that he would be easily satisfied that I had no such view, when I should tell him that my condition was worse than his, and that many ways. He looked a little concerned at the expression of my condition being worse than his, but, with a kind of a smile, said, 'How can that be? When you see me fettered, and in Newgate, and two of my companions executed already, can you say your condition is worse than mine?'

'Come, my dear,' says I, 'we have a long piece of work to do, if I should be to relate, or you to hear, my unfortunate history; but if you will hear it, you will soon conclude with me that my condition is worse than yours.' 'How is that possible,' says he, 'when I expect to be cast for my life the very next sessions?' 'Yes,' says I, ''tis very possible, when I shall tell you that I have been cast for my life three sessions ago, and am now under sentence of death; is not my case worse than yours?'

Then, indeed, he stood silent again, like one struck dumb, and after a little while he starts up. 'Unhappy couple!' says he, 'how can this be possible?' I took him by the hand. 'Come, my dear,'

said I, 'sit down, and let us compare our sorrows. I am a prisoner
in this very house, and in a much worse circumstance than you,
and you will be satisfied I do not come to insult you when I tell you
the particulars.' And with this we sat down together, and I told
him so much of my story as I thought convenient, bringing it at
last to my being reduced to great poverty, and representing myself
as fallen into some company that led me to relieve my distresses by
a way that I had been already unacquainted with, and that they
making an attempt on a tradesman's house, I was seized upon, for
having been but just at the door, the maid-servant pulling me in;
that I neither had broke any lock or taken anything away, and that
notwithstanding that, I was brought in guilty and sentenced to
die; but that the judges having been made sensible of the hardship
of my circumstances, had obtained leave for me to be transported.

I told him I fared the worse for being taken in the prison for one
Moll Flanders, who was a famous successful thief, that all of them
had heard of, but none of them had ever seen; but that, as he
knew, was none of my name. But I placed all to the account of my
ill fortune, and that under this name I was dealt with as an old
offender, though this was the first thing they have ever known of
me. I gave him a long account of what had befallen me since I saw
him, but told him I had seen him since he might think I had; then
gave him an account how I had seen him at Brickhill; how he was
pursued, and how, by giving an account that I knew him, and that
he was a very honest gentleman, the hue-and-cry was stopped,
and the high constable went back again.

He listened most attentively to all my story, and smiled at the
particulars, being all of them infinitely below what he had been at
the head of; but when I came to the story of Little Brickhill he was
surprised. 'And was it you, my dear,' said he, 'that gave the check
to the mob at Brickhill?' 'Yes,' said I, 'it was I indeed.' Then I told
him the particulars which I had observed of him there. 'Why,
then,' said he, 'it was you that saved my life at that time, and I am
glad I owe my life to you, for I will pay the debt to you now, and
I'll deliver you from the present condition you are in, or I will die
in the attempt.'

I told him by no means; it was a risk too great, not worth his
running the hazard of, and for a life not worth his saving. 'Twas
no matter for that, he said; it was a life worth all the world to him;
a life that had given him a new life; 'for,' says he, 'I was never in
real danger, but that time, till the last minute when I was taken.'

Indeed, his danger then lay in his believing he had not been pursued that way; for they had gone off from Hockley* quite another way, and had come over the enclosed country into Brickhill, and were sure they had not been seen by anybody.

Here he gave a long history of his life, which indeed would make a very strange history, and be infinitely diverting. He told me that he took the road about twelve years before he married me; that the woman which called him brother, was not any kin to him, but one that belonged to their gang, and who, keeping correspondence with them, lived always in town, having great acquaintance; that she gave them perfect intelligence of persons going out of town, and that they had made several good booties by her correspondence; that she thought she had fixed a fortune for him, when she brought me to him, but happened to be disappointed, which he really could not blame her for; that if I had had an estate, which she was informed I had, he had resolved to leave off the road and live a new life, but never to appear in public till some general pardon had been passed, or till he could, for money, have got his name into some particular pardon, so that he might have been perfectly easy; but that, as it had proved otherwise, he was obliged to take up the old trade again.

He gave a long account of some of his adventures, and particularly one where he robbed the West Chester coaches near Lichfield, when he got a very great booty; and after that, how he robbed five graziers in the west, going to Burford Fair,* in Wiltshire, to buy sheep. He told me he got so much money on those two occasions that, if he had known where to have found me, he would certainly have embraced my proposal of going with me to Virginia, or to have settled in a plantation, or some other of the English colonies in America.

He told me he wrote three letters to me, directed according to my order, but heard nothing from me. This indeed I knew to be true, but the letters coming to my hand in the time of my latter husband, I could do nothing in it, and therefore gave no answer, that so he might believe they had miscarried.

Being thus disappointed, he said he carried on the old trade ever since, though, when he had gotten so much money, he said, he did not run such desperate risks as he did before. Then he gave me some account of several hard and desperate encounters which he had with gentlemen on the road, who parted too hardly with their money, and showed me some wounds he had received; and he had one or two very terrible wounds indeed, particularly one by a pistol-bullet, which broke his arm, and another with a sword, which ran him quite through the body, but that missing his vitals, he was cured again; one of his comrades having kept with him so faithfully, and so friendly, as that he assisted him in riding near eighty miles before his arm was set, and then got a surgeon in a considerable city, remote from the place where it was done, pretending they were gentlemen travelling towards Carlisle, that they had been attacked on the road by highwaymen, and that one of them had shot him into the arm.

This, he said, his friend managed so well that they were not suspected, but lay still till he was cured. He gave me also so many distinct accounts of his adventures, that it is with great reluctance that I decline the relating them; but this is my own story, not his.

I then inquired into the circumstances of his present case, and what it was he expected when he came to be tried. He told me, that they had no evidence against him; for that, of the three robberies which they were all charged with, it was his good fortune that he was but in one of them, and that there was but one witness to be had to that fact, which was not sufficient; but that it was expected some others would come in, and that he thought, when he first saw me, I had been one that came of that errand; but that if nobody came in against him he hoped he should be cleared; that he had some intimation, that if he would submit to transport himself, he might be admitted to it without a trial; but that he could not think of it with any temper,* and thought he could much easier submit to be hanged.

I blamed him for that; first, because if he was transported, there might be an hundred ways for him, that was a gentleman, and a bold enterprising man, to find his way back again, and perhaps some ways and means to come back before he went. He smiled at that part, and said he should like the last the best of the two, for he had a kind of horror upon his mind at his being sent to the plantations, as the Romans sent slaves to work in the mines; that he thought the passage into another state much more tolerable at the gallows, and that this was the general notion of all the gentlemen who were driven by the exigence of their fortunes to take the road; that at the place of execution there was at least an end of all the miseries of the present state; and as for what was to follow, a man was, in his opinion, as likely to repent sincerely in the last fortnight of his life, under the agonies of a jail and the

condemned hole, as he would ever be in the woods and wilder-
nesses of America; that servitude and hard labour were things
gentlemen could never stoop to; that it was but the way to force
them to be their own executioners, which was much worse; and
that he could not have any patience when he did but think of it.

I used the utmost of my endeavour to persuade him, and joined
that known woman's rhetoric to it – I mean that of tears. I told
him the infamy of a public execution was certainly a greater
pressure upon the spirits of a gentleman than any mortifications
that he could meet with abroad; that he had at least in the other a
chance for his life, whereas here he had none at all; that it was the
easiest thing in the world for him to manage the captain of a ship,
who were, generally speaking, men of good humour; and a small
matter of conduct,* especially if there was any money to be had,
would make way for him to buy himself off when he came to
Virginia.

He looked wishfully at me, and guessed he meant that he had no
money; but I was mistaken, his meaning was another way. 'You
hinted just now, my dear,' said he, 'that there might be a way of
coming back before I went, by which I understood you that it
might be possible to buy it off here. I had rather give £200 to
prevent going, than £100 to be set at liberty when I came there.'
'That is, my dear,' said I, 'because you do not know the place as
well as I do.' 'That may be,' said he; 'and yet I believe, as well as
you know it, you would do the same unless it is because, as you
told me, you have a mother there.'

I told him, as to my mother, she must be dead many years
before; and as for any other relations that I might have there, I
knew them not; that since my misfortunes had reduced me to the
condition I had been in for some years, I had not kept up any
correspondence with them; and that he would easily believe I
should find but a cold reception from them if I should be put to
make my first visit in the condition of a transported felon; that
therefore, if I went thither, I resolved not to see them; but that I
had many views in going there, which took off all the uneasy part
of it; and if he found himself obliged to go also, I should easily
instruct him how to manage himself, so as never to go a servant at
all, especially since I found he was not destitute of money, which
was the only friend in such a condition.

He smiled, and said he did not tell me he had money. I took him
up short, and told him I hoped he did not understand by my

speaking that I should expect any supply from him if he had money; that, on the other hand, though I had not a great deal, yet I did not want, and while I had any I would rather add to him than weaken him, seeing, whatever he had, I knew in the case of transportation he would have occasion of it all.

He expressed himself in a most tender manner upon that head. He told me what money he had was not a great deal, but that he would never hide any of it from me if I wanted it, and assured me he did not speak with any such apprehensions; that he was only intent upon what I had hinted to him; that here he knew what to do, but there he should be the most helpless wretch alive.

I told him he frighted himself with that which had no terror in it; that if he had money, as I was glad to hear he had, he might not only avoid the servitude supposed to be the consequence of transportation, but begin the world upon such a new foundation as he could not fail of success in, with but the common application usual in such cases; that he could not but call to mind I had recommended it to him many years before, and proposed it for restoring our fortunes in the world; and I would tell him now, that to convince him both of the certainty of it, and of my being fully acquainted with the method, and also fully satisfied in the probability of success, he should first see me deliver myself from the necessity of going over at all, and then that I would go with him freely, and of my own choice, and perhaps carry enough with me to satisfy him; that I did not offer it for want of being able to live without assistance from him, but that I thought our mutual misfortunes had been such as were sufficient to reconcile us both to quitting this part of the world, and living where nobody could upbraid us with what was past, and without the agonies of a condemned hole to drive us to it, where we should look back on all our past disasters with infinite satisfaction, when we should consider that our enemies should entirely forget us, and that we should live as new people in a new world, nobody having anything to say to us, or we to them.

I pressed this home to him, with so many arguments, and answered all his own passionate objections so effectually, that he embraced me, and told me I treated him with such a sincerity as overcame him; that he would take my advice, and would strive to submit to his fate in hope of having the comfort of so faithful a counsellor and such a companion in his misery. But still he put me in mind of what I had mentioned before, namely, that there might be some way to get off before he went, and that it might be possible to avoid going at all, which he said would be much better. I told him he should see, and be fully satisfied that I would do my utmost in that part too, and if it did not succeed, yet that I would make good the rest.

We parted after this long conference with such testimonies of kindness and affection as I thought were equal, if not superior, to that at our parting at Dunstable; and now I saw more plainly the reason why he then declined coming with me toward London, and why, when we parted there, he told me it was not convenient to come to London with me, as he would otherwise have done. I have observed that the account of his life would have made a much more pleasing history than this of mine; and, indeed, nothing in it was more strange than this part, viz., that he carried on that desperate trade full five-and-twenty years, and had never been taken, the success he had met with had been so very uncommon, and such that sometimes he had lived handsomely and retired in one place for a year or two at a time, keeping himself and a man-servant to wait on him, and has often sat in the coffee-houses and heard the very people whom he had robbed give account of their being robbed, and of the places and circumstances, so that he could easily remember that it was the same.

In this manner it seems he lived near Liverpool at the time he unluckily married me for a fortune. Had I been the fortune he expected, I verily believe he would have taken up* and lived honestly.

He had with the rest of his misfortunes the good luck not to be actually upon the spot when the robbery was done which they were committed for, and so none of the persons robbed could swear to him. But it seems as he was taken with the gang, one hard-mouthed countryman swore home to him; and according to the publication they had made, they expected more evidence against him, and for that reason he was kept in hold.

However, the offer which was made to him of transportation was made, as I understood, upon the intercession of some great person who pressed him hard to accept of it; and as he knew there were several that might come in against him, I thought his friend was in the right, and I lay at him night and day to delay it no longer.

At last, with much difficulty, he gave his consent; and as he was not therefore admitted to transportation in court, and on his petition, as I was, so he found himself under a difficulty to avoid embarking himself, as I had said he might have done; his friend having given security for him that he should transport himself, and not return within the term.*

This hardship broke all my measures, for the steps I took afterwards for my own deliverance were hereby rendered wholly ineffectual, unless I would abandon him, and leave him to go to America by himself, than which he protested he would much rather go directly to the gallows.

I must now return to my own case. The time of my being transported was near at hand; my governess, who continued my fast friend, had tried to obtain a pardon, but it could not be done unless with an expense too heavy for my purse, considering that to be left empty, unless I had resolved to return to my old trade, had been worse than transportation, because there I could live, here I could not. The good minister stood very hard on another account to prevent my being transported also; but he was answered that my life had been given me at his first solicitations, and therefore he ought to ask no more. He was sensibly grieved at my going, because, as he said, he feared I should lose the good impressions which a prospect of death had at first made on me, and which were since increased by his instructions; and the pious gentleman was exceedingly concerned on that account.

On the other hand, I was not so solicitous about it now, but I concealed my reasons for it from the minister, and to the last he did not know but that I went with the utmost reluctance and affliction.

It was in the month of February that I was, with thirteen other convicts, delivered to a merchant that traded to Virginia, on board a ship riding in Deptford Reach. The officer of the prison delivered us on board, and the master of the vessel gave a discharge for us.

We were for that night clapped under hatches, and kept so close that I thought I should have been suffocated for want of air; and the next morning the ship weighed,* and fell down the river to a place called Bugby's Hole, which was done, as they told us, by the agreement of the merchant, that all opportunity of escape should be taken from us. However, when the ship came thither and cast anchor, we were permitted to come upon the deck, but not upon the quarter-deck, that being kept particularly for the captain and for passengers.

When, by the noise of the men over my head and the motion of the ship, I perceived they were under sail, I was at first greatly surprised, fearing we should go away, and that our friends would not be admitted to see us; but I was easy soon after, when I found they had come to an anchor, and that we had notice given by some of the men that the next morning we should have the liberty to come upon deck, and to have our friends come to see us.

All that night I lay upon the hard deck as the other prisoners did, but we had afterwards little cabins allowed for such as had any bedding to lay in them, and room to stow any box or trunk for clothes, and linen if we had it (which might well be put in), for some of them had neither shirt or shift, linen or woollen, but what was on their backs, or one farthing of money to help themselves; yet I did not find but they fared well enough in the ship, especially the women, who got money of the seamen for washing their clothes, etc., sufficient to purchase anything they wanted.

When the next morning we had the liberty to come upon deck, I asked one of the officers whether I might not be allowed to send a letter on shore to let my friends know where we lay, and to get some necessary things sent to me. This was the boatswain, a very civil, courteous man, who told me I should have any liberty that I desired, that he could allow me with safety. I told him I desired no other; and he answered, the ship's boat would go up to London next tide, and he would order my letter to be carried.

Accordingly, when the boat went off, the boatswain came and told me the boat was going off, that he went in it himself, and if my letter was ready, he would take care of it. I had prepared pen, ink, and paper beforehand, and had gotten a letter ready directed to my governess, and enclosed another to my fellow-prisoner, which, however, I did not let her know was my husband, not to the last. In that to my governess, I let her know where the ship lay, and pressed her to send me what things she had got ready for me for my voyage.

When I gave the boatswain the letter, I gave him a shilling with it, which I told him was for the charge of a porter, which I had entreated him to send with the letter as soon as he came on shore, that if possible I might have an answer brought back by the same hand, that I might know what was become of my things; 'For, sir,' says I, 'if the ship should go away before I have them, I am undone.'

I took care, when I gave him the shilling, to let him see I had a little better furniture* about me than the ordinary prisoners; that I had a purse, and in it a pretty deal of money; and I found that the very sight of it immediately furnished me with very different treatment from what I should otherwise have met with; for though he was courteous indeed before, in a kind of natural compassion to me, as a woman in distress, yet he was more than ordinarily so afterwards, and procured me to be better treated in the ship than, I say, I might otherwise have been; as shall appear in its place.

He very honestly delivered my letter to my governess's own hands, and brought me back her answer; and when he gave it me, gave me the shilling again. 'There,' says he, 'there's your shilling again too, for I delivered the letter myself.' I could not tell what to say, I was surprised at the thing, but after some pause I said, 'Sir, you are too kind; it had been but reasonable that you had paid yourself coach-hire then.'

'No, no,' says he, 'I am overpaid. What is that gentlewoman? Is she your sister?'

'No, sir,' said I, 'she is no relation to me, but she is a dear friend, and all the friends I have in the world.' 'Well,' says he, 'there are few such friends. Why, she cries after you like a child.' 'Ay,' says I again, 'she would give a hundred pounds, I believe, to deliver me from this dreadful condition.'

'Would she so?' says he. 'For half the money I believe I could put you in a way how to deliver yourself.' But this he spoke softly that nobody could hear.

'Alas! sir,' said I, 'but then that must be such a deliverance as, if I should be taken again, would cost me my life.' 'Nay,' said he, 'if you were once out of the ship, you must look to yourself afterwards; that I can say nothing to.' So we dropped the discourse for that time.

In the meantime, my governess, faithful to the last moment, conveyed my letter to the prison to my husband, and got an answer to it, and the next day came down herself, bringing me, in the first place, a sea-bed, as they call it, and all its ordinary furniture. She brought me also a sea-chest—that is, a chest, such as are made for seamen, with all the conveniences in it, and filled with everything almost that I could want; and in one of the corners of the chest, where there was a private drawer, was my bank of money — that is to say, so much of it as I had resolved to carry with me; for I ordered part of my stock to be left behind, to be sent afterwards in such goods as I should want when I came to settle; for money in that country is not of much use, where all things are bought for tobacco; much more is it a great loss to carry it from hence.

But my case was particular; it was by no means proper for me to go without money or goods, and for a poor convict that was to be sold as soon as I came on shore, to carry a cargo of goods would be to have notice taken of it, and perhaps to have them seized; so I took part of my stock with me thus, and left the rest with my governess.

My governess brought me a great many other things, but it was not proper for me to appear too well, at least till I knew what kind of a captain we should have. When she came into the ship, I thought she would have died indeed; her heart sank at the sight of me, and at the thoughts of parting with me in that condition; and she cried so intolerably, I could not for a long time have any talk with her.

I took that time to read my fellow-prisoner's letter, which greatly perplexed me. He told me it would be impossible for him to be discharged time enough for going in the same ship, and which was more than all, he began to question whether they would give him leave to go in what ship he pleased, though he did voluntarily transport himself; but that they would see him put on board such a ship as they should direct, and that he would be charged upon the captain as other convict prisoners were; so that he began to be in despair of seeing me till he came to Virginia, which made him almost desperate; seeing that, on the other hand, if I should not be there, if any accident of the sea, or of mortality, should take me away, he should be the most undone creature in the world.

This was very perplexing, and I knew not what course to take. I told my governess the story of the boatswain, and she was mighty eager with me to treat with him; but I had no mind to it, till I heard whether my husband, or fellow-prisoner, so she called him, could be at liberty to go with me or no. At last I was forced to let her into the whole matter, except only that of his being my husband. I told her that I had made a positive agreement with him to go, if he could get the liberty of going in the same ship, and I found he had money.

Then I told her what I proposed to do when we came there, how we could plant, settle, and, in short, grow rich without any more adventures; and, as a great secret, I told her we were to marry as soon as he came on board.

She soon agreed cheerfully to my going when she heard this, and she made it her business from that time to get him delivered in time, so that he might go in the same ship with me, which at last was brought to pass, though with great difficulty, and not without all the forms of a transported convict, which he really was not, for he had not been tried, and which was a great mortification to him. As our fate was now determined, and we were both on board, actually bound to Virginia, in the despicable quality of transported convicts, destined to be sold for slaves, I for five years, and he under bonds and security not to return to England any more, as long as he lived, he was very much dejected and cast down; the mortification of being brought on board as he was, like a prisoner, piqued him very much, since it was first told him he should transport himself, so that he might go as a gentleman at liberty. It is true he was not ordered to be sold when he came there as we were, and for that reason he was obliged to pay for his passage to the captain, which we were not; as to the rest, he was as much at a loss as a child what to do with himself, but by directions.

However, I lay in an uncertain condition full three weeks, not knowing whether I should have my husband with me or no, and therefore not resolved how or in what manner to receive the honest boatswain's proposal, which indeed he thought a little strange.

At the end of this time, behold my husband came on board. He looked with a dejected, angry countenance; his great heart was swelled with rage and disdain, to be dragged along with three keepers of Newgate, and put on board like a convict, when he had not so much as been brought to a trial. He made loud complaints of it by his friends, for it seems he had some interest; but they got some check in their application, and were told he had had favour enough, and that they had received such an account of him, since the last grant of his transportation, that he ought to think himself very well treated that he was not prosecuted anew. This answer quieted him, for he knew too much what might have happened, and what he had room to expect; and now he saw the goodness of that advice to him, which prevailed with him to accept the offer of transportation. And after his chagrin at these hell-hounds, as he called them, was a little over, he looked more composed, began to be cheerful, and as I was telling him how glad I was to have him once more out of their hands, he took me in his arms, and acknowledged with great tenderness that I had given him the best advice possible. 'My dear,' says he, 'thou hast twice saved my life; from henceforward it shall be employed for you, and I'll always take your advice.'

Our first business was to compare our stock. He was very honest to me, and told me his stock was pretty good when he came into the prison, but that living there as he did like a gentleman, and, which was much more, the making of friends and soliciting his case, had been very expensive; and, in a word, all his stock left was £108, which he had about him in gold.

I gave him an account of my stock as faithfully, that is to say, what I had taken with me; for I was resolved, whatever should happen, to keep what I had left in reserve; that in case I should die, what I had was enough to give him, and what was left in my governess's hands would be her own, which she had well deserved of me indeed.

My stock which I had with me was £246 some odd shillings; so that we had £354 between us, but a worse gotten estate was never put together to begin the world with.

Our greatest misfortune as to our stock was that it was in money, an unprofitable cargo to be carried to the plantations. I believe his was really all he had left in the world, as he told me it was; but I, who had between £700 and £800 in bank when this disaster befell me, and who had one of the faithfullest friends in the world to manage it for me, considering she was a woman of no principles, had still £300 left in her hand, which I had reserved, as above; besides, I had some very valuable things with me, as particularly two gold watches, some small pieces of plate, and some rings – all stolen goods. With this fortune, and in the sixty-first year of my age, I launched out into a new world, as I may call it, in the condition only of a poor convict, ordered to be transported in respite from the gallows. My clothes were poor and mean, but not ragged or dirty, and none knew in the whole ship that I had anything of value about me.

However, as I had a great many very good clothes and linen in abundance, which I had ordered to be packed up in two great boxes, I had them shipped on board, not as my goods, but as consigned to my real name in Virginia; and had the bills of loading in my pocket; and in these boxes was my plate and watches, and everything of value, except my money, which I kept by itself in a private drawer in my chest, and which could not be found, or opened, if found, without splitting the chest to pieces.

The ship began now to fill; several passengers came on board, who were embarked on no criminal account, and these had accommodations assigned them in the great cabin and other parts of the ship, whereas we, as convicts, were thrust down below, I know not where. But when my husband came on board, I spoke to the boatswain, who had so early given me hints of his friendship. I told him he had befriended me in many things, and I had not made any suitable return to him, and with that I put a guinea into his hand. I told him that my husband was now come on board; that though we were under the present misfortunes, yet we had been persons of a different character from the wretched crew that we came with, and desired to know whether the captain might not be moved to admit us to some conveniences in the ship, for which we would make him what satisfaction he pleased, and that we would gratify him for his pains in procuring this for us. He took the guinea, as I could see, with great satisfaction, and assured me of his assistance.

Then he told us he did not doubt but that the captain, who was one of the best-humoured gentlemen in the world, would be easily brought to accommodate us, as well as we could desire, and, to make me easy, told me he would go up the next tide on purpose to speak to him about it. The next morning happening to sleep a little longer than ordinary, when I got up and began to look abroad, I saw the boatswain among the men in his ordinary business. I was a little melancholy at seeing him there, and going forward to speak to him, he saw me, and came towards me, but not giving him time to speak first, I said, smiling, 'I doubt, sir, you have forgot us, for I see you are very busy.' He returned presently,* 'Come along with me, and you shall see.' So he took me into the great cabin, and there sat a good sort of a gentlemanly man writing, and a great many papers before him.

'Here,' says the boatswain to him that was a-writing, 'is the gentlewoman that the captain spoke to you of.' And turning to me, he said, 'I have been so far from forgetting your business, that I have been up at the captain's house, and have represented faithfully what you said, of your being furnished with conveniences for yourself and your husband; and the captain has sent this gentleman, who is mate of the ship, down on purpose to show you everything, and to accommodate you to your content, and bid

me assure you that you shall not be treated like what you were
expected to be, but with the same respect as other passengers are
treated.

The mate then spoke to me, and not giving me time to thank the
boatswain for his kindness, confirmed what the boatswain had
said, and added that it was the captain's delight to show himself
kind and charitable, especially to those that were under any
misfortunes; and with that he showed me several cabins built up,
some in the great cabin, and some partitioned off, out of the
steerage, but opening into the great cabin, on purpose for
passengers, and gave me leave to choose where I would. I chose a
cabin in the steerage,* in which were very good conveniences to
set our chest and boxes, and a table to eat on.

The mate then told me that the boatswain had given so good a
character of me and of my husband, that he had orders to tell me
we should eat with him, if we thought fit, during the whole
voyage, on the common terms of passengers; that we might lay in
some fresh provisions if we pleased; or if not, he should lay in his
usual store, and that we should have share with him. This was
very reviving news to me, after so many hardships and afflictions.
I thanked him, and told him the captain should make his own
terms with us, and asked him leave to go and tell my husband of it,
who was not very well, and was not yet out of his cabin.
Accordingly I went, and my husband, whose spirits were still so
much sunk with the indignity (as he understood it) offered him,
that he was scarce yet himself, was so revived with the account I
gave him of the reception we were like to have in the ship, that he
was quite another man, and new vigour and courage appeared in
his very countenance. So true is it, that the greatest spirits, when
overwhelmed by their afflictions, are subject to the greatest
dejections.

After some little pause to recover himself, my husband came up
with me, and gave the mate thanks for the kindness which he had
expressed to us, and sent suitable acknowledgments by him to the
captain, offering to pay him by advance, whatever he demanded
for our passage, and for the conveniences he had helped us to. The
mate told him that the captain would be on board in the
afternoon, and that he would leave all that to him. Accordingly, in
the afternoon, the captain came, and we found him the same
courteous, obliging man that the boatswain had represented him;
and he was so well pleased with my husband's conversation, that,

in short, he would not let us keep the cabin we had chosen, but gave us one that, as I said before, opened into the great cabin.

Nor were his conditions exorbitant, or the man craving and eager to make a prey of us, but for fifteen guineas we had our whole passage and provisions, ate at the captain's table, and were very handsomely entertained.

The captain lay himself in the other part of the great cabin, having let his roundhouse,* as they call it, to a rich planter, who went over with his wife and three children, who ate by themselves. He had some other ordinary passengers, who quartered in the steerage; and as for our old fraternity, they were kept under the hatches, and came very little on the deck.

I could not refrain acquainting my governess with what had happened; it was but just that she, who was really concerned for me, should have part in my good fortune. Besides, I wanted her assistance to supply me with several necessaries, which before I was shy of letting anybody see me have; but now I had a cabin, and room to set things in, I ordered abundance of good things for our comfort in the voyage; as brandy, sugar, lemons, etc., to make punch, and treat our benefactor, the captain; and abundance of things for eating and drinking; also a larger bed, and bedding proportioned to it; so that, in a word, we resolved to want for nothing.

All this while I had provided nothing for our assistance when we should come to the place, and begin to call ourselves planters; and I was far from being ignorant of what was needful on that occasion; particularly all sorts of tools for the planter's work, and for building; and all kinds of house furniture, which, if to be bought in the country, must necessarily cost double the price.

I discoursed that point with my governess, and she went and waited upon the captain, and told him that she hoped ways might be found out for her two unfortunate cousins, as she called us, to obtain our freedom when we came into the country, and so entered into a discourse with him about the means and terms also, of which I shall say more in its place; and after thus sounding the captain, she let him know, though we were unhappy in the circumstance that occasioned our going, yet that we were not unfurnished to set ourselves to work in the country, and were resolved to settle and live there as planters. The captain readily offered his assistance, told her the method of entering upon such business, and how easy, nay, how certain it was for industrious people to recover their fortunes in such a manner. 'Madam,' says he, ''tis no reproach to any man in that country to have been sent over in worse circumstances than I perceive your cousins are in, provided they do but apply with good judgment to the business of the place when they come there.'

She then inquired of him what things it was necessary we should carry over with us, and he, like a knowing man, told her thus: 'Madam, your cousins first must procure somebody to buy them as servants, in conformity to the conditions of their transportation, and then, in the name of that person, they may go about what they will; they may either purchase some plantations already begun, or they may purchase land of the government of the country, and begin where they please, and both will be done reasonably.' She bespoke his favour in the first article, which he promised to her to take upon himself, and indeed faithfully performed it. And as to the rest, he promised to recommend us to such as should give us the best advice, and not to impose upon us, which was as much as could be desired.

She then asked him if it would not be necessary to furnish us with a stock of tools and materials for the business of planting; and he said, 'Yes, by all means.' Then she begged his assistance in that, and told him she would furnish us with everything that was convenient, whatever it cost her. He accordingly gave her a list of things necessary for a planter, which, by his account, came to about fourscore or a hundred pounds. And, in short, she went about as dexterously to buy them as if she had been an old Virginia merchant; only that she bought, by my direction, above twice as much of everything as he had given her a list of.

These she put on board in her own name, took his bills of loading for them, and endorsed those bills of loading to my husband, insuring the cargo afterwards in her own name; so that we were provided for all events and for all disasters.

I should have told you that my husband gave her all his own stock of £108, which, as I have said, he had about him in gold, to lay out thus, and I gave her a good sum besides; so that I did not break into the stock which I had left in her hands at all, but after all we had near £200 in money, which was more than enough for our purpose.

In this condition, very cheerful, and indeed joyful at being so happily accommodated, we set sail from Bugby's Hole to Gravesend,* where the ship lay about ten days more, and where the captain came on board for good and all. Here the captain offered us a civility which, indeed, we had no reason to expect, namely, to let us go on shore and refresh ourselves, upon giving our words that we would not go from him, and that we would return peaceably on board again. This was such an evidence of his confidence in us that it overcame my husband, who, in a mere principle of gratitude, told him, as he could not in any capacity make a suitable return for such a favour, so he could not think of accepting it, nor could he be easy that the captain should run such a risk. After some mutual civilities, I gave my husband a purse, in which was eighty guineas, and he put it into the captain's hand. 'There, captain,' says he, 'there's part of a pledge for our fidelity; if we deal dishonestly with you on any account, 'tis your own.' And on this we went on shore.

Indeed, the captain had assurance enough of our resolutions to go, for that having made such provision to settle there, it did not seem rational that we would choose to remain here at the peril of life, for such it must have been. In a word, we went all on shore with the captain, and supped together in Gravesend, where we were very merry, stayed all night, lay at the house where we supped, and came all very honestly on board again with him in the morning. Here we bought ten dozen bottles of good beer, some wine, some fowls, and such things as we thought might be acceptable on board.

My governess was with us all this while, and went round with us into the Downs, as did also the captain's wife, with whom she went back. I was never so sorrowful at parting with my own mother as I was at parting with her, and I never saw her more. We had a fair easterly wind the third day after we came to the Downs,* and we sailed from thence the 10th of April. Nor did we touch any more at any place, till being driven on the coast of Ireland by a very hard gale of wind, the ship came to an anchor in a little bay, near a river whose name I remember not, but they said the river came down from Limerick,* and that it was the largest river in Ireland.

Here, being detained by bad weather for some time, the captain, who continued the same kind, good-humoured man as at first, took us two on shore with him again. He did it now in kindness to my husband indeed, who bore the sea very ill, especially when it blew so hard. Here we bought again store of fresh provisions, beef, pork, mutton, and fowls, and the captain stayed to pickle up five or six barrels of beef, to lengthen out the ship's store. We were here not above five days, when the weather turning mild, and a fair wind, we set sail again, and in two-and-forty days came safe to the coast of Virginia.

When we drew near to the shore the captain called me to him, and told me that he found by my discourse I had some relations in the place, and that I had been there before, and so he supposed I understood the custom in their disposing the convict prisoners when they arrived. I told him I did not; and that, as to what relations I had in the place, he might be sure I would make myself known to none of them while in the circumstances of a prisoner, and that, as to the rest, we left ourselves entirely to him to assist us, as he was pleased to promise us he would do. He told me I must get somebody in the place to come and buy me as a servant, and who must answer for me to the governor of the country if he demanded me. I told him we should do as he should direct; so he brought a planter to treat with him, as it were, for the purchase of me for a servant, my husband not being ordered to be sold, and there I was formally sold to him, and went ashore with him. The captain went with us, and carried us to a certain house, whether it was to be called a tavern or not I know not, but we had a bowl of punch there made of rum, etc., and were very merry. After some time, the planter gave us a certificate of discharge, and an acknowledgment of having served him faithfully, and I was free from him the next morning to go whither I would.

For this piece of service the captain demanded of me six thousand weight of tobacco, which he said he was accountable for to his freighter,* and which we immediately bought for him, and made him a present of twenty guineas besides, with which he was abundantly satisfied.

It is not proper to enter here into the particulars of what part of the colony of Virginia we settled in, for divers reasons; it may suffice to mention that we went into the great river of Potomac, the ship being bound thither; and there we intended to have settled at first, though afterwards we altered our minds.

The first thing I did of moment after having gotten all our goods on shore, and placed them in a storehouse, which, with a lodging, we hired at the small place or village where we landed; I say, the first thing was to inquire after my mother, and after my brother (that fatal person whom I married as a husband, as I have related at large). A little inquiry furnished me with information that

Mrs—, that is, my mother, was dead; that my brother, or husband, was alive, and, which was worse, I found he was removed from the plantation where I lived, and lived with one of his sons in a plantation just by the place where we landed, and had hired a warehouse.

I was a little surprised at first, but as I ventured to satisfy myself that he could not know me, I was not only perfectly easy, but had a great mind to see him if it was possible, without his seeing me. In order to that, I found out by inquiry the plantation where he lived, and with a woman of the place whom I got to help me, like what we call a charwoman, I rambled about towards the place as if I had only a mind to see the country and look about me. At last I came so near that I saw the dwelling-house. I asked the woman whose plantation that was; she said it belonged to such a man, and looking out a little to our right hands, 'There,' says she, 'is the gentleman that owns the plantation, and his father with him.' 'What are their Christian names?' said I. 'I know not,' said she, 'what the old gentleman's name is, but his son's name is Humphry; and I believe,' says she, 'the father's is so too.' You may guess, if you can, what a confused mixture of joy and fright possessed my thoughts upon this occasion, for I immediately knew that this was nobody else but my own son, by that father she showed me, who was my own brother. I had no mask, but I ruffled my hoods so about my face that I depended upon it that after above twenty years' absence, and withal not expecting anything of me in that part of the world, he would not be able to know me. But I need not have used all that caution, for he was grown dim-sighted by some distemper which had fallen upon his eyes, and could but just see well enough to walk about, and not run against a tree or into a ditch. As they drew near to us I said, 'Does he know you, Mrs Owen?' (so they called the woman). 'Yes,' she said, 'if he hears me speak, he will know me; but he can't see well enough to know me or anybody else'; and so she told me the story of his sight, as I have related. This made me secure, and so I threw open my hoods again, and let them pass by me. It was a wretched thing for a mother thus to see her own son, a handsome, comely young gentleman in flourishing circumstances, and durst not make herself known to him, and durst not take any notice of him. Let any mother of children that reads this consider it, and but think with what anguish of mind I restrained myself; what yearnings of soul I had in me to embrace him, and weep over him; and how I thought all my entrails turned within me, that my very bowels moved, and I knew not what to do, as I now know not how to express those agonies! When he went from me I stood gazing and trembling, and looking after him as long as I could see him; then sitting down on the grass, just at a place I had marked, I made as if I lay down to rest me, but turned from her, and lying on my face, wept, and kissed the ground that he had set his foot on.

I could not conceal my disorder so much from the woman, but that she perceived it, and thought I was not well, which I was obliged to pretend was true; upon which she pressed me to rise, the ground being damp and dangerous, which I did, and walked away.

As I was going back again, and still talking of this gentleman and his son, a new occasion of melancholy offered itself, thus. The woman began, as if she would tell me a story to divert me: 'There goes,' says she, 'a very odd tale among the neighbours where this gentleman formerly lived.' 'What was that?' said I. 'Why,' says she, 'that old gentleman going to England, when he was a young man, fell in love with a young lady there, one of the finest women that ever was seen here, and married her, and brought her over hither to his mother, who was then living. He lived here several years with her,' continued she, 'and had several children by her, of which the young gentleman that was with him now was one; but after some time, the old gentlewoman, his mother, talking to her of something relating to herself, and of her circumstances in England, which were bad enough, the daughter-in-law began to be very much surprised and uneasy; and, in short, in examining farther into things, it appeared past all contradiction, that she, the old gentlewoman, was her own mother, and that consequently that son was her own brother, which struck the family with horror, and put them into such confusion that it had almost ruined them all. The young woman would not live with him, he for a time went distracted, and at last the young woman went away for England, and has never been heard of since.'

It is easy to believe that I was strangely affected with this story, but 'tis impossible to describe the nature of my disturbance. I seemed astonished at the story, and asked her a thousand questions about the particulars, which I found she was thoroughly acquainted with. At last I began to inquire into the circumstances of the family, how the old gentlewoman, I mean my mother, died, and how she left what she had; for my mother had promised me, very solemnly, that when she died she would do something for me, and leave it so, as that, if I was living, I should, one way or other, come at it, without its being in the power of her son, my brother and husband, to prevent it. She told me she did not know exactly how it was ordered, but she had been told that my mother had left a sum of money, and had tied her plantation for the payment of it, to be made good to the daughter, if ever she could be heard of, either in England or elsewhere; and that the trust was left with this son, whom we saw with his father.

This was news too good for me to make light of, and you may be sure filled my heart with a thousand thoughts, what course I should take, and in what manner I should make myself known, or whether I should ever make myself known or no.

Here was a perplexity that I had not indeed skill to manage myself in, neither knew I what course to take. It lay heavy upon my mind night and day. I could neither sleep or converse, so that my husband perceived it, wondered what ailed me, and strove to divert me, but it was all to no purpose. He pressed me to tell him what it was troubled me, but I put it off, till at last importuning me continually, I was forced to form a story which yet had a plain truth to lay it upon too. I told him I was troubled because I found we must shift our quarters and alter our scheme of settling, for that I found I should be known if I stayed in that part of the country; for that my mother being dead, several of my relations were come into that part where we then was, and that I must either discover myself to them, which in our present circumstances was not proper on many accounts, or remove; and which to do I knew not, and that this it was that made me melancholy.

He joined with me in this, that it was by no means proper for me to make myself known to anybody in the circumstances in which we then were; and therefore he told me he would be willing to remove to any part of the country, or even to any other country* if I thought fit. But now I had another difficulty, which was, that if I removed to another colony, I put myself out of the way of ever making a due search after those things which my mother had left; again, I could never so much as think of breaking the secret of my former marriage to my new husband; it was not a story would bear telling, nor could I tell what might be the consequences of it: it was impossible, too, without making it public all over the country, as well who I was, as what I now was also.

The perplexity continued a great while, and made my spouse very uneasy; for he thought I was not open with him, and did not let him into every part of my grievance; and he would often say he wondered what he had done, that I would not trust him, whatever it was, especially if it was grievous and afflicting. The truth is, he ought to have been trusted with everything, for no man could deserve better of a wife; but this was a thing I knew not how to open to him, and yet having nobody to disclose any part of it to, the burthen was too heavy for my mind; for, let them say what they please of our sex not being able to keep a secret, my life is a plain conviction to me of the contrary; but be it our sex, or the men's sex, a secret of moment should always have a confidant, a bosom friend to whom we may communicate the joy of it, or the grief of it, be it which it will, or it will be a double weight upon the spirits, and perhaps become even insupportable in itself; and this I appeal to human testimony for the truth of.

And this is the cause why many times men as well as women, and men of the greatest and best qualities other ways, yet have found themselves weak in this part, and have not been able to bear the weight of a secret joy or of a secret sorrow, but have been obliged to disclose it, even for the mere giving vent to themselves, and to unbend the mind, oppressed with the weights which attended it. Nor was this any token of folly at all, but a natural consequence of the thing; and such people, had they struggled longer with the oppression, would certainly have told it in their sleep, and disclosed the secret, let it have been of what fatal nature soever, without regard to the person to whom it might be exposed. This necessity of nature is a thing which works sometimes with such vehemency in the minds of those who are guilty of any atrocious villainy, such as a secret murder in particular, that they have been obliged to discover it, though the consequence has been their own destruction. Now, though it may be true that the divine justice ought to have the glory of all those discoveries and confessions, yet 'tis as certain that Providence, which ordinarily works by the hands of nature, makes use here of the same natural causes to produce those extraordinary effects.

I could give several remarkable instances of this in my long conversation with crime and with criminals. I knew one fellow that, while I was a prisoner in Newgate, was one of those they called then night-fliers.* I know not what word they may have understood it by since, but he was one who by connivance was admitted to go abroad every evening, when he played his pranks, and furnished those honest people they call thief-catchers* with business to find out the next day, and restore for a reward what they had stolen the evening before. This fellow was as sure to tell in his sleep all that he had done, and every step he had taken, what he had stolen, and where, as sure as if he had engaged to tell it waking, and therefore he was obliged, after he had been out, to lock himself up, or be locked up by some of the keepers that had him in fee,* that nobody should hear him; but, on the other hand, if he had told all the particulars, and given a full account of his rambles and success, to any comrade, any brother thief, or to his employers, as I may justly call them, then all was well, and he slept as quietly as other people.

As the publishing this account of my life is for the sake of the just moral of every part of it, and for instruction, caution, warning, and improvement to every reader, so this will not pass, I hope, for an unnecessary digression, concerning some people being obliged to disclose the greatest secrets either of their own or other people's affairs.

Under the oppression of this weight, I laboured in the case I have been naming; and the only relief I found for it was to let my husband into so much of it as I thought would convince him of the necessity there was for us to think of settling in some other part of the world; and the next consideration before us was, which part of the English settlements we should go to. My husband was a perfect stranger to the country, and had not yet so much as a geographical knowledge of the situation of the several places; and I, that, till I wrote this, did not know what the word geographical signified, had only a general knowledge from long conversation with people that came from or went to several places; but this I knew, that Maryland, Pennsylvania, East and West Jersey, New York, and New England lay all north of Virginia, and that they were consequently all colder climates, to which, for that very reason, I had an aversion. For that as I naturally loved warm weather, so now I grew into years, I had a stronger inclination to shun a cold climate. I therefore considered of going to Carolina, which is the most southern colony of the English* on the continent; and hither I proposed to go, the rather because I might with ease come from thence at any time, when it might be proper to inquire after my mother's effects, and to demand them.

With this resolution, I proposed to my husband our going away from where we was, and carrying our effects with us to Carolina, where we resolved to settle; for my husband readily agreed to the first part, viz., that it was not at all proper to stay where we was, since I had assured him we should be known there; and the rest I concealed from him. ·

But now I found a new difficulty upon me. The main affair grew heavy upon my mind still, and I could not think of going out of the country without somehow or other making inquiry into the grand affair of what my mother had done for me; nor could I with any patience bear the thought of going away, and not make myself known to my old husband (brother), or to my child, his son; only I would fain have had it done without my new husband having any knowledge of it, or they having any knowledge of him.

I cast about innumerable ways in my thoughts how this might be done. I would gladly have sent my husband away to Carolina, and have come after myself, but this was impracticable; he would not stir without me, being himself unacquainted with the country, and with the methods of settling anywhere. Then I thought we would both go first, and that when we were settled I should come back to Virginia; but even then I knew he would never part with me, and be left there alone. The case was plain; he was bred a gentleman, and was not only unacquainted,* but indolent, and when we did settle, would much rather go into the woods with his gun, which they call there hunting, and which is the ordinary work of the Indians; I say, he would much rather do that than attend to the natural business of the plantation.

These were, therefore, difficulties unsurmountable, and such as I knew not what to do in. I had such strong impressions on my mind about discovering myself to my old husband, that I could not withstand them; and the rather, because it ran in my thoughts, that if I did not while he lived, I might in vain endeavour to convince my son afterward that I was really the same person, and that I was his mother, and so might both lose the assistance and comfort of the relation, and lose whatever it was my mother had left me; and yet, on the other hand, I could never think it proper to discover the circumstances I was in, as well relating to the having a husband with me as to my being brought over as a criminal; on both which accounts it was absolutely necessary to me to remove from the place where I was, and come again to him, as from another place and in another figure.

Upon those considerations, I went on with telling my husband the absolute necessity there was of our not settling in Potomac River, that we should presently be made public there; whereas if we went to any other place in the world, we could come in with as much reputation as any family that came to plant; that, as it was always agreeable to the inhabitants to have families come among them to plant, who brought substance with them, so we should be sure of agreeable reception, and without any possibility of a discovery of our circumstances.

I told him too, that as I had several relations in the place where we was, and that I durst not now let myself be known to them, because they would soon come to know the occasion of my coming over, which would be to expose myself to the last degree; so I had reason to believe that my mother, who died here, had left me something, and perhaps considerable, which it might be very well worth my while to inquire after; but that this too could not be done without exposing us publicly, unless we went from hence; and then, wherever we settled, I might come, as it were, to visit and to see my brother and nephews, make myself known, inquire after what was my due, be received with respect, and, at the same time, have justice done me; whereas, if I did it now, I could expect nothing but the trouble, such as exacting it by force, receiving it with curses and reluctance, and with all kinds of affronts, which he would not perhaps bear to see; that in case of being obliged to legal proofs of being really her daughter, I might be at a loss, be obliged to have recourse to England, and, it may be, to fail at last, and so lose it. With these arguments, and having thus acquainted my husband with the whole secret, so far as was needful to him, we resolved to go and seek a settlement in some other colony, and at first Carolina was the place pitched upon.

In order to this we began to make inquiry for vessels going to Carolina, and in a very little while got information, that on the other side of the bay, as they call it, namely, in Maryland, there was a ship which came from Carolina, loaden with rice and other goods, and was going back again thither. On this news we hired a sloop to take in our goods, and taking, as it were, a final farewell of Potomac River, we went with all our cargo over to Maryland.

This was a long and unpleasant voyage, and my spouse said it was worse to him than all the voyage from England, because the weather was bad, the water rough, and the vessel small and inconvenient. In the next place, we were full a hundred miles up Potomac River, in a part they call Westmorland County; and as that river is by far the greatest in Virginia, and I have heard say it is the greatest river in the world that falls into another river, and not directly into the sea, so we had base weather in it, and were frequently in great danger; for though they call it but a river, 'tis frequently so broad, that when we were in the middle we could not see land on either side for many leagues together. Then we had the great bay of Chesapeake to cross, which is, where the River Potomac falls into it, near thirty miles broad, so that our voyage was full two hundred miles, in a poor, sorry sloop, with all our treasure, and if any accident had happened to us we might at last have been very miserable; supposing we had lost our goods and saved our lives only, and had then been left naked and destitute, and in a wild, strange place, not having one friend or acquaintance in all that part of the world. The very thoughts of it gives me some horror, even since the danger is past.

Well, we came to the place in five days' sailing; I think they call it Philip's Point;* and behold when we came thither, the ship bound to Carolina was loaded and gone away but three days before. This was a disappointment; but, however, I, that was to be discouraged with nothing, told my husband that since we could not get passage to Carolina, and that the country we was in was very fertile and good, we would see if we could find out anything for our turn where we was, and that if he liked things we would settle here.

We immediately went on shore, but found no conveniences just at that place, either for our being on shore or preserving our goods on shore, but was directed by a very honest Quaker, whom we found there, to go to a place about sixty miles east; that is to say, nearer the mouth of the bay, where he said he lived, and where we should be accommodated, either to plant or to wait for any other place to plant in that might be more convenient; and he invited us with so much kindness that we agreed to go, and the Quaker himself went with us.

Here we bought us two servants, viz. an English woman-servant, just come on shore from a ship of Liverpool, and a negro man-servant, things absolutely necessary for all people that pretended to settle in that country. This honest Quaker was very helpful to us, and when we came to the place that he proposed, found us out a convenient storehouse for our goods, and lodging for ourselves and servants; and about two months, or thereabout, afterwards, by his direction, we took up a large piece of land from the government of that country, in order to form our plantation, and so we laid the thoughts of going to Carolina wholly aside, having been very well received here, and accommodated with a convenient lodging till we could prepare things, and have land enough cured, and materials provided for building us a house, all which we managed by the direction of the Quaker; so that in one year's time, we had near fifty acres of land cleared, part of it enclosed, and some of it planted with tobacco, though not much; besides, we had garden-ground and corn sufficient to supply our servants with roots and herbs and bread.

And now I persuaded my husband to let me go over the bay again, and inquire after my friends. He was the willinger to consent to it now, because he had business upon his hands sufficient to employ him, besides his gun to divert him, which they call hunting there, and which he greatly delighted in; and indeed we used to look at one another, sometimes with a great deal of pleasure, reflecting how much better that was, not than Newgate only, but than the most prosperous of our circumstances in the wicked trade we had been both carrying on.

Our affair was now in a very good posture; we purchased of the proprietors of the colony as much land for £35, paid in ready money, as would make a sufficient plantation to us as long as we could either of us live; and as for children, I was past anything of that kind.

But our good fortune did not end here. I went, as I have said, over the bay, to the place where my brother, once a husband, lived; but I did not go to the same village where I was before, but went up another great river, on the east side of the river Potomac, called Rappahannoc River,* and by this means came on the back of his plantation, which was large, and by the help of a navigable creek, that ran into the Rappahannoc, I came very near it.

I was now fully resolved to go up point-blank to my brother (husband), and to tell him who I was; but not knowing what temper I might find him in, or how much out of temper, rather, I might make him by such a rash visit, I resolved to write a letter to him first, to let him know who I was, and that I was come not to give him any trouble upon the old relation, which I hoped was entirely forgot, but that I applied to him as a sister to a brother, desiring his assistance in the case of that provision which our mother, at her decease, had left for my support, and which I did not doubt but he would do me justice in, especially considering that I was come thus far to look after it.

I said some very tender, kind things in the letter about his son, which I told him he knew to be my own child, and that as I was guilty of nothing in marrying him, any more than he was in marrying me, neither of us having then known our being at all related to one another, so I hoped he would allow me the most passionate desire of once seeing my own and only child, and of showing something of the infirmities of a mother in preserving a violent affection for him, who had never been able to retain any thought of me one way or other.

I did believe that, having received this letter, he would immediately give it to his son to read, his eyes being, I knew, so dim that he could not see to read it; but it fell out better than so, for as his sight was dim, so he had allowed his son to open all letters that came to his hand for him, and the old gentleman being from home, or out of the way when my messenger came, my letter came directly to my sons's hand and he opened and read it.

He called the messenger in, after some little stay, and asked him where the person was who gave him that letter. The messenger told him the place, which was about seven miles off; so he bid him stay, and ordering a horse to be got ready, and two servants, away he came to me with the messenger. Let any one judge the consternation I was in when my messenger came back and told me the old gentleman was not at home, but his son was come along with him, and was just coming up to me. I was perfectly confounded, for I knew not whether it was peace or war, nor could I tell how to behave; however, I had but a very few moments to think, for my son was at the heels of the messenger, and coming up into my lodgings, asked the fellow at the door something. I suppose it was, for I did not hear it, which was the gentlewoman that sent him; for the messenger said, 'There she is, sir'; at which he comes directly up to me, kisses me, took me in his arms, embraced me with so much passion that he could not speak, but I could feel his breast heave and throb like a child, that cries, but sobs, and cannot cry out.

I can neither express or describe the joy that touched my very soul when I found, for it was easy to discover that part, that he came not as a stranger, but as a son to a mother, and indeed a son who had never before known what a mother of his own was; in short, we cried over one another a considerable while, when at last he broke out first. 'My dear mother,' says he, 'are you still alive? I never expected to have seen your face.' As for me, I could say nothing a great while.

After we had both recovered ourselves a little, and were able to talk, he told me how things stood. He told me he had not showed my letter to his father, or told him anything about it; that what his grandmother left me was in his hands, and that he would do me justice to my full satisfaction; that as to his father, he was old and infirm both in body and mind; that he was very fretful and passionate, almost blind, and capable of nothing; and he questioned whether he would know how to act in an affair which was of so nice a nature as this; and that therefore he had come himself, as well to satisfy himself in seeing me, which he could not restrain himself from, as also to put it into my power to make a judgment, after I had seen how things were, whether I would discover myself to his father or no.

This was really so prudently and wisely managed, that I found my son was a man of sense, and needed no direction from me. I told him I did not wonder that his father was as he had described him, for that his head was a little touched before I went away; and principally his disturbance was because I could not be persuaded to live with him as my husband, after I knew that he was my brother; that as he knew better than I what his father's present condition was, I should readily join with him in such measures as he would direct; that I was indifferent as to seeing his father, since I had seen him first, and he could not have told me better news than to tell me that what his grandmother had left me was entrusted in his hands, who, I doubted not, now he knew who I was, would, as he said, do me justice. I inquired then how long my mother had been dead, and where she died, and told so many particulars of the family, that I left him no room to doubt the truth of my being really and truly his mother.

My son then inquired where I was, and how I had disposed myself. I told him I was on the Maryland side of the bay, at the plantation of a particular friend, who came from England in the same ship with me; that as for that side of the bay where he was, I had no habitation. He told me I should go home with him, and live with him, if I pleased, as long as I lived; that as to his father, he knew nobody, and would never so much as guess at me. I considered of that a little, and told him, that though it was really no little concern to me to live at a distance from him, yet I could not say it would be the most comfortable thing in the world to me to live in the house with him, and to have that unhappy object always before me, which had been such a blow to my peace before; that though I should be glad to have his company (my son), or to be as near him as possible, yet I could not think of being in the house where I should be also under constant restraint for fear of betraying myself in my discourse, nor should I be able to refrain some expressions in my conversing with him as my son, that might discover the whole affair, which would by no means be convenient.

He acknowledged that I was right in all this. 'But then, dear mother,' says he, 'you shall be as near me as you can.' So he took me with him on horseback to a plantation, next to his own, and where I was as well entertained as I could have been in his own. Having left me there, he went away home, telling me he would talk of the main business the next day; and having first called me his aunt, and given a charge to the people, who it seems were his tenants, to treat me with all possible respect, about two hours after he was gone, he sent me a maid-servant and a negro boy to wait on me, and provisions ready dressed for my supper; and thus I was as if I had been in a new world, and began almost to wish that I had not brought my Lancashire husband from England at all.

However, that wish was not hearty neither, for I loved my Lancashire husband entirely, as I had ever done from the beginning; and he merited it as much as it was possible for a man to do; but that by the way.

The next morning my son came to visit me again, almost as soon as I was up. After a little discourse, he first of all pulled out a deerskin bag, and gave it me, with five-and-fifty Spanish pistoles in it, and told me that it was to supply my expenses from England, for though it was not his business to inquire, yet he ought to think I did not bring a great deal of money out with me, it not being usual to bring much money into that country. Then he pulled out his grandmother's will, and read it over to me, whereby it appeared that she left a plantation on York River to me, with the stock of servants and cattle upon it, and had given it in trust to this son of mine for my use, whenever he should hear of me, and to my heirs, if I had any children, and in default of heirs, to whomsoever I should by will dispose of it; but gave the income of it, till I should be heard of, to my said son; and if I should not be living, then it was to him, and his heirs.

This plantation, though remote from him, he said he did not let out, but managed it by a head-clerk, as he did another that was his father's, that lay hard by it, and went over himself three or four times a year to look after it. I asked him what he thought the plantation might be worth. He said, if I would let it out, he would give me about £60 a year for it; but if I would live on it, then it would be worth much more, and he believed would bring me in about £150 a year. But seeing I was likely either to settle on the other side the bay, or might perhaps have a mind to go back to England, if I would let him be my steward he would manage it for me, as he had done for himself, and that he believed he should be able to send me as much tobacco from it as would yield me about £100 a year, sometimes more.

This was all strange news to me, and things I had not been used to; and really my heart began to look up more seriously than I think it ever did before, and to look with great thankfulness to the hand of Providence, which had done such wonders for me, who had been myself the greatest wonder of wickedness perhaps that had been suffered to live in the world. And I must again observe, that not on this occasion only, but even on all other occasions of thankfulness, my past wickedness and abominable life never looked so monstrous to me, and I never so completely abhorred it, and reproached myself with it, as when I had a sense upon me of Providence doing good to me, while I had been making those vile returns on my part.

But I leave the reader to improve these thoughts, as no doubt they will see cause, and I go on to the fact. My son's tender carriage and kind offers fetched tears from me, almost all the while he talked with me. Indeed, I could scarce discourse with him but in the intervals of my passion; however, at length I began, and expressing myself with wonder at my being so happy to have the trust of what I had left, put into the hands of my own child, I told him, that as to the inheritance of it, I had no child but him in the world, and was now past having any if I should marry, and therefore would desire him to get a writing drawn, which I was ready to execute, by which I would, after me, give it wholly to him and to his heirs. And in the meantime, smiling, I asked him what made him continue a bachelor so long. His answer was kind and ready, that Virginia did not yield any great plenty of wives, and that since I talked of going back to England, I should send him a wife from London.

This was the substance of our first day's conversation, the pleasantest day that ever passed over my head in my life, and which gave me the truest satisfaction. He came every day after this, and spent great part of his time with me, and carried me about to several of his friends' houses, where I was entertained with great respect. Also I dined several times at his own house, when he took care always to see his half-dead father so out of the way that I never saw him, or he me. I made him one present, and it was all I had of value, and that was one of the gold watches, of which, I said, I had two in my chest, and this I happened to have with me, and gave it him at his third visit. I told him I had nothing of any value to bestow but that, and I desired he would now and then kiss it for my sake. I did not, indeed, tell him that I stole it from a gentlewoman's side, at a meeting-house in London. That's by the way.

He stood a little while hesitating, as if doubtful whether to take it or no. But I pressed it on him, and made him accept it, and it was not much less worth than his leather pouch full of Spanish gold; no, though it were to be reckoned as if at London, whereas it was worth twice as much there. At length he took it, kissed it, told me the watch should be a debt upon him that he would be paying as long as I lived.

A few days after, he brought the writings of gift* and the scrivener with him, and I signed them very freely, and delivered them to him with a hundred kisses; for sure nothing ever passed between a mother and a tender, dutiful child with more affection. The next day he brings me an obligation under his hand and seal, whereby he engaged himself to manage the plantation for my account, and to remit the produce to my order wherever I should be; and withal, obliged himself to make up the produce £100 a year to me. When he had done so, he told me that as I came to demand before the crop was off, I had a right to the produce of the current year; and so he paid £100 in Spanish pieces of eight, and desired me to give him a receipt for it as in full for that year, ending at Christmas following; this being about the latter end of August.

I stayed here above five weeks, and indeed had much ado to get away then. Nay, he would have come over the bay with me, but I would by no means allow it. However, he would send me over in a sloop of his own, which was built like a yacht, and served him as well for pleasure as business. This I accepted of, and so, after the utmost expressions both of duty and affection, he let me come away, and I arrived safe in two days at my friend's the Quaker's.

I brought over with me, for the use of our plantation, three horses, with harness and saddles, some hogs, two cows, and a thousand other things, the gift of the kindest and tenderest child that ever woman had. I related to my husband all the particulars of this voyage, except that I called my son my cousin; and first, I told him that I had lost my watch, which he seemed to take as a misfortune; but then I told him how kind my cousin had been, that my mother had left me such a plantation, and that he had preserved it for me, in hopes some time or other he should hear from me; then I told him that I had left it to his management, that he would render me a faithful account of its produce; and then I pulled him out the £100 in silver, as the first year's produce; and then pulling out the deerskin purse with the pistoles, 'And here, my dear,' says I, 'is the gold watch.' Says my husband, 'So is Heaven's goodness sure to work the same effects, in all sensible minds, where mercies touch the heart!' lifted up both his hands, and with an ecstasy of joy, 'What is God a-doing,' says he, 'for such an ungrateful dog as I am!' Then I let him know what I had brought over in the sloop, besides all this; I mean the horses, hogs, and cows, and other stores for our plantation; all which added to his surprise, and filled his heart with thankfulness; and from this time forward I believe he was as sincere a penitent and as thoroughly a reformed man as ever God's goodness brought back from a profligate, a highwayman, and a robber. I could fill a larger history than this with the evidences of this truth, but that I doubt that part of the story will not be equally diverting as the wicked part.

But this is to be my own story, not my husband's. I return therefore to my own part. We went on with our own plantation, and managed it with the help and direction of such friends as we got there, and especially the honest Quaker, who proved a faithful, generous, and steady friend to us; and we had very good success, for having a flourishing stock to begin with, as I have said, and this being now increased by the addition of £150 sterling in money, we enlarged our number of servants, built us a very good house, and cured every year a great deal of land. The second year I wrote to my old governess, giving her part* with us of the joy of our success, and ordered her how to lay out the money I had left with her, which was £250 as above, and to send it to us in goods, which she performed with her usual kindness and fidelity, and all this arrived safe to us.

Here we had a supply of all sorts of clothes, as well for my husband as for myself; and I took especial care to buy for him all those things I knew he delighted to have; as two good long wigs, two silver-hilted swords, three or four fine fowling-pieces, a fine saddle with holsters and pistols very handsome, with a scarlet cloak; and, in a word, everything I could think of to oblige him, and to make him appear, as he really was, a very fine gentleman. I ordered a good quantity of such household stuff as we wanted, with linen for us both. As for myself, I wanted very little of clothes or linen, being very well furnished before. The rest of my cargo consisted in iron-work of all sorts, harness for horses, tools, clothes for servants, and woollen-cloth, stuffs, serges, stockings, shoes, hats, and the like, such as servants wear; and whole pieces also, to make up for servants, all by direction of the Quaker; and all this cargo arrived safe, and in good condition, with three women-servants, lusty wenches, which my old governess had picked up for me, suitable enough to the place, and to the work we had for them to do, one of which happened to come double, having been got with child by one of the seamen in the ship, as she owned afterwards, before the ship got so far as Gravesend; so she brought us out a stout boy, about seven months after our landing.

My husband, you may suppose, was a little surprised at the arriving of this cargo from England; and talking with me one day after he saw the particulars, 'My dear,' says he, 'what is the meaning of all this? I fear you will run us too deep in debt: when shall we be able to make returns for it all?' I smiled, and told him that it was all paid for; and then I told him that, not knowing what might befall us in the voyage, and considering what our circum-stances might expose us to, I had not taken my whole stock with me, that I had reserved so much in my friend's hands, which now we were come over safe, and settled in a way to live, I had sent for, as he might see.

He was amazed, and stood awhile telling upon his fingers, but said nothing. At last he began thus: 'Hold, let's see,' says he, telling upon his fingers still, and first on his thumb; 'there's £246 in money at first, then two gold watches, diamond rings, and plate,' says he, upon the forefinger. Then upon the next finger, 'Here's a plantation on York River, £100 a year, then £150 in money, then a sloop-load of horses, cows, hogs, and stores'; and so on to the thumb again. 'And now,' says he, 'a cargo cost £250 in England, and worth here twice the money.' 'Well,' says I, 'what do you make of all that?' 'Make of it?' says he. 'Why, who says I was deceived when I married a wife in Lancashire? I think I have married a fortune, and a very good fortune too,' says he.

In a word, we were now in very considerable circumstances, and every year increasing; for our new plantation grew upon our hands insensibly, and in eight years which we lived upon it, we brought it to such a pitch that the produce was at least £300 sterling a year: I mean, worth so much in England.

After I had been a year at home again, I went over the bay to see my son, and to receive another year's income of my plantation; and I was surprised to hear, just at my landing there, that my old husband was dead, and had not been buried above a fortnight. This, I confess, was not disagreeable news, because now I could appear as I was, in a married condition; so I told my son before I came from him that I believed I should marry a gentleman who had a plantation near mine; and though I was legally free to marry, as to any obligation that was on me before, yet that I was shy of it lest the plot should some time or other be revived, and it might make a husband uneasy. My son, the same kind, dutiful, and obliging creature as ever, treated me now at his own house, paid me my hundred pounds, and sent me home again loaded with presents.

Some time after this, I let my son know I was married, and invited him over to see us, and my husband wrote a very obliging letter to him also, inviting him to come and see him; and he came accordingly some months after, and happened to be there just when my cargo from England came in, which I let him believe belonged all to my husband's estate, and not to me.

It must be observed that when the old wretch, my brother (husband) was dead, I then freely gave my husband an account of all that affair, and of this cousin, as I called him before, being my own son by that mistaken match. He was perfectly easy in the account, and told me he should have been easy if the old man, as we called him, had been alive. 'For,' said he, 'it was no fault of yours, nor of his; it was a mistake impossible to be prevented.' He only reproached him with desiring me to conceal it, and to live with him as a wife, after I knew that he was my brother; that, he said, was a vile part. Thus all these little difficulties were made easy, and we lived together with the greatest kindness and comfort imaginable. We are now grown old; I am come back to England, being almost seventy years of age, my husband sixty-eight, having performed much more than the limited terms of my transportation; and now, notwithstanding all the fatigues and all the miseries we have both gone through, we are both in good heart and health. My husband remained there some time after me to settle our affairs, and at first I had intended to go back to him, but at his desire I altered that resolution, and he is come over to England also, where we resolve to spend the remainder of our years in sincere penitence for the wicked lives we have lived.

Written in the Year 1683

The End

NOTES

p.1 Newgate The most important criminal gaol in London, situated at the north-western edge of the historic walled city. It was rebuilt in 1672 after the Great Fire; the gate itself was removed in 1757, but the prison adjoining was reconstructed on a grand scale after its demolition in the Gordon Riots of 1780. A contemporary described it in 1756 as 'a large prison and made very strong, the better to secure such sort of criminals which too much fill it. It is a dismal place within.' The execution progress to Tyburn started from the gaol.

p.1 pretends aspires

p.2 gust taste

p.2 garbled The word meant 'to sift . . . to separate the good from the bad' (Johnson).

p.3 the park Specifically St James's Park in this context, as normally in the period.

p.3 St John's Street Running northwards from Smithfield on the northern fringe of the city, towards Islington.

p.4 cast Here 'chance from the cast of dice' (Johnson).

p.4 behind to come

p.4 midwife-keeper A 'Mother Midnight' figure, in effect one who kept a brothel: see R. A. Erickson, *Mother Midnight* (New York, 1986).

p.4 child-taker One who took in illegitimate children to foster at the expense of the parish.

p.4 every part of it Foreshadowing a possible sequel; a chapbook which appeared in 1730, *Fortune's Fickle Distribution*, delivered much of what is promised here, but it is not by Defoe.

p.7 Old Bailey   The central criminal court, situated just to the south of Newgate prison. Sessions were held eight times a year, with the Lord Chief Justice of Common Pleas regularly presiding and the Lord Mayor and Sheriffs in attendance.

p.7 steps   steps leading up to the gallows; **string**   hangman's noose

p.7 Flanders   The name suggests contraband Dutch lace.

p.7 House of Orphans   Founded in Paris under the aegis of St Vincent de Paul.

p.8 holland   Linen from Holland, generally of fine quality.

p.8 Cheapside   One of the major east-west throughfares in the city, famous for its market.

p.8 pleaded her belly   Claimed postponement of her execution by reason of being pregnant.

p.8 Colchester   Defoe had extensive links with this town in Essex, sixty miles north-east of London, and bought the lease of several hundred acres of land there in August 1722, a few months after *Moll* appeared. His plans for the site included a tile factory. It is clear from his *Tour thro' Great Britain*, vol. 1 (1724) that he made many trips to this region around this time.

p.10 plain work   i.e. plain sewing, as against embroidery

p.12 heads   caps or head-dresses

p.14 huffed   'To hector; to treat with insolence and arrogance' (Johnson).

p.16 apparently   obviously

p.16 parts   ability

p.17 Betty   A generic name for a lady's maid.

p.19 discovered   revealed

p.21 cast . . . with myself   turned my thoughts to

p.21 capitulation   'Stipulation; terms; conditions' (Johnson).

p.21 told   counted

p.22 correspondence   relations

p.22 turnover   turned-down collar

p.23 Mile End   A village some two miles north of Colchester; the land Defoe leased in 1722 lay in the parish of St Michael, Mile End.

p.25 got vent   become known

p.25 at a point   'Settled, decided, determined, resolved' (*OED*).

p.26 give jealousy   arouse suspicion

p.32 close   'Strict, rigorous, severe' (*OED*).

p.34 rout   fuss

p.35 groat   Coin worth fourpence, which ceased to be minted in 1662 but remained proverbial for a small sum.

p.35 rallied   joked

p.35 censure   professional opinion

p.38 brushed off   made off in a hurry

p.38 amuse   deceive

p.38 the doctor's an ass   Proverbial saying from the seventeenth century.

p.40 carried   behaved

p.40 broke   opened up

p.41 attacked her in form   Approached her in a prescribed way.

p.42 jointure   An income settled on the wife at marriage, to be paid in the event of her husband's death; the portion was the dowry which the bride brought with her.

p.42 Solomon   In *Proverbs* 26:4–5.

p.44 conversation   regular and familiar contact

p.45 like a bear to the stake   Reluctantly (proverbial): compare *Macbeth* V.vi.1–2.

p.46 conversation   Here, sexual congress.

p.47 happily   By a fortunate or successful arrangement.

p.47 country   Neighbourhood.

p.48 the very snare   Recalling *Psalms 9:16*.

p.49 broke   went bankrupt

p.50 the Mint   A precinct in the Borough of Southwark, where debtors could claim sanctuary; the privilege was officially removed in 1723, just one year after *Moll* appeared.

p.51 out of my knowledge   i.e. somewhere I was not known

p.51 Lord Rochester's mistress Alluding to Rochester's poem 'Phyllis, be gentler'.

p.53 lie on hand be available for disposal

p.56 Ratcliff A district to the east of the Tower between the city and Shadwell, crossed by modern Cable Street.

p.56 Rotherhithe Or 'Redriffe', a shipping and dock area on the south bank of the Thames down-river from the city. Along with many real-life seamen, Lemuel Gulliver set up home there.

p.57 Lord Rochester From Rochester's poem 'A Letter from Artemisia in the Town'.

p.58 the occasion of a character The need for a character reference.

p.58 ramble wandering, incoherent speech

p.59 uncomeatable 'Inaccessible; unattainable. A low, corrupt word' (Johnson).

p.59 nice fastidious

p.60 a leap in the dark A proverb which had evolved in Defoe's own lifetime, usually traced back to the alleged last words of the philosopher Thomas Hobbes.

p.61 to deceive the deceiver Recalling the proverb, 'To deceive a deceiver is no deceit'.

p.65 shrewdly put to it seriously embarrassed

p.66 composition partial payment on account

p.68 trained bands A citizen militia raised originally in London.

p.68 burnt in the hand i.e. branded as a felon, often in place of hanging where the accused could claim 'benefit of clergy' for a first offence.

p.71 froward self-willed, perverse

p.71 conversation behaviour

p.72 plunged cast down

p.75 policy cheat, deliberate trick

p.76 amazement Extreme fear; horror' (Johnson).

p.80 under your hand i.e. with your signature attached.

p.82 had actually strangled himself would have hanged himself

p.82 it had gotten too great a head it had grown too powerful

p.83 recruit restoration of funds

p.84 Bath By the time Defoe wrote Bath was established as the most important spa in the country, though its full rise to fashion and prosperity did not occur until the reign of Queen Anne, that is after the supposed date of the story. Defoe had known the town since his youth: in his detailed description of Bath for his *Tour thro' Great Britain*, vol. 2 (1725), he says, 'I have myself drank the waters of the Bath fifty years ago.'

p.84 a place of gallantry Defoe remarks in the *Tour* that Bath is now 'the resort of the sound, rather than the sick . . . and the town is taken up in raffling, gaming, visiting, and . . . all sorts of gallantry'.

p.85 ill house House of ill fame, i.e. a brothel.

p.87 two pair of stairs two floors up

p.88 distasted offended, disgusted

p.88 tell count

p.89 housewife We might say 'husband'.

p.89 diet board

p.89 Shepton Shepton Mallet, twenty-one miles south-west of Bath.

p.92 it is ill venturing too near the brink of a command Defoe may be thinking of *Ecclesiasticus* 3:26, which he quotes from the Vulgate in a pamphlet in 1715: the expression may be translated, 'He that loves danger shall perish therein.'

p.93 Sir Walter Cleave There was a real London banking family of this name.

p.93 Hammersmith The 'village of Hammersmith . . . was formerly a long scattering place . . . in this village we see now . . . several handsome streets, as if the village seemed inclined to grow up into a city' (Defoe, *Tour*, vol. 2).

p.96 abroad out of his house

p.98 a convincing work upon his mind A process of conviction of his own sinfulness.

p.100 frankly unconditionally

p.100 stated placed

p.100 plate silver

p.101 painting make-up

p.107 cry her down   publicly disclaim her debts

p.109 conditioned   disposed to listen

p.113 come too cheap   offer no resistance to conversion

p.114 West Chester   That is, Chester, 'a very ancient city' fully described in the *Tour*, vol. 2.

p.114 the Black Rock   A point on the east side of the Wirral, across the Mersey from Liverpool, and perhaps located at modern New Brighton, where the river enters the sea.

p.117 mere   complete

p.119 Manchester   'One of the greatest, if not the greatest mere village in England' (*Tour*, vol. 2). It was still unincorporated and without parliamentary representation, despite rapid growth in recent years.

p.119 rifle   rob

p.122 Delamere Forest   Ancient woodland between Chester and Manchester; Defoe describes a visit to the seat of Lord Delamere and his passage through the forest in the *Tour*, vol. 2.

p.122 amused   puzzled

p.123 see for a service   look for a place in service

p.123 Dunstable   A famous stage on the coach road from London to the north-west, on the route of the Roman Watling Street.

p.126 Clerkenwell   A district north of Smithfield, well known to Defoe, lying between Islington and the old city. For St John's Street, see note to p. 3 above. There was a large floating population in the area, with a concentration of immigrants.

p.128 Mother Midnight   Bawd as well as midwife: see note to p. 4 above.

p.129 the parish impertinence   The parish had the right by the Poor Law to remove an unmarried woman who was pregnant to her place of settlement; if not the place of her birth then the parish from which she had most recently come.

p.129 at the sign of the cradle   Probably located at Cradle Court, in Aldersgate, very close to the spot where Moll encounters the child with a necklace (p. 205).

p.132 Drury Lane   The street was then more famous for prostitution than for theatrical life.

p.134 nauseate   feel nausea at

p.134 **of the right hand** on the right side

p.139 **vapours** vapid and hysterical talk

p.141 **jealous** anxious

p.141 **Stone** 'A considerable town on the great road to West Chester' (*Tour*, vol. 3), actually in Staffordshire, some miles short of the Cheshire border.

p.142 **Brickhill** On the Chester road, a few miles towards London from Stony Stratford; both lie in the vicinity of modern Milton Keynes. Defoe writes extensively on the improvements to the road here in an appendix on turnpikes which he attached to the *Tour*, vol. 2.

p.143 **abroad** out

p.143 *Non compos mentis* of unsound mind

p.143 **shagreen** rawhide with a rough surface

p.145 **friends** relatives

p.146 **grimace** hypocrisy or dissimulation

p.146 **suit of knots** A set of ribbons to ornament a dress.

p.146 **bone-lace** Lace woven by means of thread being wound round bobbins, formerly made of animal bones.

p.146 **the music** That is, the 'English music' or charivari, made by a cacophonous array of primitive instruments, to give a mock serenade outside the windows of a newly married couple.

p.147 **hue-and-cry** In its old specific sense, a posse raised to pursue a fugitive suspected of a crime on the highway.

p.148 **mere** complete

p.149 **the root of all evil** Proverbial, from 1 *Timothy* 6:10.

p.150 **lethargic** In a medical sense, as then used, i.e. suffering a loss of bodily functions (Defoe himself was stated in the official records to have died of a 'lethargy'). Dr Arbuthnot called lethargy 'a lighter sort of apoplexy' (cited in *OED*).

p.151 **the vapours** 'Depression . . . hypochondria, hysteria, or other nervous disorder' (*OED*).

p.151 **the wise man's prayer** Derives from Solomon, in *Proverbs* 30:8–9. This was a favourite tag of Defoe's, used in several of his books.

p.152 Leadenhall Street Running eastwards from Cornhill, where Defoe's own business premises had lain, at the heart of the commercial district of the city of London.

p.152 Fenchurch Street Joins Leadenhall Street at the start of Aldgate; several alleys ran between the two streets.

p.152 Thames Street The main east-west thoroughfare adjoining the Thames which Moll would meet on fleeing towards the river from Fenchurch Street. Billingsgate fish market lay on the river bank on the south side of the street.

p.153 tried for my life Legislation dating from 1699 made it a capital offence to steal property valued at five shillings or more from a shop or warehouse.

p.154 Aldersgate Street Running northwards from the north-west corner of the old city, and skirting Smithfield.

p.154 Bartholomew Close A court just off the west side of Aldersgate; Moll proceeds in a loop anti-clockwise around Smithfield, crossing the insalubrious area near the Fleet Ditch, and ending up at Holborn Bridge, where the main highway passed over the ditch. The social character of this quarter is conveyed by the historian Dorothy George in her study of *London Life in the Eighteenth Century*: 'The Field Lane district was intersected by the filthy channel of the Fleet ditch (called in 1722 "a nauceious and abominable sink of nastiness"), into which the tripe dressers, sausage makers and catgut spinners, who shared the Lane with professional thieves, flung their offal.'

p.155 Lombard Street A major commercial street in the city, joining Cornhill near the Royal Exchange. Three King Court ran off southwards from its eastern end.

p.155 lustring *Or* lutestring, a glossy silk material.

p.156 forecast foresight

p.157 stood upon her legs acted in a self-reliant way

p.160 Moll Cutpurse Mary Frith, a thief and trickster of the early seventeenth century, the heroine of many criminal lives ('Cutpurse' means pickpocket).

p.161 Cheapside See note to p. 8

p.162 voted quick with child Deemed to be pregnant (sometimes by a panel of matrons) and thus allowed to have sentence postponed: see note to p. 8.

p.162 the brand of an old offender   Having been branded as a first offender claiming 'benefit of clergy': see note to p. 68.

p.163 engines playing   Reasonably effective fire-engines were a novelty which had only been seen in London since the Great Fire of 1666; the impetus came from the new insurance companies which, according to the *Tour*, covered some seventy thousand houses in London by the time *Moll* was written.

p.165 a pardon   A person convicted of burglary, or of breaking and entering, could gain a pardon and a reward of forty pounds for informing on two others guilty of the same offence.

p.165 making her market of what she knew   Buying immunity by acting as an informer.

p.166 a scouring   punishment

p.167 capitulate   negotiate terms

p.167 a certainty   a definite sum

p.169 clue   tangled web

p.169 artist   skilful operator

p.170 called myself Mrs Flanders   Defoe possibly based his heroine on a real-life criminal named Moll King: see Introduction, pp. xix–xx.

p.173 entered into recognisances   To give a surety and undertake to appear in court.

p.174 formal   For the sake of form, or circumstantial.

p.174 come post   Travel by means of post-horses, that is, relays of fresh horses.

p.175 went very near me   struck a chord with my feelings.

p.177 run a-tick   Run up a score (as in a bar), i.e. start off a new bout of criminal behaviour.

p.178 Bartholomew Fair   A great fair held every August in Smithfield, famous for its vast concourse of varied attractions and a general atmosphere of carnival.

p.178 cloisters   Arcades in front of the shops, frequented by prostitutes, pickpockets and the like.

p.178 raffling shops   gambling booths

p.178 Spring Garden   A pleasure garden to the west of London, near Hyde Park, an area known for highway robberies and other disorders.

p.179 Temple Bar Situated at the junction of the Strand and Fleet Street, it marked the boundary between London and Westminster.

p.180 Solomon says *Proverbs* 7:22–3.

p.180 the foul disease syphilis

p.182 Hampstead Then a village some way outside the city to the north, developing a bad reputation (at the time of writing the novel) for undisciplined assemblies. The *Tour* informs us that a gaming house was temporarily suppressed by the magistrates in 1722; a year later the proprietor was hiring twenty 'stout' men to protect visitors against assault on their way to and from London.

p.183 officiously helpfully, in a spirit of kindness

p.185 chairman One who carried passengers in a sedan-chair (a small conveyance borne on poles).

p.187 alleged put all the blame on

p.188 shifted hard enough had difficulty in making a living

p.189 shapes disguises

p.189 Barnet Like Totteridge and Hadley, a small town some twelve miles up the Great North Road from central London.

p.189 that came next me that first occurred to me

p.190 Charterhouse Lane Moll's escape is made through a series of streets and alleys on the east side of Smithfield, past Christ's Hospital school ('the Bluecoat Hospital'), ending up a few yards from her birthplace in Newgate gaol.

p.191 the Flying Horse A coaching inn in Bishopsgate, just beyond the walls at the north-eastern corner of the city. 'Cheston' may be an error for Chester, but it is more likely to refer to Chesterton, near Peterborough, a coaching stage on the Great North Road about eighty miles north of London.

p.191 huckaback linen A kind of coarse linen used to make towels.

p.191 ells The ell was a unit of length, three feet nine inches, still used for commercial purposes in Defoe's time.

p.191 flint glasses 'A pure lustrous glass' (*OED*), which used to be made from ground flint.

p.191 Mr Henzill's glass-house A firm of glassmakers, of French origin, based in Newcastle; Defoe knew the city of Newcastle well and refers to the glasshouses in his *Tour*.

p.191 the pitcher come safe home Proverbial for a risky enterprise, perhaps based on *Ecclesiastes* 12:6.

p.192 Covent Garden An open square north of the Strand and west of Drury Lane, combining some impressive architecture and (in Defoe's age) theatrical life with raffish and less respectable activities.

p.192 artists tricksters

p.194 not a hired officer In the absence of a regular police force, local law enforcement devolved on unpaid members of the community, selected annually by the parish; but they could pay a fine in lieu of acting, and deputies were then hired to take their place. Defoe compounded for not serving as a constable of Stoke Newington in 1721 by paying £10.

p.196 second mourning A reduced form of mourning dress worn after the unrelieved black clothes of early widowhood were put aside.

p.198 Hick's Hall The court where Middlesex sessions were held, situated at the bottom of St John's Street near the scene of Moll's earlier escapades.

p.198 pettifogging hedge solicitor A low-grade lawyer; solicitors were at this stage a sub-class of paralegal agents, not part of the recognised profession.

p.199 set myself out adorned myself

p.201 equipage outfit

p.201 tight to be neat and tidy

p.202 the Gazette The *London Gazette*, which carried official announcements, public notices and the like.

p.202 sorted consorted

p.202 at a stake coining (producing counterfeit coins) was deemed a species of treason; a woman named Barbara Spencer was burnt at the stake at Tyburn in 1721 for this offence.

p.203 part share the spoils

p.203 St Catharine's The area near St Katherine's Dock, immediately along the riverside to the east of the Tower of London. A large colony of Flemish and Dutch immigrants had settled there.

p.204 the Exchange A shopping arcade towards the west end of the Strand, sometimes known as the New Exchange.

p.204 St James's Park A royal park close to the old palace of St James, which was open to the public. It attracted fashionable loungers, especially on the Mall, a walkway between the palace and the ornamental lake. See Pope's *Rape of the Lock*, Canto V.

p.205 Suffolk Street A short street near the Haymarket, to the west of what is now Trafalgar Square.

p.205 puts myself in a rank came abreast of

p.206 the Horse Guards A parade ground between St James's Park and Whitehall, not yet surrounded by the imposing buildings designed by William Kent.

p.207 set bet

p.207 threw out Lost his bet on this throw, in the game of hazard.

p.208 told counted

p.209 rumbling Probably an error for 'rambling'.

p.209 Tunbridge, and Epsom Tunbridge Wells in Kent, and Epsom in Surrey, the leading pleasure resorts till the rise of Bath; Defoe describes his experiences in the two places in his *Tour*, admitting that he had to leave the latter because he had run out of money.

p.209 Stourbridge Fair . . . Bury Fair The former, held on the outskirts of Cambridge each autumn, is the subject of a lengthy passage in the *Tour* vol. 1. Unlike Stourbridge Fair, the rival occasion at nearby Bury St Edmunds was 'like Bartholomew Fair . . . a fair for diversion, more than for trade' (*Tour*).

p.209 bite deception or ruse

p.210 Ipswich . . . Harwich East-coast ports, known to Defoe since his youth. Both are described in some detail in the first volume of the *Tour*, and *Moll* appears to use observations which Defoe had made when planning this opening section of his guidebook (it is the portion of the *Tour* with the most recent information).

p.210 purchase plunder

p.210 fairly successfully

p.211 ducatoons Silver coins, of less value than the French pistoles, which were worth almost a pound.

p.211 wash-balls 'A ball of soap (sometimes perfumed or medicated) used for washing the hands and face, and for shaving' (*OED*).

p.212 my ends what I needed

p.212 poll crown of the head

p.212 a town This has been plausibly identified as Stratford St Mary, on the road between Ipswich and Colchester where it is crossed by the River Stour (the location of many paintings by Constable).

p.214 Forster Lane Foster Lane, on the west side of the city, running north from Cheapside parallel with Aldersgate: described by a contemporary as 'a place of good resort for silversmiths'.

p.217 the fatal tree The gallows at Tyburn.

p.219 up to my score Charged to Moll's account, as new prisoners were required to pay 'garnish', that is to treat existing inmates.

p.219 the bell The note is from the original edition; it refers to the bell of St Sepulchre's, which tolled as the execution procession set out for Tyburn from Newgate, opposite the church.

p.220 cast for my life sentenced to death

p.221 the ordinary The prison chaplain, who counselled prisoners before their execution, and published admonitory narratives of their life and death.

p.221 Guildhall The headquarters of the city corporation, where a court was also held.

p.223 the country people of the neighbourhood

p.223 the press-yard A part of Newgate near the keeper's lodging which was reserved for prisoners who could afford to pay for better accommodation.

p.223 take a tour To take to the road as a highwayman.

p.223 Hind, or Whitney, or the Golden Farmer Captain James Hind; James Whitney; and William Davis, seventeenth-century highwaymen, all of whom were executed and whose stories were well known through popular criminal narratives.

p.224 my temper was touched before Already my hard front had been pierced

p.224 the grand jury A preliminary presentment was made by a grand jury, who decided whether the accused should go to a full trial.

p.225 clout sheet

p.225 flatter To deceive with false hopes.

p.226 discovered revealed

p.228 dead warrant A list of those who were to be hanged.

p.229 of mere course naturally, automatically

p.231 **the Recorder** A magistrate, appointed by the Aldermen of London, who acted as a senior judge within the city.

p.232 **mere distemper** total derangement

p.233 **petition for transportation** Regular transportation to the colonies of convicted felons only began with an act in 1718; prior to that, criminals could make a voluntary undertaking to transport themselves, and they were given a technical pardon on this condition.

p.235 **the master's side** There were three main divisions in the Newgate gaol; the master's side was perhaps the most unappetizing, followed by the common side and then the press-yard (see note to p. 223).

p.235 **carry them off** obtain a conviction

p.236 **stupid** stupefied

p.238 **Hockley** Hockliffe, on the Chester road between Dunstable and Brickhill.

p.238 **Burford Fair** Not in Wiltshire but in Oxfordshire.

p.239 **temper** composure

p.240 **conduct** Management, hence a matter of paying a sum of money to arrange things.

p.242 **taken up** reformed

p.243 **within the term** Inside the term specified by the court, most often seven years.

p.243 **weighed** That is, weighed anchor, and made its way down the Thames to Bugsby's Reach, a stretch of the river beyond Blackwell leading into Woolwich Reach.

p.245 **furniture** private possessions

p.249 **presently** immediately

p.250 **the steerage** A part of the quarter-deck next to the cabin.

p.251 **his roundhouse** A cabin on the after part of the quarter-deck.

p.252 **Gravesend** In the *Tour*, vol. 1, Defoe describes how incoming ships were obliged to stop here, whilst outgoing merchant ships underwent a customs search.

p.253 **the Downs** A relatively sheltered anchorage off the eastern coast of Kent, near Deal.

p.253 **the river came down from Limerick** i.e. the Shannon

p.254 his freighter A private contractor who undertook the procedure of transportation (the sea-captain was an agent of this contractor).

p.257 any other country Another of the American colonies.

p.259 night-fliers As Swift observes in his poem, 'A Description of the Morning', there was an arrangement by which criminals were let out at night by their gaolers 'to steal for fees'.

p.259 thief-catchers Professional informers who brought criminals into the grasp of the authorities, having sometimes organised the crime themselves in the first place – as in the case of the notorious Jonathan Wild, whose career was still at its height when Defoe wrote (he was executed in 1725).

p.259 in fee in their pay

p.259 the most southern colony of the English Prior to the foundation of Georgia in the 1730s and the temporary acquisition of Florida.

p.260 unacquainted 'Inexperienced; ignorant' (*OED*).

p.262 Philip's Point This has been identified as a headland at the entrance of the Nanticoke River, in Dorchester County, Maryland, which flows into the eastern side of Chesapeake Bay.

p.263 Rappahannoc River Moll reaches her brother's home in Westmorland County by taking the river flowing parallel to the Potomac. This county was the birthplace of George Washington, just ten years after *Moll* was published.

p.268 writings of gift Deeds of gift, assigning the property titles to Moll.

p.270 giving her part sharing

Moll Flanders was not especially well known in the eighteenth century. By far Defoe's most famous book was *Robinson Crusoe*, and next came some of his numerous works of non-fiction – political pamphlets like *The Shortest Way with the Dissenters*, journalism like *The Review*, poems like *Jure Divino*, conduct-books like *Religious Courtship*, and general works such as the influential *Tour of Great Britain*. In fact, *Moll* initially came out as often in an adapted form or as a chapbook (see Introduction, pp. xvi–xvii). The low esteem in which the novel was widely held is indicated by these anonymous verses printed in the *Flying Post* on 1 March 1729.

> Down in the kitchen, honest Dick and Doll
> Are studying Colonel Jack and Flanders Moll.

It was with the generation of the Romantics that Defoe's broader achievement as a novelist began to be recognised. Scott and Coleridge praised his work, and Charles Lamb wrote a valuable commentary on the 'secondary' novels (that is, excluding *Crusoe*) in 1829.

In truth, the heroes and heroines of De Foe can never again hope to be popular with a much higher class of readers, than that of the servant-maid or the sailor; *Crusoe* keeps its rank only by tough prescription; Singleton, the Pirate – Colonel Jack, the thief – Moll Flanders, both thief and harlot – Roxana, harlot and something worse – would be startling ingredients in the bill of fare of modern literary delicacies. But, then, what pirates, what thieves, and what harlots, is *the thief, the harlot,* and *the pirate* of De Foe? We would not hesitate to say, that in no other book of fiction, where the lives of such characters are described, is guilt and delinquency made less seductive, or the suffering made more closely to follow the commission, or the penitence more earnest or more bleeding, or the intervening flashes of religious visitation, upon the rude and uninstructed soul, more meltingly and fearfully painted. They, in this, come near to the tenderness of Bunyan; while the livelier pictures and incidents in them, as in Hogarth or in

Fielding, tend to diminish that fastidiousness to the concerns and pursuits of common life, which an unrestrained passion for the ideal and the sentimental is in danger of producing.

Another important contribution was that of William Hazlitt (1775–1829), who wrote on Defoe in the *Edinburgh Review* in 1830.

> We find, in this style of writing, nothing but an alternation of religious horrors and raptures, (though these are generally rare, as being a less tempting bait,) and the grossest scenes of vice and debauchery: we have either saintly, spotless purity, or all is rotten to the core. How else can we account for it, that all Defoe's characters (with one or two exceptions for form's sake) are of the worst and lowest description – the refuse of the prisons and the stews – thieves, prostitutes, vagabonds, and pirates – as if he wanted to make himself amends for the restraint under which he had laboured 'all the fore-end of his time' as a moral and religious character, by acting over every excess of grossness and profligacy by proxy! How else can we comprehend that he should really think there was a salutary moral lesson couched under the history of *Moll Flanders*; or that his romance of *Roxana, or the Fortunate Mistress*, who rolls in wealth and pleasure from one end of the book to the other, and is quit for a little death-bed repentance and a few lip-deep professions of the vanity of worldly joys, showed, in a striking point of view, the advantages of virtue, and the disadvantages of vice? It cannot be said, however, that these works have an *immoral* tendency. The author has contrived to neutralise the question; and (as far as in him lay) made vice and virtue equally contemptible or revolting. In going through his pages, we are inclined to vary Mr Burke's well-known paradox, that 'vice, by losing all its grossness, loses half its evil,' and say that vice, by losing all its refinement, loses all its attraction. We have in them only the pleasure of sinning, and the dread of punishment here or hereafter; – gross sensuality, and whining repentance. The morality is that of the inmates of a house of correction; the piety, that of malefactors in the condemned hole. There is no sentiment, no atmosphere of imagination, no 'purple light' thrown round virtue or vice; – all is either the physical gratification on the one hand, or a selfish calculation of consequences on the other.

As the nineteenth century progressed, stress was increasingly laid on Defoe as a sturdy Protestant and, especially with *Crusoe*, a proto-apologist of colonial expansion.

The dissenter Walter Wilson (1781–1847) wrote one of the first major biographies of Defoe in 1830. His views prefigure many Victorian attitudes.

The story of Moll Flanders, although seriously told, and abounding in just reflections upon the danger of an habitual course of wickedness, is a book after all, that cannot be recommended for indiscriminate perusal. The scenes it unfolds are such as must be always unwelcome to a refined and well-cultivated mind; whilst with respect to others, it is to be feared that those who are pre-disposed to the oblique paths of vice and dishonesty, will be more alive to the facts of the story, than to the moral that is suspended to it. The life of a courtezan, however carefully told, if told faithfully, must contain much matter unfit to be presented to a virtuous mind. Moll Flanders is one of a low description; and gliding into the occupation of a shop-lifter, she became an adept in all the arts of her profession. The first part of her story renders her an object of pity, as the latter part of it does of respect; but the intermediate spaces are filled up by matters of a forbidding nature; and whatever lessons the whole may be calculated to afford to persons in a similar situation, it may be feared that they will weigh less with the obtuse and the profligate, than their dreams of present advantage. Those who take delight in exploring the annals of Newgate, without the moral, may here find the like scenes with the moral pointed. It is to the credit of De Foe, that he nowhere administers to the vicious taste of his reader, but takes every occasion of holding up vice to abhorrence.

Gradually *Moll Flanders* came to occupy a slightly higher place within the canon of Defoe. This is seen in the contribution of Leslie Stephen (1832–1904), critic, editor of the *Dictionary of National Biography*, and father of Virginia Woolf. He published a well-known essay on Defoe in the *Cornhill Magazine* in 1868.

We do not imagine that *Roxana, Moll Flanders, Colonel Jack,* or *Captain Singleton* can fairly claim any higher interest than that which belongs to the ordinary police report, given with infinite fulness and vivacity of detail. In each of them there are one or two forcible situations. Roxana pursued by her daughter, Moll Flanders in prison, and Colonel Jack as a young boy of the streets, are powerful fragments, and well adapted for his peculiar method. He goes on heaping up little significant facts, till we are able to realise the situation powerfully, and we may then supply the sentiment for ourselves. But he never seems to know his own strength. He gives us at equal length, and with the utmost plain-speaking, the details of a number of other positions, which are neither interesting nor edifying. He is decent or coarse, just as he is dull or amusing, without knowing the difference. The details about the different connections formed by Roxana and Moll Flanders have no atom of sentiment, and are about as wearisome as the journal of a specially heartless lady of the same character would be at the present day. He has been praised for never gilding objectionable objects, or making vice attractive. To all appearance, he would have been totally unable to set about it. He has only one mode of telling a story, and he follows the thread of his narrative into the back-slums of London, or lodging-houses of doubtful character, or respectable places of trade, with the same equanimity, at a steady jog-trot of narrative. The absence of any passion or sentiment deprives such places of the one possible source of interest; and we must confess that two-thirds of each of these novels are deadly dull; the remainder, though exhibiting specimens of his genuine power, is not far enough from the commonplace to be specially attractive. In short, the merit of De Foe's narrative bears a direct proportion to the intrinsic merit of a plain statement of the facts; and, in the novels already mentioned, as there is nothing very surprising, certainly nothing unique, about the story, his treatment cannot raise it above a very moderate level.

As we enter the twentieth century, a more searching and yet less grudging attitude begins to emerge. Thus, the novelist and critic Virginia Woolf (1882–1941) wrote some valuable pieces on Defoe, including the essay extracted here, which appeared in the first series of her studies, *The Common Reader* (1925).

From her very birth or with half a year's respite at most, Moll Flanders . . . is goaded by 'that worst of devils, poverty,' forced to earn her living as soon as she can sew, driven from place to place, making no demands upon her creator for the subtle domestic atmosphere which he was unable to supply, but drawing upon him for all he knew of strange people and customs. From the outset the burden of proving her right to exist is laid upon her. She has to depend entirely upon her own wits and judgement, and to deal with each emergency as it arises by a rule-of-thumb morality which she has forged in her own head. The briskness of the story is due partly to the fact that having transgressed the accepted laws at a very early age she has henceforth the freedom of the outcast. The one impossible event is that she should settle down in comfort and security. But from the first the peculiar genius of the author asserts itself, and avoids the obvious danger of the novel of adventure. He makes us understand that Moll Flanders was a woman on her own account and not only material for a succession of adventures. In proof of this she begins, as Roxana also begins, by falling passionately, if unfortunately, in love. That she must rouse herself and marry some one else and look very closely to her settlements and prospects is no slight upon her passion, but to be laid to the charge of her birth; and, like all Defoe's women, she is a person of robust understanding. Since she makes no scruple of telling lies when they serve her purpose, there is something undeniable about her truth when she speaks it. She has no time to waste upon the refinements of personal affection, one tear is dropped, one moment of despair allowed, and then 'on with the story.' She has a spirit that loves to breast the storm. She delights in the exercise of her own powers. When she discovers that the man she has married in Virginia is her own brother she is violently disgusted; she insists upon leaving him; but as soon as she sets foot in Bristol, 'I took the diversion of going to Bath, for as I was still far from being old so my humour, which was always gay, continued so to an extreme.' Heartless she is not, nor can any one charge her with levity; but life delights her, and a heroine who lives has us all in tow. Moreover, her ambition has that slight strain of imagination in it which puts it in the category of the noble passions. Shrewd and practical of necessity, she is yet haunted by a desire for romance and for the quality which to her perception makes a man a gentleman. 'It was really a true gallant spirit he was of, and it was the more grievous to me. 'Tis something of relief even to be undone by a man of honour rather than by a scoundrel,' she writes when she had misled a highwayman as to the extent of her fortune. It is in keeping with this temper that she should be proud of her final partner because he refuses to work when they reach the plantations but prefers hunting, and that she should take pleasure in buying him wigs and silver-hilted swords 'to make him appear, as he really was, a very fine gentleman.' Her very love of hot weather is in keeping, and the passion with which she kissed the ground that her son had trod on, and her noble tolerance of every kind of fault so long as it is not 'complete baseness of spirit, imperious, cruel, and relentless when uppermost, abject and low-spirited when down.' For the rest of the world she has nothing but good-will . . .

. . . The interpretation that we put on his characters might . . . well have puzzled him. We find for ourselves meanings which he was careful to disguise even from himself. Thus it comes about that we admire Moll Flanders far more than we blame her. Nor can we believe that Defoe had made up his mind as to the precise degree of her guilt, or was unaware that in considering the lives of the abandoned he raised many deep questions and hinted, if he did not state, answers quite at variance with his professions of belief. From the evidence supplied by his essay upon the 'Education of Women' we know that he had thought deeply and much in advance of his age upon the capacities of women, which he rated very high, and the injustice done to them, which he rated very harsh.

I have often thought of it as one of the most barbarous customs in the world, considering us as a civilised and a Christian country, that we deny the advantages of learning to women. We reproach the sex every day with folly and impertinence; which I am confident, had they the advantages of education equal to us, they would be guilty of less than ourselves.

The advocates of women's rights would hardly care, perhaps, to claim Moll Flanders and Roxana among their patron saints; and yet it is clear that Defoe not only intended them to speak some very modern doctrines upon the subject, but placed them in circumstances where their peculiar hardships are displayed in such a way as to elicit our sympathy.

From the celebrated study, *Aspects of the Novel* (1927), by Woolf's friend and colleague E. M. Forster (1879–1970):

Moll Flanders fills the book that bears her name, or rather stands alone in it, like a tree in a park, so that we can see her from every aspect and are not bothered by rival growths. Defoe is telling a story, like Scott, and we shall find stray threads left about in much the same way, on the chance of the writer wanting to pick them up afterwards: Moll's early batch of children for instance. But the parallel between Scott and Defoe cannot be pressed. What interested Defoe was the heroine, and the form of his book proceeds naturally out of her character. * * * How just are her reflections when she robs of her gold necklace the little girl returning from the dancing-class. The deed is done in the little passage leading to St Bartholomew's, Smithfield (you can visit the place today – Defoe haunts London) and her impulse is to kill the child as well. She does not, the impulse is very feeble, but conscious of the risk the child has run she becomes most indignant with the parents for 'leaving the poor little lamb to come home by itself, and it would teach them to take more care of it another time.' How heavily and pretentiously a modern psychologist would labour to express this! It just runs off Defoe's pen, and so in another passage, where Moll cheats a man, and then tells him pleasantly afterwards that she has done so, with the result that she slides still further into his good graces, and cannot bear to cheat him any more. Whatever she does gives us a slight shock – not the jolt of disillusionment, but the thrill that proceeds from a living being. We laugh at her, but without bitterness or superiority. She is neither hypocrite nor fool.

Towards the end of the book she is caught in a draper's shop by two young ladies from behind the counter: 'I would have given them good words but there was no room for it: two fiery dragons could not have been more furious than they were' – they call for the police, she is arrested and sentenced to death and then transported to Virginia instead. The clouds of misfortune lift with indecent rapidity. The voyage is a very pleasant one, owing to the kindness of the old woman who had originally taught her to steal. And (better still) her Lancashire husband happens to be transported also. They land at Virginia where, much to her distress, her brother-husband proves to be in residence. She conceals this, he dies, and the Lancashire husband only blames her for concealing it from him: he has no other grievance, for the reason that he and she are still in love. So the book closes prosperously, and firm as at the opening sentence the heroine's voice rings out: 'We resolve to spend the remainder of our years in sincere penitence for the wicked lives we have led.' . . .

Moll Flanders then shall stand as our example of a novel in which a character is everything and is given freest play. Defoe makes a slight attempt at a plot with the brother-husband as a centre, but he is quite perfunctory, and her legal husband (the one who took her on the jaunt to Oxford) just disappears and is heard of no more. Nothing matters but the heroine; she stands in an open space like a tree, and having said that she seems absolutely real from every point of view, we must ask ourselves whether we should recognise her if we met her in daily life. For that is the point we are still considering: the difference between people in life and people in books.

Although recent discussion of *Moll* has been dominated by academic studies, there are good general assessments such as that of the biographer and critic Peter Quennell, in *The Singular Preference* (1953).

Himself Defoe was a man of enormous energy who experienced considerable changes of fortune; and it is their remarkable vitality that distinguishes all the personages he created – their refusal to be downed by circumstance and the insect-like persistence with which they continue to scheme and shove. Both *Moll Flanders* and *Roxana* have moral endings – virtue is rewarded and vice, somewhat tardily, receives a rap on the knuckles; but in the last analysis each of them is an essentially moral book. No wonder that George Borrow, lounging disconsolately across Westminster Bridge after days in wringing a livelihood from the Newgate Calendar (whence he had begun to imbibe 'strange doubts . . . about virtue and crime'), was shocked to see a copy of *Moll Flanders*, black, greasy, dog-eared, in the hands of an old apple-woman who sat on the pavement, and to hear her describe its heroine as 'the blessed woman.' Her darling son, explained the apple-woman, was a transported convict; and through those eyes Moll's acquisitive and combative qualities shone with a lustre that was both unexpected and disconcerting. The protagonist's misdeeds were excused by her success and courage. Her criminal habits were not a psychological eccentricity – the idea of the *acte gratuit* derives from the well-to-do – but had behind them the impetus of a genuine social passion. Besides, Moll Flanders is an extraordinarily English character; and, as we read her story we are reminded, again and again, that

England is the country where almost everyone is conscious of being a little better than somebody else. Moll thanks her stars repeatedly that she is not as other sinners; and, although through force of circumstances she lives in the present moment, she is supported by recollections of respectability and by the relics of a good education and a middle-class upbringing. Thank God, she 'had been bred up tight and cleanly'! Among the thieves, fences and prostitutes with whom her lot is cast, she never loses sight of her own superior origins; and, when at last she finds herself committed to Newgate, what horrifies her is the indecorous squalor of her new environment: 'the hellish noise, the roaring, swearing and clamour, the stench and nastiness . . .' Later, the fact that most distresses her is that she, too, should so quickly have become acclimatised.

. . . It would be absurd, of course, to pretend that Defoe develops or builds up his heroine's character with the self-conscious artistry of a modern novelist. But, because he understood her so well and delineated her background from first-hand knowledge, the character that does emerge has an astonishing sharpness. Primarily, *Moll Flanders* is an essay in storytelling – written, one imagines, at breakneck speed, with care for the picturesque quality of every episode: but there are few incidents that could be discarded without loss to the whole.

To re-read Defoe's narrative with attention is to despair almost of the future of the English language. In detail, there is much that is slipshod; but the general effect is one of accuracy combined with lucidity. The virile prose of the late seventeenth century can hardly be over-praised. It has outgrown the euphuisms of the Elizabethans and has not yet acquired the somewhat ponderous latinistic elegance that it was gradually to take on during the Augustan age. It is a *modern* prose, made to be spoken by modern people, and admirably suited to the description of a world of muddy streets, hackney coaches, shops, warehouses, and hungry, hurrying passers-by. In that world – the universe of commercial London, shadowed by its brownish pall of 'sea-coal' fog – there is little room for spiritual airs and graces, abstract speculation or poetic fancy. The men and women Defoe deals with have always their livings to gain; and his greatest novel faithfully reflects their standards. After her first experience of romantic passion (so nearly fatal), the heroine gives a wide berth to any form of excess or insobriety. She distrusts it in herself: she condemns and despises it when she sees it in others. She may not hesitate to go to bed with a drunken gentleman, rob him during the coach-ride of 'a gold watch, with a silk purse full of gold, his fine full-bottom periwig and silver-fringed gloves, his sword and fine snuff-box,' allow her 'governess', the receiver of stolen goods, to do some quiet blackmailing, then agree to meet him again and become his mistress; but she is horrified nevertheless by his presumption and folly – 'there is nothing (she reflects) so absurd, so surfeiting, so ridiculous as a man heated by wine in his head, and a wicked gust in his inclination together . . .' She has the innate respectability of the typical prostitute . . .

Defoe seems to be looking up at us from that life itself – to partake of, and yet transcend, its confusion and drabness. Not for him the elaborate processes of aesthetic eavesdropping by which the French novelists were obliged to refresh their imagination. As he writes, the wheels are thundering along the narrow streets: the kennels swim with mud: the rain-water gurgles in leaden gutters and splashes down on to the pavements of the commercial city. Moll Flanders is any woman carrying a bundle, looking from time to time over her shoulder, hurrying independent yet furtive through fog or rain. The least 'imaginative', certainly the least literary, of English writers, Defoe is capable of a simplicity and force and eloquence that any modern novelist is bound to envy, while sudden flashes of imaginative insight redeem his commonplace. And not for a moment does he lose touch with the central drama – the tragedy of the little foundling who would be a gentlewoman and follows a will-o'-wisp of social advancement through the London underworld, pursued by the spectres of degradation and hunger and misery.

The most influential recent account of the novel has been that of Ian Watt, in *The Rise of the Novel* (1957).

Moll Flanders has a few examples of patent and conscious irony. There is, first of all, a good deal of dramatic irony of a simple kind: for example in Virginia, where a woman relates the story of Moll's incestuous marriage, not knowing that she is addressing its chief figure. There are also some examples of much more pointed irony, as in the passage when, as a little girl, Moll Flanders vows that she will become a gentlewoman when she grows up, like one of her leisured but scandalous neighbours:

> 'Poor child,' says my good old nurse, 'you may soon be such a gentlewoman as that, for she is a person of ill fame, and has had two bastards.'
> I did not understand anything of that; but I answered, 'I am sure they call her madam, and she does not go to service nor do housework'; and therefore I insisted that she was a gentlewoman, and I would be such a gentlewoman as that.

It is good dramatic irony to point this prophetic episode with the phrase 'such a gentlewoman as that', where the verbal emphasis also drives home the difference between virtue and class, and the moral dangers of being taken in by external evidences of gentility. We can be certain that the irony is conscious because its tenor is supported by Defoe's other writings, which often show a somewhat rancorous spirit towards the failure of the gentry to provide proper models of conduct: there is a similar tendency, for example, in Moll's later ironical description of the eldest brother as 'a gay gentleman who . . . had levity enough to do an ill-natured thing, yet had too much judgment of things to pay too dear for his pleasures'. Here, the combination of stylistic elegance and demonstrable consonance with Defoe's own point of view makes us sure that Moll Flanders's reflection after she has been duped by James is also ironical: ' 'Tis something of relief even to be undone by a man of honour, rather than by a scoundrel'. The verbal hyperbole drives home the contrast between overt and actual moral norms: 'undone' is a calculated exaggeration, Moll Flanders being what she is already; and the ambiguity of 'a man of honour' seems to be used with full consciousness of its subversive effect.

These examples of conscious irony in *Moll Flanders*, however, fall far short of the larger, structural irony which would suggest that Defoe viewed either his central character or his purported moral theme ironically. There is certainly nothing in *Moll Flanders* which clearly indicates that Defoe sees the story differently from the heroine. There are, it is true, a few cases where such an intention seems possible: but on examination they are seen to have none of the hallmarks of the conscious examples of irony.

The passage is also typical in content, because the suspicion of irony is aroused by a bathetic transition from sentiment to action which is very common in Defoe's novels, although it is never certain that he intends it ironically. There is the occasion, for instance, when Moll, in her unwonted transport of feeling, kisses the ground her son has trodden on, but desists as soon as it is urged upon her that the ground is 'damp and dangerous'. It is perhaps possible that Defoe was laughing at his heroine's unabashed mixture of sentimentality and common sense; but it is surely more likely that he had to get Moll off her knees before he could get on with the story, and that he did not ponder the means of doing so very carefully.

The lack of insulation between incongruous attitudes seems particularly ironical if we are already predisposed to regard one of them as false. This happens with many of the moralising passages, and Defoe certainly does nothing to obviate our incredulity by the way he introduces them. One glaringly improbable case occurs when an as yet impenitent Moll relates to the governess how she was picked up by a drunken man whom she later robbed, and goes on to improve the occasion by quoting Solomon in the course of a lay sermon against drunkenness. The governess is much moved, Moll tells us:

. . . it so affected her that she was hardly able to forbear tears, to

think how such a gentleman ran a daily risk of being undone, every
time a glass of wine got into his head.

But as to the purchase I got, and how entirely I stripped him, she
told me it pleased her wonderfully. 'Nay, child,' says she, 'the usage
may, for aught I know, do more to reform him than all the sermons
that ever he will hear in his life.' And if the remainder of the story be
true, so it did.

The two women then combine to anticipate divine retribution, and
to milk the poor gentleman of his cash, in order to drive their lesson
home. The episode is certainly a travesty of piety and morality; and yet
it is very unlikely that Defoe is being ironical; any more than he is later
when, by some very human obliquity, Moll Flanders excuses herself
from the prison chaplain's appeal that she confess her sins on the
grounds of his addiction to the bottle. Both episodes are plausible
enough psychologically: the devotees of one vice are often less
charitable than the virtuous about the other ones they happen not to
favour. The problem, however, is whether Defoe himself overlooked,
and expected his readers to overlook, the very damaging nature of the
context in which his homilies against alcohol occur. There is every
reason to believe that he did: the lesson itself must have been intended
seriously, and not ironically; as for its context, we have already seen
that there was no way in which Defoe could make good his didactic
professions except by making Moll double as chorus for his own
honest beliefs; and there is therefore good reason to believe that the
moral imperceptiveness which is so laughably clear to us is in fact a
reflection of one of the psychological characteristics of Puritanism
which Defoe shared with his heroine . . .

One famous instance is the passage when she consoles herself for
having stolen a child's gold necklace with the reflection: 'I only
thought I had given the parents a just reproof for their negligence, in
leaving the poor lamb to come home by itself, and it would teach them
to take more care another time'. There is no doubt about the
psychological veracity of the reflection: the conscience is a great
casuist. There is, however, some doubt about Defoe's intention: is it
meant to be an ironical touch about his heroine's moral duplicities, her
tendency to be blind to the beam in her own eye? or did Defoe forget
Moll as he raged inwardly at the thought of how careless parents are,
and how richly they deserve to be punished?

If Defoe intended the passage to be an ironical portrayal of spiritual
self-deception, it becomes necessary to assume that he saw Moll
Flanders's character as a whole in this light, for the incident is typical
of her general blindness to her own spiritual and mental dishonesty.
She always lies about her financial position, for instance, even to those
she loves. Thus when the mutual trickery with James is revealed, she

conceals a thirty-pound bank-bill 'and that made freer of the rest, in consideration of his circumstances, for I really pitied him heartily'. Then she goes on, 'But to return to this question, I told him I never willingly deceived him and I never would'. Later, after his departure, she says: 'Nothing that ever befell me in my life sank so deep into my heart as this farewell. I reproached him a thousand times in my thoughts for leaving me, for I would have gone with him through the world, if I had begged my bread. I felt in my pocket, and there I found ten guineas, his gold watch, and two little rings . . .' She cannot even in theory attest the reality of her devotion by expressing her willingness to beg her bread, without immediately proving that it was only a rhetorical hyperbole by reassuring herself that she has enough in her pocket to keep her in bread for a lifetime. There is surely no conscious irony here: for Defoe and his heroine generous sentiments are good, and concealed cash reserves are good too, perhaps better; but there is no feeling that they conflict, or that one attitude undermines the other.

Defoe had accused the occasional conformists of 'playing Bo-Peep with God Almighty'. The term admirably describes the politic equivocations about common honesty and moral truth so common in *Moll Flanders*. Defoe there 'plays Bo-Peep' at various levels: from the sentence and the incident to the fundamental ethical structure of the whole book, his moral attitude to his creation is as shallow and devious and easily deflected as his heroine's on the occasion when her married gallant writes to her to terminate the affair, and urges her to change her ways, she writes: 'I was struck with this letter, as with a thousand wounds; the reproaches of my own conscience were such as I cannot express, for I was not blind to my own crime; and I reflected that I might with less offence have continued with my brother, since there was no crime in our marriage on that score, neither of us knowing it.'

No writer who had allowed himself to contemplate either his heroine's conscience, or the actual moral implications of her career, in a spirit of irony, could have written this seriously. Nor could he have written the account of James's moral reformation, in which Moll Flanders tells us how she brought him the riches given by her son, not forgetting 'the horses, hogs, and cows, and other stores for our plantation' and concludes 'from this time forward I believe he was as sincere a penitent and as thoroughly a reformed man as ever God's goodness brought back from a profligate, a highwayman, and a robber'. We, not Defoe, are ironically aware of the juxtaposition of the powers of God and Mammon; we, not Defoe, laugh at the concept of reformation through hogs and cows.

A leading Defoe critic, Maximillian E. Novak, is one of many to have responded to the arguments of Ian Watt; this extract comes from Novak's essay, 'Conscious Irony in *Moll Flanders*', in *College English* (1964).

> Moll's words are those of a woman in a state of prosperity and repentance. As a character she tends to be blind to her situation and to reveal only the dimmest understanding of her true moral state. We cannot know her tone of voice, but Defoe will vary his style to suggest sincerity or sophistic rationalisation.
>
> 1. *Morality:* In his fiction Defoe operated on two levels of morality. The first was a standard Christian morality with charity as the highest of virtues. It is difficult to determine the degree to which the Christianity of the fictions is eccentrically puritan. The second was that connected with natural law. This view sees man as a creature motivated mainly by self: self-love, self-interest, and self-defense. Natural law was codified by Grotius and Pufendorf in the seventeenth century, and Defoe drew upon them for his moral judgments concerning natural behavior. 'Natural' is a key word in *Moll Flanders*, and Defoe draws some irony from the disparity between the judgments of the repentant Moll concerning her life passed under the laws of nature. Thus when she says that she was driven by the devil to steal and then excuses herself on the grounds of her poverty, we can see her upbraiding herself for an act which not for a moment could she have avoided. The great virtue of the heroic follower of natural morality is activity, and Moll is one of the most active of his protagonists. Vices include the unnatural: ingratitude, incest, and doing evil to others where there is no excuse to be found in self-preservation or self-interest. It is a moral code which is peculiarly modern in its implications, for it abstracts the individual from specific social institutions and religion and establishes a 'natural' standard based on the sophisticated view of human customs which voyagers to foreign lands had made available to the European.
>
> 2. *Repentance:* Defoe was not being ironic about Moll's repentance and conversion in Newgate. That we are told in the preface that she is no longer as penitent as she was may make us question some of the attacks upon her natural morality in the name of a more conventional Christian morality, but the conversion and repentance in Newgate follows the pattern of a true repentance which appears in Defoe's other writings. Defoe would have allowed for the possibility that a woman like Moll could repent, and the sincerity of tone in these passages should leave little question about the suspension of irony. Here the repentant narrator is dealing with her greatest moment. The remark in the preface merely suggests that Moll remains true to her essential character – a character which fits ill with a perpetually fervent convert.
>
> 3. *Sex, Love, and Marriage:* Defoe once noted that God did not

put the sexual instinct under the control of the reason, and in this it differed from the passions which might be controlled. Sex, then, subjects men and women to a universal comedy in which the main joke lies in the human condition. Thus his most sympathetic hero, Colonel Jacque, is continually cuckolded by his wives, and poor Robin, Moll's first husband, whose defense of marriage for love rather than money Defoe would have found admirable, marries his brother's mistress, who goes to the wedding like 'a bear to the stake.'

A large part of *Moll Flanders* is devoted to the comedy of sex, love and marriage, and Defoe's sympathies remain divided. He thought that the women were worse off than the men, for they cannot buy a husband if they do not have money, and once they marry, they are at the mercy of their husbands. Defoe's only solution was to advise women to become as capable as men – to educate themselves for survival in a masculine world. Moll's rather masculine nature does not appear until her disillusionment, and, unlike the feminist, Roxana, she always prefers to assume a feminine role. But her ideals should not be confused with Defoe's. Her desire for a 'gentleman' husband, who proves useless in the American plantation, is part of the marriage comedy.

Defoe's ideal is one which we can still understand – a marriage for love, a wife who is understanding and helpful, a husband who is a companion and a conscientious provider. Ideally both should be religious and of the same religion. But Defoe seldom presented this ideal and regarded any workable compromise as acceptable. He did not regard polygamy as the worst of sins, for natural law had shown that it was a common institution, and by the same standard of natural law, he regarded desertion as equivalent to divorce. Incest was considered to be contrary to the law of nature, and Moll cannot endure her incestuous marriage to her brother. Even her desire for security must yield to her natural detestation of this relationship.

4. *Children:* The injunctions of natural law state that parents must care for and educate their children, but that in cases of necessity, [they] may give them away. Moll gives love and care where she has the money to afford it. The important point here is that self-preservation was allowed to take precedence over parental love. Defoe seems to have accepted Moll's attitude toward her children as natural enough.

5. *Servants:* After her training with her foster mother, Moll becomes a servant in the home of the Colchester family. She speaks of herself as if she were an adopted daughter, but she is called Miss Betty (the generic name for chamber maids) and is at best a servant-companion to the daughters. Defoe wrote a variety of works attacking the insolence of servants, but he also admired the clever servant who has the ability to rise in the world. Like Mandeville, he knew that the social structure was in flux, but he was much more an exponent of *la*

carrière ouverte aux talents than his contemporary. In Moll, then, Defoe illustrates the servant who is not clever enough to trick the heir of the family into marriage but pretty enough to win a younger son. Defoe's attitude toward the young Moll, who dislikes servitude and admires the independence of the town whore, is detached, amused, critical, and ironic. The irony of the first part of the book which ends with the death of Robin is perfectly clear and free from the complications of more serious themes – the possibility of starvation and destitution.

6. *Poverty (Necessity):* When a person falls into a state of destitution which makes starvation a possibility, he may do anything to preserve his life. Some writers on natural law believed that such a state dissolved the bonds of society and made all goods common. Defoe placed the following limitations on man's freedom when confronted by this 'first and great principle of nature': (a) He must not harm someone in the same condition as himself (a condition of equal poverty or danger). (b) He must try to make restitution of whatever he steals or repair whatever harm he has done when it is possible. (c) His degree of guilt depends to some extent on the degree to which he is to blame for falling into a state of necessity. When Moll blames herself for her crimes she judges herself from a standpoint of divine law and excuses herself on grounds of natural law. The paradox lies in the limitations of the human condition. She condemns herself for her failure to resist temptation, but then argues that human nature is too frail to resist the laws of nature.

7. *Positive Law:* Even Coke argued that no national law could overrule the laws of nature or the laws of God. Such laws could not be regarded as valid. But Moll lives in a society which will punish her for violating its laws. English law tells her that she cannot steal no matter how hungry she is, and she cannot remarry while her husband is alive. Moll always follows the laws of nature, but the contrasts between the three levels of law are responsible for much of the paradoxical morality in *Moll Flanders* and in Defoe's other works.

8. *Thieves and Tradesmen:* Defoe frequently contrasted the honesty of the thief who will steal through necessity and the dishonesty of the grasping tradesman. He suggested that the worst pirates were more honest than the capitalists of his time and superior in every way to the directors of the South Sea Company. He even suggests that Jonathan Wild destroyed honor among thieves when he organised them as an industrialist. Defoe blamed theft and piracy upon the laws of England and English society with its unfair treatment of debtors, its failure to care for the poor, and its ill treatment of seamen. But he also recognised that a society must punish crime or fall into anarchy.

9. *Prostitutes:* Defoe attacked Mandeville's suggestion concerning legalizing prostitution, but he objected to the manner rather

than the matter. Defoe sympathised with the prostitute and argued that she does not support society by consuming its goods (as Mandeville suggested) and that her life is miserable, for he did not believe that she experienced any sexual pleasure in her job. In sketching the decline of women into prostitution he argued that the primary guilt lay with the man who first seduced her. Moll is hardly reluctant but the rake who seduces her is still more at fault.

10. *Gentlemen:* Moll has affairs with three 'gentlemen'. The first robs her of her virtue and refuses to marry her. The second is a 'gentleman-tradesman,' who spends all her money and leaves her destitute. The third is a 'gentleman-highwayman' who tries to cheat her but proves to be a loving spouse. All of these men have in common an aspiration to a life of leisure. Moll's aspiration toward gentility and her disapproval of her Lancashire Husband's idleness in America suggests an appropriate 'muddle' in Moll's mind which is hardly in Defoe's. Defoe frequently attacked those rakish gentlemen who added nothing to the wealth of the society and were a plague to the women. The Lancashire Husband is the best of the group both because he reveals a good heart and because he led an active life of crime to support himself.

11. *Economic Individualism:* Defoe was fully aware of the movement in feeling and ideas which Tawney and Weber described and stood staunchly against it in the name of older mercantilist ideals. He was continually proposing state intervention in trade, the establishment of cooperative communities and societies from orphanages to homes for the aged. In 1704 he complained that 'it is now almost become a Maxim with them [Dissenting ministers], that poverty proceeds from want of Grace, Inverting the Scriptures. That only with [rich?] Men, can enter the Kingdom of Heaven, at least into their Congregation.' Though he dramatised the struggle for wealth in his fiction, Defoe's ideal was always that of retirement when a moderate wealth was achieved. There may appear to be a paradox in his admiration for both activity and retirement, but Defoe did not insist that the activity had to be economic. Colonel Jacque seeks gentility and an education after he has gained wealth.

12. *Projects:* Defoe has Moll remind the reader that some nations have hospitals to take care of orphans and much time is spent on the home for expectant mothers operated by the woman who later becomes her 'Governess'. These are both ideas which Defoe is advancing with some seriousness, but in both cases he uses them dramatically. Moll is given what ought to be a perfectly good training for servitude by the parish. Her inability to accept servitude has something to do with heredity (she sucked her mother's milk in Newgate) and something to do with environment (she was raised by gypsies until the age of three). She should have been spared both

experiences and trained more thoroughly. The Governess has some excellent ideas, but Defoe would have disapproved of her sly suggestion about abortion; and we are not surprised to find that the establishment slips into evil ways.

13. *Colonial Propaganda:* Defoe presents the possibility of a new life in America for the transported criminal in both his fiction and didactic works. He believed that the criminal might become a wealthy property owner through hard work and ingenuity. Though Jacque feels that he needs the official status of an army officer, education, and travel before he can regard himself as a gentleman, Defoe recognised the relativity of status in such a society.

In a collection entitled *What Manner of Woman*, edited by Marlene Springer (1977), John J. Richetti discusses 'The Portrayal of Women in Restoration and Eighteenth-Century English Literature'. He compares the two strong Defoe heroines, Moll and Roxana.

Defoe's two indomitable women claim to be surrounded by desperate circumstances and do indeed endure specifically female trials. They are seduced, forced into crime and a sort of defensive prostitution and mercenary marriage; they have children, marry, and speak at length of the woe that is in marriage. Roxana, for example, develops a clearly articulated ideology of freedom which outlines with subversive vigor her desire to 'be a *Man-Woman*; for as I was born free, I wou'd die so.' One of her lovers proposes marriage and its attendant submission, arguing 'that a sincere Affection between a Man and his Wife, answer'd all the Objections that I had made about the being a Slave, a Servant, *and the like*; and where there was a mutual Love, there cou'd be no Bondage; but that there was but one Interest; one Aim; one Design; and all conspir'd to make both very happy.' Roxana's answer to that conventional wisdom is contemptuous of the male dominance and female risk such arrangements involve . . .

But Roxana and Moll are female impersonators, not simply strong and self-reliant but unperturbed by the implications of female experience. For them, sexuality is simply an available and efficient means for self-advancement and survival. As their tendency toward multiple identity in their stories indicates, they are playing at being women. They are essentially male creations, characters who use their dreadful female problems as opportunities for demonstrating their skill and cunning in survival. They remain to all intents and purposes untouched by the special quality of female experience.

Marie-Paul Laden is the author of *Self-Imitation in the Eighteenth-Century Novel* (1987), a study of ways of representing the self in the English and French novel. In this extract she compares *Moll* to picaresque novels including *Gil Blas* (1715–35) by Alain-René Le Sage (1688–1747).

On the surface level, the narrator's outlook on her life is that of the Christian reformed sinner: '. . . the publishing of this Account of my Life is for the Sake of the just Moral of every part of it, and for Instruction, Caution, Warning, and Improvement to every Reader . . .'. Not unlike Alemán's Guzmán de Alfarache, Moll's stated purpose in writing about herself is not self-glorification, but rather the confession of her crimes for the moral edification of the reader. This purpose, which bears the stamp of her present prosperity, accounts for the larger amount of moralising in Moll's discourse than in Gil Blas's. However, even the casual reader of Moll Flanders's memoirs soon realises that the temporal gap that should exist between the 'I' of the criminal protagonist and that of the penitent narrator is not as wide as one might expect in this form. Contrary to what happens in most of Gil Blas's memoirs, in Moll's the act and the content of the narrative event are often impossible to distinguish. Although Ian Watt qualifies this aspect of Defoe's narrative technique as 'somewhat primitive,' Defoe's perception – unconscious or not – that a tale of the past is an inseparable compound of past actions and present attitudes constitutes the modernity of *Moll Flanders*, and probably accounts for its continued popularity . . .

What renders Moll's memoirs so problematic, and why they have puzzled several generations of critics, is that Moll's manoeuvres to deflect the reader's attention from her culpability constantly and deviously destroy rather than construct any consistent point of view toward herself. Though particular comments or narrative details in a passage can be identified with various points of view, the incongruities are so noticeable, and the shifts from one point of view to another are so rapid and frequent, that they leave only an impression of instability. Moll's 'voice' becomes first polyphony, then cacophony. Blurring matters further is the changing nature of Moll's perspective (a notion that refers to the extent of the narrator's knowledge and understanding of events, as distinguished from the notion of point of view). *Moll Flanders* provides an excellent illustration of the fact that in a personal novel the one who speaks is not necessarily the one who sees, since the perspective can be that of the narrating 'I,' or of the experiencing 'I,' or even of a mixture of both. Hence the need to distinguish between point of view and perspective. In many first-person narratives, such as most of *Gil Blas* and *Great Expectations*, one may easily distinguish between the retrospective voice of the narrator and his contemporary perspective. This separation is next to impossible in the case of *Moll Flanders*, for many reasons: not simply because the narrator is dishonest and twists her tale, as has often been pointed out, but also because, in spite of her experience, Moll does not see certain aspects of her life in retrospect any more clearly than did the protagonist.

For instance, when she explains in a sentence already quoted that she became a compulsive thief because of her love for money, she is still blind to her real motives. It is clear that both Molls love money and 'things' – as demonstrated in the endless lists of stolen items that the narrator remembers – but her main motive for continuing her thieving when she could have retired is her sheer love for her 'Trade.' This she will not admit, and probably does not even recognize. Although she carefully blames her past crimes rather than herself, as we have seen, what emerges from the narrator's discourse is the real zest with which she tells about her past pranks. She piles up story after story of thefts involving various disguises, on which she dwells with relish, when a few examples would have been sufficient to convey an idea of her corruption. In the same manner as for Rousseau, confessing or writing about a sin functions as a repetition or reenactment of the sin. Moll, unconsciously or not, relives her perilous and seamy life through writing while paying lip service to convention through her moralising. Although she may be unaware of it, the narrator manifests the pride of the skillful craftsman in her trade, even calling it her 'Art'. In the following passage she can hardly conceal her glee at the thought of her past exploits: 'I could fill up this whole Discourse with the variety of such Adventures which dayly Invention directed to, and which I manag'd with the utmost Dexterity, and always with Success'.

In what is now the standard biography, *Daniel Defoe: His Life* (1989), Paula Backscheider describes the background to the transportation of criminals, as this affects Defoe's novels, *Moll Flanders* and *Colonel Jacque*.

The Transportation Act of 1718 allowed courts to sentence even clergied felons* to transportation to America. On a very limited scale, transportation had been used before the Restoration as an alternative to capital punishment, and by 1700 it had become a fairly common form of conditional pardon. The judge could pronounce it, or the criminal could petition as Moll Flanders did for transportation. A typical text written by a justice of the peace read:

* Some lesser felonies (such as damaging trees or poaching) allowed the offender to claim the ancient 'benefit of clergy' for the first conviction only. Before the Restoration, *male* criminals read 'the neck verse', Psalm 51, and were turned over to a representative of the Church for punishment. By the early eighteenth century, such offenders were simply released, as were women who committed these 'clergyable' crimes. Public dissatisfaction grew, and demands for fewer releases led to a decrease in the number of clergyable offenses and then to the provision for the transportation of clergied felons.

I reprieved them because it did not appear to me that either of them had committed any such offense before, or were ingaged in any society of offenders ... But they are lewd idle fellows, and it is fitting the country should be clear'd of them. They are strong able body'd men and may do good service either in her Majestys Plantations or army.

The secretary of state would then endorse the pardon upon condition of the prisoner joining the army or accepting transportation. Until 1718 merchants or the prisoners themselves paid their passages to the New World. Because the infirm and female had no market value there, they and the indigent were hanged or simply released. Defoe himself had transported people to Maryland in 1688. He paid £1.7.6 for the transportation of each, and another £1.7.0 for shoes and a coat for them. His expenses were typical. Transportation and board never cost more than £5 or £6 pounds, and Defoe, then a partner for the ship's voyage, was probably paying the actual cost rather than cost plus the profit expected by the captain or shipowner. The trade was profitable; for instance, Defoe made an £8.5s. profit on one of the men he sold. Not all people shipped were convicts; companies and colonies recruited servants, and unemployed people chose to immigrate. Some courts paid up to £8 per person to merchants willing to take women, but so sure were profits from the sale of the prisoners that most required the merchant pay jail fees and even the clerk's charge for drawing up a pardon. Between 1580 and 1650 some 80,000 people went, voluntarily or otherwise, to be servants in the North American colonies; between 1651 and 1700 the figure rose to 90,000. Colonial planters sometimes purchased them by the shipload.

The 1718 act gave merchants contracts granting them £3 for each convict transported. In addition, the merchants could sell the prisoners' services at auction in the colonies where men brought an average of £10, women £8 to £9, and craftsmen as much as £25. By 1722, the year *Moll Flanders* was published, about 60 percent of the convicted male, clergyable felons and 46 percent of the women were transported. In fact, about 70 percent of all the felons convicted at the Old Bailey were deported and only about 7.5 percent executed. Between 1718 and 1775 the courts sent 30,000 convicts to the North American colonies, primarily Maryland and Virginia, Moll's and Jack's destinations. Although the contract holder might protest, prisoners could still arrange their own passage to the colonies. The experience of Moll Flanders is authentically rendered.

Defoe's depiction of her life and Jack's included powerful propaganda for the recent act. Because convicted felons had often been released with a punishment as mild as being branded on the thumb, large numbers of criminals were quickly and repeatedly released.

Because there were no satisfactory penalties between branding and whipping at one extreme and hanging at the other and judges and juries often felt the inappropriateness of either, the lighter sentences were imposed. Moll's and Jack's cases were designed to show the appropriateness of transportation. Jack's crimes were just the kind committed by most of the felons sent over, but he had not been caught, tried, and sentenced. In any event, his kidnapping and sale were realistic. The Mansion House Justice Room Charge Book records several instances of men 'spirited' 'beyond the Sea without Consent,' and Virginia seems to have been the most frequent destination (2 December 1701, fol. 130). So frequently were people tricked, made drunk, or forced that a series of laws against kidnapping were passed in England and the colonies. Even the most prominent merchants were occasionally prosecuted; a 1682 diary entry reads, 'Two great Merchants are this Term Cast for Kidnapping, you know how many merchants use to buy young people that say they are willing to goe into forraine Plantations.' Moll, although an old offender, is tried only once, for theft of goods valued at £46. To have hanged a person who was technically a first offender for that crime would have seemed cruel indeed.

Defoe presents transportation as both opportunity and the means to break an addictive pattern. Transportation gives Moll and Jack, and other characters in both books, a new chance. Had Moll's husband not been her brother, she might have lived as peaceful and productive a life as her mother had.

Contemporary approaches to Defoe illustrate a new sophistication in describing his formal devices, and an ever-increasing understanding of the social and literary milieu in which *Moll* was produced. This is exemplified in the work of J. Paul Hunter, who has written one of the most important studies of early British fiction, *Before Novels* (1990). This passage describes the way in which *Moll* foreshadows effects and strategies of the later novel.

Much of what happens in the novel for two hundred years is suggested by what happens in *Moll Flanders*. The title page sounds daring, and its enticements are bold and almost leering: *The Fortunes and Misfortunes Of the Famous Moll Flanders, &c. Who was Born in Newgate, and during a Life of continu'd Variety for Threescore Years, besides her Childhood, was Twelve Years a Whore, five times a Wife (whereof once to her own Brother), Twelve Year a Thief, Eight year a Transported Felon in Virginia, at last grew Rich, liv'd Honest, and died a Penitent.* The book is not, however, inflaming and lurid. It is not that the title page lies (except for a few numerical details and the fact that the report of Moll's death is greatly exaggerated), but that pickpocketing, robbery, adultery, bigamy, and incest – things that are categorically clear when they are bared in an outline – tend to lose their labels and most of their shock in the context of day-to-day narrative. Part of Defoe's accomplishment – an accomplishment repeated in kind in novels ever since – is in making Moll's life seem ordinary even though it violates community standards in ways unthinkable to most readers. The novel is aimed at readers very different (at least in circumstances) from its narrator: that is part of its strategy of demonstrating the commonality of repressed desires and disapproved behavior in a human history controlled by intrusive circumstance.

SUGGESTIONS FOR FURTHER READING

BIBLIOGRAPHY

J. R. Moore, *A Checklist of the Writings of Daniel Defoe* (Bloomington, 1960; rev. edn, 1971). A few dubious items included.

P. N. Furbank and W. R. Owens, *The Canonisation of Daniel Defoe* (1988), challenges many of the attributions which have been made to Defoe.

LETTERS

The Letters of Daniel Defoe, ed. G. H. Healey (Oxford, 1955).

BIOGRAPHY

P. Backscheider, *Daniel Defoe: His Life* (Baltimore, 1989), the most comprehensive survey of Defoe's career.

EDITIONS

Moll Flanders (1722), ed. G. A. Starr (1971).

Along with Starr's, the most useful editions of *Moll Flanders* are those by J. P. Hunter (New York, 1970); E. Kelly (New York, 1973); and D. Blewett (Penguin, 1989).

CRITICISM

Important recent criticism can be found in four useful sources:

Daniel Defoe: A Collection of Critical Essays, ed. Max Byrd (Englewood Cliffs, N. J., 1976).

Twentieth Century Interpretations of Moll Flanders, ed. R. C. Elliott (Englewood Cliffs, N. J., 1970).

Moll Flanders, ed. J. P. Hunter (New York, 1960).

Moll Flanders, ed. Edward Kelly, Norton Critical Edition (New York, 1973).

These works are keyed **B**, **E**, **H**, and **K** respectively to indicate items they include among the materials listed below (either in full or in extract).

Daniel Defoe's Moll Flanders, ed. H. Bloom (New York, 1989) contains similar material, but with annotations removed.

General books on Defoe which throw light on *Moll Flanders* are these:

I. A. Bell, *Defoe's Fiction* (1985). The background of popular fiction.

P. Earle, *The World of Defoe* (1976).

P. Rogers (ed.), *Defoe: The Critical Heritage* (1972).

M. Shinagel, *Daniel Defoe and Middle-Class Gentility* (Cambridge, Mass., 1968).

G. A. Starr, *Defoe and Spiritual Autobiography* (Princeton, 1965).

— *Defoe and Casuistry* (Princeton, 1971). **E, K.**

The following books contain sections on *Moll Flanders*:

D. Brooks, *Number and Pattern in the Eighteenth-Century Novel* (1973). Numerological approach.

J. Bender, *Imagining the Penitentiary* (Chicago, 1987). A challenging modern interpretation.

R. A. Erickson, *Mother Midnight* (New York, 1986). Good on the midwife.

G. Howson, *Thief-Taker General* (1970). **K.** A life of Jonathan Wild.

A. D. McKillop, *The Early Masters of English Fiction* (Lawrence, Kansas, 1956). A good general account.

N. Miller, *The Heroine's Text* (New York, 1980). Feminist approaches.

M. E. Novak, *Realism, Myth, and History in Defoe's Fiction* (Lincoln, Nebraska, 1983).

M. Price, *To the Place of Wisdom* (New York, 1964, repr. 1970). **B, K.** A wide-ranging survey of the period.

P. Rogers, *Literature and Popular Culture in Eighteenth-Century England* (Brighton: 1985). On chapbook versions.

D. Van Ghent, *The English Novel: Form and Function* (New York, 1953). **B, E.** An influential reading.

I. Watt, *The Rise of the Novel* (1957). **B, E, H, K.** A standard work.

V. Woolf, *The Common Reader* (1925). **B, E, H, K.** A classic survey.

Articles which discuss the novel include:

H. O. Brown, 'The Displaced Self in the Novels of Daniel Defoe', *ELH*, vol. 38 (1971).

D. Donoghue, 'The Values of *Moll Flanders*', *Sewanee Review*, vol. 71 (1963).

H. Koonce, 'Moll's Muddle', *ELH*, vol. 30 (1963). **E.**

M. E. Novak, 'Conscious Irony in *Moll Flanders*', *College English*, vol. 26 (1964), E, H.

P. Rogers, 'Moll's Memory', *English*, vol. 24 (1975).

M. Shinagel, 'The Maternal Theme in *Moll Flanders*', *Cornell Library Journal*, vol. 7 (1969). K.

I. Watt, 'The Recent Critical Fortunes of *Moll Flanders*', *Eighteenth Century Studies*, vol. 1 (1967).

TEXT SUMMARY

Born in Newgate gaol, to a woman convicted of shoplifting and subsequently transported to Virginia, Moll is cast abroad as an infant, and spends some time among the gypsies. At about three, she is rescued by the parish authorities in Colchester, and put out to nurse in the town. At the age of eight she is told that the magistrates intend her to go into domestic service, a fate at which she rebels, having already conceived the idea that she will eventually become a gentlewoman. When her kind foster-mother dies, Moll – now fourteen – is taken in by a prosperous family, where she is given some of the education and accomplishments of a real gentlewoman, along with the daughters of the house. There are also two sons, and it is with these young men that Moll's sexual education begins. [pp. 7–16]

Awakened to love by the elder brother, she experiences her first, and possibly deepest, affair of the heart. But the younger brother Robin has designs on Moll, and when she finds out that the elder will not marry her she suffers a severe emotional breakdown. When she recovers, she continues her relations with the elder brother, but ultimately agrees to marry Robin. Their marriage lasts five years, after which Moll is left an attractive young widow with a large store of capital (the basis of her later prosperity), as well as two children, taken conveniently off her hands. [pp. 16–47]

Moll now moves to London. There she meets and marries a profligate 'gentleman-tradesman' who, after financial reverses, decamps to France. She takes refuge in the sanctuary of the Mint, and takes the name of 'Mrs Flanders'. Through the friendship of a sea-captain's widow, she begins to learn more of the way to negotiate the contemporary sexual minefields. She decides to mark out one of her admirers for attention, and in due course he marries her in the belief that she has a large fortune. When this illusion is dispelled, Moll's new husband takes her to his estates in Virginia. There she learns the story of her mother-in-law, a former transportee who had prospered in the colony. Moll realises that this is her own mother, and that therefore she has incestuously married her brother. Horrified by this revelation, she eventually plucks up courage to tell him the true state of affairs. He is deeply afflicted by the news, whilst Moll can see no other course than to return to England. [pp. 47–83]

After she comes back, her first liaison is with a gentleman whom she meets at the resort of Bath. This irregular union lasts for six years, ended when the gentleman undergoes a religious conversion and forswears his immoral life. Once more Moll is, as she sees it, 'loosed from all the obligations either of wedlock or mistress-ship.' Now in her early forties, she enters a relationship with a banker who had assisted her in financial matters. Whilst waiting for this man to obtain a divorce from an allegedly unfaithful wife, Moll takes a journey to Lancashire. Here she meets an apparently wealthy gentleman from Ireland, later identified as Jemmy. Each party deceives the other with regard to his or her wealth: the outcome is Moll's 'fourth' marriage. When all is revealed, Jemmy proves surprisingly loyal. He accompanies her on the way to London as far as Dunstable, then leaving for mysterious business connected with his Irish affairs. [pp. 83–126]

Back in London, Moll resumes relations with the banker. She has now formed a close friendship with a 'midwife', in reality a bawd and receiver. The banker obtains a divorce from his wife, who promptly 'destroys herself' in her distress. All now looks set fair for another marriage; but no sooner has the wedding taken place at Brickhill, on the Chester road, than Moll catches sight of her 'Lancashire husband', Jemmy, riding by. The next day a hue and cry is set up after three robbers, and Moll belatedly begins to suspect that Jemmy's business may lie in the trade of highwayman. However, she is able to return to London without revealing her secrets, and begins a tranquil period of five years as wife to the banker. (pp. 126–150)

At the end of that period, her husband suffers a large financial loss, pines away and dies. This is the main hinge in Moll's career: now quite poor again, approaching fifty, and subject to acute depression, she passes two years of loneliness and despair. One day, reduced to bare necessity, she is tempted to steal a bundle of fine lace and money from a shop in the city. Appalled by what she has done, she realises that she may now be heading down the same road to Newgate as her mother had taken. But her scruples are overcome by her desire for comfort, and gradually she embarks on a regular career as a thief. Needing someone to handle the stolen property, she gets in touch with her old 'governess', the midwife. This draws her firmly into the criminal world, and she starts to lose her bad conscience about this way of life. She perpetrates some particularly mean thefts, deceives her fellow-criminals, and takes to working in disguise, once in male clothes. Despite a number of lucky escapes, she refuses to heed the warning signs, and pursues her career undaunted. She even ventures outside London, and takes a thieving tour of East Anglia, returning through her old haunt of Colchester, only to find that her former contacts are either dead or gone from the district. [pp. 150–213]

Eventually her luck runs out, when on Christmas Day she attempts to carry off some silver from a shop in Foster Lane and is caught red-handed; but her presence of mind allows her to wriggle out of the charge. Just three days later, 'not at all made cautious' by this event, she is finally trapped in a mercer's shop: this time there can be no escape, and her worst fears are realised when she is carried off to Newgate. Whilst awaiting trial, she is astonished to meet Jemmy, also a prisoner, and learns of his doings as captain of a gang of highwaymen. Her trial goes ahead and the inevitable sentence of death is passed. Now finally cowed, she is brought to repentance for all her misdeeds after visits from a minister of the church. Through his intercession, her petition for the sentence to be remitted to transportation is granted. Jemmy, finding the evidence against him weak, is able to appeal for the same remission, and eventually the pair are dispatched on the same ship across the Atlantic. [pp. 213–43]

The story is not yet quite ended. By bribery and crooked dealing, Moll is able on arrival in Virginia to gain immediate freedom. She discovers that her mother is now dead, and her brother has moved to another part of the colony. She sails with Jemmy across Chesapeake Bay and sets up an estate in Maryland. After some time she returns to Virginia, locates her brother (now old and frail), and meets the son she had borne to him. She learns that Moll's mother had bequeathed her a plantation nearby. She returns to the Maryland estate, which soon begins to prosper. A return visit the following year finds Moll's brother now dead, and she is legally free to acknowledge her marriage to Jemmy. The book ends with the aged couple returning to England, their terms of transportation ended, prosperous thanks to their American estates, and resolving to spend the rest of their lives 'in sincere penitence'. [pp. 243-72]

ACKNOWLEDGEMENTS

The publishers and the editor are grateful for permission to quote from the following:

E. M. Forster, *Aspects of the Novel*, London, Hodder & Stoughton, 1927; Peter Quennell, *The Singular Preference*, London, Collins, 1953; Ian Watt, *The Rise of the Novel*, London, Chatto & Windus, 1957; M. E. Novak, 'Conscious Irony in *Moll Flanders*', in *College English*, vol. 26, 1964; J. J. Richetti, 'The Portrayal of Women in Restoration and Eighteenth-Century English Literature', in *What Manner of Woman*, ed. Marlene Springer, New York, New York University Press, 1977; Marie-Paul Laden, *Self-Imitation in the Eighteenth-Century Novel*, Princeton, Princeton University Press, 1987; Paula Backscheider, *Daniel Defoe: His Life*, Baltimore, John Hopkins University Press, 1989; J. Paul Hunter, *Before Novels*, New York, W. & W. Norton & Company, Inc., 1990.

WOMEN'S WRITING
IN EVERYMAN

A SELECTION

Female Playwrights of the Restoration
FIVE COMEDIES
Rediscovered literary treasures in a unique selection **£5.99**

The Secret Self
SHORT STORIES BY WOMEN
'A superb collection' *Guardian* **£4.99**

Short Stories
KATHERINE MANSFIELD
An excellent selection displaying the remarkable range of Mansfield's talent **£3.99**

Women Romantic Poets 1780-1830: An Anthology
Hidden talent from the Romantic era, rediscovered for the first time **£5.99**

Selected Poems
ELIZABETH BARRETT BROWNING
A major contribution to our appreciation of this inspiring and innovative poet **£5.99**

Frankenstein
MARY SHELLEY
A masterpiece of Gothic terror in its original 1818 version **£3.99**

The Life of Charlotte Brontë
MRS GASKELL
A moving and perceptive tribute by one writer to another **£4.99**

Vindication of the Rights of Woman and The Subjection of Women
MARY WOLLSTONECRAFT
AND J. S. MILL
Two pioneering works of early feminist thought **£4.99**

The Pastor's Wife
ELIZABETH VON ARNIM
A funny and accomplished novel by the author of *Elizabeth and Her German Garden* **£5.99**

£4.99

£2.99

£5.99

AVAILABILITY

All books are available from your local bookshop or direct from
Littlehampton Book Services Cash Sales, 14 Eldon Way, LinesideEstate, Littlehampton, West Sussex BN17 7HE. PRICES ARE SUBJECT TO CHANGE.

To order any of the books, please enclose a cheque (in £ sterling) made payable to Littlehampton Book Services, or phone your order through with credit card details (Access, Visa or Mastercard) on 0903 721596 (24 hour answering service) stating card number and expiry date. Please add £1.25 for package and postage to the total value of your order.

EVERYMAN

MOLL FLANDERS
Daniel Defoe

Edited by Pat Rogers
University of South Florida, Tampa

**The cautionary memoirs of an outrageous
female rogue**

Abandoned at birth and threatened with a life in service,
Defoe's young rebel sets her heart on independence.
One fatal seduction and five husbands later she resorts
to a life of self-supporting crime.

On her downward path from the relative respectability
of London's underworld, Newgate Prison and eventual
deportation, the indestructible Moll Flanders gives her
frank opinion of temptation, flattery, fortune-hunters
and innocence corrupted in the world of men.

**The most comprehensive paperback edition available,
with introduction, text summary, selected criticism
and chronology of Defoe's life and times**

*Cover illustration: Detail from 'Before' by William Hogarth
(Fitzwilliam Museum, Cambridge)
Cover design: The Tango Design Consultancy*

ISBN 0-460-87287-7

9 780460 872874

UK £3.50
USA $5.95
CAN $3.95